Dear Erica,

I am so glad I have you as a friend. Your support, caring, and humor are things

OIL AND WATER

I will be eternally grateful for!

Lara Ann Danielle

OIL AND WATER

by

Lara Ann Dominick

For Michael

Contents

Chapter 1

Elsie

I looked up from the book, having finally finished it, and sighed. The hard, glossy cover rested on my thighs, which were bouncing up and down with the adrenaline rush the book had engendered. I was done, but it was hard to put down- literally. I stared back down at the blank inside cover and silently willed the story to continue- a futile effort since this was the final chapter. I had flown through the series, reading all of the books, one right on the heels of another, finishing now, several hours after I ought to have been asleep. Tomorrow was going to *suck*.

It was an easy read, both in terms of the writing and the way I'd found it far too easy to get absorbed into the unrealistic romance; to lose myself in the somehow simultaneously overdone and watered down action; to picture myself living within the impossible realm of the story. And yet it was so hard to let go of the book, to put it on the shelf and force myself to return to reality. I closed it, finally, and traced my finger over the title, which was slightly raised on the cover.

I stared at the design on the front of the book for close to a quarter of an hour, unraveling in my head the way the colors highlighted certain parts of the picture, drawing my attention to them. It took a long time for me to pry my eyes away; it felt like hours. Once I abandoned my reverie, I placed the book back on the shelf, not with the spine facing out, as all my other books were, but flat against the spines of the others so that I could see the cover from my perch on my bed. I wanted to see the cover art, to take it in, to continue to ponder what it meant to the story. I passed my mirror as I returned to my bed and looked at my reflection.

Many of my favorite books were the same basic formula- trashy young adult fantasy romance- and I *loved it*. Most of those had a similar main character type. The leading lady was always just a touch shy, or "odd," or antisocial, but she was beautiful, and always in a way that she couldn't see for herself. She needed to be *shown* how beautiful she was- even though it was evident from her interactions with others. That was something I couldn't exactly relate to. I glanced at the mirror above my dresser.

I wasn't about to win any beauty pageants (mainly due to being too short and, at this point, old to do so), but I definitely thought I was cute. I was athletic but curvy, strong but soft. I could have afforded to lose a few pounds, but, hey, in the era of fast-casual food delivered to your door with the click of a button, who couldn't? My skin wasn't perfect, but I'd never struggled with heavy acne- just a little uneven tone and texture that some tinted moisturizer usually took care of. My hair was a natural shade of dark blonde that got killer highlights when I spent a lot of time outside thanks to the relentless Florida sun. My eyes were a deep shade of gray-blue I liked to call "shark-skin," but with a ring of gold around the pupil that made them look like a stormy teal from a distance. I *loved* my eyes, especially as they were at that moment, very lightly made up with just a hint of eyeliner and mascara to make them pop.

I glanced back at the book, lamenting my normal life. I'm not the only person from my high school (or even my university) who still lived at home. My Bachelor's in Liberal Arts was *not* as helpful as I (or my parents) might have hoped when they refused to let me major in Fine Arts (in favor of something "better"), and we all took out obscene loans to pay for it. As a result, I was working an hourly job that I desperately needed to slowly chip away at my crippling debt. *Thrilling.*

I always compared myself to the main characters of the books I read, but it was getting harder and harder to mentally insert myself into the world of a teenager whose first love is a sensual, mature, immortal being who happens to look like another teenager. For one thing, I could barely remember what it felt like to be a teenager. I was already getting to the age where I not only couldn't relate to juveniles, but I actively found them aggravating. Even my little sister wasn't an adolescent anymore, so I had minimal contact with anyone in that age bracket.

For another, I was already in love. Well, kind of. Sam and I were off again, but he'd been calling more often. I always answered, because... well, of course, I did. I couldn't even say that Sam was my very first love. But I did lose my virginity to him, so he was my first *something*, even if he missed out on the "first love" title by a few years. I just wasn't sure I was ready to make that choice.

It was also hard to imagine being a loner like those girls. They always seemed to be on the outside of any social circle, without a true, close friend; this made it easier for the girl to be whisked away by some mysterious figure who would bring her to a fantastical new life filled with danger and romance. I, on the other hand, had a great circle of friends that had been lovingly cultivated from friendships made in high school, college, and the years after to create a support system I could count on for anything. Need a shopping trip? Call Ashley- she had no student loan debt and even less self-control and would never make you feel bad about retail therapy. Want to go ride bikes at the trails? Jack is the guy (if you could deal with his ego for any length of time), and he was usually already on his way there. Need to cry because Sam dumped me again? Jess would be at my door with a bottle of wine, in her pajamas, ready for a Netflix binge. Need to indulge in way too many margaritas *because Sam dumped me again?* Charlotte and Matt were good for getting me home without making any stupid mistakes.

I also had a great relationship with my family. I mean, my sister Danielle and I rubbed along okay, but she was in New York getting her Law Degree, so we didn't see each other much. My parents had supported me in everything I'd ever pursued... except for that Fine Arts degree, which would have been no more useless than my current degree; I may be bitter about that one until the end of time.

Even when I was away from home (which was never that long, because to go anywhere would require more money than I could spare), I spoke to my parents every day. We still did family dinners whenever everyone was available to do so, which was surprisingly often for four adults with different schedules, one of whom lived a thousand miles away.

All of this to say, I could never be like the girls in those books. My family life was too commonplace. My friendships were too commonplace. My love life was too commonplace.

This life was too commonplace.

I sat up in bed for hours longer, still riding the adrenaline high of finishing my book and knowing I was going to have a bitch of a time getting to sleep anyway. So I turned on my TV and started mindlessly browsing for something to stream.

It's very disconcerting when your mind is focused on a particular topic and your predictive recommendations seem to be tuned into that. Of course, my taste in movies and TV wasn't too far off from my taste in books, so naturally, my recommendations would all be "trashy young adult fantasy romance."

Watching the trailer for a few options that, at first glance, seemed appealing sadly left me wanting. Even though the characters in my books were teenagers, I aged them up in my mind, something I couldn't easily do with real people portraying them. I could imagine, while reading, that the characters were my age, much closer to thirty than twenty or a little older- not borderline children like the actors on the screen. It was hard to get into a movie where you were supposed to be attracted to the "sexy vampire guy" when he looked like a fresh-faced little baby. I couldn't even enjoy the fantasy properly. The book is always better, right?

Just for once, I wanted to feel like the story could be *my* story. If such stories could really happen, that is. I wasn't naïve or crazy; I knew reality from fantasy. But it didn't keep me from taking pleasure in the mythology and folklore around immortal beings- gods, deities, vampires. Vampires, most of all. Go ahead, laugh at me.

I have been fascinated by the undead since I was old enough to understand what a vampire was. From the moment I saw *Dracula* as a child (when I walked in on my parents watching it when I was definitely too young for that movie), I was captivated. When I was younger, I used to be terrified of the idea of vampires, convinced that they lived in my creepy crawl space that we never used. As I got older, I began to read young adult vampire novels- the ones that now covered my bookshelf. They spoke of vampires with souls, who try to be good, who are appealing, friendly, and, in many cases, hot as hell. I watched movies and TV shows devoted to the heartthrobs without heartbeats religiously.

I had yet to find anything to make me doubt the existence of creatures outside the realm of what most consider normal or natural. Having always believed in a higher power, the idea of superior supernatural or preternatural beings was nothing strange to me. I harbored no uncertainty that there existed things I could not see or understand. Nearly every religion in the world, my own included, speaks of evil creatures that live solely for the destruction of humankind, and of protectors of the human race. Even humans could be considered our own enemies- I don't know if there even exists another species that destroys each other and themselves with such enthusiasm. But I hoped that someday I would happen upon something that would help me feel less...

Commonplace.

Chapter 2

Opal

I awoke, opening my eyes into the comforting, dim illumination of twilight. I rolled over, pulling my soft down comforter around me, enjoying the smooth feel of the luxurious Egyptian cotton sheets on my skin. I relished one last moment under the covers before I threw them off of me and rolled to the edge of the plush king-sized bed. I put my feet on the floor, feeling the supple fibers of the white shag rug as they caressed my feet.

I walked toward the floor to ceiling windows that dominated the west-facing wall of my flat, looking out over the bay where the horizon was a lovely shade of deep purple. With every exterior wall being a window, my home on the very top floor of my building had a perfect view of both the water and the city, filled with people enjoying an evening stroll along the river, dining along the water or downtown, rushing to this meeting or that.

I tilted my head as I wondered what drove them to it. Mortal motivations eluded me and always had. Then again, I had only ever known life as a vampire, so I suppose I couldn't be expected to understand what made humans tick.

I turned and walked to my bathroom, where I stood, admiring my reflection in the full-length mirror. My body was strong and toned, but with feminine curves; I had long champagne-blond hair that shone even in the evening light with a natural body wave most women would kill for; smooth, lightly tanned skin, compliments of the Florida sun (yes, sun); a perfect pout that sat equally perfectly above a heart-shaped jawline. Anyone looking at me would see a model-beautiful bombshell with a kind smile and energetic eyes enjoying a night on the town. They would never know what I really was until it was too late.

I saved looking at the reflection of my eyes for last. They were a bright emerald green... tonight, anyway. Some people have eyes that may shift their shade in response to a change in lighting or to reflect a color they wore. My eyes underwent a more extreme change. The color of my eyes at any given point reflected the state of my soul at the moment. I was unique in that regard; other vampires' eyes reflected their soul, but in a single color that settled shortly after their death. Mine could change as quickly as my mood. Tonight, the spritely tone meant I was ready for some fun.

I smiled as I thought of what the night might offer, and noticed that my canines had elongated and sharpened. I touched one with the tip of my finger, drawing a drop of blood that I sucked absent-mindedly as I thought of the dream I'd had. It had been the promise of a night filled with sex and blood. No wonder my fangs had come out- I was hungry in more ways than one.

I let my fangs retract, smiling into the mirror, then pulled on a white dress that showed off my curves and a pair of bright blue heels that gave me legs for days. I walked back to my window to look over the prey milling about the city and to plan my night. Living in paradise had certain benefits over other locations. It was mid-April and warm enough in the twilight hours that the people below wandered around with their necks, arms, even legs exposed. I licked my lips, feeling the fangs threaten to reemerge. *Later*, I promised myself.

I left my condo, walking to the elevator. I strode through the lobby, the doorman giving me a polite, "Good evening, Miss Opal," as I waved to him, walking out into the night. The "Miss" was only acceptable because of our familiarity, him having been my doorman for nearly a decade. Most of my kind needed to show a bit more respect.

My name, Opal, was the result of my "birth." Not the birth where I came screaming into the world as a human child, but rather when my human body died and I became what I am now. By vampire standards, I was young, but I was still regarded with respect (and some fear) by many of my fellow vampires. This was thanks in large part to the events that took place the night of my rebirth, though I didn't fully understand them...

My eyes had opened that night, nearly ten years ago, under a palm tree in the woods. The wind whipped around me and I felt the beginnings of rain.

I had no memory of how I got there or even who I was. Since then, I've heard from others that my inability to remember my life as a human was not typical, and I'd never known why that was the case with me.

As I lay there, I felt damp sand beneath me and ran my fingers through it, feeling the details of every grain. I pushed myself easily to my feet, moving lithely and quickly, something that felt natural if only because I had no point of comparison from my time as a human. I glanced around, wind whipping my wet hair into my face. There appeared to be a rather large amount of nearly-dried blood where I'd been laying, on the tree, and all over my clothes. I did a quick mental inventory and decided I wasn't hurt. I was, however, hungry. I caught a whiff of something sweet on the air and tried to follow it to the source.

It didn't take long. A few yards away, a man lay sprawled across a large boulder, a trickle of blood in the corner of his mouth. His eyes were closed. He was either dead or unconscious, but that little stream running down his cheek was the sweetest smelling thing I could imagine. I leaned down and licked it away, feeling my canines elongate into the lovely fangs I've been fond of since that very moment. There was a moment where I relished the feeling of that one drop on my tongue. I savored the stillness before I would feed, before I would kill for the first time, even though I wasn't yet fully cognizant of what I'd planned to do; I was running on pure instinct. Dropping my head to his throat, I sensed more of that nectar just below the skin and let my fangs graze the length of the vein and artery there. I felt a sensation not unlike the thrill of sexual arousal just before I sank my fangs deep to open a fount and felt the decadent rush of blood over my tongue.

I gulped it down, not stopping even when I felt him stir and groan, "No..." *Not dead*, I thought. *Not yet.* I wondered if remembering my human life might have changed my actions, or at least might have made me feel guilt or hesitation, but I was entirely driven by the animal inside. I grabbed him by the hair and pulled his head back to keep him from moving; I had no intention of releasing him before I was finished.

The rain was falling freely as I drank until it seemed there was nothing left inside of him. When I pulled away, his eyes had fallen open, glassy in death. They had been lovely- a rich and earthy shade of hazel. I nearly felt a sting of regret at the beauty, but I felt a power coursing through me that made me immediately forget any concerns I'd had up until that point. I had felt normal upon waking- normal for a vampire, anyway- yet after feeding, I felt like the Gods themselves dwelled within me, granting me a strength and confidence that rivaled their own.

I walked through the woods I'd been in and found myself on a beach. I could hear the waves crashing and the wind whistling relentlessly, the rolling thunder and the musical sound of the raindrops pounding on the sand and water. There was no natural light. Any man-made lights were too far off to be of any use, and yet I could see every grain of sand; I could see the fish splashing just below the surface of the water; I could make out the vibrant and clear green-blue of the sea; I could even sense when someone came up behind me, despite the fact that they'd been quiet as a ghost.

"So you've fed already," a woman's voice said. "That's good."

I spun around, my instinct and the strength I'd felt after feeding prompting me to lash out at the intruder. It was a young woman. She was classically beautiful, but something dark flowed beneath that beauty.

"Whoa, girlie," she said, putting her hands in front of her as though to calm a wild horse, but with a shift in her weight, I saw she was ready to fight if need be. "I'm just checking on you. That first wake up can be a real bitch, what with the primal hunger, the need for the first blood and all."

It was the first real thing anyone had said to me since waking up, except for my first kill who'd simply said *No*. I very quickly started checking off boxes in my mind that had just as quickly been thought of in the first place. Shared language: check. Not aggressive: semi-check. Name: big fat question mark. "Who are you?" I demanded.

She gave a slight smirk. "You don't remember me?" She asked.

"No," I admitted, not feeling any calmer, and ready to strike. "I don't remember *anything*." My aggravation was growing. I nodded back toward the woods behind her. "And

I've already killed someone tonight, so unless you want to be next, you'd better tell me what I need to know."

The woman's smile never moved, but her eyes widened as though she'd heard something exciting. They were an intense shade of bright orange-gold and surveyed me in a way that made me feel exposed. "Well, that makes two of us with a body count tonight," she said, letting me know that she was as dangerous as I was. "Why don't you come with me and we can chat, girl to girl." She winked at me and motioned for me to follow her. I let the rain fall on me for a moment more before I obeyed, my thirst for answers nearly as intense as my earlier thirst for blood.

She led me to a car that was parked in a lot through the woods and told me to get in. I hesitated, unsure if I could trust her, but I had no other options. Plus, I had the sensation that if it came down to a fight, I would win. I decided I may as well be warm and dry with the opportunity to find out more about who I was and what had happened to me, rather than cold and wet, wandering the woods.

Once in the car, she started to drive us off of what appeared to be some kind of barrier island- wherever we were- and through several others. After nearly half an hour of silence, I finally spoke. "So are you going to tell me who the hell you are? Or who I am? Or why I woke up on that island?"

The woman smirked again. Her honey-colored hair had begun to dry out and, somehow, looked as perfectly coiffed as if she'd been to the salon rather than in a tropical storm.

"I'm Amber," she said, looking at me and batting her lashes. "Like my eyes. I'm your sire."

"What's a sire?" I asked.

"It means you have me to thank for your new life. You were going to die in those woods. When you did, I made sure you came back even better than before." She looked at me, realizing I wasn't getting it. I felt a heat behind my eyes, a rage

12

beginning to build. "Hm, but as far as who you are, I'm think-ing maybe you're... Scarlett."

"You don't know?" I asked, my frustration peaking. "I thought-"

"Oh, I know what your name *used* to be." She waved her hand dismissively. "But it's not your name anymore. My name wasn't Amber when I was a human. And the old name doesn't matter, for either of us. Eyes are the key, and yours are a stun-ning shade of red."

I pondered this for a moment, my anger subsiding. I didn't know if I was like this before, but my emotions seemed more than a little volatile. "Scarlett?" I tried the name out.

Amber looked back at me and opened her mouth to speak, but then paused. "Wait..." she stared into my eyes, con-cerned. "Your eyes had definitely settled on red."

"Okay," I said. "So, what's the problem?"

"They're not red. Not anymore." Amber sounded trou-bled. "They were bright and fiery *red*. They're... softer now. Lavender, or grey. Maybe a little of both?"

"That sounds pretty. Is it bad?" I asked. There was no in-security in the question. I was merely curious.

"It's definitely not normal," she replied, a look of unease coming across her face. "I'm going to hold off on naming you for a bit, though. Shit, I thought you were difficult when you were alive. For now, just assume I'm talking to you unless I di-rectly address anyone else until your eyes finally settle."

I pondered the strangeness of the moment. I sat in a car, in terms of both information and destination completely at the mercy of someone who claimed that she had saved my life, but that I was *not* alive even though I felt decidedly so; who had claimed that she (and had implied that I) was not a human. I could remember what humans were, and I had the sensation I should have been one, but was unbothered by the indication I may not be. She assumed responsibility for naming me, yet refused to do so. And she seemed to have no issue with either of us killing humans. Not that I had any kind of love or affinity for humans- I couldn't even remember any I'd ever known personally, unless you count the man I'd killed in the woods.

"Who was he?" I asked out loud, suddenly interested.

"Who?" Amber asked, her own mind elsewhere.

"The man in the woods. You said I would have died back there if you hadn't come along, which I guess I did anyway. You also said you made sure I came back, which means you were there when whatever happened to me happened. I feel fairly certain that an unconscious and injured man would not just coincidentally be lying a few feet from where I died and came back to life, so I have to assume you knew who he was."

Amber raised an eyebrow at me. "You're smart. That's good. It'll get you far in this life." She turned the car onto a highway and hit the gas hard. There was a pregnant pause before she said, "He had drugged you and taken you to those woods."

"But *why*?" I asked, unable to comprehend why he would do that.

"No good reason, girlie. I was already there and saw you both. Thankfully, I'm stronger than he was, but you were wounded- badly. You were probably going to die, but thankfully, I'm a vampire and you needed vampire blood to survive. I gave you some of mine, but by the time you had enough to heal up and pull through, your wounds had already turned fatal. When you died, because your blood bonded to the vampire blood, you became like me. Then you found the only living body in the area to feed on and finish your transformation to secure your new eternal life."

"So he deserved to die," I said, staring out the window at the rain, trying to make sense of what I knew and what I felt. "Because he drugged me and kidnapped me and killed me."

Amber laughed. "Sure, if you want to justify it, but *why*?"

"I don't understand." I felt surprisingly calm, despite her patronizing tone. I had the feeling that death shouldn't be random or cruel, but I also didn't know why I felt that way. There was a detachment that never struck me as odd; it was just how I felt. I couldn't remember anything from before waking up in the woods, but there were certain emotions I sensed I *should* feel, or things I sensed I *should* be thinking; but they were distant, as though I was trying to see them through fuzzy binoculars. I needed Amber to explain.

She shook her head. "At the end of the day, does anyone expect the lion to justify killing a gazelle? Or the spider, a fly?" She smiled at me, her fangs showing- not threateningly so, but to prove the point. "Kidding. Mostly. I actually agree with you; there are certainly some people who deserve our wrath, and we have that right. We are gods to them. We can mete out justice and pain as we see fit, because we are the predator. They are the prey. All we have to do is find the fun in it."

It made sense. If we were truly superior- and given the euphoric rush I'd experienced after that first kill, I believed that we were- there was nothing to stop us, and no reason to care about the insignificant deaths of those beneath us, especially of those who would harm others. I stared out the window as we drove into a city. "And how do we do that?"

"That's up to you."

Chapter 3

Elsie

The black oblivion of sleep (all two hours of it) was shattered by the shrill caterwauling of my alarm. I reached out from under the covers and slammed my finger onto my phone screen over and over until it stopped. It was still dark out. I groaned and rolled over, seriously debating closing my eyes and going back to sleep. But I was paid by the hour and deeply in student loan debt; I couldn't afford to skip. Plus, I'd have Jimmy's smiling face to brighten my day in just a few hours. I could have slept an hour longer, skipping my morning run, but I knew I'd need that runner's high to be ready for the insanity that was sure to greet me when I stepped through the doors for Monday at Shining Stars.

I dragged myself out of bed and threw on my running clothes. I laced up my bright blue trainers and put my headphones on. It was barely spring, but central Florida was already hot and humid, and at the height of the day, it could make even the locals start sweating. Just my usual jaunt around my neighborhood left me drenched. Know where vampires (if they were real) would never go? Florida. And the burbs. The bright, sunshiney, sweaty, Gulf Coast *burbs*.

Flushed and winded, I darted back into my house, scratching my dog Oso behind the ears before he could bark and wake up my parents. I jumped into the shower, letting the water wash away the sweat and grime, and trying to force it to wash away that tugging in my soul to revisit the story I'd been so wrapped up in the night before.

I debated wearing the cute new blouse I'd bought the day before. It was nice and light, and on a day like today, that was threatening to be a scorcher, it would probably be fantastic. The thought, however, of having my white shirt covered in whatever would be thrown at me today (probably literally) in front of everyone, especially my "clients," was not the most appealing concept. So I pulled on my old standby shirt: a once-oversized black unisex tee that I'd gotten at the planetarium when I was a kid. I hadn't worn it much back then because it was too big for anything other than sleeping in, and it had a giant glow-in-the-dark picture of the moon, so it was very distracting when I tried to sleep. I'd grown into the shirt since then and my clients really got a kick out of it. Jimmy, in particular, loved that shirt and always told me so.

I grinned at the prospect of seeing him, and my outlook brightened considerably. I ran a brush through my hair and pulled the disaster into a messy bun, then stuck my sunglasses on top of my head and dashed into the dining room.

I took a deep breath. Mom was up and making eggs. The sizzling sound of the butter in the frying pan alerted me to the fact that I was hungry. I rushed into the kitchen and saw Oso sitting patiently at Mom's feet, drooling on her shoes and hoping she'd drop something.

I walked around her to the cabinet and pulled out a mug. I poured myself a big cup of coffee and dumped a load of milk and sugar into it.

"I thought you were cutting back on that," Mom said pointedly, eyeing my cup.

"Which?" I asked, feigning ignorance with wide, innocent eyes.

She glared at me. "The sugar! We were going low carb together!"

I resisted the urge to roll my eyes, knowing that as a grown-ass woman, I shouldn't have to justify a cup of sweet coffee, but also knowing that my parents were allowing their grown-ass daughter to live with them rent-free- a situation that could end any time they saw fit. "I do know," I said, the exhaustion in my voice making me come across as sarcastic, even though that was not the intent. "Look, I slept like shit and I can't stand to drink it black. It tastes like sour dirt."

"Then why drink it at all, Elsie?" Mom sighed. "You said I wasn't going to have to deal with this misery alone."

"I know!" I snapped. She glared and I glared right back. I knew she was trying to look out for me (kind of), but like any adult who still lives with Mommy and Daddy, it was sometimes hard to find the line between being treated like *their* child and being treated like *a* child. It's a tricky distinction, but one side of the line makes you feel loved; the other makes you feel smothered.

I continued, trying to defuse the situation. "I *do* know. I'll forego the sugar tomorrow. But for today, my loan bills are going up, not down, and I need to be able to function at work. It's not like they'll take it easy on me if I'm tired. *They smell fear!*" I said, sounding like the voiceover in a horror trailer.

Mom continued to glare as she tipped the eggs into a serving bowl and pulled a big tray of Cuban toast out of the oven. I held my tongue at the hypocrisy. Sugar in coffee? *Bad.* Big chunks of white bread? *Totally fine!*

We sat and ate, joined by Dad a few minutes later. The only sounds were chewing and Oso breathing wet spots onto our pants, still hoping for a morsel. I ate everything but a couple bites, and, walking to the sink, "accidentally" tipped the eggs onto the floor. Oso bounded over, his shaggy black fur rippling around him.

"Elsie!" Mom cried.

"Whoops!" I said with a laugh. "Love you, bye!" And I grabbed my bag and ran out the door.

I had a great ten-minute commute, despite the crazy local traffic. I used a shortcut through the back of my neighborhood that skipped two of the worst intersections and brought me out to the main road at a point where I was thankfully driving against the traffic rather than with it. If the drive to work had been a stressful one, there was no way I could put up with my duties, especially the one where I had to keep my cool. I was pretty much an open book. It was a big part of why I quit working in retail. I was great at customer service, but really bad at customer ass-kissing.

I pulled in to a spot at the end of the row and climbed out, dodging the cars speeding through the lot that were trying to get back onto the main road as fast as possible so they could sit in traffic a few seconds sooner. I punched in my code at the door and walked in.

The smiling face behind the desk greeted me. "Morning, Miss Elsie," she said in a lovely, deep southern drawl. People always think of big cities up north or out west as being these melting pots full of people from all over, but I found that more people had moved to my tiny corner of the world near Tampa than were born and raised here. *This* was where diversity thrived.

"Morning, Miss Tracey," I responded, returning her smile. Miss Tracey was our receptionist and was always so put together- makeup perfectly in place, hair cut and styled into flawless curls around her face, fingernails immaculate, like she'd never used them to touch a thing in her life. I loved

Tracey because she was an absolute sweetheart. But I hated how she made me feel like a Goddamned slob, even if it wasn't her fault.

I clicked onto the computer on the desk to sign in. "Anything I should know before I walk in there?" I asked, half teasing but wholly hoping she didn't have anything to tell me.

"Well..." she started, her smile faltering. *Shit.* "I think Margot had a bad weekend, and I don't know if it's a full moon tonight, but everyone walking through this door seems all out of sorts, like something's in the air. Add that to everyone is sniffling and coughing, and no one will admit that it may be more than allergies..." Tracey realized she'd begun to ramble and perked herself back up, putting the smile back where it belonged, though with a hint of insincerity. Or maybe that was just because I'd already seen behind the curtain. "But I know you're gonna have a great day, Miss Elsie!"

I leaned in and spoke quietly as someone else used the computer to sign themselves in. "Thanks, Tracey. How's my boyfriend doing?" I asked with a wink.

The smile was full wattage now and Tracey winked back. "He was asking about you when he came in. Make sure you don't get too crazy with the PDA- his friends will be jealous."

Hearing that Jimmy asked about me before he even started the day was better than coffee. Suddenly ready to tackle anything, I waved at Tracey and walked to my room.

The sound of screams assaulted my ears the second I opened the door. There was bedlam, with everyone running all over. Some were laughing, some were crying, and some were being dinosaurs.

Oh, wait. Did I not mention my job was as an assistant preschool teacher?

Miss Margot, my lead teacher, walked over to me with a scowl. "About time you got here. Breakfast is barely over and it's already chaos in here."

"Margot," I sighed, speaking softly and trying to make it seem like the conversation was pleasant to not let the little ones all around know what we were discussing, "I'm early. Like 15 minutes early. If you want me here earlier, talk to Dana because I'm not even allowed to clock in any earlier. I'm going to go put my bag- *oof!*"

A tiny battering ram struck me around my lower belly and squealed. "Miss Elsieeeeeee!"

Looking down at my assailant, I saw a mop of unruly dark brown waves. "Hi, Jimmy," I smiled. He lifted his face and looked up at me, his grin nearly reaching his ears and showing every one of his adorable little teeth. He squeezed me tightly before turning around and running back to play rough with some of the other little boys.

Margot frowned at me and sighed. She didn't like Jimmy much and was very up front with me about it. He could be hyper and wild and definitely struggled with paying attention and following directions, but Margot couldn't see past that. Something about Jimmy caught my eye- and to be honest, my heart- the first time I met him, and I worked hard to break away the rough edges around the little diamond inside. He still got negative marks for behavior fairly frequently, but while he used to lash out in anger when it happened, he had started to come to me to talk about why he acted out and to ask for guidance on how to do better next time. For a four-year-old, that's an amazing amount of self-awareness.

There was also the fact that I knew things at home weren't great. His parents had been on the brink of divorce when they'd gotten pregnant again. His little sister was now in the infant room at the school. People wouldn't believe the things you learn about a family as a teacher, but with Jimmy coming to trust me as he had, and seeing the interactions between him, his parents, and his sister, a few things were pretty obvious. His parents were fighting again; his mom had always wanted a daughter and would make awful, snide comments to Jimmy about how like his father he was; and his dad was disengaged from the family to the point that he may as well have not been there at all. Margot had long since decided that this was why Jimmy was a lost cause. It just made me love on him harder.

Plus, he gave the best hugs.

"Well," Margot huffed, "Go put the bag down and let's get these kids going with the schedule, okay?" Margot was a great teacher to small kids, but not so great with adults- at least not at work. Her only real failing as a teacher was that she definitely didn't think that the "problem kids" were worth too much of her time since they took away from all the other kids. That was the benefit of being the assistant teacher; I could focus on the "problem kids" that would otherwise not get the attention they needed and deserved. I know I'm not alone in that line of thinking, but sometimes, especially when teachers were as overworked and underpaid as we were, it was so hard to see through the weariness to find what drew them to the job in the first place; especially those like Margot who'd been here for a few decades and had become jaded. The Jimmys who walked through that door were my "why"- as in why I put up with Margot's shit. I could go back to retail management in a heartbeat... if not for these kids.

The rest of the day proceeded as usual, with Margot's occasional sniping at me. When nap time hit and it was time for me to take lunch, I fled as quickly as I could. Just because I loved "my" kids didn't mean that they didn't stress me out to a crazy degree and that I didn't need some "me" time. Margot didn't help, always making things just a little harder and tenser than they really ought to have been.

I sat in the staff break room while the other ladies watched some talk show that I couldn't care less about. I sipped my smoothie; it tasted like a peanut butter cup, but it was full of all kinds of healthy stuff I guess I should have been eating as long as I was pumping my body full of beer several nights a week. I pulled out my phone and headphones and started mindlessly scrolling social media, waiting for...

Bzzt. There it was. Lunchtime in text-land. As many of my friends sat down to their own lunches, they began lamenting the tragedy of Monday and looking toward the weekend to see who wanted to hang out and where and when.

Beach and barz? Ashley (always the poet- bars with a "z." She's probably smarter than the rest of us combined, but you'd never know it from the way she texts) asked in our group message, naturally leading the conversation into territory the rest of us would either, depending on what time of the pay cycle it was, jump on board or-

Unsubscribe! Jack (our token health nut) replied. *Beach for sure, but I have a race Sunday morning and can't be hungover.*

"Ugh," I said out loud. Then in my head, *Heaven forbid Mr. Fitness pull the stick out of his ass for a weekend and actually act like a human being who had fun.* Jack annoyed the shit out of me sometimes. I liked to run, but he liked to act like he was getting paid to do it. Spoiler: he wasn't.

Ever the diplomat, Jess chimed in, *We could do both anyway. Jack can just go home when he needs to.*

Charlotte responded, *Sounds good, y'all, but can we keep it low key? As in just stay at one cool place and not hop all over DTSP?*

Downtown St. Pete, or DTSP, was pretty much the only choice to go party after a day at the beach, unless we just stayed at one of the little beachfront joints that were usually overrun with spring breakers, which, no thank you.

Ashley answered back with a string of emojis indicating her exasperation.

Bzzt. Not in the group message. Just Sam. *Hey.*

I stared at the phone, debating whether or not to answer. Sam was a good guy. I won't even pretend that a lot of our fights and breakups weren't due to my desire for a more intense relationship like those in books I read, such as the one from the night before. It's really hard to be content in a good, stable relationship when a part of you craves excitement and danger. Sam wasn't perfect either, but his impatience (one of *his* worst qualities) wasn't helped by my constant need for things to be just a little... *more.* That wasn't my only issue, but, hey, no one is perfect.

My fingers hovered over the keys for a few more seconds while the group message blew up, making the phone buzz as I finally typed, *Hey.*

He sent back, *So what do you think it's gonna be? "Beach and barz?" Or do we end up just going to The Watering Hole for a few brews and wings?*

I smiled. Our group had a 50/50 shot of actually following through on big plans. It was one of the peculiarities of living close enough to the beach and beach towns to go over for a few hours, but far enough for it to be a production to get there and home- especially if we'd been drinking. And The Watering Hole was a great little local place that had a mix of house-made brews and other local beers and wine. Plus, there was always something happening, like live music or trivia, and there was usually some kind of food truck to satisfy all your greasy cravings.

WH is ALWAYS a solid choice, I answered, *but we haven't done the beach and barz in FOREVER. Plus Friday is payday. I'm thinking... BEACH AND BARZ!*

A few seconds later, the group message popped up. This time it was Sam. *Let's get CRAYYYY!* He interjected a crazy faced emoji into the message. *Well, not too cray. We all know how Matt gets...*

As Matt jumped to defend himself, another private message came in from Sam. *WH tonight? Just us?*

This was what I'd been expecting for a couple weeks now. After our last breakup, I didn't take his calls for nearly a month. I'd avoided group events, and I even blocked him on social media. It didn't last long. It started with one phone call... then another... then a few late night drinks that turned into breakfast. The sex was never bad with Sam. I just didn't know if it could be better. I mean, I knew it could be *different.* But that was only twice, and I don't think Sam knew about either time... at least, I hoped he didn't.

I took long enough answering that I saw, "..." as Sam started to type, probably to say he was joking or something to save face. I typed as quickly as I could, *Sure! What time?*

Chapter 4

Opal

I walked down the alley to a thick steel door. I rang the bell beside it and waited.

"Name!" A voice called through a grate in the door.

"Opal," I said lazily.

The door opened, and the doorman behind it gave a little bow. "Madame." I was used to that. It came with being borderline royalty.

The Speakeasy I'd entered was not like the trendy bars humans seemed to frequent, where they pretended to enjoy a forbidden night of debauchery as experienced during the prohibition era, all while engaging in what was currently perfectly legal and socially acceptable behavior. If *this* place was ever found, my kind would be in big trouble. We may be stronger, faster, and smarter than human cattle, but they outnumbered us a few thousand to one and could overpower us if united.

The room was dimly lit in red light, making it feel even darker and more dangerous than it already was. I tossed my hair behind my shoulder and walked up to the bar, behind which were several lounge chairs containing humans who had been so drunk or otherwise inebriated that they'd followed the owners willingly into the establishment. Here, they were hooked up to an IV that would be opened up when their blood and alcohol or drug type was ordered. Then they would be released to a colleague who worked in the hospital before they were drained enough to cause lasting damage. The idea was to prevent questions from family and friends of deceased humans.

Pity that they cared so much; I was not the only one who might have paid a premium to enjoy the last drops.

I perched on the edge of a barstool and the bartender came to me and set down a cocktail napkin. He was a rugged looking Latino man with rust-colored eyes who went by the name Colorado. "The usual, Madame Opal?" He asked, by which he meant a red wine infused O-neg.

"Not tonight," I said. I raised my eyebrow as though thinking hard. "Something more... fun. I'm feeling feisty."

"How feisty?" He asked, his eyes drifting to a young man with track marks up and down his arm.

I looked at the boy in disgust. Humans and their weaknesses for hard drugs were something I couldn't fathom even if I cared to try. I had no taste or desire for whatever the man had used that led to him being brought here. "No," I said simply to Colorado. He knew I wouldn't touch the stuff, but I suppose my tone had made him question just how far I wanted to go down my rabbit hole tonight.

He smiled. "I got just the thing for you, Madame," he said and went to pour a glass from the IV of a young woman with brown hair. "Tequila Jell-O shots and A-neg. I know you don't love the positive."

I tipped the glass to him. "Right you are." I took a sip. It was sweeter than my usual fare, but delicious and smooth. And, like all blood I drank, slightly disappointing.

I had never yet found the equal of the sweet and satiating blood I'd had on my first night in this life. I didn't know if it was simply because it was my first kill, or if it was because it had been the blood of the man who tore me from my human life, but it was the best, most decadent drink I'd ever had. I occasionally wished I'd had that final drop from him, which I now know I had somehow missed. But knowing what Amber had told me about how we'd ended up in the woods together, it was probably for the best I didn't take it.

I downed my glass quickly and tapped the bar, indicating I wanted another. Colorado obliged, checking the girl's vitals. "One of the last few from this tap before I call Azura." Azura was our contact at the ER. She worked as a night nurse who made sure that any intake paperwork didn't indicate how the victims had been found. Colorado leaned close and whispered, "Whatever you're planning for your 'feisty' night out, Madame, it's probably best that you didn't go for the harder stuff. Zilpher is here tonight."

My eyes widened slightly at the news. Zilpher was one of the oldest vampires I'd ever known (hell, that most people had ever known) and, as such, was held in such high esteem that he was able to claim a spot on the Council without having to contend for it. He may have even helped found the Council; no one was quite sure anymore. His eyes were the color of cold steel, and his demeanor was about as warm- at least toward me. But then, he had reason to dislike me.

With Zilpher in town, I would be on a leash that I didn't appreciate. I'd intended on a much more "satisfactory" night than what I could get away with under the nose of a Council member, especially one who didn't particularly care for me.

"Thanks, Colorado," I said sincerely, making a mental note to not kill anyone in what could be construed as a "reckless" way. Sure, I could just not kill anyone, but where's the fun in that? And with Zilpher in town for who knew how long, I'd need as much extra juice as I could get in case things turned... unfriendly.

It was during my third helping (and the last that my source could handle before she was carried off to be treated at the hospital) that I finally heard Zilpher's voice carry from across the room.

I turned around to face him, leaning casually against the bar, knowing he'd probably had one eye on me since he'd walked in. I was right. As soon as I looked at him, his steely eyes locked onto mine and I tipped my glass toward him. It might have been a friendly gesture, if not for our history.

*   *   *

The night I'd died and been reborn, Amber had brought me to her condo in Tampa (which would later belong to me) and had gotten me cleaned up and changed.

She stood next to me and looked at our reflection. "Well, damn," she said. "I thought *I* had a lock on the sexiest vampire in town, but you changed over like a dream." She brushed a hand through my hair, tousling it just enough to give it a care-free look. "I just wish we could figure out your Goddamned eyes. They're mint green now." Her brow creased. "I've never seen anyone's eyes take so long to settle."

"What if they don't?" I asked, mildly concerned that maybe something had gone wrong when I'd come back, and I might go back to being regular dead rather than undead.

"They always do," Amber said, shaking her head. A thought seemingly occurred to her. "Maybe... what happened when you killed that guy in the woods?"

I looked at her in the mirror. "What do you mean?" I asked. "I drank his blood and he died."

She put a hand to her mouth thoughtfully. "So, you didn't drain him completely."

"Yes, I did," I insisted.

She seemed half-lost in thought. "I don't think so. The last drop contains their dying memories, the life flashing before their eyes. If you'd drained him to empty, you'd have relived his most prominent memories in your mind, and that would definitely be something you remembered. Maybe you haven't completed the change yet... We need to get you some more sustenance. I know a place."

She took me by the hand and led me out onto the street and to the large steel door where the doorman had asked for a name, and, upon hearing Amber's, opened the door for us.

It had been a shock the first time I'd walked in, not because I was horrified at the human kegs behind the bar, but because I was so overwhelmed by the sight and smell of them that I had a moment where I nearly went feral with bloodlust. Amber stopped me and sat me in a booth in the corner. "Chill, bitch," she'd said frantically. "Council members are here, and we cannot go savage with them looking on. Cool?"

I restrained the instinct, then cocked my head to the side, eyes still on the blood in an IV line that was waiting to be poured. "What Council?"

"*Our* Council. For vampires. We didn't get to a point where some of us were literally thousands of years old without having some rules for ourselves. It makes it a little easier to cohabitate with others of our kind and to stay hidden from humans. Of course..." she glanced across the room with a curl to her lip. "Sometimes it just makes it less fun. Especially when," she nodded her head in the direction of her gaze, "the high and mighty see fit to pass judgment on us for simply acting like what we are."

"What do you mean?" I asked, my hunger dulling the curiosity I felt.

"I mean that the man and woman at the bar are Zilpher and Orla. Silver and Gold," she spat, sarcasm dripping from the words. "They're some of the highest ranking Council members, and they're so fucking old and powerful they've forgotten how to actually live like the rest of us do."

I looked in the direction she indicated. There were two vampires at the bar who were being given treatment that fringed on reverential. Zilpher appeared to be in his early 40s but with hair as grey as the stylish suit he wore, and, I realized when his gaze swept the room every so often, his eyes. He was tall and slender, but in a way that added to the overall sensuality of his look. While he opted for the monochrome look, the woman beside him, Orla, I supposed, was head to toe contrast. Appearing to be about the same age as her companion, she was dressed in an all-white pantsuit over golden stilettos. Her black hair was styled close to her head in tight curls like a 50s pin-up girl. With the addition of bright red lips and winged black eyeliner, her golden eyes seemed to be practically glowing. She could have been the face of a Parisian perfume ad with her elegance and style.

And yet, I was unimpressed. "Why not just ignore them then?" I asked Amber.

Amber laughed, that lilting laugh that sounded innocent and sweet. "You can't ignore them. They get so far up our asses if they expect that we're breaking a law that you could taste them. And they're constantly changing up what is and isn't 'acceptable' behavior. The only way to change a Council ruling is to actually challenge a member of the Council to combat and win. Meaning you'd have to kill one of the *several thousand year old* vampires. Believe me, if I thought I could win, I'd have tried."

"Why?" I asked. What did they not allow that she wanted to do?

"Well..." Amber seemed taken aback by the question. "For one thing, they don't think any of us should be killing in the first place. Totally hypocritical, since they've been killing for millennia so no one can win against them if they ever get challenged."

"What do you mean?" I asked, feeling like a broken record. Amber made it sound like killing was necessary to our lives- it certainly was necessary for finalizing my transformation from human to vampire, since leaving behind a single drop seemed to have caused something to go wrong with my eyes.

She struggled for a moment to find the words. "We need human blood to survive, but we don't *need* to kill. Draining someone to the last drop does a few things to us. First, we get to see their dying thoughts, that whole 'life before their eyes' thing, which is a high like no human drug can give. Second, and most important, it makes us stronger than just drinking human blood without killing. It's part of why they have their bullshit 'guideline' about it. If the rest of us aren't allowed to kill, we can't challenge them. But they've been at it so long, someone would have to do a *lot* of killing to stand a chance, and they'd have to do it quickly enough to not draw the Council's attention. By the time you did it, you'd have a body count that would draw the attention of human authorities and risk our secrecy." She said this all very fast and with aggravation. "The Council claims that modern technology is the reason we have to be so discreet- people can spread information about someone missing or dead faster than we can hide the bodies. And they're kind of right, but it's still fucking annoying. Believe me, babe," she patted my head condescendingly, "I've thought this all out. For centuries."

What Amber didn't realize was that I had woken up from my death with little to no impulse control or care for rules- not that I was sure if I'd ever had any before. So when she looked at me after I sat silent for several moments, staring at the backs of the Council members, she gasped. "Whoa! Black? Your eyes are pitch black now... What are you doing?!" she'd said with shock, but it was too late. I walked over to the Council members and tapped Orla on the shoulder.

She turned her golden eyes on me. They were full of reproach and distaste. "May I help you?" She asked, seeming uninterested in whatever I'd come over to say.

"Yes," I said simply. "I want to challenge you."

Everyone in the bar went still except for Orla, Zilpher, Amber, and I. Orla and Zilpher laughed, while Amber buried her face in her hands, embarrassed. I, on the other hand, crossed my arms, annoyed that I wasn't being taken seriously. "Unless you think you'll lose," I taunted.

Orla stopped laughing, turning her haughty gaze on me. "How old are you?"

I set my chin defiantly. "I don't know. I don't remember anything from my human life."

She raised an eyebrow at me. "How long since you've not been human?"

"A couple hours," I admitted without shame.

Orla stood up and looked around. She saw Amber staring at us with a mix of horror and amusement and called to her. "Do you know this fledgling?"

Amber hurried over. "Yes, Madame Orla," she said. "She's new, just changed tonight, and if I could have a word with you alone..."

She urged Orla to a far corner of the room, Zilpher following, where they spoke in voices too low for me to hear. Their body language and expressions never once shifted, but I could feel an amalgam of tense emotions coming off of them, even if I couldn't exactly figure out what they were. Humans have a saying, "you could cut the tension with a knife." To humans, it's hyperbole; to a vampire, the feelings that cause such tension are physical, tangible things that we can see and feel in the air. It's highly beneficial on a hunt and when defending yourself.

When they returned several minutes later, Orla said, "Amber," her lip curled slightly, "has convinced us to allow your challenge to be forgotten. Don't let it happen again." She sat back on her barstool and put her glass to her lips before turning away from me in what I'm sure was intended to be a dismissal. All it did was piss me off.

I glared. "I don't want it forgotten," I said. I felt reckless and strong, and wanted to test what I was capable of. I had no patience for being ignored. I had woken up in the woods with no memory. If I lost this fight, I decided, I lost nothing. If I won, I realized, I would have complete agency over my life, or afterlife. "I challenge you."

Orla was larger than I; she stood about half a foot taller and easily had twenty to thirty pounds of muscle that I lacked despite her slender build. This was in addition to the millennia of human kills that had given her vampiric strength I should never hope to match as a fledgling vampire. So when she stepped close to me, I should have felt threatened. Instead, I felt exhilarated.

I stared her down, feeling the thrill come over me. Orla laughed, a rough, cruel sound. She had barely finished her cackle when she struck out with one hand and hit me in the chest so hard I flew backward twenty feet and hit the wall. I reached up and felt my lip, which had smacked against my descended fang when I landed. There was a trickle of blood, which I licked away before standing.

"Stay down, young one, and I'll let you live," she said in a bored voice.

Despite the blow, I didn't feel any pain, which itself was a wonder. My excitement level blossomed like jasmine in the evening hours. She thought she'd dealt a crushing blow, but I was just fine. I stood and locked eyes with her. "No thanks," I said, confidence infusing my entire being.

A strange look entered Orla's eyes as I walked slowly back toward her. At first, I couldn't place it, but as I approached and she began to take a more defensive stance, I realized the emotion I saw was *fear*. I should have questioned more why she feared me, with every possible factor in this fight being in her favor, and yet, she had dealt a blow that had done nothing. I felt that delicious fear emanating from her, and it was intoxicating.

I lashed out with one hand, which Orla blocked, but as she prepared to send a blow back at me, I twisted away, my foot coming around the other side and connecting with her face. She staggered back and I, using her moment of surprise, landed a second blow to the other side of her face, and a third to her chest. She fell backward, trying to regain the high ground, but she'd lost it before we'd even started; she just didn't know it. And it wasn't until much, much later that I'd find out why.

I had Orla pinned to the ground, bloodied and beaten. Instinct came over me and I knew what I had to do. I leaned over and sank my fangs into her neck, feeding from her, imbibing all of her strength, collected over millennia. I had been a vampire for hours, and yet I now stood amongst others of my kind, stronger than most, with power I'd never expected. Zilpher watched as I destroyed his lover, as Amber handed me a piece of broken glass from a mirror that had shattered in the exchange, looking at me with a mix of fear and awe.

"You have to finish it," she said, her eyes only briefly glancing toward Zilpher, who had now looked away from his defeated lover. "You drained her blood, but you have to deal the final blow- you have take off her head. If you don't finish it... if you don't kill her, you don't win, and they'll kill you for harming a Council member."

I took the jagged glass from Amber and stood over Orla, whose eyes were now closed. She didn't look nearly as stunning now, more like a skeletal caricature of the woman I'd seen drinking confidently. In a swift motion and with no hesitation, I slashed the makeshift blade across her throat, cutting deeply, severing the spine, decapitating her. Having drained her of every last drop of blood, it was a bit anticlimactic when the wound opened and nothing happened, but I'd won, and easily.

As I looked up and into the eyes of everyone who'd been watching, I saw shock on their faces that hadn't come from watching me best a Council member.

"*Mierda*," Colorado (whom I hadn't yet officially met) said.

Zilpher gave me a calculating stare, his eyes very carefully not drifting to Orla's body. He turned to Amber. "What is that?" He asked her, perturbed.

"What?" I asked. I had just violently murdered a member of vampire royalty and they all seemed to be much more concerned about something on my face. I lifted the weapon in my hand to peer into the reflection there and saw what they'd been looking at. My eyes, which had been slowly changing all night, suddenly shone like a kaleidoscope with every color and shade, undulating between waves of varying tones, with sparks of this color or that flitting across the iris.

Amber came to my side. "Well... I have no idea what the fuck made you so damn special, but I think you're not quite like the rest of us... Opal."

Zilpher's calculating expression had turned into one of distaste. "Opal..." he seemed to be tasting my name on his tongue and not liking it.

And that had been good enough for me. If Zilpher hated it, I loved it.

"Opal. Yes. I think so," I said regarding my new name, admiring my still changing eyes. They slowly changed to an icy blue that rivaled Zilpher's eyes in their coldness, and I stared him down. "Well, I won the challenge. Which means you get to leave me alone to do what I want."

Zilpher laughed humorlessly while everyone else looked at me in a way that let me know I'd said something stupid. "You killed a member of the Council," Zilpher said, venom in every syllable. "You'll never be left alone again. This is a pack system- if you challenge and win against an alpha, you become the new alpha. The difference is that you're not the only one- there are dozens of us spread across the globe, and while we make the laws, we're still beholden to them." Then he looked between Amber and me with disgust etched all over his face, and my stomach felt leaden as his words took hold in me. "Perhaps you should have understood what you were doing before you killed someone." With that, he swept from the room and out into the night.

Amber looked at me with that same mix of elation and terror and pulled me back to our booth after calling for two B-positive with Jack Daniels. Once there, she stared at me until the drinks came. I reached for one, but she threw her first one back, followed quickly by the one I thought had been for me.

"Know what, Colorado?" She said to the barman. "Just leave a bottle of Jack, maybe."

He nodded.

I would learn a lot in my first night. I just wish I'd taken the time to learn it before I had challenged Orla and sealed my fate.

Chapter 5

Elsie

Sam rolled over, kissing me good morning. "I'm really glad you came out last night, El," he said.

I smirked at him. "I bet you are." I climbed out of the bed and went to the bathroom to shower. Sam had his own place, which was a really nice escape when you were well into your late 20s and living at home. It may have been a shitty little studio with no interior doors except the one to the bathroom, but it was private and made me feel free- compared to how I felt at home anyway.

When I'd gotten home from work the night before, I changed and told mom I was going out and to not wait up. Of course, it wasn't that easy. One thing that doesn't change from your teens is that your mom will still want to know details. "Who are you meeting?" Mom had asked, though, by her face, I figured she already knew.

"Sam," I said, spraying my hair with some dry shampoo and avoiding meeting her eyes. We'd never talked about the physical nature of my relationship with Sam, nor had I ever allowed anything sexual to happen in my childhood home for my parents' sake (and my own- I had zero desire to have that conversation), but I didn't exactly hide it.

Her disapproval was thicker than syrup. Mom thought we shouldn't be having "sleepovers," as she liked to delicately put it, before we were at least engaged, and certainly not when we weren't even a couple. "By don't wait up, do you mean you're not coming home tonight?" She eyed the bag I'd packed. I still hadn't reclaimed my drawer at Sam's. That was committing to more than I was sure of just yet.

"Yes, Mom. That's a possibility. I could be home at 9, I could be home tomorrow." I caught her glowering at me in the mirror while I put on some eyeliner. "Mom, I don't know where things with Sam are going, but I won't find out by *not* seeing him. We need to talk things through, one way or another."

"It seems like y'all have already decided where things are going tonight," she snapped. Every time. Every time I even hinted that I was staying over, the fight came up about whether I should, like Sam, have my own place. "*Sure, Mom,*" I'd always retort, "*Kick me out or force me to pay rent. Guess what won't get paid? I'll give you a hint. It's not rent. It's not the phone bill. It's that student loan you co-signed. Mutually assured destruction isn't on my agenda this week. Is it on yours?*"

As I washed the previous night off of me in Sam's shower, I tried to decide if this meant more than our last few nights together or if it was just stress release- for him *or* for me. Looking back, the evening had been so effortless, and coming back here after felt natural. But now that I had a few minutes alone...

Never mind. If it *was* just about the sex, who said we had to stop because it was morning? Certainly not Sam, who'd come to join me, making it entirely impossible to continue down that train of thought.

*   *   *

The rest of the week flew by without much happening. Work was standard, as was Sam's and my inability to have a real discussion about what we wanted from each other. By the time Friday rolled around, I knew I couldn't wait for our beach day Saturday to go let loose or I'd crawl out of my skin. But after spending Thursday night at Sam's again, I wanted a little distance to think. Or not think. Just because the week was uneventful didn't mean it wasn't stressful.

I called Jess and asked her to meet me at The Watering Hole. Jess was the most laid back of our group, unless you counted Charlotte and Matt, who weren't married yet but may as well have been; they could still have fun, but they didn't have the carefree single(ish) spirit the rest of us did.

I'd hoped that Jess and her level head would keep the night from getting too crazy since I didn't want to miss out on the beach day because of a hangover. We each ordered one of the weekly special beers and sat at one of the outdoor tables, watching people of all ages (literally- some people brought their kids) playing corn hole and enjoying the cooler evening air. We hung out and pointedly *didn't* discuss my relationship with Sam.

"Jimmy drew me the cutest picture today," I told her over my fourth beer (whoops- so much for taking it easy). "He said it was the two of us eating a pizza, because that's his favorite food and I'm his favorite lady."

Jess, still on her second beer, said, "Awwww! You are so lucky to have such an adorable reason to go to work. The only thing I got handed today was a notice that people will be getting laid off soon, so, *that's* fun!"

I almost dropped my beer. "Jess, what?!" She smiled sadly at me. "You might get *fired?*"

"Technically laid off is different from fired," she pointed out. Jess worked at a local tech firm specializing in software for... well, I don't really know because I honestly didn't understand it. She explained that their business was based entirely on contracts from other companies and organizations, and there hadn't been as many big contracts, so they couldn't keep all the staff on.

I gave her a big hug made all the bigger by my dwindling inhibitions. "I'm sorry," I mumbled to her. I wasn't drunk, but I certainly wasn't sober.

She patted me awkwardly, realizing this. "I'm not down and out yet, Elsie. Let's have some faith that my work is good enough for them to want to keep me." She backed out of the hug and looked into my eyes. "You wanna head home?" She asked. Jess was a master at "momming" you without making you feel "mommed." But as I looked around, I realized it was still early. The sun had just barely cleared the horizon; it was still light out.

I thought about it. "Not yet," I decided, thinking suddenly that a menthol would be awesome. "I want to smoke."

Jess tilted her head to the side and frowned. "We haven't smoked in five years. Remember how hard it was to quit?"

I laughed. "Not for me!" It was true. Somehow I woke up one day, declared I was quitting, and that was that. But I remembered how hard it had been for Jess, who'd had to use almost every quit aid there was. "I just... it's been a week. Okay? Let me have this one, without judging. Please."

"Well, you go ahead then," she said with a hint of resentment in her voice. She'd be fine by the time we left. "I'm going to go use the bathroom and settle up. Meet you back here?"

"Sure!" I sang, getting up to go find someone I could bum a cigarette off of since, as a "non-smoker," I didn't exactly have any of my own. The first person I saw lighting up, leaning against a high top table off to the side of the crowd, was a man, probably a few years older than I was. He had on a white button-down with the sleeves rolled up to his elbows and dark jeans that were slim cut, but not too tight. He was fit, but in an

41

understated way, just enough that you could see toned and defined muscles under the lines of his shirt, but without being built up. His shoes were fashionable sneakers that sat perfectly under the hemline of the pants. His black hair was styled in that way that looked natural and carefree but probably took an hour to get just right. In fact, every part of his look was very casual, but altogether there was something about him that came across as just *decadent*. He was the apotheosis of average. The only odd thing was that he was wearing sunglasses, even though the sun had set, but hey, that was his prerogative, and it just added an air of mystery.

I walked over with the confidence of three-point-five beers. "Hey," I said. "Mind if I borrow one of those?"

He glanced up at me, having been watching the same corn hole tournament. "Hello," he replied with an amused half-smile. "I'd prefer if you didn't borrow it as I probably I don't want it back once you've finished, but I'm glad to let you keep one." He was definitely not from around here. He had an accent that caused him to hit certain syllables just a little harder than I did. It was faint but noticeable; distinct but nearly unplaceable; vaguely Anglo with many years of living stateside to make it difficult to figure out exactly where he hailed from.

I smiled back, taking the cigarette and leaning against the high top next to him and toward him so he could light it for me. The first pull filled my mouth and I almost moaned with how wonderful it was. I resisted the urge to do so, not only because I chose to inhale, but also because moaning at a stranger who just gave you a cigarette was probably some kind of social taboo.

I looked down at the little stick of paper and leaves. "I haven't had one of these in five years," I said. "I'd forgotten how *nice* they are." Okay, maybe I was a bit closer to drunk than sober. If I hadn't been, I'd never have even considered smoking. The reason I'd woken up that one day and decided to quit was because smoker's cough the morning after drinking and smoking and drinking and smoking was a bitch. I could smell the stale smoke on my body and breath all day, no matter how much I showered or brushed my teeth, and I hated it. It also wasn't exactly helpful for a runner to have reduced lung function, and I enjoyed running much more than smoking... usually.

But if I hadn't been four beers deep in half as many hours and craving a cigarette to go with the alcohol and stress combination, I wouldn't have met the man who would change my life...

And bring about its end as I knew it.

Chapter 6

Elsie

When Jess came back out, I was shoving what was left of the butt into one of those cigarette disposal podiums that was next to the table where I'd been chatting with-

"Cyrus," he'd said, reaching for my hand while Jess was still inside.

"I'm Elsie," I replied coyly.

"That's a lovely name," he mused, "and not one you hear often. Is there a story there?"

His smile was nearly blinding. I thought I was going to need a pair of those sunglasses if he kept flashing those pearly whites my way. Slightly intoxicated wasn't my best presentation, but hey, I was single(ish) and he was attractive enough that I'd have been flustered had I been stone cold sober.

"I don't really know," I flirted. "Is there a story behind 'Cyrus'?"

His eyebrows shifted for a millisecond before he replied, "Yes. Perhaps I'll share it with you. But not today."

Catching the hint that he was asking to see me again, I felt my breath catch in my throat and took a long drag to cover. I hadn't yet worked out my feelings for Sam or about our future together, but being hit on by a guy like Cyrus was unexpected and, frankly, a major boost to my self-esteem. He had the effortless grace of someone who was simply sure of himself, and it was captivating. For everything about Sam that kept me coming back, he had lingering insecurities that kept rearing their heads, usually in response to me complaining about a lack of excitement in our lives.

"Sure," I said to Cyrus, smiling. "Give me your number."

I handed him my phone and he added himself as a contact. "There. It's under Cyrus Kelley. And..." he grinned down at his own phone. "Thanks for *your* number." He held his phone up, showing a text from me. He made sure he'd gotten my number as well. I was torn between being flattered and mildly annoyed.

I decided to change the subject. "I've never seen you here before. Are you local?"

"As of recently," Cyrus answered. "I'm still getting my bearings, but so far, I think I'm settling in well." He took a long drag, not of the cigarette, but of the not-too-warm breeze that ruffled the magnolia trees that had just begun to bloom. "It helps that we're basically in paradise."

"Actually," I teased, "We're in a sectioned off area of a parking lot."

He laughed and lightly pushed a loose strand of hair behind my ear. "This is true."

My heart jumped at the touch. It wasn't a love-at-first-sight or a meant-to-be reaction. It was more that I barely knew him and he barely knew me, but his touch was welcome and exhilarating.

I also thought about how Sam would feel if he saw the moment, and I felt guilty. It was one thing to flirt with someone when Sam and I were an uncertainty. It was another to go beyond that if we were already becoming more.

That was when Jess came back out and I had finished my cigarette. I smiled at Cyrus, thanked him for the cigarette, and followed Jess to the car, ushering her away quickly.

"Elsie!" Jess squealed once she pulled out of the parking lot. "*Who. Was. That?! YUM!*"

I tried to give an easy laugh. "I just bummed a cig off of him," I said, rolling my window down to let the warm breeze dispel some of the smoke smell in case Mom caught a whiff. If she smelled cigarette smoke on me, she would have an even bigger fit than she did when I went to Sam's. "His name is Cyrus. He's new to town."

Jess smirked. "Seemed like he wanted to be new to *your* town!" Then she did a little mock-sexy dance.

I laughed, this time without trying. "That doesn't even make sense!" I lightly shoved her arm. "I don't know. Things are so fucked up with Sam, and I don't know if they ever *won't* be. Sometimes it's just nice to have someone else notice me- to make me feel like being with Sam is a choice and not an inevitability."

The laughter faded from Jess's eyes. "Elsie..." she paused, working out what she wanted to say. "If Sam isn't the guy, he isn't the guy. But don't let him think that he might be forever just because *you* don't know. You're both good people who care about each other. But you both have lives to live and either need to give each other permission to do that, or you need to be totally honest and lay everything out and decide to make it work." She paused. "Does he even know about that time you 'went home early'?"

My gaze fell. Jess had called me out on one of my most shameful moments. Technically, we hadn't been a couple at the time, but Sam and I had been working things out when, after a night at The Watering Hole, I told Sam I was going home.

He didn't know I was going home with *another guy.*

It only happened the one night (with that guy, anyway), and Jess was the only other person who knew because I was bursting with guilt and had to tell someone. She'd come over in her signature way- in her pajamas, with wine.

"You and Sam aren't a couple," she'd consoled me at the time. "You can fuck anyone you want. But don't let Sam think this is going somewhere if it isn't."

It was the same advice she was giving me after I met Cyrus. Jess and Sam had been friends longer than most of us, so she treated him like a brother. She would never betray a confidence, but her love for him combined with a maturity that went beyond what most of the rest of us displayed, often manifesting in some occasionally hard-to-swallow advice.

She didn't even know about the time I *really* betrayed Sam...

And that one was my secret. And as long as *he* kept the secret, so would I.

But Jess was right. I needed to figure things out with Sam, and soon. Because-

Bzzt. My phone lit up with a text from Cyrus. *It was a pleasure to meet you, Elsie. Sleep well.*

I turned the phone over as Jess gave me a suspicious side-eye. Her advice was right. But it wasn't her decision. It was mine, and that meant I didn't have to share *everything*.

Chapter 7

Opal

Zilpher walked over from his corner booth to where I was enjoying my drink at the bar. "Hello, Madame Opal," he said, his voice as steely as his eyes. "Lovely night out. I'm surprised you're holed up here and not out on the prowl." His eyes glinted dangerously on the last word. I knew that he knew about my activities as much as I knew about his.

I turned so that I no longer faced him, but he still had a perfect view of my profile as I gave a wide, would-be friendly smile. "All in good time," I said. "What brings you to our charming little parish, Master Zilpher?" My voice dripped with sarcasm. Tampa was hardly a tiny, quaint village.

Zilpher climbed onto the barstool next to me and waved Colorado over to order a drink. "We understand that Amber may be alive and back in town. You haven't heard anything about that, have you?" His voice was accusatory and taunting, but masked in the cordiality you might observe in business associates vying for the same position.

I tried not to let the shock show on my face. It had been years since I'd even heard from Amber. I had actually believed her dead, something Zilpher of all people should know and, even more than I, be concerned about. I wasn't sure if it hurt that she didn't contact me, but it certainly took me by surprise that she would be in town and not reach out. I wasn't going to give Zilpher the satisfaction of knowing that I actually cared on any level, even though the idea alone gave me chills. I took a sip of my drink to cover. "If she is, that's news to me." Amber was a rolling stone- never one to sit still and gather moss. If she was back in town, however, it explained why Zilpher was here. He had been charged with dealing with her after the incident, which meant he was responsible if she was alive. At the time, Amber had blamed me for her predicament and swore eternal hatred if she made it out. If she was back... I had reason to worry. "I'd think it would be very embarrassing for you if she was."

"We know that you and Amber have history," he said, ignoring my accusation and sounding like a cop on a procedural crime show who was trying to get someone to rat out a friend, "what with her being your sire. But as a member of this Council, *Madame*, you need to be willing and ready to enforce the laws we have in place. Amber has a pattern, and she seems ready to act on it."

Amber rarely operated with a pattern that she herself had devised. It was what had made her so unpredictable and difficult to find. And I'd never wanted to be on their damn Council. I'd only wanted to show that I couldn't be pushed around. Killing the man in the woods had been so satisfying. I wasn't about to let some Grandma and Grandpa vampires tell me what I could or couldn't do, especially if that meant I couldn't hunt how I wanted.

I rolled my eyes, the smile I'd been faking falling into an expression of boredom. "Fine, Zilpher," I conceded. "Tell me what I need to be looking out for- other than Amber herself- and I'll do my best to keep her in line."

He frowned at me. "I certainly hope so. Her rumored existence is concerning enough, but she's gotten reckless about this particular activity in the last few centuries. Not that I blame her." His eyes narrowed. "It's easy to lose control when you've lost a lover."

I ignored his thinly veiled suggestion that I wouldn't do my job and instead focused on his mostly false statement. "She didn't *lose* him," I said, "but I imagine you already knew that."

"Not the same way I did," Zilpher growled. He was a broken record about Orla. "But yes. He *left* her, and she took it poorly. She has a... ritual, but she's taken it too far of late."

I shrugged. "Sounds like Amber."

"As members of the Council, *Madame*," his voice dripped disdain, "We have to be concerned about certain activities. Killing, if done at all, needs to be done discreetly. I think we can agree that discretion is not one of Amber's strengths."

He was right on that count. Amber had made that much clear to me on many separate occasions, although one, in particular, had been such a mess I'd had to call Zilpher himself in to help with the fallout.

I turned to Zilpher to look him in the eyes. I leaned back on the bar, my head tilted to show my contempt for him and the whole conversation. "Is that all? You just came to warn me about Amber? Fine," I said with finality. "Message received, *Master*. Can you let me enjoy my night? I have *prowling* to do, as you put it."

He raised an eyebrow at me. "I suppose so." He stood, adjusting his suit and downing his glass in one gulp. He gave me one final disdainful glare. "Take care, Opal."

With that, he walked out.

Chapter 8

Elsie

The beach was the perfect remedy to a long week. The powder-fine white sand, bright blue-green waves, and salt-water smell were like medicine. Sam stayed close, which was frustrating because it didn't really give me an opportunity to think about him. His sun-bleached blonde hair was cropped close. He was fairly active, but beer and junk food had softened his frame- much like my own. I didn't care. His big brown eyes were warm and kind and so was his smile, which was more than enough for me. I just didn't know if Sam himself was enough for me anymore.

I finally broke away for a bit on my own under the pretense of going to use the restroom up at the main building. Instead, I walked up and down the beach, just out of sight, letting the waves whisper to me. The sound of the water beating against the sand, of the children playing, of the seagulls calling to each other, was an elixir, clearing my mind and helping me to think clearly.

Tonight was going to be the turning point for Sam and me, I decided. I just couldn't decide which way I wanted it to turn. If I didn't make the call, he would do it for me and I would be along for the ride again, which never ended well. I wanted to feel in control. I needed to know that I chose the path we went down, and this time I didn't want to be running in circles. Whether I stayed or not, I wanted that to be it. My final decision. Like Jess said, we both needed to give each other and ourselves a chance to live our lives, either together or apart.

I sat on the sand and hugged my knees as I tried to picture my life as Sam's friend or as his future wife. I could be content, I concluded, married to a good man like Sam. But was content the same as happy? There was my question. Was it worth giving up Sam in the hopes that something better was out there? And could we even just have a constancy in our relationship? Would we always revert back to old habits, to on-again, off-again? I didn't want that. I wanted all or nothing. Could we just be friends? It would be hard, but the thought didn't make me quite so sad as I might have imagined.

By the end of my reverie, I realized I hadn't been keeping Sam on the hook because I still loved him. I had loved him once, and I still had love for him, but that had changed to a friendly affection. It occurred to me that I was more afraid of losing someone who loved *me* than of losing someone I loved.

I stood up and brushed the sand from my legs and wandered back to my friends, but not before pulling out my phone and texting Cyrus back. *Sorry, just saw this. Thanks!* Followed by an emoji of a smiley face blowing a kiss.

*　　*　　*

I sat with Ashley as we waved goodbye to our friends. It was getting late and Jack had already left, but Charlotte and Matt had offered to drive the rest of us home. I knew I couldn't get in the car with Sam after our conversation, and

Ashley, who had wanted to stay out anyway, had offered to stay and share a ride home with me.

We'd gone back to Matt's sister's house earlier, where we all got to shower and get ready for the night out. I had just wrapped my towel around me to start doing my hair and makeup when there was a fast yet quiet knock at the door, followed by Sam slipping in.

"Sam!" I hissed.

"Shh," he smiled at me in that mischievous way he always did. He reached out and pulled me close, laying a hard, hungry kiss on my lips. I kissed him back, feeling his hands lower to grab at my towel-covered backside. It was a few minutes of kissing and groping before he reached to pull my towel off, and I remembered my decision from the beach.

"Wait!" I said, grabbing at the towel and stepping back. "Sam, wait."

He flashed that smile at me again, stepping forward and reaching for me again. "Don't worry. We have time," he drawled, putting his lips close to my ear.

"I know," I barely managed, steeling myself. "And I think we should use that time to talk." I gave him a grim smile and perched myself on the edge of the tub, motioning to him to take a seat on the toilet.

The nerves in his face gave way to sadness and anger as I spoke. I didn't blame him. We'd been going back and forth leading each other on for so long, I don't know if he really believed that I meant every word at first, but he seemed to understand that, at least for now, we were over. I didn't even blame him when he stormed out of the bathroom.

I *did*, however, find it particularly unkind when he started flirting with the server at our favorite rooftop bar, aptly named The Roof. Emily, her name was, recognized us, and clearly took notice of Sam and I sitting far apart- not our norm. I shouldn't have been mad when she flirted back, or even when she gave him her number, but I was stung. It was shortly after that that Sam, Jess, Charlotte, and Matt left. I pulled out my phone for a momentary distraction and saw a missed text. Cyrus. *You are most welcome. I haven't had a chance to make too many friends in the area yet, and it was refreshing to have a friendly conversation.*

My mood considerably brighter, I turned to Ashley. "Wanna hop?" I asked with a wicked gleam in my eye. I wanted to go somewhere we could dance.

"Hell. Yes." Ashley nearly shouted. I knew I could count on her.

We ended up at one of the nicer dance clubs, on the second floor of a historic looking building. While our usual place was full of young entrepreneurs and had an atmosphere like you'd expect in a beach town, this place had music loud enough to drown out nearly anything outside and had an atmosphere of people desperate to get laid. I wasn't sure if I was on board with that tonight, but who knew? Maybe tonight *would* end with a one night stand. After all...

There's a third time for everything.

I made my way over to the bar. Ashley got separated from me in the crowd, but I could see her coming over. Having her with me at a place like this was both a blessing and a curse. Ashley was one of those girls who shined like a diamond 24/7. She had bountiful blonde waves (not terribly unlike mine, but much more voluminous and with spectacular highlights that shouldn't even be allowed) around a face that was just tanned enough to bring out her freckles. Her deep royal blue eyes were big and bright and lined with a perfect black wing at each corner. She had the kind of body I could only dream of having, slim but strong and the exact proportions you would see in a lingerie catalog, and she had a warm smile and a laugh that was more musical and noticeable than the pounding bass around us. What was both great and not great about that (for me) was that she acted as a buffer for any guy who came over. That was awesome when the guy was a creep. It was less awesome when I was actually interested.

Of course, once we got there, I felt very much like I wasn't interested in any of it. Not the music, not the dancing, and not the guys. Certainly not any guys like the one who came up to me after Ashley went to dance with a man who had dressed to impress- something not easy to do with Ashley.

I had thrown back my first drink quickly and ordered another. The bartender offered me a water while I waited for her to make it. I ran my fingers through the condensation on the side of the glass, feeling the cool water cover my skin and run down to the table. I was beginning to question my decision to break things off with Sam. I pulled my phone out and glanced at my notifications. Nothing new from Cyrus, since I'd responded to him before: *I'm up for friendly conversation anytime,* followed by a smiley face. I'd hoped he would take "anytime" to mean now, to distract me from my first distraction, but he obviously didn't get the hint.

I looked around me. I realized I really meant what I said to Cyrus. I wanted to *talk* to someone, not start dry humping them in public. I knew in that moment I was full of shit. I couldn't even lie to myself. I wasn't going home with anyone that night. I'd been so full of regret after the first two times I'd had a one night stand, I swore I would never do it again. I had nothing against the act itself; heaven knows I was no virgin. But for me, sex needed to mean something. Jumping into bed with someone I barely knew (or even whom I knew well, but should never have gone there with) wasn't for me. I craved a connection to the person I was sharing my body with. A part of me wanted to cry as I thought about how it may not have been earth-shattering with Sam, but it was always meaningful, and I'd given that up.

The bartender, Betty- and she *looked* like a Betty, with big black curls around her pale face and red lips- was putting the finishing touches on my drink when a thick fingered hand covered in gold rings came down on the counter next to me, followed by its twin on the other side.

A slurring voice spoke in my ear, making me cringe. "Lemme buy you a drink, sweetheart. Something a little stronger than water." His heavy northeast accent and the smell of cheap cologne, not to mention the patronizing endearment, caused my lip to curl. I leaned forward to reduce contact and turned to look at him.

Black hair slicked back with way too much gel; a white wife beater that showed off a very obviously steroid-enhanced physique; an inexpertly trimmed chin strap; and enough gold jewelry to feed a family of four for a year all contributed to the leaden feeling in my stomach. This man was *not* my type. I didn't want him touching me, and yet, here he was, helping himself to my personal space.

"Excuse me," I sneered, speaking as coolly as I could over the music. "I already bought myself a drink. Try someone else. Thanks."

Instead of leaving, he dropped himself into the seat beside mine, resting his hand on my lower back. I began to fill with rage, but also dread. He was twice my size and, while I could always get Betty to alert the bouncers, I knew his size, his persistence, and his drunkenness were going to make it very hard for me to just walk away.

Luckily for me, despite my own intoxication level, *my* size was in my favor. I spun the barstool around and away from the person I'll call Greasy Pete, hopping to my feet and moving as quickly as I could into the crowd to try to lose him. I didn't make it far- in fact, it was only a couple of feet- before I felt myself slam into something. I stumbled backward and there was the tiny sound of plastic cracking, then the sensation of cold.

Not just cold, but wet.

Looking down at myself, I noticed that my white blouse was covered in sticky, pungent brown liquid. Ice had managed to fall into my hair and was scattered around my feet. Face burning with shock and humiliation, I looked up to see what I'd run into and was met with the brightest, most vibrant blue-green eyes I'd ever seen. I was so stunned, I didn't even notice who they belonged to until I went back on alert at the feeling of a hand wrapping around my lower back.

"Cyrus?" I gasped. My heart fluttered at his touch once again, but then it sank as I realized one of his hands was on his now shattered cup and the other was at his side. It wasn't his hand on me.

Greasy Pete had come up behind me, unwilling to hear "no," and had yet again helped himself not only to my space, but to my body. He squeezed the flesh along my hip as he looked at Cyrus.

"Hey, man," he snarled. "You gonna say sorry or what?"

Cyrus looked at the man touching me, then raised an eyebrow at me, asking a question I answered with a shake of my head. No, this was not okay. No, I was not here with this man. No, I didn't want him touching me. No, please don't let him take me from here. I was too stunned- from cold, from wet, from shock, from the booze- to do more. He looked up at my aggressor and raised the same eyebrow. This time it was not a question.

It was a threat.

"You should let her go," Cyrus said. His voice was polite, but there was something about the way he said it that, had it been directed at me, I'd have been a bit frightened. Greasy Pete, whether from the alcohol or just an overinflated ego, ignored the warning.

"Me and my lady here are gonna go get her out of these wet clothes," he said with a leer that would have made me roll my eyes if he hadn't been holding on to me in a way that made the look terrifying.

"I'm n-not your l-lady," I stammered, barely able to form words, both chilled from the icy drink and frozen with fear. "Let me go!"

Cyrus looked at me and back at Greasy Pete. "You heard her. Let. Her. Go."

Suddenly Greasy Pete's hand left my side. I was filled with relief- until it soared past me and made sickening contact with Cyrus's face.

"Oh, my God!" I screamed and dove for him.

The next few moments went by very quickly. The bouncers came over to break up the fight, though, by that point, there wasn't much of a fight to break up. Cyrus was sitting on the floor, cupping his bleeding nose; I was kneeling next to him, trying to see if it was broken; Ashley had seen the commotion and come running over. She may come across as a ditz, but I'll be damned if she can't read a situation in a second and a half or less. She took one look at Cyrus and me, then at Greasy Pete and started screaming for the bouncers to eject him. Which was completely unnecessary because they were ready to throw us all out until Betty piped up in my defense, having been about to have security intervene on my behalf anyway.

"There's a single stall bathroom over here," she called over the still too-loud music, shoving a handful of cocktail napkins at me and pointing to a small alcove behind the bar. "Go get your boyfriend cleaned up."

Ashley and I helped Cyrus to the bathroom since he was holding a giant wad of napkins in the center of his face. Once he was seated on the toilet, Ashley gave me a questioning look. It said, "*Are you okay? I can stay, but if you want I can give you two a moment.*"

I gave her the slightest nod and she piped up, "I better go make sure Tim... Tom... Ted- whatever his name is hasn't forgotten about me in the chaos!" She showed all her teeth in a winning smile and ducked out.

Cyrus and I were silent for several minutes while I made use of the sink and the nice absorbent paper towels (the kind meant for employees) to clean him up. He was dressed exactly the same as the night before, except that his white shirt was covered in the same brown liquid as mine, as well as some droplets of the blood from his nose and mouth. The smell of the liquid had finally registered with me, and I realized he'd been drinking a Jack and Coke when I'd spun around and crushed the cup between us, essentially causing it to erupt into a sugar and booze volcano around us. He kept staring at me with those startling eyes that I hadn't gotten to see the night before because of the sunglasses he'd never taken off. The stare wasn't leery like Greasy Pete's had been, or angry like I'd have expected given how we'd *run into each other*, literally.

Instead, there was something questioning about it, as though he was working through a puzzle or trying to figure out a dilemma he couldn't quite get a hold on.

Finally, I broke the silence. "Yes?" I asked him, both eyebrows up in a semi-defensive, semi-flirtatious (I hoped) expression.

He frowned slightly. "You didn't have to clean me up," he said.

Okay... not what I was expecting. "And you didn't have to help me chase that douchebag roid-head off. But you did. Thanks for that, by the way." I paused, looking down at my hands and the pink-tinged paper towels. "I'm usually pretty good at looking out for myself and not getting into situations like that, but..." I was very close to telling him, *But I just broke up with my boyfriend of, like, forever and got way too drunk and careless,* but that seemed like the wrong move. So instead, I

59

said, "But I guess guys like that will always find you in the exact moment you can't. Look out for yourself, that is."

He gave a sad half-smile. "That's sadly true. Bad people will do bad things. Nothing we can do about that," he said. A devilishly handsome grin replaced the sad one and he continued, "Except to rescue the damsel in distress when the time comes."

I laughed. "I am so not a damsel, regardless of my distress level." I spread my arms to indicate my current sugar-soaked state. "Right now, I'm just ant-bait."

We both laughed heartily, the kind of laugh that doesn't fit the situation, but the relief you feel from a high-stress event that has passed overwhelms you, and you just can't stop.

"You know," I said, wiping at the drying blood on his face again, but still smiling, "None of this would have happened if you'd just responded to my text."

He raised that same eyebrow at me- I was going to start calling it the "The Brow"- with a sarcastic smile playing across his face. It was a good look for him; the expression highlighted the best of his face- the angular jaw, the straight white teeth, and the eyes... those eyes were like looking into Caribbean waters when the tide was still. "So you mean to say that you weren't already here, drinking and getting into trouble?"

"I haven't the slightest idea what you mean," I said very seriously before giving back that same sarcastic smile. "As a matter of fact, I was here all day." Suddenly I started rambling as the adrenaline began to wear off and my brain remembered I was still intoxicated. "There were a bunch of us- we came to the beach and- oh my God, it's awesome- you should totally come with us sometime. Our friend's sister has a place here, so we went there and got cleaned up then we went to the Roof and then everyone else wanted to go home so Ashley and I came here because she wanted to go dancing and I just didn't want to ride in the car with Sam and-" I cut myself off, realizing I'd probably said too much. Not only had I mentioned Sam, but I'd invited him to hang out with all my friends and I didn't even know him. So far, we'd only shared a few minutes over cigarettes, a few texts back and forth, and a dance club brawl over my honor. Not exactly the foundation of trust needed for personal conversations or to invite him into my circle.

As I stood there with my mouth clenched shut to prevent the word-vomit from spilling out, Cyrus said, "That's very kind of you to invite me along. It would be nice to meet some new people. But if you'd rather get to know me yourself first, before bringing me into your circle of friends, I understand that as well."

It was so unexpected of him to say precisely what had gone through my own mind, that this was so close to moving too fast, that I ignored everything that I had thought and that he had said; I acted without thinking and grabbed him around the neck and pressed our faces together in a rough kiss, doffing my own internal advice. My inhibitions were low to begin with, and feeling so understood and *seen* prompted the assertive action. After all, isn't this why people came to nightclubs?

Cyrus grabbed me around the waist and pulled me close until I ended up in his lap. He smelled amazing, his cologne something like the fresh, salty, invigorating fragrance of seawater itself. My hands worked their way across his chest- much more muscular than it appeared under his stylish shirts- and his crept under the front of mine. I pulled back for only a second, opening my eyes and seeing him do the same, but it was just enough. It had been so long since I'd opened my eyes and seen anyone's but Sam's, the color of rich chocolate. The vibrancy of Cyrus's blue- or were they green?- eyes set my head spinning and I pulled away.

Cyrus held tight to me as he asked, "What's wrong?"

61

What was wrong? My head spun. "Everything about this," I said, without really meaning to. He let go, stung, and I stood up to pace the room as I rambled. "Not you, I mean. I mean... We're in a shitty nightclub bathroom covered in booze and about to fuck each other in that shitty bathroom, and I'm way too drunk to be fucking anyone, anywhere, and I just ended things for good with a guy- a *good* guy- who I've been seeing for years, and I was upset and *-shit!-* you're so fucking hot, and I was thinking about you all day, and then you were just *here,* and you saved me from that dirtbag asshole, and then you were hurt and I wanted to help because you helped me and I don't know, I just feel like there's something about you I can't even explain and you're just a really weird kind of perfect and you said exactly what I was thinking at exactly the right moment and I just... I just..." I had finally burned myself out and looked back at Cyrus, who had an alarmed look on his face. There it was. I'd scared him off. The first time in a long time, I'd been excited about getting to know someone new, and I'd blown it because I couldn't control myself when my emotions were high and my defenses were down.

It was just like the time I'd slept with Jack... while Sam and I were dating.

Chapter 9

Elsie

It had been two years before. Sam and I had just reconciled (again), and we'd gone out for "beach and barz" as Ashley would have described it. We'd gone to the beach, where Sam and I were all hands and smiles. Jack had been relentlessly flirting with Ashley, but without any real hope as she'd made it clear long before that she had no interest in a steady boyfriend until she turned at least 30, and even less interest in complicating friendships by adding benefits.

When we'd gone to Matt's sister's to get cleaned up, we all pregamed hard with both shots and shotguns. I got to that point of drunkenness where rather than slowing down as you should, you want to go harder. Sam then pissed me off by insisting I only order water "or maybe a coffee or something?" because he was worried that I was going to be sick. He was probably right, even though I didn't want to admit it; I didn't like being told what I should do, even by someone who I knew had my best interests at heart. The end result was that my hard and fast intoxication became a hard and fast same-day hangover, and I was sick regardless- just without all the fun.

I'd gone to the bathroom to throw up and dig through my purse for some pain relievers. I was still kind of drunk but had sobered up enough to be in control of myself and the choices I made, just in case there could be any doubt about what happened next and who is at fault or not. So when a bathroom stall opened up while I gargled with some mouthwash I'd had in my bag, I wasn't expecting Jack to come out.

"What the fuck are you doing in the ladies', Jack?" I'd cried with indignation.

He chortled and said, "I think what you mean to say is, 'What the fuck am *I* doing in the *men's*, Jack?'" Then he laughed at his own joke, a habit of his I couldn't fucking stand. He came up next to me to wash his hands.

I turned around and leaned against the sink, crossing my arms. "You should let up on Ashley," I chided. Normally I'd let it go, but I was already annoyed and still just tipsy enough to be bold with my words. "Even if it worked, it wouldn't go anywhere. She likes being single, and she doesn't want to complicate the group dynamic."

He sneered. "Like you and Sam complicate the group dynamic every time you break up and get back together?"

I bristled with anger. "Okay, Jack," I charged ahead, not caring anymore. "What the actual *fuck* is your issue with me? You've been such a dick ever since college. You *used* to be cool, but half the time I don't even know why I hang out with you."

Some kind of wall went up behind his eyes and he said, "Me neither. But I guess we're stuck as long as we have the same friends." He dried his hands but didn't leave. He stared at me with a look I'd never seen in him before.

"*We* used to be friends, Jack," I lamented. "What changed?"

His stony expression changed to a dark one. "Do you really want to know?" He asked. There was a warning there, and I couldn't fathom what it might be. Had my mind not been *just* clouded enough, I might have figured it out before he leaned close and said, "Sam. Sam changed things. You and I should have been…" he trailed off. His hand had crept onto mine. He gave it a squeeze. "You never got it, and then it was too late."

My heart stood still. Sam and I were in such a good place, but for how long? Maybe not even the rest of the night if he kept acting so controlling. The fragile nature of my relationship with Sam; the slight intoxication; the way his voice had hit a timbre that sounded like sex itself; all of it came together in a perfect storm and I kissed him, with the same intensity I would later kiss Cyrus, also in a bar bathroom. Jack lifted me off the floor, my legs wrapping around him. He carried me to the bathroom door and locked it before bringing me back to the sink, where we proceeded to undress just enough to make the worst mistake I'd ever made.

Afterward, we didn't talk about it for weeks. I broke up with Sam again. I'd lashed out at him over something stupid, a side effect of my guilt, and he blew up, giving me the excuse I needed to break things off and retreat into myself. During that period, Jack called me a few times, probably thinking that if it was over with Sam, he had a shot. After ignoring a few of these calls, I finally answered and explained that even if I wanted to give us a try, it would never work because it would forever be tainted by that night in the bathroom of The Roof. I would never be able to be with him without thinking of what I'd done behind Sam's back.

Luckily Jack valued his friendship with everyone else just as much as I did, so we went back to a cool indifference that to everyone except us had appeared unchanged. But *I* knew how fucked up it really was, and Jack never forgave me. He'd gone from being frustrated that I wouldn't date him to hating me for dangling the carrot and taking it away. I didn't entirely blame him, but he could be really shitty to me when he could do it without anyone else noticing.

It was for this reason, as I stared at Cyrus, that I knew I'd made the right choice to stop things, even if it meant that I really had scared him off. I still struggled with the guilt of that night and had just accepted that I probably always would. Just because I was now single didn't change the fact that it was happening in an almost identical way, and I *knew* if I had any desire to get to know Cyrus better, I had to *not* screw him in this bathroom.

"I'm sorry," I said at the end of my rant to him. I looked down at my feet, which made a suctioning sound when I moved them from the liquid my shoes had absorbed. "I've made some... bad decisions in situations like this before." I looked up at his eyes, which were trained on me like a hawk's. I decided to be brave with my words. "I like talking to you, and I think you're interesting. I want to get to know you more, but I can't do *that* if we do *this*, here and now. And even if you say you don't want to get to know me because this was just way too much for you, my answer is still no." I held myself in a defiant stance. "Because I need a real emotional connection before I jump into a physical one. So... sorry, Cyrus. Not sorry."

I stared at him, waiting for him to walk out silently, or to try to convince me to reconsider, or even for him to try to grab me and kiss me again (which I honestly might not have minded if that's as far as it went, because when we'd kissed, *oh my God!*). He did none of those things. He gave me a calculating look and said, with a tiny shrug, "Okay."

Just that. *Okay.* Like I'd said I wanted ice cream. *Okay.* To a crazy person's ramblings and rejection. "Okay?" I probed. There had to be more to what he was thinking than, "*Okay.*"

He sighed, one corner of his mouth quirking up in a sympathetic look. "Don't get me wrong. I had little intention of stopping you *completely* if that was where you were going to take things. But I'm not an animal. I have *some* self-control, and likely- hopefully- would have not let it get too far since I don't think you're of a state to make sound decisions." He winked and I almost melted. "And like I said, I haven't met too many people here. As long as you were sincere in wanting to talk and get to know each other, I would be happy to get to know you, Elsie. And, by all means, please call me Cy." At that, he leaned toward me. I pulled back, still a little on edge, but then realized he wasn't going for my lips. He planted a soft kiss on my cheek before giving me a breathtaking smirk and, grabbing for my hand, led me out of the bathroom.

He didn't let go until we had found Ashley, who was ready to go home herself, having decided that Tim- Tom- Ted wasn't worth her time after all. Cy even waited with us outside and offered up cigarettes for each of us, standing by until our ride came to make sure we were all set to get back to Ashley's house safe. It was already past 1am, and if I walked into my house half-drunk and smelling of smoke, I'd probably get kicked out on the spot; not even the threat of mutually assured destruction would save me then.

"What about you?" I'd asked. He had to live much closer to us than the city; no one left St. Pete to come to The Watering Hole. "Don't you want to ride back with us?"

"No, no," he'd said. "You girls have a safe ride. You by no means have to, but I'd love it if you told me when you've made it home safely." The deference seemed a bit excessive, but I could tell he was trying to make sure I knew he was respecting my boundaries. It was nice, but also strange. When you've spent eight-plus years with the same person, over time, boundaries kind of dissolved. I wasn't used to them being there without having to fight for them. I waved as the driver took off through the streets.

Ashley was throwing me a wicked grin. I realized I was smiling from ear to ear and couldn't stop. "What?" I asked her, feigning innocence.

"Where in God's beautiful heavens did that guy come from?" She squealed.

"You mean tonight or in general?" I asked, stalling for time to decide how much I wanted to share.

Too bad for me, Ashley read between the lines. "You mean you *know* him? No wonder you dropped Sam like a fucking rock! Spill. I need all the details!"

"It wasn't like that! And I don't have too many details yet. I only met him... recently," I told her. "His name is Cyrus, and he's new to the area. I literally *ran into him* when that douchebag wouldn't leave me alone."

The wicked grin was back. "And after *I* left you two alone?"

"I cleaned him up, we talked, and then we came out to find you," I said, feeling confident that I sounded believable.

"Well," Ashley's smile had faded, "That's a little disappointing."

I shrugged. "Sometimes things should move slowly if you want them to last longer than a night."

Ashley snorted. "I meant it was disappointing that you're a *goddamn liar!*" Seeing the shocked expression on my face, she continued, "Your shirt was tucked in when I left you. It's completely untucked now, and there are little boozy fingerprints all over the hem. And your lipstick is smeared all over. Girl. Spill."

"Fine," I relented, trying to fight the grin that was spreading across my face. "We just made out a little. I meant it when I said I don't have many details about him; we only just met yesterday, but... I don't know. I think I like him. And I didn't dump Sam because of that. Sam and I... it hasn't been right for a long time. It's why we're off and on and off again. I just finally decided it wasn't fair to either of us to keep that up until we either settled for each other and lived life in mediocrity or went our separate ways, resenting each other for having missed out on some of our best years."

Ashley squeezed my hand sympathetically. The wild one of our group, it was easy to forget she also had a big heart that showed itself to those she loved most. "I get it," she said. "Look at me! I won't date anyone seriously until I'm 30 because I don't want to settle down too early and regret not having lived my best life first. Just..." she paused, obviously struggling with what she was about to say, "You've been in relationship-mode for so long, and I think a lot of us know that's why you and Sam have lasted past your expiration date- you both were too comfortable to consider whether you were actually happy. If you really *do* want to take things slow with this guy, do it. Don't jump in headfirst just because you crave the comfort of being in a couple. Jump in- when you're ready- because this guy makes you excited for the future."

I smiled at Ashley, tears pooling in the corners of my eyes. She was wild, crazy, and unpredictable, but that unpredictability also applied to her intuition, caring, and heart. I squeezed her hand back, and we rode the rest of the way to Ashley's house in silence.

Well after 2am, we curled up on either side of her plush queen-sized bed and began to doze off. Right before sleep claimed me, I pulled out my phone and typed a message. *Thank you for everything tonight. Hope you made it home alright. Talk to you soon.*

Chapter 10

Opal

Amber had spent months with me in the beginning. She taught me our laws and the ways we have to protect ourselves. Sunlight is deadly to our kind, but not in the way most old myths tell it. We can survive the sun's rays, and most, myself included, enjoy basking in its light. It does make us sleepy, but it's nothing we can't power past. It is true, however, that it can hurt us. Eyes are the windows to the soul, as they say, which is evident in the coloration of our irises. But it goes beyond that; if any direct UV light enters our eyes, even after the sun itself has cleared the horizon, it begins to burn away- quickly- at the vampire blood in our veins until none remains and we rapidly age and die, decaying swiftly to catch our bodies up to what they would look like in that moment had we died instead of being changed. So she bought me sunglasses with a special polarization that kept the UV rays from our eyes and had to be worn in the presence of any sunlight- even the fading rays of dusk.

She taught me about the ecstasy of the kill, and how to dispose of a body if you took too much, since the Council would bring swift justice on any who threatened our secrecy. She taught me how to drain someone just enough that they could still live, and how to prevent them from remembering you'd ever been there.

She taught me that not much could destroy us as long as our blood remained within us, animating our walking corpses. Aside from the sun, the only way we could be killed was by being drained and decapitated. Our blood could heal just about anything we suffered quickly. As long as any of our own vampire blood remained in our bodies, we could recover even from having our head cut off, but not if the blood was taken and the head was separated from our body. I had no heartbeat, yet the humans I bedded and bled would tell you otherwise- all part of the illusion. I could breathe, I could smell, I could smoke a cigarette if I chose to (not like it could kill me), but I required nothing from the air.

The condo she'd taken me to the night I was reborn was built by vampires for vampires and could be mine, she'd said, since she preferred to travel. Just as long as she had a place to crash when she came back through for a visit, she'd hand it over willingly. As a member of the Council, I had to stay close to my city as much as possible in order to oversee and regulate vampiric activity in the area, so it worked out well.

As far as any other rules... I regretted killing Orla every time I was confronted with one of my "responsibilities" on the Council. Being a vampire could be *so* much fun... except for the *rules*.

I was no stranger to killing young women who'd wandered into rough areas of town. It was so easy to disguise their ends as suicides or drug overdoses (a bit trickier due to the exsanguination, but possible if you knew what you were doing). I could have as many as a Jane Doe a week attributed to me, but women were just easy prey- nothing more. Despite those occasional unfortunates who crossed my path, my evenings much more frequently ended with a bit more play than prey. I would find and seduce a human male to bring back to my place for some erotic fun... before I fed. But with Zilpher in town, I had to be careful. It was against the rules to let a human find out about us, and it was hard to bite into someone's neck to drink their blood without questions coming up, no matter how well we tried to cover up our nature. Death usually put an abrupt end to the questions, but risked unnecessary attention. Because of this, I'd had to sate my hungers differently the previous night.

I slid out of bed, the sun just rising, casting its rays all around my room and giving everything a golden glow. I stood fully naked in front of the large windows, knowing that they had been specially engineered to not only prevent people from seeing in, but also to keep out UV rays that could be fatal to me. I opened the mini-fridge in the corner of the room, which held several packets of blood from the blood bank. I poured a wineglass full and took a lingering sip before I lit a cigarette near a vent on the wall that kept the smoke smell from the rest of the room.

"Good morning." The voice came from my bed, under the covers.

I turned grumpily toward the sound, pure contempt written in the set of my body and face. I took a long drag, then replied, "Good morning. Thank you for last night. Now," I nodded my head toward the door, "get the fuck out."

Zilpher sat up, a smirk tickling the corners of his mouth. The expression wasn't friendly- his eyes and his countenance were still cold. Nothing about last night had been about attraction or passion, unless that passion was borne out of sheer hatred. He walked over to me, taking the cigarette from my hands and taking a long pull from it. "If you insist," he said. He then drained the rest of my glass and set it down on top of the fridge before placing the cigarette back in my mouth. "But the sun is up, which means I'm in no hurry." I took a drag from the cigarette as he wrapped a hand around my waist and leaned forward to kiss along my jaw. I felt a thrill as he did so. I *hated* Zilpher, a feeling I knew to be mutual, but I'd be damned (more than I already was) if he didn't know exactly when, where, and how hard or soft to touch a woman. It was infuriating and arousing at the same time. Besides, if I hadn't taken him home, I'd have been making breakfast for some human (since killing was out of the question with Zilpher around) rather than being touched just so by someone with a couple thousand years of experience.

I finished my cigarette with one long, extended breath as his hands began their journey across my body, finding its most exquisite peaks and valleys, and I allowed myself to be directed back to the bed.

It was like this every time Zilpher came to town- after the first few times, that is. The first two or three years went by fairly uneventfully for me as a Council member. Amber had long since left to go "travel" as she had once put it, and I was more or less on my own. I didn't mind. Tampa was full of other vampires, and I was essentially their ruler. Friendship wasn't really in my wheelhouse anyway; I had adoration and fear, not to mention the willing body and less-than-willing blood of almost any human man I came across to keep me warm.

It took me the better part of a year to work out the vampiric hierarchy. While the Council was technically made up of equals across the globe and of all ages, we were regarded by our peers and our subjects as having different "ranks." Zilpher was very nearly at the top, while I hovered just below him, an "honor" for someone as young as I was.

Fuck honor.

The Council more or less existed to make sure that vampires stayed hidden from humans and to police disputes between other vampires. Possible complaints ranged from porch pirates stealing deliveries from the blood bank all the way up to murdering another vampire, which, except in very rare circumstances, called for quick and decisive sentencing and execution from the Council. I would occasionally receive a call to weigh in on such matters, usually nothing more than a fledgling who had gone mad or feral and needed to be dealt with quickly. Such an action had to be approved by a two-thirds Council majority of the two dozen members in eastern North America. I was lucky enough to be across the world from where the global meetings were held for the greatest controversies (Geneva, ironically, considering its fame as the home of a great agreement about human rights), which meant I could be phoned in and it wasn't too much of a disruption. That was not the case when other Council members "dropped in" to check on the newest, though not lowest ranked, Councilor.

I realized early on that part of the reason for my rank was my power. Somehow I'd gained unprecedented strength immediately upon my rebirth, which caused the others to fear me. Good. Better they fear me and leave me alone than to have oversight I didn't care for. It didn't seem to matter, though, since I was only one of many. I tried to at least maintain an appearance of following the rules, though. Even with my strength, if it was decided that I was a danger, I could be "removed", which is a really nice way of saying they'd take turns draining me to empty to imbibe my strength and then dismember me.

Being so highly esteemed meant I was watched much more than I wanted to be, but I did my best to flout the authority of the other Council members without drawing their wrath. My subjects also tended to look to me for cues on what was or wasn't acceptable behavior in our area, so I had to hide my kills from them as well, lest they show my same disregard for protocol, and the Council decided to wipe Tampa off the map.

Any time Zilpher, in particular, came to town, I was usually the first to know, though not always; sometimes, as with the present visit, I'd hear about it from Colorado. In cases like this, Zilpher would end up at the Speakeasy before coming to see me. To be fair, that's usually where he could find me anyway, and where I could often find him abusing his power, making himself known to fledglings who may as well have been groupies for the fawning over him they did.

In my third year in this life, he'd come for routine business, just to make sure that I was behaving as I should, and that there were no suspicious deaths in the area that would need to be appropriately taken care of before the authorities got too suspicious. It was his fifth visit in less than a year, and I was getting tired of his presence in my city. In this case, he'd found me on my way to the Speakeasy, and had accompanied me the whole way there, much to my annoyance. Not only did I not want to talk shop while I was out for the night, but I certainly didn't want to talk with him.

He didn't care. Once at the bar, he'd continued the impromptu meeting and ordered drink after drink for both of us, putting everything on his own tab. Say what you will about me, but I'm rather bloodthirsty, even for a vampire, and never one to turn down blood, especially when it was alcohol-infused, and I was being forced to listen to someone I hate ramble on about things I don't give half a shit about. It was on this visit, however, after he'd ordered several rounds of various infusions, all positive, that I realized I disliked the taste of positive as much as I disliked everything about Zilpher; or maybe it was just that my mind began to make the association between the two. He talked at me the whole night, ruining any chance I'd had of finding anyone on the street or in one of the human bars to take home or even just feed on, but never failing to interrupt his unending stream of word-vomit to thrill some young, weak vampire with a wink or a gratuitous touch. A few millennia of life had not made the slightest impact on his sense of propriety. He looked all the gentleman, but believed his power gave him the right to do anything to anyone at any time without consent or consequence.

But, hey, I'm one to talk.

I had walked along the water, intending to leave Zilpher at some point, a slow undercurrent of anger and frustration building. When he followed me up the elevator of my building, I finally turned to him.

"Zilpher, I think that's enough for one night. I get the gist. Feel free to call me tomorrow if you need to tell me more. I won't answer," I said, every word filled with venom, "but you can tell it to my voicemail. It's not long before sunrise, anyway, so you may as well go." My mind was exhausted, not only from the approaching sun, but from all of the information he'd relayed about the global communities as well as what they were saying about my area from the outside. "I'll take it all under advisement," I said, my voice dripping with sarcasm.

He stepped closer, threateningly. "You should take this more seriously," he scolded. "Need I remind you that you *killed* for this?" His lip curled at me in disgust.

I finally snapped. "I didn't know what I was killing *for!*" I admitted to him for the first time. "I was brand fucking new with no memory of who I was before, and I felt reckless and impulsive. So, yeah, I killed Orla. I'd say I'm sorry, but I'm really not. You've killed plenty of people yourself, including others of our own kind." I didn't know if I should admit this to him, but in my anger, I did. "I've had you followed. You kill often enough that you never have to worry about being dethroned because no one beneath you could ever match your body count. You're just like me," I accused, "an animal, hunting and fucking and killing when it suits your fancy. You use your power over the other vampires who would happily die to feel just a taste of that power. You abuse. You murder. You rape. You're a beast. You just hide it behind your title and a tailored suit!"

He stared at me as I turned the key and walked into my condo. I closed the door, but as I did, he stuck a patent leather dress shoe in the opening and shoved it back open, allowing himself inside.

"You," he scolded, sticking a finger in my face, "Are infuriating! You claim to want none of this power, but you use it to your advantage. I've had you followed too, and yes, I know about your body count and how it rivals my own. You killed another vampire- supposedly, I now discover, on a wild, newborn impulse- yet claim you don't want the consequences that came with that. You could have ingratiated yourself to Orla and me to learn and benefit from our wisdom and power, and in-stead you chose to end her very long, very rich life, which you will have no benefit of knowing and understanding. You were born, for whatever reason, with strength and power most of us could never dream of, and you use it purely for selfish, irresponsible reasons!"

I reached up to slap him, but he caught my hand. I could have fought back, but after killing one Council member (and being burdened with responsibility I would happily give up if I could do so without inviting my own end), I decided to employ some restraint and allow him to stop me. But I wasn't going to let him think he won, either. "Get the fuck out," I growled.

He stepped closer, his lips curled into a snarl. "Make me."

It was then, when we were centimeters apart, my wrist held tightly in his hand, that the tension broke and, in the same instant, we brought our lips together. Up until that point, I'd only slept with human men, who had no idea what "rough" could really be. Had my house not been built with people exactly like me in mind, Zilpher and I may have demolished the entire thing. Any time Zilpher came over, it was almost always violent and exhilarating.

It still was. Which was why, as the midday sun came over the roof of my building, eliminating the shadows throughout the city, I could still be found enjoying (or not) his company. His presence was both provocative and evocative, and once we'd burned out all of our frustration on each other and anything that was unfortunate enough to come between our raging bodies, I couldn't be rid of him quick enough.

He went to my bathroom to shower and I reached for my tablet. I had to keep track of things that happened in the area as Councilor, but unlike my colleagues around the world who kept to the old ways they knew in centuries past, I was a child of this millennium and opted for a more high tech approach. The majority of vampires I knew had kept up with the times, but, possibly due to their lack of connection with the real world, I was one of the only Councilors who even had social media, let alone a full-scale surveillance system for my area. It made the work much faster, if no less tedious.

I had my feed set up with news alerts from every national and local outlet to keep track of the area. Certain patterns emerging could indicate a vampire who'd gone rogue or a turf war. I also had access to most of the traffic cams for the city and surrounding areas. I opened the database and started combing the feeds from the previous night, looking for anyone who might be Amber.

One woman caught my eye, but as quickly as I noticed her, I realized it couldn't possibly be Amber. She was conniving and would go to great lengths to create a false sense of security in her prey, finding the act of betrayal as satisfying as the actual kill, but I couldn't imagine she'd go so far as to create a long term false relationship, and this girl was very obviously romantically involved with the tall, dark-haired man she was frequently with.

I reflected on this, the idea of relationships, of monogamy, of marriage. Mortals swore themselves to each other "until death." Which was really a joke since so many of them never actually held to the vows, either divorcing or being unfaithful to one another. But the idea of "until death" was a strange concept to me, knowing that such a promise, to a human, would last a century at most. If a vampire were to make a similar oath, we could be bound together for millennia, more even, unless we were killed. I thought about Zilpher and Orla, how they'd been partners, but not in the way humans saw their spouses. They were far from monogamous, yet they had been a constant in each other's lives. I had heard from others of the decades, even centuries, between their love affairs. They might spend a human lifetime together, then separate as though they were strangers, only to come back together. Were any of my kind actually monogamous, in an eternal sense?

I continued to digress. For me, the promise of blood was as arousing as the promise of sex, and often they were so intermingled for me that I could hardly think of one without thinking of the other. I knew there were vampires who didn't kill as I did, who saw blood as a necessary sustenance and only consumed just enough to prevent the rapid decay we experience without it, who possibly could separate the lust for blood and the lust for flesh. Perhaps those vampires *could* make a commitment as I never could.

Zilpher's phone buzzed from his suit pocket. He was still in the shower. I thought he must have heard it, but I listened closely and couldn't even pick up a change in the flow of the water that would indicate he'd turned his head at the sound. I'd never had any insight to his duties other than what he told me, and he had so often held those duties and his seniority on the Council over me, that I decided a brief imposition on his privacy was in order.

I pulled the phone out of the pocket. Of course, it was locked, but the home screen told me he was continuing to receive messages from the same unknown number over and over. It wasn't saved to a contact. Then the phone rang. I could answer without inputting a password, so I held as still as I was able so as to not make a sound, and picked up the phone. After several seconds of silence, the caller spoke.

"Zilpher? Are you there? Zilpher!"

I nearly dropped the phone. It was Amber.

Chapter 11

Elsie

I felt myself being dragged back into consciousness. I tried desperately to cling to the dream that was rapidly fading; I knew it had been important, but it was hard to focus while the sunlight was beating against my eyelids, turning them red.

I opened my eye a fraction of an inch and immediately squeezed it closed again. The sun, even at the early hour, was absurdly bright. The Florida sun was a take-no-prisoners kind of bitch.

The dream had been so strange and unsettling. It began to slip away, like sand through a screen. I managed to hang onto pieces, and I knew that the final moments would linger.

We were near the beach, at one of the tiny local restaurants that had a great view of the sunset over the Gulf. My friends were all there, and they were upset. I wanted to go to the beach and stand in the surf as the sun set, but they didn't want me to go. Ashley was crying. Sam was angry. They were insistent that I stay, but I knew that I had to go to the beach. Something was waiting for me there...

I had walked onto the beach, which was unusually empty, devoid of the usual hordes of tourists who came from all over. The sand had been whiter than I'd ever seen it, and softer. The water was its usual hue, but shone with a vividness that caused it to seemingly glow in the twilight. The sun had just set and the sky was a thousand different colors: red along the horizon, swirling with pink and orange as it darkened overhead to blues and purples. I stood ankle-deep in the waves and let them wash over my feet as I spread my arms wide, welcoming the warm ocean breeze. As I looked out over the vibrantly blue-green water, the color began to bleed upwards into the sky; looking down, it had changed the sand as well. It started slowly, then moved faster and faster until I was surrounded by that effulgent hue.

The waves had shifted the sand around my feet, creating a quicksand effect, and I felt a thrill of fear and euphoria. I wanted to escape, fearing I'd be pulled down and drown, but I was so calmed by the radiance of that dazzling, virescent shade of blue that I didn't even fight. It was permeating my being, surrounding me as though it- a color- had physical arms that had wrapped around me in a way that was both protective and invasive; familiar and strange; comforting and frightening. The pressure increased and I closed my eyes tightly, trying to shut out the scene before my eyes, which had become so overwhelming that I was about to scream, at which point I felt a gentle kiss on my lips. My breath left me, and as whoever had kissed me pulled away, I opened my eyes.

My vision was still filled with that color of the tropical surf, but now it wasn't surrounding me. It was staring back. Cy had me wrapped in his arms and was smiling at me. I smiled back, pleased that he'd found me here. It calmed the anxiety that had been gripping me, but only for a moment; as he leaned in to kiss me again, I felt a shot of panic as I realized the sand had swallowed me up to my chest. I clutched at Cy, begging him to help me. Instead, he shook his head at me, his face a mix of sadness, fear, and helplessness; he was trapped too. Tears pooled in both of our eyes- tears the color of his irises. I leaned into him, resting my head on his shoulder. I knew I was in too deep to run, literally, but at least we wouldn't be alone. I looked back at him as the sand came up over our heads, saturating my vision with the color of his eyes...

It was at this point that I had been torn from the scene and shoved violently back into reality- several hours before reality should have begun to exist, in my opinion.

I groaned and pulled my blanket over my head. Even with the extra covering, the light managed to break through. I squeezed my eyes tightly shut and tried to go back to sleep.

It had been a late night the night before, but one I was still riding the high of as I awoke. It also explained at least part of the dream- the part where everything was saturated with that color. Oh, that color! It sent tingles down my spine even thinking about it and how the previous night had changed everything.

*   *   *

It was two months after the incident at the club, and Cy and I had been in almost constant contact. We had spent several lunches together, but always careful to keep it casual and platonic, trying to get to know each other as friends. I'd learned more about him and how he'd ended up moving here. A former coworker was involved in a new business venture and had asked Cy for help, but, due to a non-disclosure agreement about a mile long and worth more than my parents' house and retirement fund combined, he couldn't say more. He was staying in one of those residential hotels until the job started paying enough for him to get a place of his own.

He'd met each of my friends during that time, and, with Ashley leading the charge, they had all given silent approval to start including him in our plans together. Sam was resistant, understandably, but since he had started bringing Emily around as well, he didn't put up too much of a fight. That's how we'd all ended up at The Watering Hole together for Friday Night Trivia.

Cy and I didn't sit next to each other, but we certainly interacted with each other more than with anyone else at the table. Sam and Emily, by contrast, were pushing the limits of what could be considered family-friendly PDA. It was a mark of how hopeful I was for the future that it honestly didn't bother me.

We enjoyed the challenge of exercising our brains through the fog of beer. When one of us gave an incorrect answer, causing us to lose a point, we booed and teased the offender. It was carefree, easy, and fun. Life had gotten to a point where I no longer felt that yearning for some fairy tale, star-crossed romance simply because I was truly content; not like I thought I'd been with Sam, which in retrospect had really been more like placated, but because I was actually pleased with the trajectory of my life. Friendship with Cy was wonderful, even if I knew I wanted it to grow into something more. I could wait.

During a break between rounds, Cy stood up, pulling a pack of cigarettes from his shirt pocket. He very rarely changed up his look, I'd noticed. I couldn't complain; the white button-down rolled up to the elbows and dark, slim-fit pants of varying materials over either dark sneakers or semi-dressy shoes (and always the sunglasses, for which he'd given a perfectly reasonable explanation) was a good look for him. But thanks to the light fabric and small pocket, I could always see if he'd been planning on smoking that day. Like me, he wasn't a full-time smoker, but enjoyed the pairing of it with alcohol from time to time.

"Anyone care to join me?" He asked, waving the little box invitingly. He raised The Brow at me directly, but I'd been off of smoking again since waking up with that awful mouthfeel after the night at the club. Besides, I'd been trying to get out and run more to balance out the effects of so many happy hours and nights out, and smoking certainly didn't help with trying to breathe while working out.

"No, thanks," I said. "I'm going to pass tonight." I was just about to offer to keep him company anyway when Jack chimed in.

"I'll have one," he said.

We all stared. If I was concerned about my running, Jack was *obsessed* with fitness, to the point that he counted the calories in every beer he had; and if a calorie count wasn't available, he didn't partake. He did nothing to hinder the performance of his "machine," and so often could be heard lamenting the lack of laws restricting smoking even outdoors.

Ashley, being the bold one, was the only one to speak up. "For real?" She erupted. "Jack. Is going to smoke. Am I on a reality show?" She looked all around mockingly, like she was expecting to find hidden cameras.

"Yeah," Jack said with a smirk. "It's called 'Mind Your Fucking Business, Ashley.'" He laughed to show he was joking, and everyone chuckled along. Except me. Because as his eyes found mine, there was a coldness I didn't trust. Our tryst had driven a wedge between us as friends, and some part of me had thought we had gotten past it, at least enough to be coolly indifferent to each other. One glance from him that night was enough to make it clear... I'd been so wrong.

I couldn't say anything to combat what happened next. Jack followed Cy out the door, and my heart began pounding louder than the music they were playing to fill the time until trivia started back up. I tried to stick with the conversation, hoping that the cold sweat coming across my forehead wasn't apparent to anyone else, since Jack's and my brief dalliance was still a secret.

The minutes stretched on forever while I waited for them to come back inside. When they finally did, the anxiety I'd felt gave way to dread. There was something closed in Cy's expression, and he avoided my gaze for most of the rest of the evening. Jack, on the other hand, had a hint of what seemed like triumph in his smile. I thought no one seemed to notice the tension that came in with the smell of smoke, but at one point, Ashley's eyes met mine and, in that moment, I knew she had sensed the fizzle in the atmosphere. I sent her a silent plea to not call it out, and was about to send her a text to promise to explain later, but the Trivia Master called out, "Cell phones away! Time to get back to some questions!"

Afterward, Ashley drove the two of us home and she wasted no time.

"Okay, what the hell was that?" She asked the second the car doors were closed. I tried not to read accusation in her voice, but my guilt was practically a cloud around us, and I knew that just because she wasn't already aware that what had happened was due to a royal fuck-up on my part, she was about to find out and that was enough to break me. I sobbed while I told her all about what had happened that night in the men's room of The Roof, while her eyes grew wide and horrified; I explained that part of why Sam and I continued to break up was because the guilt ate at me constantly; I explained how that entire situation was the reason I'd stopped myself from going further with Cy in the bathroom at the club.

Ashley listened without making a sound until I finished, "And I bet that's why Jack went out there. To tell Cy what a skank I am- to hit me one more time- all because I didn't love him back, or at least because I wouldn't fuck him again, since he didn't seem to mind that I was with Sam while he was railing me in the men's room." My words gave way to noisy, uncontrollable sobbing.

Ashley continued to sit in silence for a moment longer. Then, in a thoughtful and clear voice, she said, "Well... fuck that." My tears stopped instantly in the shock of her response. I stared. "You heard me. Fuck. That," she reiterated. "Jack is a grown-ass man, and if he's going to play bullshit games, you need to play them better. There is no room for that kind of drama at our age." I realized why, despite her wild side, I still felt like I could confide deep, personal, painful things to her. She had a way of putting things into perspective and reminding you that there was always a path forward. She continued, "I know what I said, about taking it slow and making sure actually you want Cyrus the person and not just a relationship, but Jack just changed the play, and you need to respond. It's been two months of you getting to know this guy. Decide. Do you like Cy? Like, actually like him?"

We were pulling around the corner to my house.

I tried to think hard about it, but the truth was that I already had given it a lot of thought. He was handsome, and sweet, and unexpected; he made me feel like there was something to look forward to. Even if it was a mistake, I wanted to see what kind of future Cy and I could have together.

"I do," I squeaked, throat constricted from the tears. "I like him."

She pulled into my driveway, but instead of putting the car in park, she put it into reverse and drove out of my neighborhood.

"What are you doing?" I asked.

"I'm taking you to his place," she said. "You better give me directions."

Chapter 12

Elsie

When we pulled up to the hotel, Ashley leaned over and hugged me. "You sure you're okay to get a ride back by yourself?"

"Yeah," I said. I knew I'd want to be alone to deal with whatever feelings I'd have after seeing Cy. "Thank you." I smirked at her. "Don't ever let me tell you that you're just a pretty face."

"Oh, I'm definitely a pretty face," she laughed, tossing her hair over her shoulder. "Just don't forget about what's underneath it." She winked and unlocked the door to let me out.

I waved at her and turned around to go into the hotel, nearly getting flattened by some woman rushing out. Whoever it was was clearly in a hurry and didn't even slow down to apologize. "That's fine, I'm okay," I mumbled to myself, not wanting to get into a confrontation right now- I needed to get this over with.

I took the elevator to the second floor and walked down the hall to Cy's door. I knocked, but before he could answer, my phone vibrated. *Bzzt.*

I pulled it out and looked at the name. Jack. I was about to put it away without even looking at what he sent, but I noticed from the text preview that he'd sent an oddly angled photo of a man with black hair, wearing a white button-down with the sleeves rolled up. Cy, obviously. What made me stop dead in my tracks was that he was embracing a drop-dead gorgeous woman who was wearing the warmest, most intimate smile I'd ever seen. And I'd just seen her in person, slamming into me outside.

I realized now my mistake. Jack hadn't *done* anything. He'd *seen* something. Jack had seen Cy and this woman, whom he obviously was very familiar with; and it was pretty safe to assume that she wasn't family since he'd told me he had no one in the area when we'd met.

The door opened while I was still staring at the picture.

"Elsie?" Cy asked, sounding both surprised and concerned. "Are you alright?"

I didn't move, I just stared at the photo, unsure whether I was crushed or angry. I couldn't rationally be angry with him since I was the one who'd wanted to slow down and be friends, but since when is anger rational? After several seconds, he reached out to put his hand on my arm, and I spun away from his touch. "I'm sorry," I said with a deadened voice. "I just—never mind. I gotta go." I started to walk away, and he stepped around me to look at my face. It was then that he glanced down and saw what I was looking at. When he spoke again, his voice was soft and urgent.

"Elsie, please come in. Can we talk?"

I looked up for the first time. His sunglasses were off and his eyes bored into mine, that brilliant shade of blue-green acting like a missile to cut right through my defense.

My body acted against what I tried to do. Instead of telling him, "*No*," and walking away, I nodded curtly and stalked inside. He didn't remove his hand from my arm the whole time, even when he closed the door and led me to the two-seat dining table in his kitchenette. His hand wasn't possessive or controlling; I couldn't place the emotion in his expression, but the way his hand was gently resting on my arm, it almost seemed like he was worried that if he let go, I'd leave forever. And he probably wasn't wrong. I was humiliated. I had made such a fool of myself, thinking he actually might feel the same way I did, and was happy to just be friends and see where things went. Someone who looked like he did, who acted like he did, who was as smart and funny and humble as he was didn't have to wait around. I'd dropped the ball, and someone else had picked it up.

"Elsie," Cy paused. "Elsie, I... I should explain." There was that look again. It was making me angrier. We still barely knew each other. What did it matter if I walked out and we never saw each other again? Especially knowing he'd found a "friend" in the area to spend time with.

"You don't have to." My voice was cold. "It doesn't matter. Look, I made a mistake coming here, so-" I started to stand up, but he grabbed my hand.

"If you want to leave, I won't stop you," he said. Now his eyes were resigned. "But I wish you'd stay. I want... I don't want you to leave like this." He gripped my hand tightly as though steeling himself to let go, which he did. "I want you to understand, because it's not what you think."

It was new. He hadn't tried to control me or the situation. He gave total authority to me, something I wasn't used to. When you spend the better part of a decade in a relationship (even if it's not a constant one), you get used to both people trying to steer the ship. I'm pretty sure most fights that couples have are the result of everyone trying to drive. Cy wasn't going

90

to make me stay or even force me to listen to him. He gave me a choice. It was such a curious situation for me that I sat back down.

"I don't-" I started, the words not coming out right. "I don't even know what you have to explain. I'm such a dumb-ass. I thought just because we were getting to know each other as friends that the door was still open for..." I sighed. "I'm happy to be your friend. I just misunderstood and..." I broke off, worried that if I continued, I'd start to cry and I didn't want to be crying when I left. Drivers tended to get a little weird when you got into their cars sobbing.

His eyes never left my face, even as I tried to look everywhere but at him.

"May I?" Cy asked, motioning toward my phone. I nodded and handed it over. He stared at the picture for a moment, a stony expression covering his face. He blew air through his nose. "Hm. I'm assuming Jack took that picture from under the table when he and I went out for cigarettes?" He asked. I nodded in response. He shook his head, half speaking to himself. "I hadn't expected to see her there."

"Who is she?" I asked. "It's not my business," I added quickly. "I've never heard you mention her, is all."

"That's..." he steeled himself, "My ex. Her name is Amber. We were together for a long time, but she..." He broke off. "It didn't work out. She wasn't who I thought she was."

"What happened?" I asked, half intrigued, half concerned.

"The details don't matter now. It was a betrayal. I left." He laid his hand near mine, not touching it, but the way his eyes settled on the space between them made it clear he'd close the gap if given the invitation to. Goosebumps ran up my arm while I tried to tell myself to relax. He looked back at me. "I promise to tell you one day. I just can't yet. Not while she's still following me around," he spat.

That surprised me. "Following you around?"

Cy grimaced. "She found out where I moved. Never mind that the whole reason I was willing to uproot my life in the first place was because of her. I saw her that night in St. Pete. She'd found me at the restaurant I'd gone to for dinner. I went into that club to try to go somewhere she couldn't pick me out of the crowd. She's here 'for vacation' with friends, but I haven't seen a one of them. And," he digressed, "if we really want to dissect her story, why has her vacation lasted two months?" He shook his head and returned to his narrative. "When she showed up at The Watering Hole earlier, I confirmed a suspicion I've had for a while: Amber still has me tracked by GPS through our phones. I didn't want to make a scene in front of your friend, so I played nice (a mistake, I now see, since it was entirely misinterpreted), but I checked when I got home. By then, she'd obviously already seen where I was staying." He motioned around himself to the hotel room. "She showed up here tonight, but I told her to leave." So that was why he'd acted so weird for the rest of the evening. Not because Jack told him my secret, but because his ex was stalking him.

"Yeah," I grumbled. "Well. You and Amber definitely have something in common. You both tend to get in my way when I'm not looking where I'm going." He gave me a questioning look, and I said, "We collided downstairs, I just didn't know it was her. I got this text right outside your door, after I already knocked."

A flash of something crossed his face, but it vanished almost as quickly. His eyes scanned my face, looking for something in my expression- what, I wasn't sure- but there was a tangible concern there. Finding nothing, it seemed, he said, "I'm sorry. She's angry because I sent her away." He seemed to be done talking, except that his eyes were screaming something that he hadn't voiced. And then he did. "You didn't mistake anything. I feel... Well... That door is open for you whenever you want to walk through it." He gave a small, hopeful smile.

My heart leaped for joy. It was everything I ever could have hoped. I opened my mouth to tell him, "*Yes! Please, be with me. Let's do this! Jump in together headfirst and the fuck with everyone else!*"

Instead, what I said was, "I want to. I do. But you need to know why Jack took that photo and sent it to me, and why I really came here tonight. I thought... I wanted to tell you how I feel, but I also needed to explain something."

I told him everything, knowing that since he had been betrayed, it was only fair for him to know that I myself had betrayed someone I cared about. I told Cy how Sam and I were still working things out when I'd met him, and didn't really break up until after Cy and I had already started texting each other. I told him that I thought Jack had told him I was unfaithful to Sam, and that's why Cy had shut down after they'd gone outside together. I told him how I thought he could do so much better than a girl who had already fucked someone in a bar bathroom behind her "good guy" of a boyfriend's back, and had nearly done the same with Cy before shutting him down when those memories ruined the moment. I told him if he did feel that way, I understood, and I wouldn't hold it against him.

"But... dammit, Cy," I groaned through my teeth, rising to my feet, looking anywhere but at him while I said what I needed to. "I've never felt anything like this before. I've always just been in relationships of convenience, and this is so not like that. I didn't expect you, and I didn't expect to be so attracted to you, or to keep running into you until you managed to get stuck in my brain, in my heart, or whatever, and I couldn't stop thinking about you and couldn't help but start to feel..." I sighed heavily. "Which I know all sounds stupid and sudden, but... just dammit!" I took a breath to slow myself. "Please say anything so I can shut the fuck up."

There was a long pause as I saw him looking at me from the corner of my eye. His face was impassive and he simply stared for the better part of an eternity. When he finally spoke, his voice carried no emotion. "You've never told anyone about this," he said sagely. "This thing with Jack. Have you?"

I bit my lip. "Not until tonight. I told Ashley after we left The Watering Hole. She knew something was wrong, so I told her because I needed someone to finally unload this on. I needed to talk about it... I didn't want to lose you before I had a chance to really have you." I covered my eyes with my hands, a plethora of overwhelming emotions threatening to cause tears to fall. "She drove me here so I could tell you how I feel."

It was then that I felt his hands on mine and he gently pulled them from my eyes. "Thank you," he smiled.

That was the last thing I expected to hear. "Thank *me*?" I asked a bit stupidly. Then I exploded in frustration. "Did you listen to a word I said? I don't know what the fuck Amber did, but I'm no angel, Cy. I'm a devil- a slutty little devil who can't think of you as just a friend because I want you in ways that... I've been with other people, but never- *ever*- have I wanted someone this badly and somehow still don't want it because I'm so terrified it will ruin *everything*." My heart was pounding and my chest heaved with every breath, each of which felt like they were being ripped out of me; it was akin to the shortness of breath the morning after smoking a whole pack of cigarettes.

"Yes. Thank you." Cy's smile widened as he changed his grip on my hands so that he was holding them between us like he planned to plant a kiss on my knuckles. Goddamn it, he was frustrating. That smile made my heart flutter, and yet I wanted to hit him and run away for daring to make light of what I'd told him. It was like being on an elementary school playground with the boy you think is cute.

He leaned forward to emphasize what he said next. "Thank you for telling me that. Thank you for being honest, even when you were embarrassed and when you knew it might drive me away. Thank you for coming here." He stepped closer, pulling one of my hands to rest on his chest. "Because you've managed to get stuck yourself, in ways I didn't expect to feel after my last heartbreak."

Backflips. My heart was doing backflips. *Did he just say he felt the same?* I thought. *Holy shit, he did.* And he didn't laugh at me for sounding like some shitty romance novel that might be on my bookshelf; he *thanked* me for telling him how I felt and for telling him about my past.

Suddenly, the tension dissolved and I started laughing, the same way we had laughed while cleaning blood off of his face- free and very nearly hysterical. He seemed taken aback and nervous at first. I tried to explain through the tears of laughter streaming down my face that it was all so cheesy and I'd never heard anyone actually declare their feelings like this except in those same shitty romance novels on my shelf, and then I cackled, "And I'm j-just so overwhelmed because I'm h-happy and I can't believe you feel the same and-" I forced myself to take a breath and calmed down to try to explain, but on the word "*happy*," his shoulders relaxed and he began to laugh too.

My right hand was still on his chest, the left still held in his. I felt the laughter leaving me, and heard him quiet as well. He closed the last few inches between us. With his free hand, he brushed my hair back. His fingers rested behind my ear for a breath, then trailed to the back of my neck, where he gently pulled me forward. I leaned in and we kissed.

This, I thought as butterflies tried to murder each other in my stomach, *should have been our first kiss. Not a violent osculation on top of a grubby bar toilet. This, with all its sweetness and with actual, caring feelings for each other.*

It wasn't a passionate, hungry kiss; it was soft and sweet. Our hands didn't wander this time, and we didn't finish what we'd started that second night after we'd met. We stayed in the kiss for a few more moments, and then parted. We sat back at the table, our hands intertwining as we basked in the simplicity and warmth of the moment. We talked a few more minutes, mostly about making plans, including a real first date for the following evening, and then I called a ride home. He walked me to the lobby and waited with me for the car. He then placed a gentle peck on my lips before saying, "Goodnight, Elsie."

"Goodnight, Cy," I'd replied.

He opened his mouth to say something else, but seemed to change his mind at the last second. Instead, he said, "Let me know when you get home," and closed the car door.

Chapter 13

Opal

I laid back down in my bed, carefully arranging my face into the same mask of contempt I'd had before Zilpher showered. I had hung up on Amber without saying a word and stowed his phone back in his pocket. When he came out, he saw me as I stared intently at my tablet, swiping through various screens and video feeds without really seeing them. He put his suit back on and walked out without a glance or goodbye. I hadn't expected one; it wasn't like we'd ever exchanged such pleasantries before he'd left any other time.

Once he was gone, I began frantically combing the feeds again, looking for more angles of the blonde woman who carried herself so much like Amber, in case I'd been wrong and it *was* her. Whoever she was, she did a great job, whether intentionally or not, of making sure her face wasn't seen by any cameras on the street.

Why was Amber back? And *why* was she not only in contact with Zilpher, but calling him frantically? The questions battered my brain, pleading for an answer as I reflected on the last time I'd seen Amber, though not the last time we'd spoken.

It was seven years prior, and she had come and gone and come again, ever the rolling stone. When she showed up at the Speakeasy, I was pleased to see her, in my way. Pleasure was relative to me by that point. I had become content in my detachment from not only humans, but from others of my own kind. I had found a joy in my solitude, a peace in my violence. Most vampires who remembered their human lives seemed to struggle for years (or decades, even centuries) with the internal paradox of remembering what it was like to be the prey while having to live as the predator. Many never achieved the level of disregard for mortal morality and human impulses that I (the only vampire I knew with not a single memory of my human life) managed to achieve so early in my afterlife.

But Amber being in town meant something very important. She avoided the Council like the plague, which meant that they were unlikely to be in town and breathing down our necks; it meant we could let loose. Hunting with a partner was always more fun, successful, and satisfying; this was true even in a relationship as tenuous as it must always be between two forces of nature such as Amber and myself.

We had gone over the bridge into St. Petersburg, where there were a number of bars and clubs we could choose from. These were populated by the young entrepreneurs that had flocked to the area for years, as well as the children of the old money in the area. Old money, new money... it was all the same green, and their blood all ran the same red.

We had set ourselves up in a corner booth at a lovely rooftop bar, which seemed to be a place for the young, hip, and moderately wealthy. They'd come here to drink just to the point of excess before moving on to a seedier establishment. We were an arresting image: two fit, young, exuberant beauties looking for a good time on the town, without a care in the world.

We had managed to attract a pair of young men, very close to my age and a few years older than the age Amber appeared, since it seemed she was several years younger than I was when she became a vampire. One of the men was investing in the other's new business, and they behaved and spoke in a way that suggested we should feel lucky to have gotten their attention. When men's blood runs south, the hubris that follows is borderline comical. These were the kinds of quarry I found most appealing- those who see other humans as prey for their own desires and ambitions.

We invited them back to our hotel because, of course, we were there for the weekend on a girls' trip, a getaway from the rigors of life, from the monotony of work, all the things we knew to be true of the human condition. My victim (the tenderfoot businessman) had agreed, but Amber's worldly wastrel had been more aggressive. Had we not been the proverbial wolves in sheep's clothing, I would never have let her go with him. In hindsight, I shouldn't have let her go regardless.

The wealthy young man led Amber away while I took the green one back to a room I'd rented for the night, under a false name, of course. It wasn't like there was an official record of "Madame Opal, the Vampire Killing Vampire" anywhere.

The interesting thing about men is that some genuinely believe that *they* are the prize, and they present themselves to women as such. It's why the dating apps humans use (as well as the more tech-savvy vampires such as myself- it's so easy to find willing prey on the internet) end up with women looking at inboxes full of unsolicited erections. In the absence of his friend, the businessman I had seduced was much less full of himself. He was kind and gentle, and generous in every regard. Had I been human, I would likely have been smitten; he was genuinely *likable*. He spoke to me for longer than I would typically have cared to listen about the business he was so excited about; about how if he hadn't needed the money he wouldn't have accepted it because his "friend" was arrogant and controlling, and he really couldn't stand people like that.

I faltered in my plan to kill him. It felt wrong, like slaughtering a fawn who'd wandered off from its mother. His naïveté struck a chord in me I didn't know existed, and I let him live. Instead of going for the kill, I bedded him, drugged him to sleep, fed enough to feel satiated, and left him to be awakened by housekeeping sometime the next morning.

I went back to The Roof (the name of the bar we'd been at) and followed what little of Amber's scent I could still pick up. Vampires have predatory senses to begin with, but when we choose to hunt together, we can deliberately leave a trail of our own scent for our fellows to follow, making it easier to stay together. I traced the trail to a large house along the water. From the number of cars in the driveway, it seemed to be host to either a party or a place where lots of people lived, like a small commune or fraternity, in order to share the price and afford such a place.

I opened the door slowly, finding it to be unlocked. I had caught a whiff of something that filled me with a sense of foreboding from outside, but thought I must be wrong. I could smell dozens of warm, pulsing bodies, booze, drugs... *Party it is*, I thought. It would make it easier to move through the house unnoticed, which I knew would be necessary once another scent came to me. The moment I entered, I felt woozy and overcome with both hunger and revulsion. The smell of blood was overwhelming; there wasn't just one victim. I could smell at least half a dozen different casualties, and at least one of those scents had the reek of death.

I walked through the foyer, filled with gyrating bodies who had no idea that somewhere nearby, a slaughter had occurred, and that death herself walked among them toward it. If

I'd had a heartbeat, it would have been racing with anticipation and anxiety over what I was expecting to find. Men not unlike the one who'd brought Amber here were doing lines of cocaine off of the breasts of a half-naked woman lying on a couch. Still others were swapping prescription bottles or sharing joints. No wonder no one noticed the death in their midst- they were too busy numbing themselves to anything at all that might be occurring in their short, meaningless lives.

My disdain for humans growing as I watched them become lost in their escapism, I felt gratitude for whatever had happened to cause my inability to remember my life as a human. If it had been anything like this, my current life was the greatest blessing I could have ever hoped for, Council bullshit and all.

I overheard a scuffle and voices shouting about who had the real power in town. "We're the ones who run this town! The old names! The Elite!" one blowhard was yelling. I imagined him beating on his chest like a gorilla in a zoo, only less civilized. Little did he know that he and his Elite brethren, his old names, could be completely wiped out if I had the slightest inclination to make that happen. Humans had no idea of the fragility of those things they held so sacred.

I walked up a grand staircase, past people doing things in plain view of others that, even as an immortal being devoid (mostly) of shame, I'd only kept behind closed and locked doors. For me, it had less to do with modesty, however, and much more to do with the blood that often entered the equation, and the attention that would bring. These people just didn't care who saw or even who joined in.

I walked to the end of a long hallway (the house hadn't looked quite so big from the outside) and found myself at the door of what appeared to be the master bedroom. I stood stock-still, reaching out with my senses to feel for danger inside. I braced myself and opened the door. I didn't knock. I could tell before I turned the handle that there were only two survivors inside.

I opened the door and found Amber standing over a sobbing, half out of her mind girl, younger than either of us in appearance- practically a child. Amber was covered head to toe in blood and gore, but was unharmed. The girl was hurt, but her wounds were superficial and definitely not caused by one of us. Around the room, the mutilated bodies of young men dripped what was left of their life onto the floor, walls, bed, couch, chairs...

Amber stared at me, a wild look on her face I had never seen before. She looked feral, unable to discern friend from foe as she stepped protectively between the crying girl and me, a snarl forming on her lips.

"Fuck," I whispered. She continued to stare me down, blood dripping from her fingers and mouth. "Fuck, Amber!" My voice rose, thankfully unable to be heard over the deep bass resonating through the house from downstairs. "*What the fuck did you do?*" I closed the door quickly behind me. I looked around, the scene grisly enough to nearly cause *me* to become squeamish. Nearly.

"You didn't see," she growled, her eyes blazing, "what they did to her! What they would have done to me... or you... or anyone they could."

It was only then that I realized the other smell. It was another fluid from each of the men in the room... And I could smell a lot of it on the girl. And suddenly it hit me what had happened, and I was horrified. The girl was out of her mind from what they'd done, but also from the cocktail of alcohol and drugs she was on. She'd been an easy target, and they had taken advantage- to a magnitude even I couldn't fathom. This was entitlement taken to the highest limit. I may be a predator, but never had I *hurt* anyone like they had. This was abhorrent. Amber's violent reaction, I felt, was undoubtedly appropriate in terms of the emotional response. The scene before me nearly shattered my aloof attitude toward humans and their exploits. I hated them. I was filled with a rage that threatened to send me flying back down the stairs to do just the same thing to everyone else in the house.

I knew I would never, because I had to maintain control, both as a Council member and as a vampire who lived in this area and needed to maintain our secrecy. Something like this could expose us. It was beyond what we could easily cover up; the rest of the Council would find out, and I would be responsible for both assigning and carrying out Amber's sentence. I knew I wouldn't be able to, and not only because I think these fiends probably deserved what they got. Amber could be cold, selfish, and a queen bitch when she wanted to, but she had saved my life by making me into what I am. She had done her best to educate me and make sure that I could function as both a fledgling and a Council member when I had no way of knowing how to be either of those things. She held a tender place in my cold, dead heart, and I knew I was prepared to fight for her.

My mind worked quickly. We had two choices. When someone eventually entered this room, they would have to come to some kind of conclusion. I could never get rid of the evidence before that happened, so I needed to devise a scenario people would believe when they walked in. The two I could work out were both terrible, and this poor girl was going to pay the price for the actions of the men who had died here no matter which outcome we chose. Either we could kill her and make it look like someone had broken in and left by the same window, slaughtering everyone inside, or this girl was about to become a murderer- not by her own hand, but when we framed her for the killings.

I pulled Amber aside and told her my plan. Her eyes widened with horror and rage at what I suggested. "Opal, no!" She growled. "Do you really expect me to believe you haven't considered the third option?" Her eyes wandered over to the girl, still sobbing and hugging her knees, staring madly around the room.

In that moment, I actually *felt* my eyes change in warning to her. "*What* third option?" I asked. I knew what she meant. It was a dare, one I hoped she would back down from.

"She comes with us," Amber said, her golden eyes still alight with that same fire. "Opal, she doesn't have to live a wretched mortal life filled only with the fallout from this night forever, and she doesn't have to die here either. What they did..." Her face was ashen as she looked at each of the bodies strewn about the room. "Opal... it was done to me."

Chapter 14

Elsie

I had awoken from the strange dream about Cyrus, that beautiful morning after we'd shared our feelings. I lay in bed, going over and over the previous night in my mind, trying hard to fall back asleep and knowing I'd never be able to as long as the sun was shining directly on my face.

I threw the blanket off and, squinting, lowered the blinds over the window and yanked the thin mesh curtains (which probably didn't help at all) closed. It was a marked difference, but it was still bright.

"Elsie?"

Shit. I had been heard. It was Saturday morning, and that meant Mom was on the warpath, intent on obliterating any and all dust accumulated in the house over the last week.

I debated responding, but my mind was still preoccupied and blissful, so I quickly dove back under the covers and tried to pretend to be asleep, hoping it wouldn't be faking for long.

I made my breathing even and deep. Just as I was nearly calm enough to possibly fall back into my slumber, I heard my bedroom door open.

"Elsie?" my mother repeated at the same volume she'd used to call from the living room. I glared through closed eyes. She wouldn't have seen the expression; I was facing the other direction.

Then my entire body moved as she sat down and leaned over and touched my head. "Elsie, are you awake?"

Well, if I hadn't been before... I decided to ham it up, so I made my voice hoarse and croaked, "Wha...? Hi, Mom." Then I turned my head away in an obvious gesture of "*let me go back to sleep.*"

Mom didn't pick up on that. Or maybe she did and ignored it. "Morning, sleepy," she crowed. "Look, I have a lot to get done in the house today. I'm going out with the girls for Andrea's birthday tonight."

I tried to ignore her, but she pulled the covers off of me. I immediately curled myself into a ball to try to stay warm.

"Get up," she said, dropping the sugar-coating.

"What time is it?" I asked, genuinely curious and moderately aggravated.

"It's almost eight-thirty," she responded impatiently.

I opened one eye at her. "I hope you mean at night."

She stood up and turned my light on. I reached for my blanket, but she grabbed my hand and tried to pull me to my feet. I took my hand back and returned to my little ball.

"Come on, Elsie, I'm leaving at six."

I opened the other eye and stared at her. Never, even at its worst, was our house messy enough to merit nine-plus hours of cleaning.

"So, what time are we expecting company?" I was sure that people must be coming over beforehand to justify so much housework.

"No company," she chirped. "I'm just sick of looking at the mess."

"'S not that bad," I mumbled, sleep threatening to take me before I could react.

"Get up. It's not my fault you stayed out all night. You live here, you can help keep it livable for everyone."

I reached for my blanket again to make my point as I said, "I wasn't out all night. I'm here, home, in my bed, trying to sleep. I can help after I'm actually awake, Mom."

"Sleep is a waste of your life," she spat and threw my blanket back over me. She turned and stormed out, leaving my light on and door open.

"Not when I need it, Mom. Let me sleep 'til noon, and I'll help you out," I called after her. I stood up and turned off the light. I had almost gotten the door closed when Oso stuck his nose into the door and jumped on my bed for attention. He smiled his goofy smile and looked hopefully at me.

I growled and tried to make him get off, but he lay down and became dead weight. I put my hands under him, forcing him to stand and then to jump down before ushering him into the hall. I slammed the door behind him and crawled back into bed, but Oso had accomplished his goal- I was now wide awake. I could go down and just get the cleaning over with, but with my luck, Mom would find a way to extend it until her dinner party.

And of course, Danielle was away for a few more weeks at least, and as such, I would be expected to go pick Mom up later since Dad's sense of direction was hopeless. Not that he was likely to be around anyway; on Saturdays, he usually went to the movies with his best friend, unless they were golfing.

Too bad for them, I was also leaving at six for my date with Cy and would be unavailable to be my mother's taxi.

I picked the book I'd finished weeks before off of the shelf and started flipping through it. It had been so enthralling when I'd read it, but now... real life was just so much better.

Even so, I read a few pages, hoping that reading would exhaust my eyes enough that I was ready to attempt to sleep again. It very nearly worked, and I rolled over and felt oblivion pull at me.

At which point, Oso started to scratch at my door.

*　　　*　　　*

I slumped onto the couch and sighed. I reached for the remote and turned on the television. I wasn't really in the mood to watch anything, but I scrolled through all our streaming services to see what was new. I had cleaned the guest bathroom, the kitchen, the living room, and the dining room. Mom had taken care of the family room and her master bathroom and was now chattering away on the phone.

As I clicked and swiped mindlessly, Oso came to lay by my feet. He was part lab with a mammoth amount of fur and looked a lot like a black bear cub, hence the name. I used my foot to scratch behind his ears, and he let out one of his funny groaning noises.

I finally settled on one of my favorite sitcoms that I'd seen enough times to know the jokes by heart. I put it on as background noise and leaned my head back, closing my eyes. After Oso had prevented me from returning to sleep, I had succumbed to a day of chores. Now, at two o'clock in the afternoon, I had finished everything Mom had set down for me, and I decided to rest before I got ready.

It was at this point that Mom entered the room, pacing while on the phone. She stood next to the speakers I had been counting on to drown her out. I turned the volume up to give her a hint. I closed my eyes and tilted my head back, trying to listen to what the characters were saying. It was a cute scene between the main character and her boyfriend and would have made me smile, especially given my current situation, except...

Suddenly the volume decreased. I looked up to see Mom turning it down. She was still talking.

"Mom!" I whined. I knew I sounded childish, but the lack of sleep was wearing on me.

She glanced at me and put up a finger. After a few seconds, she whispered to me, "I'm on the phone, Elsie."

I blew my breath out in a huff. I could see she was on the phone. Why she planted herself next to the television every single time she had a phone call, I would never know. I debated using the remote to turn it back up, but decided that angering her would not be the best course of action- I could wind up cleaning out the attic tonight rather than enjoying a nice dinner on the bay with Cy. Instead, I forced myself to my feet and stomped to my room, where I fell into bed.

I smiled at the promise of a nap and rolled over onto my side. I sat up immediately and crossed the room to close my door and turn out the light. I had almost made it back to bed when- *Bzzt*.

I groaned, but held my phone up to read the message anyway.

Girl! Ashley texted. *Deets! What happened?*

I smiled, taking a small moment to be grateful for my friends. Sleep could wait after all. I started to type out the answer but realized quickly I'd be writing a small novel. So instead, I figured I'd escape my house, get a little energy for the evening, and avoid Mom's inevitable request to help her with something she either "forgot" or decided should be done.

Coffee? One hour?

Ashley sent back a thumbs up, and I launched out of bed and into the shower.

*   *   *

"... So *please* don't say anything about Jack," I begged, "Because I think he was totally planning on telling Cy until he thought Amber showing up was perfect for wrecking things." I glared down at my coffee. "I can't believe I ever thought we were friends."

I'd told Ashley everything that had happened after she dropped me off at the hotel. She had gasped in horror when I pulled out my phone to show her the photo that I'd received at his door; she had squealed with delight when I told her that we'd kissed; and when I finished, she was frowning as deeply as I was.

"Jack needs to get his ass kicked," Ashley said, shaking her head. "I still can't believe he'd do all this. It's so high school. I would have thought by now that he'd have grown up a little, but I guess his ego outweighs his sense."

I shrugged, and steered the conversation back to the happier side. "Yes, but I couldn't even care less anymore. Cy knows all about it- my worst secret- and he wants to be with me anyway." I hadn't even realized that I'd started smiling again, but it became clear when my cheeks started to hurt. "We have a date tonight," I said with a sly grin.

Ashley dropped her jaw in an exaggerated expression of shock. "What?! Where?"

"Down by the Riverwalk," I told her. The Riverwalk was a beautiful walkway along the Tampa Bay downtown. There were all kinds of restaurants, bars, live entertainment venues, and amazing views of the water and the city. "He made reservations somewhere... Trusty's?"

Ashley choked on her latte. "How the fuck did he pull off last minute Saturday night reservations at Trusty's? Oh, my God! And you're sitting here with me?" She sputtered. "Instead of getting ready?"

110

I wasn't ready for that reaction. "Why?" I asked. "I've never heard of this place. Is it fancy?"

She shook her head, appalled by my ignorance. "You have spent way too much time *not* being taken out." She was right. Sam and I rarely went anywhere nice because it just wasn't a priority. We had gotten so comfortable when we were actually dating that we usually just had bar and bedroom dates. "What are you going to wear?"

I felt like a deer in headlights. "Um... I hadn't thought about it. Maybe a sundress? Or dark jeans and a nice top?"

"Get your coffee," she ordered, shaking her head in horror. "We have to get to the mall. Now."

*　　*　　*

I stood in front of the full-length mirror in the hall of my house. The dress Ashley had helped me pick out was like nothing I'd ever worn, and the price tag had been like nothing I'd ever spent, except on a prom dress. It had thin black straps that came out from the neckline, which was cut into a gentle sweetheart shape. The base of the dress was black silk and chiffon with pale pink, yellow, and orange flowers swirled all over. The hem, which fell halfway between my knees and ankles, had a built-in petticoat, and the top layer was such a light material and was cut into such a pattern that every time I so much as breathed, it swirled around me like smoke. My style had always been more classically inspired, but in that dress, I felt like a real-life princess, or a European heiress, or Jackie O. reincarnated.

Ashley had also helped me pick out the perfect shoes, which were thankfully on clearance since I'd already blown my wardrobe budget for the whole year on the dress. They were strappy suede heels that matched the pink in the dress. The heels were just the right height that they were dressy enough for the occasion, but comfortable enough to spend some time walking along the Riverwalk.

She had offered to come do my hair and makeup, but while I went for a less is more approach to makeup, she liked to try daring looks from online video tutorials, so I declined. I may have been dressed up like a pretty, pretty princess, but I still wanted to look like myself.

So with my hair in loose curls around my shoulders and some minimal makeup, I looked at myself in the mirror. I felt more than cute- I felt gorgeous. I hadn't even realized people actually got dressed up like this except for engagements or anniversaries or meeting the Queen. I would *totally* wear this if I was going to meet the Queen.

My mom glanced up at me as she rushed past to go out for her girls' night. She did an almost comical double-take. "Elsie?" She gasped. "What...? You look beautiful!" She grabbed my shoulders to look at me, then hugged me tightly. After she took a step back, she asked, "Where are you off to, all dressed up?"

I realized that we hadn't really talked at all since the previous day before I'd gone out; I'd gotten home too late, and she'd launched us so quickly into cleaning that morning that I hadn't had an opportunity to tell her that I had a new boyfriend, but I'm sure the blush I felt creeping over my cheeks gave away that there was something she didn't yet know.

"I have a date," I said shyly. "At Trusty's."

Mom's eyes widened, impressed. "Sam is taking you to Trusty's? Finally! That boy was frustrating me with how little effort he puts in with you," she lamented.

"Um..." I frowned. "It's... not Sam," I corrected her.

Her eyes stayed wide, but now there was accusation in them. "Not Sam? Who are you dating that is taking you out somewhere this fancy that I don't know about? Is it Jack? I always felt like he had a crush on you."

I felt my lunch threaten to make a reappearance at the thought of dating Jack, knowing now the kind of person he truly was. "No, Mom. Not Jack either. I've mentioned Cy- Cyrus- to you."

"The one who just moved here?" She asked, a crease forming between her eyebrows. "I didn't realize you two were a thing..." Hurt and accusation colored her words.

I put my hands out, trying to calm her, feeling her emotions teetering dangerously close to anger. She clearly thought I'd been hiding it. We'd always been so open with each other, but me living at home as an adult had driven a wedge into our relationship, making things perpetually tense. I knew I hadn't been totally honest with her about what had gone on when Cy and I met (I mean, who wants to talk to their mom about trashy nightclub hookups?), but I still respected her and our bond. "It's new, Mom. We've been friends, but last night I told him I like him as more than that, and he feels the same. Mom..." I gushed. "He's so *hot!*"

At this, she laughed and hugged me again. "I'm happy for you, sweetie." Then she looked at me with a wink. "But I hope you like him for other reasons than how *hot* he is."

I gave a genuine smile. "He's kind. And smart. And, it's still *so* new, but..." My smile turned sheepish. "I don't feel like an afterthought with him. He makes me feel special."

"Good," she said. "Because you are." Mom squeezed my arm, then looked over my shoulder at the clock. "I have to run. Is he coming to pick you up?"

"Yeah, he should be here in a few minutes."

She looked thoughtful. "I could be a bit late..."

Now *my* eyes went wide. "Mom, no," I commanded. "I promise to introduce you soon, but please. I know I live with you, but I'm a grown woman, and I need my new boyfriend to not feel interrogated by my mommy on our first real date."

She pursed her lips at me. "Fine. But soon." Then she smiled, but it didn't reach her eyes. Uh oh. "Have fun. What time will you be home?" By which she meant, *will you be home at all?* Subtle.

"I'm not sure, Mom," I sighed. It was the truth; Cy had told me to plan for a "night on the town," but I didn't know what that entailed after dinner at Trusty's.

There was an awkward silence before she kissed me on the forehead and left. I hated having our relationship be so tense. I wished I could afford to move out so that we could get back to how we used to be.

Mom had barely cleared the end of the street when Cy pulled around in a white sedan and climbed out to greet me. I realized I'd never seen him drive, and therefore had no idea what kind of car he had. It wasn't some wild sports or luxury car, but it was a nice full-size sedan with a sunroof, and probably bursting with options. Fancy, but not in a garish, over the top way. The apotheosis of average. It suited him.

I walked toward him, feeling the dress ripple around my legs. He had on his usual white button-down, but tonight it was under a suit that was just relaxed enough that it would look casual if it hadn't been perfectly tailored. No tie, top button loose. Good lord, he was handsome. My heart was going to either burst through my chest or stop altogether, I couldn't tell.

He smiled at me, those fucking sunglasses hiding his eyes from me. He'd told me a few weeks earlier why he always wore them. "When I was younger, I had a degenerative disease that targeted my eyes. They were able to save them, but they're so sensitive that I need polarized lenses whenever there are any UV rays that could damage them, or I may lose my sight completely." He rocked the look, but I wished I could see his eyes sparkling in the daylight.

He opened the car door for me and I climbed in. He got in on the other side, continuing to smile at me. Then he leaned across and kissed me gently on the cheek. "You look absolutely lovely." He motioned to the dress. "That's going to be perfect."

I gave him a look as though I was onto his mischief. "Perfect for what?" I asked.

"You'll see."

Chapter 15

Opal

"What the fuck do you mean 'it was done to you'?" I hissed at Amber. In all of our nights drinking together, hunting together, her teaching me, turning me into a vampire, she had never once mentioned this.

The pain in her eyes was so startlingly human at that moment, I nearly forgot that she was my ageless, immortal mentor. At that moment, she and the girl huddled on the floor were sisters in a way I could never understand.

Amber spoke to me in a frequency humans couldn't hear, but was clear as a bell to our kind. "Bring her with us. Do it, and I'll tell you." A tear fell from her eye. "Please." I had never heard Amber beg for anything- I didn't think she was capable. I knew in that moment I couldn't refuse her, not if she was willing to show this level of weakness. This was going to be a mess no matter what we did, anyway.

Once we smuggled the girl out through a window, we did some work to make it look like the robbery I'd planned to stage, just with one less victim. We somehow managed to get the girl back to the hotel and into our room without anyone noticing. My "date" was still lying unconscious on the bed. Amber gave me an exasperated look. "Really? The one night you *don't* kill your food?" Her voice was heavy with criticism.

Her attitude set me off. "Well, you've killed enough tonight to pump up half the Council. Shall we invite them to partake?" I asked aggressively. "Besides, we have hours before the shit I gave him wears off." The girl between us was limp but for a shivering that seemed to have come over her in her shock and withdrawals. Her eyes didn't seem to be focused on anything- they just rolled around the room.

Amber looked at him thoughtfully. "Well, I suppose it's good he's here. We'll need him before sunrise, anyway."

Amber took the girl into the shower and cleaned her up, whispering to her the entire time. I could hear her through the wall, but I knew the words weren't for me and I tuned them out.

Once she was clean of the blood and other fluids, Amber brought her to the empty bed, continuing to talk to her. I caught briefly that the girl's name was Melody. "Melody," Amber crooned at her, "I want to help, and there's one way I can do that." Her voice sounded as musical as Melody's name, full of promises of comfort, of peace. I didn't believe that was what lay in store for poor Melody, but I let Amber continue without interruption. "I can give you a gift. I can give you the power to right this wrong for others, like I did for you." Melody seemed to stir and focus at these words, but there was a fear in her eyes. She had seen what Amber had done, and recognized that, as monstrous as what had happened to her was, Amber was frightening in an entirely different way.

"Amber," I called softly, speaking in our frequency so as not to have Melody hear. "Amber, think about this. You didn't want her mortal life to be filled with this night over and over for whatever years she has left, but you would give her immortal life to relive this for all eternity?" I shook my head at her. "Don't do this, Amber. End it here."

Amber looked at me, that all-too-human pain resurfacing in her golden eyes. "I'm giving her the only way through: vengeance and justice." With that and without so much as another word to me, she drew a razor-sharp nail across her collarbone. She turned to Melody, as if to allow the girl to rest on her shoulder, but she instead turned her face to the wound. Melody pulled back at first, her eyes widening in fear at the sight of more blood, but as the decadent drink filled her mouth, she relaxed, and an expression of pure rapture came over her. She suckled like a newborn at its mother's breast, letting the irresistible fount fill her with its strange sustenance until Amber pulled her away.

Melody's lips were stained and she seemed to be slowly regaining her focus. I had heard of this process from others, but had never seen it done. I didn't even have the memory of my own experience, but Amber had said it was much like this; the major difference for me was that I had been given the blood because I was dying, not losing my mind. Amber's blood was beginning to sharpen Melody's focus on her surroundings, to heal her wounds- the ones on her flesh, anyway. I wasn't convinced all the vampire blood on Earth could heal the other kind.

Amber kissed Melody softly on her cheek. "When you wake, you'll be truly awake for the first time." Then she swiped the same nail she'd cut her own skin with across Melody's soft, supple throat, and we watched together as she gasped and thrashed. The remaining human blood left her, the vampire blood already bonded to her body and clinging to it. Then she was still.

"How long?" I asked. Watching the exchange had stirred something in me, a true longing for the first time to know my life before, at least the part where I'd been changed. I wanted to remember the sensual event as it had happened, not as I saw it happening to another. "How long until she wakes?"

Amber sighed. "Depends. Could be an hour, could be five. It's always before sunrise, though, so we know it won't be longer than that." She sat on the bed next to the body that was once Melody, the poor human girl who'd been unlucky enough to walk into a party with more than one kind of evil creature in attendance.

I hadn't moved an inch since walking into the room. I spent the entire time leaning against the door to the hotel room, arms crossed, watching the process. I turned my darkened eyes- the menacing deep gray of a storm cloud, complete with flashes of bright yellow lightning, from what I saw in the window reflection when we walked in- to Amber.

She stood and mirrored my posture, but she failed to imitate my aura. Warning, fury, and (limited) patience spilled from me, while Amber exuded defensiveness and shame.

"I guess you're going to force me to tell you," she practically whined.

I cocked my head to the side. "I could. You know I could." It wasn't a threat, and she knew it. It was simply a fact. I was stronger than nearly any vampire either of us knew, and certainly stronger than she was. Why? I'd never found out why my fledgling strength far surpassed my sire's accumulated power of centuries, why I was able to defeat Orla with little to no effort.

This wasn't about my strength, though. This was about information owed to me. "As your Councilor and *friend*, I hope you'll choose to tell me about what happened, since knowing might have helped me to prevent the events that occurred tonight, and will hopefully help prevent it from happening again."

Amber glared. "As long as men take what they want from women who have no choice in the matter, I hope there will always be me or someone like me there." I didn't say anything, just continued to stare her down. Then she sighed and began her story,

"When I was alive, in the 11th century, I was the daughter of a Viking Jarl, a lord in our village. I should have been quick to marry off, but I wasn't as... desirable as other girls in the village. I'm beautiful now, but in my mortal life, I certainly wasn't. My younger sisters married before I did, and I was nearing twenty, the age at which Norse women became independent. It should have been liberating, but it was terrifying. I was never smart enough to be good at political matters and not powerfully built enough to become a warrior, though my father had always hoped... He loved his girls. Norse women weren't seen as inferior the way women were in other places. I was the firstborn, but the least pretty, least smart, and least strong. I had little hope for any kind of decent future.

"There was a boy... because of *course* there was a boy. He was a Thrall, one of our slaves, and I knew my parents would never allow the marriage. Legally independent or no, a marriage was still decided by the family. But he was so handsome and strong. We fell in love hard and fast, and we were secret lovers an entire summer.

"We'd hoped that we could find passage on a ship headed south somewhere where no one knew us once I was able to leave of my own accord. I was prepared to give up my dowry, my titles, everything for him. His name was Hemming."

Her eyes took on a strange quality I'd never seen. The raw emotion was so unlike what I was used to not only from Amber, but from any of our kind. Even the fresh vampires who remembered every moment of their human lives rarely expressed such deep and complex emotion, knowing to do so would label them as weak. She was remembering love, joy, and, somewhere deep down (I felt certain she was about to tell me why) she was remembering exquisite pain.

"Hemming and I went to the new Christian priest in our village, who agreed to marry us privately. Most of us tried to hold onto the old traditions despite the arrival of the new religion, but we were losing. Hemming himself was very interested in Christianity, and had begun to cling to many of the teachings and values it brought with it.

"It was a difficult decision for me, to leave my father, who always loved me best, but I hoped he would understand that I could never have what I needed if I stayed. I went home after the agreement took place, and I gathered what I could of my belongings, none of which meant a thing to me more than the love I felt for Hemming, my future husband. I sold nearly everything and went to wait for Hemming at the church.

"When I arrived, the priest told me Hemming had been there before, but would not be coming. His parents had requested permission from my father to marry Hemming to a Karl girl, middle-class, from another village. He said that while he was grateful for our time together, he had fallen in love with this other girl, Sigrun, and would be marrying her.

"In that time, you have to understand," she said, her lip curling in disgust, "we had spent centuries with our own rules and rights as people, even the women. Taking a lover before marriage, even being an unwed mother, was not seen as shameful to my people. But Hemming had told the priest that he and I had lain together, that we had sinned, which was why he wouldn't marry me after all. Sigrun had been a virgin, supposedly, and so he chose her.

"The priest took the matter to my parents, telling them that by the new religious laws, I was no longer fit to be married at all. What little prospects I had left for a possible marriage dried up as word spread throughout our village that I had sinned against the new Christian God. I was damaged goods.

121

My father tried to find a way for me to continue as his aide in trade and political matters, but the priest stepped in and shipped me off to a convent in Denmark to live out the rest of my life. I never made it there.

"I traveled with a merchant ship that was overtaken by pirates in the North Sea. Almost everyone on board was killed. There were three of us who were spared, and all for the same purpose. We were taken to their ship and confined to quarters... chained to the beds..."

Her eyes took on a glazed quality. I stopped her from continuing, feeling sick at the thought of where her story was heading. "I can put two and two together from there," I said. "You don't have to tell any more."

"You got me to tell this much, and you don't want to hear the rest?" Amber snapped.

I was surprised. I had thought I was doing her a kindness by ending the story. It seemed, however, that she was finding the experience of speaking of her pain as cathartic as the slaughter she'd committed earlier in the evening. I never felt anything that strongly, and wondered briefly if this was what truly set me apart from the rest of my kind, even old ones like Amber or Zilpher; it was as much the lack of human weakness as it was the vampiric strength. I motioned for her to continue.

"They... kept me. For weeks. They all didn't come to me every night, but every night some did. I was broken to the point of no longer resisting, but that only made some of them worse... they liked my pain. But finally, after what I believed to be nearly a month, we docked in Scotland. One night, one of the more brutal men left me so wounded and bloodied that they left me behind a monastery, of all places, to die when they moved on...

"It was there and then that Sapphire found me." Sapphire was Amber's sire, and a very high-level member of the Council, somewhere above Zilpher. "Sapphire offered me what I offered

Melody tonight. At first, I didn't understand; I just wanted to die, and to be released from my pain. Do you know what my human name was?" She gave a barking, humorless laugh. I shook my head. "Oydis. It means 'lucky.'" She shook her own head then. "I suppose I *was* lucky that Sapphire walked that way, but nothing in my entire life up until then felt very lucky. Once she made me, I was glad to abandon that cosmic joke of a name and all the pain that came with it. I even went back home. First, I dealt with that priest who'd sealed my fate. Then Hemming and Sigrun came next. They fell at my feet, convinced I was Freya, come to bring their deaths. I obliged happily, knowing I had finally rid myself of everything that had destroyed the person I was."

"Except you clearly didn't," I pointed out brutally. "You're still carrying that human weakness around with you."

Amber lurched forward with a movement like she planned to attack me, but thought better of it, knowing she would likely lose. She settled, instead, for taking a more aggressive stance as she retorted, "Ask those assholes bleeding all over that house if I was *weak*."

I narrowed my eyes, not speaking. She knew I hadn't meant physical weakness. She was lashing out, allowing her past to control her present.

She glared at me for a while, but backed down before I did, looking at the window without really seeing it. She sighed. "I have shaped my entire afterlife around finding justice for myself and women like me. Women who have been so hurt by men that..." she seemed unable to finish the thought. Something seemed to occur to her, and she looked at me and said, "Need I remind you how you ended up on that island with no memory of your life? Should I have not saved *you*? Given *you* a second chance?"

That gave me pause. I hadn't exactly forgotten the details of my rebirth, but since I had no memory of how I'd gotten there, it wasn't something I dwelled on. It had never occurred to me that Amber might have saved me because of her own history.

I was spared having to answer as Melody began to stir, the wound across her throat having knitted itself together; the only indication it had ever been there being a thin pink line that was already fading. She sat up and looked at us with a mix of wonder and fear. I marveled at the change she'd undergone. Her appearance had changed subtly; if you didn't know that it was her, you might have just thought her someone who reminded you of Melody in vague ways. Her cheekbones and jawline had sharpened, giving her natural contours and highlights. Her mouth was fuller, more expressive and sensual. Her skin was now without flaws, no blemishes, no enlarged pores, no fine lines. Her body, while slim before, had filled out in terms of musculature and her curves were more pronounced. With her lustrous, chocolate-brown hair, she could have walked off the set of a Golden Age movie and into this hotel.

I excused myself to give Amber time to explain to Melody about her new life. I had to make a phone call anyway. I stepped into the hallway and dialed Zilpher.

It rang once. "What?" He snarled. "I'm eating."

"Hello to you, too," I said, quietly enough that even if anyone had been in the hallway next to me, they couldn't have heard me. "Feel free to eat while you listen. I need to tell you before it hits the news..."

I filled him in on the highlights of the evening, leaving out the unnecessary parts.

"And where is Amber now?" Zilpher growled. I could practically hear the headache this was giving him. Not literally, of course, since we don't get minor maladies such as headaches.

"With the fledgling."

"I cannot believe you let her make someone," Zilpher said. "You know the rules-"

"Yeah, I know," I snapped. Making someone into a vampire was supposed to be a process in which they were made aware of what was happening and had time to accept the decision with a sound mind. If they refused, they were killed, as we couldn't have humans living free who knew about us. Few ever refused. It was never supposed to be a knee jerk reaction to an emergency situation, no matter how often that was the actual case. I myself could be put to death if I were to share my blood, since Council members were forbidden from passing our own strength on to fledglings for multiple reasons. One reason was that they might end up like me, unable to control their impulses, and, also like me, they might put a challenge to an older vampire, which would end in someone's death either way. The other was political stability. We couldn't have one Councilor creating an army to overthrow the rest of us. "But I'm grateful those rules were broken for me, and it seemed the least costly option under the circumstances."

"We can agree to disagree whether it was the right choice," he said. I knew perfectly well that he could have meant that for either the girl formerly known as Melody or me. "We will come to help with PR once it hits the news. Is that all?"

I fucking hate you, I thought. "Goodbye, Zilpher." I hung up and went back inside.

There were tears on her cheeks, but the fledgling vampire seemed to have stopped crying. Amber was explaining to her that she would need to feed. She pointed to the young man I'd allowed to live. It was certainly easier than taking her out to hunt.

Melody shook her head, no, she wouldn't hurt anyone, but she was fighting the inevitable; her fangs had already descended at the scent of the living body. I walked over to the boy and made a small nick in a medium-sized vein along his arm. I ran my finger through the blood and walked over to the girl, wiping it across her lip. Her eyes suddenly became wild and ravenous, and she moved quickly, yet almost mechanically to kneel at his side. She began to lap at the gently dripping wound. I grabbed her by the shoulders and moved her to the boy's throat and told her, "Bite."

All of her protestations were lost the moment she tasted the blood. She took him passionately, gulping like someone who'd found a spring in the desert. The first blood, the first chip away at her humanity. It was amazing to watch. It goes by so quickly and without much thought when it's your own first time. To see it in another... it set my skin on fire.

Amber and I agreed that she would take Indigo (Melody's new name, for the deep, night-sky blue of her eyes) to another city while I dealt with the Council and the media fallout of the missing girl. Indigo was just changed enough from her mortal countenance to not trigger any facial recognition software, and enough that even friends and family could doubt her identity if they saw her, but it was still better for her to not be in the same city she vanished from. Amber and I said goodbye, and she took Indigo, still reeling from the change of direction her existence had taken in a single night. And like that, they were gone.

Chapter 16

Elsie

Dinner was like nothing I'd ever experienced. They led us to a small room sectioned off by a heavy curtain. The absence of natural light- not only in this room, but in most of the restaurant- allowed Cy to take off his sunglasses, which made dinner conversation so much more enjoyable for me.

The restaurant was beyond anything I could have expected, having never been in such a place before. The menus had *literature* about the food. It took me forever to order simply because I was enthralled with the story behind each dish. After dinner and several glasses of wine which the server had recommended, Cy turned to our server and said, "We will be enjoying dessert tonight, but can you please let Jett know that Cy is here and would love to say hello?"

The server blanched but kept his smile firmly in place. "Of course. Cy, you said?" Then he hurried off to find "Jett."

I looked at Cy in wonder. "What was that about? I thought he was going to pee himself when you asked that."

Cy gave an easy laugh and leaned back in his chair. "Jett owns the place and is a friend. I'm sure the server was nervous, considering I know his boss. But he needn't worry. I felt he did a spectacular job. Did you?" He asked, almost as an after-thought. "Because if not, I could certainly mention to Jett-"

"No!" I interrupted. "I mean, no, don't mention any-thing. I agree, he was great." A friend? I thought he had no friends in the area. "How do you know Jett?"

Jett entered at that moment, and Cy stood to shake his hand. "Jett! Good to see you!" Jett was tall and tanned, built like a Mack truck, with a thousand watt smile. His inky black eyes sparkled jovially.

"Cy, how are you?" Jett asked before his eyes moved to me. "Is this the girl? She *is* stunning. Well done, sir!" He took my hand and kissed the knuckles. I would normally pull away from an uninvited touch from a stranger, but it was somehow very non-threatening when Jett did it. There was something about his whole demeanor, probably a result of working in fine dining for long enough to be the boss. Certain outdated man-nerisms still worked in this setting.

"Thank you, Jett," Cy said, not returning to his seat. "The service and the food were both top-notch, as always."

As always? He'd said he had no friends in the area, so how did he know Jett? Had they met after Cy moved here? And how often did he eat here to get to know the owner if this was a new friendship? Did that mean this was standard fare for him? If so, why did he bother coming places like The Watering Hole at all? I suddenly felt like a backwater redneck. Living in a small town in Florida, there was always some level of that feeling, but right now, I felt like I may as well have brushed my tooth and mullet before hugging my uncle-dad and going to sleep on a camp cot by the river.

Questions swirled in my head while Cy and Jett chatted together for a few moments. I did my best not to look like the slack-jawed hillbilly I felt like, but I could tell my cheeks were beginning to burn.

Cy seemed to notice and cut Jett off. "Jett, thank you for coming to say hello, but I wanted to take Elsie to the dessert room. Would you mind escorting us?"

Jett obliged, but insisted on first showing us the wine cellar, which was just past the kitchen, and allowing us to sample a bottle from a collection he'd just brought in. It was some of the richest, smoothest wine I'd ever tasted. It was also thrilling to see the master chefs at work creating beautiful and delicious works of art as we passed through.

He led us to an entirely different wing of the restaurant, where we were seated in a private booth, separated from the rest of the room by floor to ceiling barriers. Jett pointed out a call system on the wall to let our server know if we needed anything, then pulled a thick curtain closed, and Cy and I were alone again. He smiled at me and tipped his wine glass (refilled before we'd left the cellar), in hopes of a toast. I cradled my glass, hesitating to reciprocate. Cy tilted his head to the side. "What's the matter? You don't like it?"

I snorted softly, looking down at the glass and running my finger in circles around the base. "It's the best wine I've ever had," I said glumly.

There was a pause, during which I glanced up and noticed that Cy was bewildered. "I don't understand..." he said slowly. "If it's the best wine you've ever had, why are you upset? Is it something else?"

Before I could stop myself, I whispered, "It's everything else."

Another pause. "I don't understand," Cy repeated, completely befuddled.

I looked into his eyes and they nearly took my breath away as I knew I was potentially ruining everything. But I needed to know, and for him to know. "It's... honestly, it's mostly me. Cy..." I gave a small, dry sob, then started speaking very softly but quickly, and without taking a breath. "I've never set foot in a place like this before, and we come here and you apparently *know the owner*, but you didn't know anyone locally when I met you, so you're clearly here a lot, and this is just another dinner to you, and you met me at a dump like The Watering Hole- and why would you even bother with a place like that when you can come eat fancy five-star steaks and drink fancy five-star wines with fancy five-star people? And this is all so new to me, I mean, I had to go buy this dress so I wouldn't look like a fucking slob walking in here, and it didn't even matter because I'm just the country bumpkin who doesn't know how to act in a place like this!" Then I gave a mighty *Humph!*, crossed my arms, and sat back in my chair, looking at the closed curtain that separated us from other diners.

"I..." Cy sputtered. "I don't even know where to begin. But Elsie..." I looked up at him and his eyes were reproachful. "If this was bothering you, you should have said something." I nearly interrupted him to shoot back, "*I just did!*" but I held my tongue, deciding to let him have his chance to speak. "I met Jett shortly after I moved here- even after I met you- because he and my business partner knew each other from years ago, and Jett invested in our business. But we don't spend much time together, only when we have our investor meetings, which yes, he's kind enough to allow us to hold here. I'd only hoped by saying hello that he'd do just what he did and offer you a glimpse of what few see. Most people don't get to see behind the curtain of how a place like this operates. And this is *not* my usual fare, but I don't mind sharing such things with you. And for the record, The Watering Hole is a delightful place- much more lively and fun. And lastly, you are not a country bumpkin. You're talking about my date and my girlfriend, and you *will* respect her." For a moment, I thought he was angry, but by the time he'd finished, I could tell he was disappointed that I'd ruined what he felt was a special evening.

"I'm sorry," I mumbled. "That was stupid of me."

"Stop," he snapped. I was so startled, I quit staring at the curtain and saw that his eyes were pleading with me. He reached across the table to grab the hand I'd been playing with the wine glass with. "It wasn't stupid. I should have thought better about something like this for a first date. I wanted to make an impression, but, clearly, I made the wrong one. I want us to enjoy ourselves and to *be* ourselves as we usually are. That's how I like us." He smiled and I couldn't help but smile back, feeling the embarrassment washing away. "So let's enjoy an extravagantly overpriced but delicious dessert together, and go for a walk along the water. Would you like that?"

I responded by pointing to the menu and smiling. "This one is made for two."

*   *   *

The full moon made the Riverwalk, lit up for pedestrians regardless, look almost enchanted. It was a cooler night than usual at this time of year, which, at the start of hurricane season, could be oppressive without the sun to dry out some of the humidity. It seemed to be the perfect night for a walk by the bay, however, and he wrapped his arm around me as we strolled along, occasionally stopping to look at a street artist who'd finished a piece, or to listen to a freestyling musician who seemed to be playing just for us.

We arrived at a park about halfway along the pathway and sat on a bench. He wrapped his arms around me, but it was sweet rather than sensual. Groups of teenagers ran around, roughhousing and flirting; other couples, out for a similar stroll, were entwined intimately despite the publicity of the location; evening runners and cyclists zipped past, getting their workouts in before bed. The soft sound of the water, and the occasional rumble of a boat trolling at a no-wake speed toward the marina, was soothing; add the wine from dinner, and I was feeling relaxed, yet... excitable.

I tried to look like I was just enjoying the scenery, but I kept glancing at Cy, hoping he'd notice the invitation in my eyes. But he seemed to be preoccupied with something, even though he was trying not to show it.

"Hey." I tugged at his hand, the fingers of which were wrapped around my own. "You okay?"

He looked down at me and gave me a light kiss. "Never better."

"You seemed like you were thinking about something there," I probed further.

"You'll see soon enough," he said, raising The Brow in a teasing expression.

He had barely said the words when suddenly loud music started playing in the park, but it didn't sound like a song I'd ever heard before. I looked up and saw that several of the teen-agers who had been messing around were now gathered in an area near a small pavilion at the water's edge, and were holding orchestral instruments. They were warming up, it seemed.

I watched while they got situated, and felt Cy squeeze my hand. He looked at me with a wild and excited expression. I re-alized that, somehow, he'd set this up- these musicians were here because he'd arranged it. But why?

The sound of disjointed chords died down, and there were several seconds of silence; we weren't the only ones hold-ing our breath to see what would come next. When they began to play, I felt a soaring sensation in my chest.

"Swan Lake," I breathed. I'd taken ballet for nearly a dec-ade as a child, and every young ballerina is familiar with Tchai-kovsky's famous composition. Most were willing to do nearly anything for the lead in that show. My skills had been just average, so I was never even on the shortlist for such an honor, but I still listened to the score from time to time, imagining myself flowing with the melancholy music as though it was water and I was an actual swan. He knew this about me from a conversation we'd had over lunch a few weeks earlier, in which I told him all about my dashed childhood ballerina dreams.

Cy stood, gently moving me so that he didn't knock me over as he did so. He reached out a hand and pulled me first to my feet, and then to him. He placed my hand on his upper arm, then wrapped an arm around my ribcage, and held my other hand up lightly at his shoulder level.

"Cy," I whispered, looking around as people began to notice what we were doing. "Cy, I haven't danced in years. And I never took any kind of ballroom lessons."

"It's easy," he whispered back, his voice and his eyes reaching inside me to calm my nerves. "I do all the work. You just follow."

It turned out he wasn't far off with that advice. He kept the steps simple for me, and after a few missteps where my training as a solo dancer tried to take over, I began to feel for his movements before making my own. Suddenly, we were twirling around gracefully, with my flowing dress creating a halo around us, and I felt more graceful than the White Swan herself.

The musicians played through several of the more well-known excerpts from the ballet as others joined us in our dance, finally ending their piece after nearly half an hour. Cy took a step back and bowed like a gentleman from the Victorian era. I giggled, half finding it funny and half feeling so giddy I couldn't help it.

He chuckled back at me. "How was that for a surprise?"

I found myself speechless, unable to do anything but smile, my hands covering my mouth for fear that the joy would escape. It was as good an answer as any.

The music started up, a new piece, and he pulled me to him again.

Chapter 17

Opal

I had been tracking the movements of the blonde woman I'd seen in the area, first using traffic camera feeds, then in-house security systems (yes, I had access to private feeds- *nothing* is as private as you think it is), then attempting to follow her movements on foot. This proved difficult since she didn't seem to live in the city proper. The more I followed her, the less convinced I was that it could actually be Amber. This woman, whoever she was, had a full life here, complete with a circle of friends, a job, and a lover. I couldn't imagine Amber having the forethought and tenacity to put years worth of effort into whatever pattern she was carrying out, but Zilpher *had* said she had upped her game in recent decades, so I kept looking into her.

It wasn't easy. I still had to fulfill all of my other Council duties and find time to actually feed so that I didn't weaken and risk becoming a victim, although I was getting absorbed by my task to the point of failing to take in sufficient blood. I made a point of setting myself up at places I knew the blonde woman frequented, hoping to finally see if it was Amber, and, if it was, to confront her. One of these places was The Roof, the bar in St. Pete, where Amber and I had started our evening that ended in a small massacre years before.

I walked in and took a seat at the bar, my hair tumbling over my shoulder and hanging into the cleavage that was classy, yet prominent. My fitted grey dress brought out the almost perfect shade of violet of my eyes that night. I was feeling famished, having gone over a week without a kill, and only twice did I have fresh blood- not from a bag. I needed a good, clean kill tonight, and I wasn't going to waste a drop.

I ordered a martini (gin, light vermouth, twist of lime), and waited. I had hoped the blonde woman would arrive before I found a potential victim, and I was disappointed.

A reasonably attractive man, possibly in his early 30s, with black hair and eyes hidden by sunglasses like my own, had approached me and offered to get the next round, introducing himself as Cyrus. There was something about him that drew me in. At first, I thought it was how easily he could be mistaken for one of my own kind with his strong, graceful build and the eye coverings, but then I noted the odd but entirely appealing scent of him: salty and crisp, like he was made of a sea breeze. It struck me in a way I seldom experienced, having been nearly depleted of the level of strength I was always so careful to maintain. I was starving and he smelled like a feast. My fangs nearly dropped- I might have ripped him open there in the bar had I the composure of a lesser vampire.

I excused myself to the ladies room before we left under the pretense of checking my makeup. In reality, I was concerned I felt my eyes shifting. I was right, but thankfully it wasn't a shade too far off from the violet- they had changed to a more muted shade of purple. I was fading faster than I thought.

As I looked in the mirror, I was startled as a bountiful mane of golden hair breezed through the door. It was as if time stood still, and I watched her enter. Her scent came in with her, and I realized it before she'd taken even a single step beyond the doorway. She joined me at the sink, and I couldn't tell if I was pleased or disappointed that it was not Amber after all.

She was beautiful in a very natural, human way. She looked older than I did by a few years. When she looked up and saw me staring at her in the mirror, she startled and stared back, her heart rate spiking. It wasn't unusual for this to happen to humans who got too close to us if we weren't actively trying to put them at ease. It was like a mouse sensing a cat nearby. She finished freshening her makeup and washed her hands. She kept stealing glances as she did so, and finally, I gave her a small grin to ease her nerves, which seemed on edge. She had no reason to fear me. I had no intention of attacking her here.

"Hi," she said, the unease in her vibrant blue eyes seeming to dissipate ever so slightly. "Just FYI, that dress goes *amazing* with your eyes! They're so beautiful, by the way!"

And with that, she flashed a winning grin and walked out. Humans were so strange. She sensed something about me that set her on edge, and, rather than defend herself against me, had made a point of complimenting me, as though flattery could protect her from whatever ill will I bore her. I looked back to the mirror, reeling from the encounter when it hit me. Just like that, all of my work and dedication on this task had amounted to nothing.

I took a moment to consider the waste of the last few weeks. Tracking this woman had occupied so much of my time, and it hadn't been Amber at all. I realized that a small part of me had been hoping it was her, wanting to see her. I had put myself in danger for the sake of finding this human, and when I could have vented my rage on her in this bathroom, feeding until I was surfeited, I let her go. I hadn't even considered taking her blood, let alone her life. I was frustrated with myself for allowing such human emotions as hope and affection to rule me at the expense of maintaining my strength.

Well, at least I had another kill already lined up.

I rearranged my angry expression to one of delight and went to invite my date back to my place.

Cyrus and I shared a ride back into Tampa and to my condo. While we waited for the car, he had offered to buy coffee or tea from a café next to the bar... for stamina. I needed neither, but asked for a water to keep up the human appearance. In hindsight, I shouldn't have cared so much.

When we got back to my building, I felt the fatigue borne of the vampire blood in my veins slowly dying off with nothing to bond to. I needed human blood soon- and a lot of it- or the physical effects would come on quickly. I knew once we were upstairs, I wouldn't waste time with the foreplay- we'd be getting right down to the main event.

I let him inside and closed the door behind us. He had walked over to admire my view, taking off his sunglasses. I came up behind him and wrapped my arms about his waist, smelling the sweet and salty blood pumping through him, nearly ripping a hole in his shoulder, where my lips reached, to get to it. But that would be far too messy. I had to get him to the bed, where it would be easier to hide the body and clean up after.

I waited for him to turn to me and I kissed him, putting all the lust I felt for his life into the passion behind my lips, carefully concentrating on not allowing my fangs to drop just yet.

He lifted me off the ground and spun us around so that I was pressed against the window, where I wrapped myself tightly around him, a snake gripping an unwitting rabbit. I pulled my face away and he kissed down my neck. "Bed," I gasped. To him, it probably sounded like I was too revved up for more than a single word. In reality, I was feeling the fatigue progress quickly and it was getting harder to control myself.

He laid me down on the bed and stood, I assumed to take off his clothes, but then he just stared at me, unmoving. I noticed in that moment that his eyes were a rich shade of hazel. It reminded me of the first time I killed, and the sweetness of that first blood. With the enticing scent of the man before me and the memory of my first kill, I suddenly felt even hungrier than I had before.

I waited for him to lean down so I could strike, but he didn't move. I went to prop myself up on my elbows and found that I lacked the strength to even do that. It was too fast... I should have been slightly weakened at this stage, not unable to control my limbs. I looked at Cyrus, coming to a slow realization.

"What..." My words were slurred, as though I were drunk. "What did you do...?" my brain was chugging along, having difficulty finding the pathway to the truth. I shouldn't have succumbed to a normal sedative... my blood should have bound it and eliminated it... but my blood was weak... and maybe... maybe it was a more potent drug... I was losing my focus on Cyrus's face, but when it was clearer, his expression was cold.

"Why...?" I asked.

I lost consciousness before I could hear the answer.

*   *   *

When I woke up, I was in the basement of my building on a mattress. I knew the place well, having disposed of many a body down here. I felt clearer-headed than I had the night before, and tried to stand, ready to fight. It didn't work.

I realized a number of things very quickly: one, I had fed. I knew this both from the reduced sensation of slowly dying as well as from the dried blood around my mouth and on the otherwise spotless white sheets. Two, I was chained to the wall using some of the wall mounts found in the condos upstairs explicitly created to withstand vampire strength. Three, I was not alone.

Leaning against the opposite wall was Cyrus. He was staring at me with the same cold expression he'd worn as I had lost consciousness. "Sleep well?" He asked. His voice carried none of the warmth of the previous night.

I didn't answer. I stayed as still as I could, attempting to level my most superior gaze at him, to match him measure for measure in stoicism. I failed horribly; I had never experienced fear like I did now, and I knew it was etched on my face.

"You don't have to answer me," he said, walking closer and pulling a chair around so that he could sit just out of my reach. His expression was cold, but there was a glint in his eye. He was aiming for indifference, but the malice wouldn't hide. "I wouldn't expect you to. I say that because I know you. I know that you, *Madame* Opal, are a member of the Vampiric Council, and the youngest member by more than a few centuries. Amber was your sire, and she is both alive and back in the area. I know exactly what her plan is and how she had planned for you to factor into it. You are here because Amber killed the love of my life, and now she's planning for the two of you to kill someone else- someone who was important to my dearly departed lover- the same way. I won't let that happen."

I was flabbergasted, unable to figure out how some human had all of this information. How did he know not only what we are, but details of our existence? How did he know Amber's plan? Who the hell did she kill and leave enough of a trail for some mortal to find her out- to find me? I wanted to ask all of these questions but felt it best to draw him in to draw him out. I shrugged, wiping some of the crusted blood off my mouth and sucking it off my finger for effect. "Thanks for the blood." Then I laid down, putting my hands behind my head as best as I could with the chains restricting my movement.

"You are very welcome," Cyrus said with an over-the-top politeness and an ironic bow.

We sat there in silence for a long time. It might have been minutes, it might have been hours. Finally, my curiosity and concern got the better of me and I asked, "Did Zilpher send you?"

Cyrus laughed; it was a guttural, humorless sound. "Zilpher? Zilpher doesn't know I exist."

"But you know *him*." It was a statement, not a question.

He smirked. "I know much more than you realize," he said, a glint in his eye.

"Like what?" I asked, my voice trembling and giving away how anxious I was to hear what he'd say next.

He leaned in just a bit closer and said, "Well, for one... I know how you died."

Chapter 18

Elsie

My first date with Cy had been such a success that I soaked in the afterglow for days. Not even Margot's bitchiness could dampen my spirits, and Jimmy Molina made a comment about my "great bigger smile." But the best way I celebrated was that I'd had a coffee date with my girls the day after to spill the tea.

Ashley walked in first and ran over to wrap me in a big hug. "You can buy my coffee to thank me," she offered. I rolled my eyes at her, but even though she was half-kidding, she was completely right. Without her push (and her driving), I wouldn't have gone to Cy and confessed my feelings.

I ordered, and by the time the drinks were made and we sat down, Jess and Charlotte had arrived. Ashley had called them after she left my house the previous day and told them Cy and I were officially dating.

"But," Ashley reassured me, looking around the circle, "it's just between us girls for now. We don't want word to get back to Sam until Elsie has a chance to tell him in person."

Charlotte grimaced. "Matt already knows," she admitted.

I waved her concern away. "That's fine. Just please ask him to not mention it to any of the other guys." Charlotte nodded and I shot Ashley a grateful glance. We both knew asking Jess and Charlotte to keep it quiet had little to do with Sam, who seemed to be enjoying his post-me life with Emily. It was more about Jack and what we now recognized as an ego-driven streak of cruelty. Either way, I wanted to make sure when Jack found out that his plan to keep Cy and I from getting together failed, that it happened on my terms. "But, I still wanted to tell y'all everything!" I paused for effect and took a long sip of my latte.

"So?" Jess searched my face for a hint, but she didn't have to look so hard; I was beaming.

I told them all about dinner at Trusty's, including my meltdown.

"Well," Jess said in her characteristically sage way, "You've never been treated like that. Sam is a great guy, but y'all got together in college. No one does that kind of thing when they're that young, and by the time you'd gotten old enough for that to be a thing, it was too late. You were too comfortable."

Charlotte shrugged. "I don't know, Matt and I have been to Trusty's."

Ashley rolled her eyes. "For your anniversary, Char. Elsie, did you and Sam ever even really have an anniversary? I don't remember you ever dating for a full year at a time." I shook my head no, and she continued. "Dating someone new as an adult- not a college adult, but a *real* adult- is different than dating someone new while you're in school, or even than dating someone you've been with for years. There's a whole new level of needing to show someone a good time. Which it sounds like he did, and I want to hear more!"

I told them about the surprise dance in the park, and how, afterward, he'd walked me further down the Riverwalk to a beautiful high rise with a view of the water.

"What do you think?" He had asked.

"It's very nice," I said. "Is this your big business venture?"

He laughed, "Yes, I successfully completed an entire building full of luxury condominiums in the last two months, already filled with well-established and long-term owners since I arrived." I narrowed my eyes so he knew I understood the sarcasm. "No, I've just closed on a little one-bedroom unit on the twelfth floor. So..." he repeated, "What do you think?"

I stared up at the building. "Luxury" was certainly the correct term. The walls seemed to be made entirely of one-way glass. I couldn't even fathom what the views from his new place would look like.

"Cy," I breathed, "Are you kidding?" A crease formed in his brow. I continued. "It's... it's beautiful! I can't wait to see inside!" I heard the words as I said them and hoped he would understand what I had meant.

Thankfully, he figured it out. He grabbed my hand and silently asked the question. My heart leapt, and I felt a pleasant shudder pass over me. I nodded, and he pulled me into the lobby, where a doorman greeted us. Cy showed the man a key card; the doorman then nodded to the elevator attendant (*there was a fucking elevator attendant!*) who took us up- all the way up- to the twelfth floor.

Stepping out of the lift, I realized there was only one door on the landing. "Cy," I broached, "Is your 'little one-bedroom unit' the entire fucking top floor?"

He raised The Brow as he cast a devilish grin over his shoulder before unlocking the door.

Immediately upon entering, what struck me was how open it was, and how it felt even more so with the floor to ceiling windows that wrapped all the way around the unit, showcasing the bay, river, and city, sparkling with boat lights and cars and buildings still lit up. I found myself wandering toward the window where the full moon hovered over the water. It was like a painting. My hand reached out as though I could cup it in my hand, and I felt hands close around my waist.

Cy had come up behind me and buried his head in the hair that fell over my shoulder. "I take it you like it?" He murmured, beginning to plant little kisses along the soft side of my neck.

I grasped at his hands as he pressed closer against my back, and I let out a soft moan. "Yes," I breathed. "I like that- it." My breath was coming short and fast. "I like it."

He gave a soft sound that could have been a growl as he spun me around, and suddenly his lips were no longer gentle and upon on my neck- they were ravenous upon my own lips. Not that I was complaining, because I kissed him back just as hungrily. It was sudden and intense, but certainly better than a one-night stand in a bathroom- again.

He lifted me off the floor and led me to the only surface available since he hadn't yet moved in- the kitchen counter. It was here that I peeled off his suit jacket, and he snaked his hand up under my petticoat to better run his hand up my leg and under the thin fabric of my panties to pull me closer with his hand wrapped around my bare backside.

His kisses returned to my neck as he felt for the zipper on the back of my dress, when I slid a few inches to the side and my hip collided with the sink.

"Ow!" I cried, unaffected for a few seconds as Cy continued exploring further down along the neckline of my dress with his lips; then memories came rushing in uninvited and, for the second time, I told him in an urgent gasp, "Wait. Cy. Wait."

He pulled back reluctantly. "What's wrong?" He asked, "I can go slower..." But his hands weren't slowing down at all. I hated what I was about to do and say, but I couldn't go further. Not tonight, now, like this. Not with Jack's ghost in the room.

I'd hit my hip on the sink at The Roof in exactly the same way, on the same hip, when I was there with Jack. And while the circumstances and partners were so different between the two nights, it was too familiar and killed my whole drive. Once my brain had started functioning again, it was easier to figure out why I wanted to wait, but no easier to explain.

"Cy, I just... I can't. Not tonight, like this." I motioned at the counter beneath me. "Please, believe me, I want this so badly that it's almost a physical *ache,* but this isn't how I want it. It's too..." I paused, knowing that mentioning another man while I still had my legs around his waist would not go over well. "I don't ever want it to be like this- not the first time. I had something like this once and it was terrible after." I held his face in my hands. "You're such a different person than that other time, but it would always be tainted, knowing how similar it was." I looked into his eyes. That color consumed me; the concern lying under the desire that I saw there made me brave. "I need it to be different with us. I need it to be real, and I need it to be special. Because I... care about you. And us, and this. Please understand."

Cy sighed resignedly. "Okay." *Like I said I wanted ice cream.* "I won't pretend I'm not a little disappointed..." He licked his lips before exhaling in a big bluster. He then lowered his gaze and helped me off the counter, his hands smoothing my dress back down and returning to the more PG placement of my hips. "But I agree. If this isn't right, it isn't right. This-you and me- is real, so it *should* be special." He leaned forward and kissed me once, gently, and then grabbed my hand and showed me the rest of the condo (all stunning, of course- I couldn't wait to see how he furnished it) and led me back to the elevator, then to the car.

*   *   *

"And then he drove me home," I finished lamely. I had left out the part about *why* I had stopped before we went any further, considering only one person listening knew the truth about that.

"Oh my *Gawd*," Jess drawled. "Is he just dreamy or what?"

Charlotte nodded, but Ashley cut to the chase. "So, what will make it special?" She demanded. "A golden set of sheets? A diamond set of handcuffs?"

I rolled my eyes at her and pretended I planned to knock over her coffee. "No. I think..." I hesitated because I didn't know how my friends would react. "I want to really be in love this time. Like, 'we've both said it and mean it' love."

They were all silent for a second, but then Charlotte asked, "Well... do you think you could love him? Do you think it's headed there?"

It was a simple question with what I thought was a simple answer. "I think maybe I already do," I said.

But Ashley was quick to make me think twice. "No. El, you have gotten so used to saying you love Sam, even when you really didn't, that it's lost any meaning for you. Those words aren't beads you toss to a pretty girl at Mardi Gras. Those words, that you love someone, they mean that you've really thought about it and your feelings go beyond what you can express in other words. 'I love you' should be hard to say to someone for the first time, because putting those words out there is like exposing your actual heart, knowing the other

147

person could break it into pieces. If it's easy, if it doesn't scare you, it's not true."

Chapter 19

Opal

Of all the things I had anticipated Cyrus saying, I did not expect it to be that. "You know how I died? How?" I asked, unable to keep up my icy front any more. He had information he had no way of having, and I was as thirsty for him to divulge more as I had been- and still was- for his blood. It was then, as I heard his words, evoking the memories of that night, that it came back to me.

In my mind's eye, I saw the scene before me as I awoke, the man bruised and broken and laying across that stone. The man whose blood I took, whom I killed... whose blood had the same salty sweetness I could smell just a hint of on Cyrus...

"You!" My eyes were wide with horror and rage. "*You* killed me?" I cried, but then realized the impossibility of what had occurred. "How are you here? I killed you!" I demanded imperiously, affecting the air I wore when on Council business to feel more powerful. "You're not a vampire. I'd smell it on you."

"Would you?" He asked, just enough mystery to his question that I paused. "Did you never wonder why you were so strong, right at your rebirth? Why your eyes change as no other vampire's do? It was because the first time you fed, you fed on a vampire." His hazel eyes, so human, appeared darker to me, hiding some emotion I couldn't decipher.

"What?" The word escaped me before I could stop it. Cyrus had exposed me yet again. He had killed me, abducted me, burst the illusion of my lofty secrecy, and had now reduced me to confused utterances. All of my weaknesses, unknown even to me in my arrogance, were laid bare before me.

It was then also that the true horror of the night came back to me. Amber had told me I'd been drugged and brought to that island by the man before me for "*nothing good.*"

"What did you want with me that night?" I snarled. "Why did you take me there?"

He looked at me curiously, his eyes never losing the darkness that he directed at me. "What do you remember?"

"Nothing!" I roared. "I woke up, bled you dry, and Amber found me and told me how you drugged me and took me to that island!" I was filled with the rage I'd seen in Amber that night in the party house, but it was a distant emotion. I knew that I had been his victim, but I couldn't remember it. It was like it happened to someone else, and my indignation was on their behalf.

"Did you, though?" He asked in the same tone. It was maddening.

"Did I what?" My voice was at its highest volume, loud enough to shake the walls if they had not been made specifically to withstand a creature like myself. He simply stared at me, waiting for me to arrive at the answer myself.

I remembered the reason that I never saw the memories contained in his final drop of blood was that I hadn't bled him dry- I hadn't finished the job. He'd held onto it, and it was how he survived... maybe.

A doubt about many things began to creep into my mind. I stuffed it down, intent on hearing more information and unwilling to allow this wretch to extract any from me.

"Okay, so I missed some," I said as if it didn't matter to me in the least. "Is that how you survived?"

He smiled and stood. "Maybe I'll tell you tomorrow." He turned and walked toward the stairs.

Fear gripped me. He was really going to leave me here, and I wasn't strong enough to break free, having gone without a kill for as long as I had. "Wait!" I cried, trying to sound annoyed rather than afraid. I failed. "You can't leave me here to starve!" Then I looked to the tiny window at the top of the room. It was soundproof and difficult to see from outside. No chance of rescue, but the sunlight would be problematic- and soon; it was not the same special glass as in my flat. "If you leave me down here, I die. You could have killed me already, taken my blood and left me starving while I was knocked out, and you didn't. Whatever you want from me, you won't get it if I burn up."

He shrugged and tossed my sunglasses and a plastic packet from the blood bank over his shoulder. "I suppose you're right," he said. He put on his own sunglasses. At the top of the stairs, before opening the door, he called back, "I have an engagement to attend to. Until tomorrow... *Madame.*"

And he closed the door behind him.

*   *   *

I lay in the semi-darkness of the basement most of the day. I had ripped into the blood packet almost immediately after Cyrus left, but forced myself to leave some for later. I had no idea what time he might return, or if he even would at all.

I stared at the lines in the wall, studying the masonry, hoping for a weakness to reveal itself to me, the way I'd revealed my own to Cyrus. Furious with him, furious with myself, I raged at the chains on my wrist and found them beyond my strength to break, weakened as I was. It was a new feeling for me.

And now I knew why. My first feeding as a fledgling had been another vampire. Not just any vampire- one who had planned to kill me and do who knows what else. Well, I already knew I came into this life a fighter. Just look at what happened to Orla...

Orla. There was the other question. Why didn't I see *her* memories either? I had my first two kills on the same night, both vampires. Was it our shared nature that prevented me from seeing their memories? I'd never asked if we saw the memories of other vampires; it seemed taboo. Or could I have really missed the final drop for both? And if I had missed some blood, and if Cyrus could be alive and well and clever enough to have me captive in my own basement, couldn't Orla also be alive and looking for revenge when I least expect it?

And if she was alive, did Zilpher even know? Perhaps Orla had orchestrated this entire thing; had Cyrus abduct me to carry out her vengeance, while keeping Zilpher in the dark... No, that didn't resonate as true. She would have sought out Zilpher immediately, and they'd have been in on this together. And Cyrus had said that Zilpher didn't know him...

What was even true? Could I trust a word he said?

I screamed and roared incoherently at the walls, at the window, at the door, hoping against all hope that I could make myself heard, seen, sensed, but I knew it was hopeless. This basement was built for us to dispose of our kills. They needed to make sure that no one, human or vampire, could know what happened down here.

I slumped onto the mattress, absently scraping my finger-nail along the sheet, ruining it. I went deeper, pulling out tiny tufts of cotton from the mattress. It was then, holding the bits of fluff, that I hatched my plan. It would be a slow play, and it may not work- it might even weaken me enough that I'd never survive once I did escape, but I knew it was the only way to try.

Chapter 20

Elsie

I thought about what Ashley had said for days. I didn't want to rush things with Cy, and I certainly didn't want to tell him I loved him if I really didn't mean it. But that didn't mean I couldn't let him know how I felt in other ways.

As such, I could be found on my lunch breaks texting him about how wonderful our date had been, and how amazing the dance was, and how lucky I felt to have such a thoughtful and respectful man in my life. He always responded by thanking me for spending the time with *him*, as though I was doing him a favor. He then suggested we save our second official date for the following week so that we could go out with my friends for trivia night again.

It was going to be really hard to hold that word back if he kept being so considerate.

Of course, that upped the timeline of making sure Jack knew about my relationship with Cy, and of making sure that he behaved like a Goddamned adult about it.

I called Ashley on my way home Monday after work. Her voice came over the Bluetooth system in my car. "Hey!" I greeted her.

"Heyyyy," she replied. Ashley's phone voice was a little 90s Valley Girl, but it suited her.

"Ashley, I have a problem."

Suddenly "phone Ashley" disappeared and "friend Ashley" took over. "What's wrong?"

"Well," I started, "Nothing's *wrong* per se, but..." Why was I hesitating when she already knew everything? Oh right, because I didn't know how to handle this situation and needed her help. "Cy and I are coming out for Trivia Friday, but we don't want to hide our relationship, so I need your help. What the fuck do I do about Jack?"

"Hmm..." Ashley pondered. "Well... maybe there's an opportunity here to shut him down for good about this. It would really suck for you, but since you've already got me on your side, it would put Jack in the position of either backing down or backing out of the group."

I didn't want to cause any friendships to fall apart, but I had let my guilt over the situation with Jack control me for too long. "Okay," I said. "What's the plan?"

"You have to call Sam and tell him everything," she said.

"*What?*" I exploded. "Ash, *no*, I've kept this secret for this long because it would destroy him!"

"Would it, though?" She asked. "You and Sam were together a long time, but you weren't exactly a power couple. And you've both moved on. I don't expect him to be pleased about it, but it's not like you're getting back together and need to worry about rebuilding trust for that. Your friendship might take a temporary hit, but it already has- y'all are so cool towards each other it's chilly to watch."

"But what if everyone else blames me? Sam and Jack together could make life pretty miserable for me..." I paused.

"I'm just not sure it's worth risking all my friendships. Maybe I should just see what happens when we show up..."

"First of all, it's not all your friendships," Ashley reassured me. "No matter where the hammer falls, if it even does, you have me. I couldn't give two shits about keeping Jack around. And I'd be sad about it, but if Sam would rather side with the asshole who bent his then-girlfriend over a sink (and who has zero remorse about that, by the way) than the then-girlfriend who was honest with him about it (and who actually feels bad about what happened), then that's his stupid fucking decision. And I think- I hope- knowing that I'm on your side, Jess and Char won't dump you, and Matt comes with Charlotte."

I thought about this, not entirely convinced. "What if they don't?" I asked, feeling small. "What if they blame me?" I took a breath and admitted to Ashley something I hadn't yet told anyone. "I blame me... Jack wasn't in a relationship. I was. He probably thought he was winning me over or something. I..." My throat constricted. "I made the first move."

"Yeah, well, I remember that night," Ashley said. "You may not think you were all that drunk, but you were. You were drunk enough that Jack should have walked you straight back to the table, and instead, he figured he'd get his dick wet. You did wrong by Sam, I won't pretend otherwise. But Jack did wrong by all three of you. And I think it's really time you came clean to Sam and everyone else, and gave Jack an opportunity to either eat crow or show his true colors."

Tears had begun to pool in the corners of my eyes. I wanted to keep up the fight and just pretend this conversation never happened, to just let people naturally find out about Cy and I and see how they reacted, and to respond if needed. But I knew she was right. I'd kept this secret from Sam for too long, and I needed my girls, at least, to know about this.

It was funny. At first, I had wished I could talk to Jess about this because she's so much more grounded, but Ashley turned out to be the best person for it. While Jess might have spent half the conversation trying to be diplomatic, Ashley called everyone on their shit in real-time. That girl was worth her weight in diamonds.

"Okay," I said. "You're right." I had just pulled into my driveway. "I guess I need to make some calls. Ash... thanks."

*   *   *

I sat at The Watering Hole, my fingers nervously running up and down the sides of my beer glass, making designs in the condensation. I hadn't even taken a sip. I wiped off my wet fingers to respond to a text from Cy.

Good luck, he sent. *Call me when it's over.*

Thanks, I typed back. *I will.*

It was only a few more minutes before Sam walked in. No Emily. Good. I had been worried he'd bring her out of spite, but I'd asked him specifically if we could talk alone.

Hey, I'd texted him earlier. *I know things have been weird with us lately, but there's something I really need to talk to you about. It's been weighing on me for a long time, and I need to get it off my chest before you find out from anyone else.*

He'd agreed to meet me after dinner Thursday, and so we ended up at what was once our usual high-top, with our usual order.

Nothing else was usual about it, though. He was leaning back in his chair, as far as he could with his hands folded across his chest, rather than leaning across and holding my hand. I continued to stare at my beer, still untouched.

Sam blew his breath out in a huff and dropped his arms. "Was there *actually* some reason you asked me here?" He accused. "Or is this just more weird Elsie mind-games?"

That stung. "I don't play mind-games."

He rolled his eyes. "Yeah, okay. All that 'let's make-up, I love you, baby,' 'Just kidding, let's call it quits,' for years. You want to tell me you didn't love keeping me on your leash? Or is that exactly what this is- begging to get back together again? Because I heard you better than you think last time. I'm done."

I glared at him. I wanted to blow up at him and throw the Jack thing in his face, just to make it hurt. But that wasn't why I wanted to meet face to face. I owed it to Sam, after nearly a decade of being lovers and years of lying, to tell him the worst thing I ever did to him, and I owed it to him to say it to his face. So I took a breath and counted to five under my breath.

"Sam..." I started. My throat was dry and I took a big gulp of beer. Suddenly my glass was half empty. "Sam. I don't want to play mind games, and I'm not here to get back together, either. Exactly the opposite. I want to lay all my cards on the table, to tell you the truth, so that hopefully I can begin to earn your forgiveness and be your friend again. Because I *do* care about you. We have too much history for me not to. So..." I drained the rest of my beer. "Do you remember that one night at The Roof, about two years ago? We'd just gotten together, and I got too drunk at Matt's sister's, and you were pissing me off by trying to make me sober up?"

"Yeah, I remember you being unable to hold your liquor, as always, and going to the bathroom to barf for like, half an hour."

My heart constricted and it took every ounce of courage and strength to get the next words out. They were barely audible. "I wasn't barfing. Not the whole time. I felt so shitty that I accidentally went into the men's room. Jack was in there. He told me he'd always wanted to be the one I ended up with, not you. And I was so *angry* with you, and it made no rational sense, but... I slept with him."

Sam's eyes were wide with anger and hurt. "After we broke up again that weekend?" He knew, but wanted me to keep lying. Too bad.

A single tear fell from my eye as I shook my head, no. "No, Sam. That night. In the bathroom at The Roof."

Sam stood up, pulled out his wallet, threw down a ten, and walked out without looking at me once.

I stood quickly and followed him out. I'd be back since I'd opened a tab in case the conversation went south and I needed some comfort. Looked like I'd been wise to do so.

"Sam!" I called once I was outside. He walked to his big white pickup and climbed in, ignoring me. I didn't blame him, but I had more to say. I stood behind the truck, preventing him from backing out. He threw it into reverse and jerked it backward, threatening me. By now, people began to watch. Noticing this, he put it in park and yelled out the window.

"Move!"

"No," I said defiantly, my arms crossed. "I'm not finished. Get out and come inside. Once I'm done, I'll watch you leave and never contact you again if that's what you want. But you deserve to hear this from me. So get the fuck out and come back inside!"

His face was a mask of rage, and he looked utterly torn between running me over or listening to me. In the end, he turned the truck off and walked back inside, as he passed me, throwing out an angry, "You're buying."

I proceeded to tell him about how I'd met Cy the day before I'd finally broken things off, and how Cy and I were now an item. His face never changed during the whole conversation. "I needed to tell you because Jack is trying to use what happened with us to hurt me now. Last week at trivia, he went out to smoke to tell Cy to make him think twice about dating me. He didn't end up saying anything, but now that Cy and I *are* dating, I didn't want him to blab and for it to become public knowledge before you had a chance to hear it from me. After all we've been through, I owed it to you." More tears. "And I don't blame you for hating me, but I needed you to know I never wanted to hurt you, and I'm really happy you seem so happy with Emily. And... I hope maybe someday you can forgive me, and we can be friends again, but I won't try to force anything."

I stood up and started toward the bar to pay, then turned back. "We'll be at trivia tomorrow. I hope I'll see you there."

With that, I walked out to my car, where I sat and cried long after I saw the white pickup leave. Once I could breathe normally, I called Cy, and he talked to me the whole ride home.

Chapter 21

Opal

For two weeks, Cyrus came back every night, always dressed the same, as though it was a uniform. Dark jeans or slacks and a white button-down, casually unbuttoned at the top with the sleeves rolled to the elbows. He never showed up at the same time, though. Sometimes he'd come right at sunset; on others, like the first time he returned after trapping me, he came back so late that sunrise wasn't far off when he appeared.

"So I have to ask," I said when he finally showed up that night, my voice dripping with contempt. "How did you manage to get me down here? The doorman knows me well enough that he should have at least alerted someone if you carried me down here."

Cyrus laughed, sitting back in his chair. "Braun, you mean?" His voice carried judgment. "I don't think you even knew that was his name. He certainly didn't think so when he agreed to keep others from coming down here. You've lived in that lovely penthouse for ten years. Maybe what you see as strength- your arrogance- is actually weakness."

I glared. He was right- I hadn't known Braun's name. I had passed by him every day, thinking it didn't matter who he was because all that mattered was that he showed the proper respect for me- because it only mattered who *I* was. But I wasn't going to let him know that I thought he was right. The fear, the hunger, the isolation with this fiend... they were all beginning to wear on my mind. I would never have entertained such trite notions as mutual respect before. Fear is greater than love, and those who elicit fear earn respect- at least, that's what I had always believed.

"You owe me a story, I think," I deflected, leaning back on the wall, allowing my arms to relax by my sides with what little slack there was in the chains.

"I suppose so," he teased. He pushed back on his chair so that he was leaning as casually as I was attempting to. "Should we chat about the weather first?" He motioned sardonically to the window.

"A little foreplay before we fuck?" I shot at him, sarcasm infusing every syllable. "No, thanks." I wanted to steer the conversation. "How did you get out? You should have died there, or held on with just enough life to make it until sunrise when the daylight would have killed you. How did you survive?"

He chuckled at the desperation in my voice, then paused. He was staring at me curiously. Even with my ability to hold perfectly still for as long as needed, his gaze held for too long, and I found myself looking away first. His stare made me uncomfortable for reasons I couldn't quite pin down.

"Look, this isn't going to be some bullshit Stockholm situation," I said, trying to throw him off-balance, hoping he'd divulge more. "Amber killed and probably ate your girl, not me. I don't even know who she was, and after all you've done, you *deserved* to lose someone, just the way I lost who I was before. Was she another vampire? Was it *Orla*? A human? Maybe if you narrowed it down-"

"No," he interrupted. His voice had a resonance that, for the first time, alerted me to the fact that he really did have at least some of the same abilities that I did, faint though they may be.

"Then tell me," I demanded, my more powerful voice drowning out the echoes of his own, "how you survived."

He looked out the window at the lightening sky. "Sorry, darling." I scowled at the patronizing endearment. "I guess we'll have to wait another day." With that, he tossed another blood packet at me and left.

Each night that first week, he came in and we started with easy banter and small talk, then receded into stoic silence. We spent so long sizing each other up, just staring and puzzling about one another, that we said little, despite my insistence that he tell me how he came out of the woods and ended up here, ten years later, physically unchanged yet utterly mortal. I supposed I shouldn't have been surprised- he had the secret to being murdered by another vampire and living to tell about it. Why shouldn't he possess my same ability to wait someone out in cold silence?

Daytime, when I was alone, was the worst. I did my best to sleep, but often my thoughts kept me awake. I found myself going over the previous night with Cyrus in my mind. Re-examining our conversations, looking for hints of exploitable weakness. All I succeeded in doing was casting doubt upon my own assumptions, my own truths.

I knew how strong I was, but had I allowed my ego to outgrow my power? It certainly seemed so, given my situation. My disregard for human emotion, for useless mortal percep-tions, had created a world for me in which I struggled to under-stand the motives of others, especially those so ruled by that which I ignored.

163

Then there was Cyrus himself. The more nights we were alone together, the more I began to question all I thought I had known about the night I died. *He could exact vengeance on me at any point,* I thought. *He could leave me to starve, take my sunglasses... I don't know, shoot me with a harpoon gun or something, and, once I've bled out enough, take my blood and strike me down.* For someone who had once supposedly intended on being my rapist and murderer, he was very careful not to cross any lines. He intrigued me, and I hated him for it.

It wasn't until the eighth night of my captivity that the conversation began to flow again.

When he walked in, much earlier than most other nights, I ignored him, laying staring at the ceiling. He sat in his chair and pulled a phone out, laying it on his knee. He had never done this before.

"Waiting on a call?" I asked, not expecting a real answer.

"You could say that," Cyrus replied, his voice worn and tired. "I'm waiting for news about someone I care about."

This got my attention. I sat up, my eyebrows threatening to become one with my hairline. "You care about someone."

If he had hackles, they'd have reached the ceiling. "I care about many people," he said, bristling. "Just because Amber took away the most important person to me doesn't mean everyone else doesn't matter."

I shrugged, suddenly less interested in the details, but more interested in the emotions behind the words. I didn't believe in such selflessness. "Sure, it does. No one else *does* matter. Anyone who claims they're not out for number one is full of shit. Amber is my only friend, and I'd throw her under the bus in a heartbeat to save myself," I admitted.

He raised an eyebrow. "And yet you covered for her when she massacred a room full of rapists." It was a statement with a question underneath, but what he said struck a chord with me.

"Would you describe yourself that way?" I asked in disgust. "After all, I don't believe for a second you would drug and abduct a young woman with good intentions. So I'm interested in why you'd throw the word 'rapist' around like it doesn't apply to you as well."

He seemed ready to say something back, but decided against it. He checked his phone to buy time and, clearly not seeing what he'd been waiting for, he laid it back down. He glanced up at me, his hazel eyes looking more like fire than earth. "Why don't I just answer your other question?"

I sat up, looking at him cautiously, not sure I was understanding his meaning. Was he going to tell me how he made it off of the island when he should have perished there? "Really?"

Cyrus shrugged his shoulders. "Why not?" His face had a strange expression. "I think we both know I don't intend to kill you at this point-"

"Why is that?" I interrupted.

He ignored me. "And as long as you're going to live regardless, I may as well tell you. Besides, you're unlikely to be as lucky as I was that night. It would take a miracle."

I scoffed. "A miracle?" He raised his brow and leaned back, threatening to stop talking. I shut up and motioned for him to continue.

"While you lay dying and changing, Amber and I battled. She won and laid my body where you found me. I was still aware but unable to move. I had been weakened earlier-"

"How?" I interrupted again.

He snapped at me, "Do you want to hear how I survived or not? Because that's the only story you get."

I crossed my arms and waved my hand again.

"Since I was already weak, when you began to feed, I couldn't fight back. I could only make little noises. I wasn't even sure if they were audible."

"You said, 'No,'" I told him. "Otherwise, you just made the normal dying sounds." The memory made my mouth water. I avoided glancing at the hidden hole in my mattress.

"Mm," he said, remembering. "Well, I felt you draining me and did my best to hold on to my blood, even if it was only a single drop. You know the power of the last drop. It contains our memories, our souls, all that we are. I kept it from you. I held onto myself and my life. I didn't even realize I could, but it worked, so I suppose it's possible. It took a few hours, but I was found by some well-meaning humans walking back to their campsite-"

"But you should have been too weak to move, too weak to feed." I wasn't used to being narrated to like this. I usually did the talking; I enjoyed exercising my power even in conversation, so sitting quietly was proving challenging.

"You're right. But that last drop did what I needed it to. They found me, and they felt a heartbeat." Vampires have no heartbeat, but part of our predatory camouflage is that if a human checks for a pulse, they will feel one unless we choose to drop the illusion. "They called emergency services and the paramedics came. They had no idea how I was still alive, having been almost completely exsanguinated, but they gave me a blood transfusion." He looked down at his hands and flexed them. "I still have that drop of my own blood, the vampire blood, but human blood is what flows through my veins now. Because of how it happened, because I didn't feed on it, it didn't bind to the vampire blood the way it normally would. What's left of the vampire in me keeps me from aging, and it gives me a higher than normal ability to read human emotions, greater strength than average for my size, but not inhuman. But..." He glared icicles at me. "You took my eyes."

The color, he meant. The rich, vibrant colors our eyes become when we are changed. So I made him into an immortal human, and therefore his eyes were those of a human. Now I understood why I smelled that alluring scent on him- it was the last remaining drop of his immortal blood, the blood that had given me my God-like strength. Even now, with my thirst growing more and more, day by day, I could smell it, and I wanted it.

"What color were they?" I asked, curious.

He stared hard at me, then sidestepped my question. "Sometimes they show. Sometimes I can enjoy them being that color again, if I focus, or if I feel something strongly. But it's hard to do, and it doesn't last long. Not like you, whose eyes seem to change every few minutes without a thought."

Had they been changing that often? That was curious. I shouldn't have been surprised, considering the isolation was causing major mood-swings. Not to mention the strange roller coaster of feelings I felt about Cyrus. To deflect, I looked at the sunglasses perched on his black hair. "You still protect them, though," I pointed out.

He took them off and looked at them. "Mostly habit at this point. But it does burn to see the sunlight too much. Like getting a sunburn, but I feel it in my eyes, and going deeper down. And... I won't lose my last drop. Not for sunlight. Not for anything. Not yet."

I found myself pitying him and tried to catch myself. He had intended to sound stubborn and strong, but the effect made him seem defeated, which I suppose he was. He had hurt me (the girl I used to be before, anyway), or had planned to, and I had not only risen from that moment, but I had defeated him in every way except ending his life. In return, he had exposed my weaknesses in this basement because I had robbed him of everything except for weakness. Well, almost everything. He still had rage. He had taken from me and, without even knowing it, I had taken from him. Now I was here, trapped. But not for long.

The air was pregnant with our mutual hatred, rage, and weariness. When Zilpher came around, the tension felt something like this, but I couldn't see myself ever falling into Cyrus's arms, even if it was just for a night. And yet... there was something about him that continued to captivate me. Amber had taught me, trained me, and given me the eyes to see what was truly evil. *I* was evil in my wanton killing, but I never caused unnecessary pain. In fact, I often provided my victims, who more often than not were no great loss to the world, with carnal pleasure before I indulged in a very different carnal pleasure of my own. Cyrus, however...

"Why did you take me to that island?" I realized I had never gotten a straight answer. I knew what Amber had insinuated, and the conclusions I was able to draw on my own, but I wanted to hear it from his own lips.

"Why do *you* think I took you there?" He asked. His face had quickly and completely emptied of all emotion.

I studied him for a moment. I knew what I'd believed all along, what Amber had both implied and told me outright, the natural assumptions, but something about the story, having now met Cyrus, having talked with him, having spent hours alone in his company, didn't sit right with me. *Christ, I'm a fucking liar. It only took a week for Stockholm's to set in,* I thought. This guy was literally holding me prisoner, and I was questioning what he would or wouldn't have done to the human I used to be, when it was once so clear. "I've always had assumptions," I hedged around the answer. I narrowed my eyes to angry slits. "I want to hear it from you. I want you to say it."

He seemed to be getting angry, but was trying to hide it. Interesting. Why would this be a hot topic for him? Was it shame? Had I been wrong all along, and I was being insulting? What was causing him to burn up like this?

"Well, that won't happen," Cyrus said, his voice barely above a growl. "You won't even say what you think I was supposed to have done, or planned to do, yet you expect me to confirm or deny it." *Bzzt. Bzzt.* He looked down at his phone, which was ringing. He stood and threw a packet of blood at me. "See you tomorrow," he spat at me and walked up the stairs, closing the door behind him before answering the call.

I pulled at the opening in my mattress, looking at a collection of stashed blood packets. I crammed the new one down in with the collection. I pulled out the oldest one, which was very nearly spoiled and took a small amount, just enough to not appear like I was succumbing to blood fatigue. The taste was foul from the rot, but it did the job. I stuck the packet back down in and took stock. A few more days of this and I would have enough for one great binge, and hopefully, it would give me the strength I needed to break free.

Chapter 22

Elsie

I was honestly surprised when Sam and Emily were at Trivia, but less than surprised when Sam avoided my eyes at all costs, even when talking to me (but only about the trivia questions; otherwise, I didn't exist). By now, everyone knew about what had happened between Jack and me at The Roof because I'd told Jess and Charlotte the night before. I called them once I was home after telling Sam. They were shocked but supportive, and seemed glad I finally opened up about it, and Jess had said, "Now I understand why you wanted to keep your relationship with Cy a secret. Not because Sam would be hurt about who you're seeing now, but because he'd be hurt by who you'd been with in the past." Of course, there was still a secret in the air...

Jack didn't know everyone else knew.

Cy and I held hands and occasionally shared sweet little kisses. Sam never looked in our direction, but Jack couldn't keep his eyes off of us. There was something brewing behind his eyes and it began to worry me; right up until the break hit, and suddenly everything changed.

Emily gave Sam a peck on the cheek and said, "I have to run to the ladies'. Can you order me another one of the same?"

"Sure, babe," Sam replied, smiling at her, then watched her hips sway as she walked away.

Jack stretched his arms out wide with a groan and said, "That's not a bad idea. I'll be right back, too." He stood to walk to the bathroom.

Suddenly Sam leaned forward, his eyes with a look in them that actually frightened me. His face had never been filled with passion like that the whole time we were together, and now that fire was aimed right at Jack. "Or why don't you sit the fuck down and don't move a muscle until my girlfriend gets back from the bathroom?"

Sam never touched Jack, but the way Jack's face went slack, it looked like he had been sucker-punched. It took a few seconds for him to realize that Sam finally knew about The Roof.

The tension around the table was so thick that no one spoke for what felt like forever. Everyone was resolutely looking away from Sam, Jack, and I, only further confirming for Jack that the secret was out. Finally, Jack said, while looking like he was going to choke on his own tongue, "Bro, what...?" He couldn't finish. His eyes bulged out as he tried to find something to say. I don't know if he was trying to lie, or to come up with an excuse, but he never got a chance.

"I'm not your bro," Sam said coldly. "Your shit's out in the open now. You should just go. You probably have some kind of long run or bike ride tomorrow anyway. Not as exciting as dirty bathroom hookups-" *Ouch.* "-but something to occupy you that's not here."

Jack glared at me and pointed. "This fucking whore cheats on you- comes on to *me*- and you're going to throw *me* out? Come on, Sam-"

"No," Sam said. It was one word, and it was final.

Cy, on the other hand, had something more to say. He walked around the table to Jack, stopping about a half a foot away and putting his hands casually in his pockets. He was smiling, but there was nothing friendly about the smile. Jack, several inches shorter, stared up into his own reflection in Cy's sunglasses. "Trying to cast the blame for your own disloyalty is a coward's approach. Take your disrespect for everyone here and leave. Now."

Jack seemed to toy with the idea of throwing a punch, but looked around at everyone staring at him and thought better of it. He gave a small growl, then turned and walked out of the door. The entire table seemed to breathe a sigh. Sam caught my eye for the first time all night. I knew from that glance that while he blamed Jack more, there was still plenty of blame left for me.

When Emily returned from the bathroom to a completely silent table and a tense Sam, she was understandably perturbed, but Sam gave her a kiss and said quietly, "Hey, I'm not feeling too great. Do you mind if we bail out and just head back to my place?"

Emily nodded, trying to hide her concern, and they paid their tab and left.

The rest of us stayed to finish up trivia, but it was clear our hearts and mind weren't in it, as we had one of our worst finishes ever. Afterward, while Cy and Matt went to pay the remaining tabs (Cy picked up Jack's since he left without doing so; they didn't want the bar to suffer for Jack's inability to behave as a human), the girls and I all stepped outside to wait.

"I'm really sorry I never told y'all about all of that sooner," I said for the millionth time. "I don't know what I expected, but this wasn't it. I thought Sam would hate *me*, and I'd be the one getting told to leave."

"Men are fucking weird," Charlotte chirped. "Matt's always doing and saying stuff I just don't understand."

Jess chimed in, "And stop being sorry. We've all done stuff we're ashamed of. I can't speak for anyone else, but if my biggest shame came bundled with someone constantly reminding me of it to get one over on me, I'd probably do exactly what you did."

Ashley eyed Jess from the side. "What's *your* biggest shame?" She asked, curious.

Jess flipped her dark hair over her shoulder with a grin and said, "So, Elsie, about that boyfriend of yours... any brothers? Because *damn.*"

This made me laugh. "You know you've all met him before tonight, right?"

"Yeah," said Jess, "But now we have a direct line to details about things I may have only had one- or two- dreams about..."

I feigned jealousy and shoved her arm away. "Well, quit dreaming. That's mine, and you'd better tell your subconscious."

We all were laughing then, until Charlotte very thoughtfully asked, "He makes you happy, though. Right? It seemed for a long time like you were just giving up on love. Is that where you see things heading with Cyrus?"

I blushed at being asked this question again, knowing my answer was the same. "I don't know... I feel like maybe I already-"

"No!" Ashley interjected. I was startled at the intensity of her outburst. She explained, "I'm sure you're sick of hearing this, but too many years with Sam made you lose all connection with that word. We literally had this conversation like, last week. You say it *way* too easily. You cannot just say it because he does something you like. When you tell him you love him, it

173

needs to be because it carries the heaviest meaning that word can carry. In fact," she pointed at me. "I'm giving you an order. You don't say it until he does. Do you understand?" I nodded. "Good. Because *I love you,* and I think you've found something really great and I will not let you fuck it up."

At that point, the men had paid and we all climbed into our cars and drove off. Cy had given me a ride, and asked if I wanted to go hang out longer at his place. I squeezed his free hand and said, "I really, really do... but with everything that happened tonight, I think I just need to go home and sleep it all off. Thank you, by the way." I pulled his hand to my cheek and nuzzled it. "For stepping in when Jack said... well, when he called me... you know." My eyes lowered and I gave a small, dry laugh. "It's bad enough to be called a whore. It's even worse when you deserve it."

Cy turned to face me full on in the red glow of a traffic light. "You do *not* deserve to be called a whore. You made a mistake. But no one I've ever met has been more honest about their transgressions, nor been so open about how badly they feel about it as you. You could have lied to me or just kept it to yourself and never let me know about any of that, but you wanted me to know before you'd agree to be with me so that I would know the worst of you. You care about other people more than anyone I've met in a very, very long time. You deserve much more than to be called a whore by a pillock who would go behind the back of someone he calls a friend, and then hold that secret of that over your head." He kissed the palm of my hand, and then continued the drive back to my house as the light turned green. It was dark along the road through my neighborhood, but my smile could have lit the whole street brighter than the sun.

*   *   *

174

When I awoke the next day, I immediately pulled on my running gear, having been slacking on my longer weekend runs since spending so much time out in the evenings. While most weekdays were quick three- or four-mile jaunts, weekends were usually reserved for double-digit distances. I figured, for today, I would lace up and see how far I could go.

The sun was already peeking over the horizon when I began. The humidity of late June in Florida, constantly threatening rain, was lightened ever so slightly by the sun's rays, which seemed to dry the air out a bit; why, the humidity may have been at a mere ninety percent!

I was used to this, though, and knew that all I had to do was to slow my pace and focus on my breathing. A day like this could sneak up on you while running, causing your heart rate to suddenly spike, and even the most experienced and seasoned runners could end up in trouble. I was pretty good about keeping an eye on my heart rate as I ran, and would often examine the running report after I'd finished to compare speed versus heart rate over the course of the run.

If I had seen the report from that morning's run on any other day, I'd have wondered how I hadn't died. Because that day, my heart rate maxed out.

And it had nothing to do with the run.

Right about at the point where I was thinking I would turn around to head back home, I noticed a figure stretching at a red light ahead of me, waiting for the green. I slowed down to a walk, not wanting to get any closer, because even at a distance, I recognized Jack. I nearly ran home without taking a step farther, but I saw him pull out his phone and begin to speak to someone, completely missing his chance to cross the road. Something in his posture changed, and he started arguing with whoever he was talking to. Then he hung up the phone and took off at a sprint towards the coffee shop- the opposite direction he'd been waiting to go.

I knew it wasn't my business and tried not to care, but Jack had never, in the whole time I'd known him, changed his training for anything other than illness. Who had been on the phone, and what had they said? His rage at the bar last night left me with a bad feeling, and I felt compelled to see what he was up to. I could go a bit farther before I turned around anyway...

I followed at a distance, pushing my pace more than I should have in the heat, but letting curiosity best me.

He slowed as he approached the parking lot of the coffee shop and looked around, pulling his phone back out and typing something. After a moment, he put his phone away and walked to a corner of the lot, obviously having found whatever he was looking for.

There was a deep blue convertible parked in the back corner of the lot. I couldn't see through the tinted glass, especially as far away as I was; I was unwilling to get close enough to be noticed. As Jack approached the side of the car, a slender woman with bouncing flaxen hair stepped out. *Ashley?* I couldn't believe she'd be here meeting Jack after everything that had happened the night before. Something was definitely strange, and I'd never even seen that car before.

As she flipped her hair back, I saw the sunglasses atop cheekbones that were definitely not Ashley's, and I breathed a bit easier, but then I felt my heart begin to race- and considering I'd just been running, the pounding was painful.

It was Amber, I realized. Cy's ex, the one who had run into me outside of the hotel where Cy was staying. She and Jack had met briefly when he'd taken the picture of her and Cy to send to me, but I didn't realize they knew each other.

Then again, maybe they didn't. Jack's posture was defensive and he kept a bit of distance between them. She, on the other hand, seemed at ease and sidled right up beside him and guided him into the coffee shop. Right before they went inside, she turned her head and, though I couldn't be sure with her sunglasses on, I was convinced she looked directly at me before tossing her hair and walking through the door.

Chapter 23

Elsie

"No, Ash, it was *definitely* Amber," I insisted. "I swear to God, I thought it was you at first."

"Thanks for thinking so little of me as a friend," Ashley grumbled. I'd told her about Jack and Cy's ex meeting up.

"I don't!" I cried. "I completely trust you. That's why I was floored when I thought it *was* you. It was so weird, though..." I thought back to the whole situation. "Jack was on his run. He had a path he was heading for, and he answered his phone, and he completely changed his course. Jack hasn't changed his training mid-course in his life! And when she got out of the car, he wouldn't go to her. She had to walk to him and drag him inside the coffee shop. I mean, Ashley..." I needed her to understand. "That's fucking weird, right?"

Ashley paused. "Yes, it's weird, but, El..." she sighed. "Maybe just let it go. Jack showed us all what an asshole he was last night. We don't have to deal with him anymore. If he acts weird with your boyfriend's ex, let him. Cyrus said she's a psycho too, right? Let them deal with each other if that's what they want." She said the next part slowly: "It's. Not. Your. Business. Let it go."

The whole event made me uneasy, but of course, Ashley was right. I didn't know Cy's ex, but I knew Jack. He was an egotistical piece of shit, but he was also a coward. What could they possibly do? Date to annoy us?

I pushed it all to the back of my mind and carried on with my day, helping Mom with her weekend clean. Cyrus and I were going on a very tame dinner-and-a-movie date that night, and I promised Mom and Dad they could meet him- briefly- before we went. So by early evening, when he came to pick me up, Mom and Dad were waiting in the living room with me, wearing frightening clown-like smiles.

"Y'all," I pleaded. "*Please* try to be normal."

"Aren't we always?" Dad asked, legitimately confused. I guess he wouldn't know how to act normally around the adult man taking their adult daughter out; the last time he'd met one of my boyfriends, I was still in school and we were, in every way but the ability to vote, kids.

"Just act like he's someone you'd meet at a work function, Dad," I advised. "Polite, friendly, but don't ask weird, prying questions. Okay?"

Mom hadn't spoken in about an hour. She was having some kind of internal war, and I had some guesses about what. She obviously thought, after she and I had sparred about it the week before, that Cy and I had slept together on our first date. Because we didn't really talk about my sex life other than to snipe at each other using incomplete and indirect statements, I could see how she came to that conclusion (not to mention the fact that we really had almost had sex in his kitchen), but I was still annoyed that she was acting weird when it didn't happen.

179

The doorbell rang and both Mom and I jumped up. I shot her a look and practically ran to the door, no easy feat in the heels I was wearing.

I wasn't as dressed up as I had been on our date the previous week, but I certainly put in more effort than I would have if we had been heading to The Watering Hole. I had felt like a princess being twirled around in my beautiful dress on our first date, and wanted to wear something to feel pretty again. I had a white sundress, printed with various citrus fruits; it was fitted around the bust, but flared out at the waist into a very flattering A-line. It came about halfway between my knees and hips, so with the addition of the heels, I got to show off the shapely legs that running had helped to tone.

I opened the door and Cy smiled at me from behind his shades. I grinned back, little butterflies threatening to start chomping away at the lining of my stomach from nerves. He handed me a single, perfect magnolia- my favorite. I took a big whiff, then grabbed his hand and pulled him inside before he could even say hello.

I did my best to keep the conversation short and sweet, but parents will be parents, and they asked a few questions that I had already answered in advance.

"So, what's with the sunglasses?" Dad asked.

"I told you about his eyes, Dad," I reminded him.

"That's such an interesting accent, Cyrus," Mom said, almost before I had even finished speaking. "Where are you from?"

That one I had gotten an answer to shortly after we starting seeing each other as friends: "I was born in Ireland," he'd told me. "I grew up there, in a small fishing village called Ballycastle. As soon as I could, I left Ireland and came Westward, arriving in New England and moving around from state to state until I settled in New York. Then a friend reached out with an opportunity in the area, and here I am."

After repeating this information to my parents, my Dad chimed in with, "And what exactly is that business?"

I glared at him, but Cy spoke before I could. "Sir," he said, "nothing would make me happier than being able to boast about this particular venture, but with the NDA I had to sign, I'd likely have to sell everything I own as well as the rights to my first- and second-born children if I told. But once things are final, I'll be glad to regale you with the details over a pint."

Between the "sir" and the promise of beers together, my Dad seemed mollified, but Mom looked like she was having a stomach cramp. I knew it was because she wanted to say something and was trying not to, but finally, she lost the battle with herself and burst out with, "And what exactly, with a transient life like yours, do you hope to get out of a relationship with Elsie?"

"Mom!" I snapped. I stood up to leave, ready to say something biting before we left, but Cy grabbed my hand gently to pull me back down beside him and looked at Mom.

"Mrs. Taylor, I understand why you would be concerned, and I appreciate it because I have concerns about the future as well." He gave my hand a squeeze. "You've raised a level-headed daughter who cares so deeply about those around her, that she's like a beacon of kindness. She's honest, something so few people are in this world today, and that's nothing she learned on her own. She learned it from you, so I would like to display the same honesty. I care about Elsie, and I don't want to see her get hurt. I plan to do everything I can to prevent that, and I hope that doing so involves her being by my side."

I beamed at him, feeling my cheeks burning and my eyes welling up with tears. He wasn't exactly the strong and silent type, but he rarely spoke so openly about his feelings. To hear him declaring his feelings to my parents was a bit embarrassing, but mostly enchanting.

I looked over at Mom and Dad, who seemed both surprised at Cy's candor and pleased with what he said. I don't think Mom had expected such a satisfactory response to what she'd likely intended to be a stumper of a question, and she was back to looking like she had indigestion.

I stood as I said, "If we don't get going, we're going to be late for the movie after dinner. Mom, Dad, I love you. Don't wait up."

Cy called a goodbye over his shoulder as I practically dragged him out of the house and to his car. Once we were inside, he turned to me. Before he could say anything, I leaned forward and kissed him, trying to convey all of the emotion I'd felt as he'd spoken to my parents. My fingers interlocked behind his head, holding him to me. I felt him reach one hand to my waist and the other to my hair. We stayed that way for several seconds- maybe even minutes, but for all I know it could have been hours. I never imagined there could be a real-life romance that gave me as much of a thrill as the fictional ones I used to enjoy, but this was so much better.

When I finally pulled back, I took a moment to catch my breath and said, "Thank you for that. You were perfect. I mean, you're always perfect, but you were so amazing in there, with what you said, it was exactly what they needed to hear, and even if it was all for them, I so appreciate you saying it because it was so sweet and-"

Cy cut me off with another quick kiss, then smiled at me with The Brow creeping just a hair higher than its partner. "You're cute when you ramble," he said. "And I meant every word."

*   *   *

Over dinner, I told Cy all about that week at work.

"… And Jimmy is such a sweetheart, but it's the most heartbreaking thing to see him labeled that way. No one else even tries with him because they see him as a lost cause. I don't believe any kid is a lost cause, do you?"

Cy smiled at me. "I've never really worked with children, so I don't know. But if you believe that, it's probably true."

It was sweet, but my stomach also gave a funny lurch, and I couldn't figure out why. It wasn't until we were looking over the dessert menu and my eyes settled on the coffee list that it occurred to me. He trusted my gut. And my gut was screaming at me to tell him what happened on my run.

"So…" I hesitated. Ashley had told me to let it go, but I felt like Cy deserved to know what I'd seen that morning since it involved his ex. "Cy, something weird happened on my morning run today."

His expression changed to one of cautious concern at my tone. "Oh?" He asked in a would-be calm voice, except that his entire body had gone still.

"Yeah. I saw Jack."

Cy's eyes went wide and he asked urgently, "Did he do something? Did he hurt you?"

"No!" I shushed him, not wanting to make a scene. "He didn't see me. But… Cy, you should know that he was meeting Amber."

"Amber?" Cy's face went ashen. "Are you sure?"

"Very sure," I said. Then I told him everything I'd seen.

"And I know it was stupid of me to even follow him, but I guess they've decided to date to try to get back at us or something. It was just really fucking weird," I finished, repeating what I'd said to Ashley.

Cy was silent for a few moments. He stared at me, his jaw tensing and releasing. He was anxious. I'd never seen that look on his face… except, I realized, for a split second after I'd collided with Amber outside his hotel. What about her made him this nervous?

"Elsie..." he started, then seemed to falter. "Can we skip dessert and the movie? We need to talk in private, I think."

*   *   *

We arrived at the hotel and he let us into his room, locking the door behind us. His face had been taut with worry the entire ride home, and his eyes had darted everywhere. Clearly, there was something serious he hadn't told me, but I guessed that he was about to.

Upon entering, I saw that all his belongings (what little of them there were) were either stacked up or in boxes, ready to be taken to the condo. I wondered briefly if he had other things packed away in storage, or if the lack of personal belongings was due to his "transient life" as my mother had put it.

Cy wrapped his arms around me in a way I could only describe as protective. He held me close, so tightly that it was on the verge of hurting. His hands seemed to be clammy, and his lips shook ever so slightly.

"Cy," I said, feeling his worry spreading to me. "What is going on?"

He took a breath and pulled himself away, sitting on the edge of the single couch in the suite and motioning for me to sit on the cushion. Once I did, he seemed to rethink sitting and started to pace restlessly.

"Cy!" I nearly shouted. "You're really freaking me out. Talk to me! Why are you acting like a pig in a slaughterhouse?"

My words seemed to bring him back to his senses enough that he stopped pacing and looked at me. "I'm not. I..." He sighed, pulling off his sunglasses now that the sunlight had completely faded from the sky outside. He turned his eyes away from me and continued, "I should have told you everything before. You were so honest with me, and I didn't return the courtesy. Not that I believe for a second it would have stopped her, but maybe..." He looked up at my eyes. "Amber... she's dangerous, Elsie. And I'm not the pig in the slaughterhouse. It's you."

I felt the bottom drop out of my stomach. "What do you mean dangerous?" I asked woodenly. "And why am I the pig?" Cy crossed the room to sit next to me, grabbing for my hands, but I was shocked and angry that there was something big enough to frighten him this much that he hadn't told me, even after I'd spilled my guts to him about every skeleton in my closet, so I pulled away. "Explain. Now," I said, my voice suddenly full of fire.

Cy's eyes were full of regret and something else. He steeled himself with a deep breath and said, "I was engaged once. Years ago." I hadn't expected that, but it also didn't explain why I was in danger. Yet. "Her name was Fiona. I loved her... the way anyone loves their first real love. The day of our wedding, she left me a note that she had fallen in love with someone else, and had eloped with him." His eyes dropped, but when he brought them back to mine, there was a rage burning low in them. "Amber and I found each other at that time, and she was all I'd needed to heal from the devastation of my first heartbreak. Where Fiona had been bold and kind, Amber was just as bold, but cruel. She shouldn't have, but she captivated me. It was far too long before things began to gnaw at me. She would tell me how she did everything to make sure we were together. Then, during a fight, she mentioned something about Fiona, something I never told her, and suddenly all the things she'd said made sense... Elsie, I have no way to prove it, but Fiona didn't leave me- I'm sure of it. Amber did something to her. She hurt her, or worse. When I say she's dangerous... she's a psychopath, and she will hurt you if given the chance."

It felt like my heart had stopped. His ex- Amber- had possibly killed his fiancé in order to be with him? I felt something inside me break.

"Fuck you," I whispered, glaring at him.

His face fell. "Elsie-"

"Fuck. You," I repeated, jumping to my feet. "Do you not think that's information I should have had? That someone who you knew was in town and stalking you might want to do actual physical damage to me?" I was nearly screaming, but I sounded much less hysterical than I felt.

"Elsie," he held his hands out like a cowboy trying to calm a wild horse. "I thought I'd managed to scare her off after the night you came here and saw her. I'd told her I had found evidence she was following me, and told her if I saw her anywhere near you that I would call the police." He looked thoughtful. "I imagine she contacted Jack to try to get information about our relationship, to try to find a way to hurt one or both of us."

"How?" I asked. "How did she contact him? Did they exchange numbers outside The Watering Hole while y'all were out there smoking?"

"I don't know how," Cy admitted. "She showed up that night to let me know that she'd found me. She and Jack introduced themselves, but then she left. I wouldn't put anything past her, though. She could have illegally obtained Jack's information, and if she found out about what happened last night (or perhaps if she'd been there watching), she would, of course, try to take advantage of Jack while he was licking his wounds," he finished with a look of disgust.

I tried to process this. "But... why?" I asked.

Cy looked bewildered. "Why what?"

"Why do any of this? Why follow you to Florida? Why hurt people when it doesn't win you over? Just... why?" I sputtered.

Cy reached for my cheek, and although a part of me wanted to pull away, I also craved comfort from him. He ran his thumb across my cheekbone as his fingers wrapped around to my hair. "The fact that you have to ask that question is exactly why I care for you as much as I do. You could never understand the motivations of someone so driven by cruelty and malice as Amber is... that's why I love you." Despite their cool tone, his eyes were like fire. My lips parted ever so slightly as they burned into me and his words took hold, and he took it as an invitation to lean in and press his lips to mine.

I'd always read books where there was a big climactic kiss while the characters were in danger, and it was always such a thrilling thought; two lovers who could be killed any moment, needing to express their love- just in case. The danger only added to the sexiness of the moment.

It was nothing like that. Rather than feeling the fire of passion for Cy, I felt cold. He'd told me he loved me, and kissed me, and none of it mattered because he'd put me in danger. People I loved were in danger. I stepped back.

"Thank you for telling me," I said, my voice breaking. "I think I'd like to go home now."

The look on his face might have shattered me. He'd confessed his love, and not only had I not said it back, I had told him I wanted to leave. I knew he'd been trying to protect me from an unpleasant truth, and even now was trying to impress upon me the danger I may be in, but I couldn't process my feelings about all of this if his hands and lips were on me. I needed to be alone to work it out.

"Okay," he said, as simply as he had in the bathroom in the nightclub. *Like I said I wanted ice cream.*

He drove me home, and I started to get out of the car when he asked me to wait. I looked down at his hands, rather than into his eyes.

"Please be careful. I should have told you sooner, and I didn't. I... I fucked up. Please don't put yourself in harm's way because of my mistake." He paused. "I'm moving into the condo tomorrow- you saw the boxes, and I have furniture coming. I hope you'll come by and see it soon. Maybe we could talk more."

I nodded tightly. "I'll call you." Then I looked up at my house, the lights- thankfully- were turned off, which would allow me to sneak to my room without any questions or conversations that I couldn't handle. I got out of the car and, as fast as I could in my heels, ran to the door of my house. Once inside, I locked it behind me.

In my bedroom, I kicked off my shoes. My eyes settled on the bookshelf, with that same book still facing out at me. I stomped over to it and slammed it onto the shelf with the others, furious at the thought of any kind of romance, and especially at ones where the lovers drew closer together in light of a conflict with a dangerous villain. I checked that there were no gaps in my curtains, convinced if I looked out, I'd see Amber watching me. Then, without even taking off my dress, I fell into bed and sobbed myself to sleep.

Chapter 24

Opal

I stared at the dark ceiling, waiting for my captor to return, just for something to do. I had awoken as the sun was setting and hours had passed since then, hours in which I pondered the situation that had plagued me for weeks, that had knocked me so off guard I had been able to be abducted by the same man who had abducted and killed me in my mortal life.

I knew when I finally escaped that I would be in danger until I had fresh blood and a kill to strengthen me. I had no idea what they were doing, but I knew that Zilpher and Amber were coordinating, which couldn't mean anything good for whomever they were targeting.

Naturally, I had to assume it was me. If I was incorrect, the worst I did was defend against an attack that never came. If I was correct, I would hopefully be prepared for whatever assault was headed my way.

I loved Amber, but the last time we spoke had not been a kind or gentle conversation, and she'd sworn that if she came out alive, she would never forgive me. I hadn't heard from her since then, and naturally, I'd assumed she was killed.

It had been two years after I'd seen her last, when she'd taken off with Indigo to teach her about being a vampire and, I had assumed, to either do what she did with me or to bring her along to carry out a crusade against sexual predators of the worst kind. I couldn't officially approve of this as a Council member, but as a woman, even an undead one, I relished the idea of such monsters being rightfully punished.

It had been just before sunrise, and I was cleaning up after a long night, down in this very basement, when Amber called. I let the phone ring, knowing I could call her back, but she called two more times in quick succession.

Finally, I answered. "What, Amber?" I snapped, exasperated. I had drained the body of blood well enough, but there were other fluids to contend with when dismembering a corpse before immolating it in a furnace. I was doing my best to keep things contained and was annoyed at the distraction.

She was screaming. "Fuck, Opal! Fuck! Indigo went rogue, she went way too fucking far, and I don't know what to fucking do!"

She sounded scared, and I'd never heard her like that. Even on the night she'd turned Indigo, she had exposed her sadness and pain to me, but never fear.

"Relax," I commanded, using my most imposing tone. I threw the body to the floor, frustrated but knowing it could wait a bit longer. "Tell me what happened."

She told me all about how she and Indigo had traveled the country and even overseas for years, seeking out the men who got away with their crimes against women. The date-rapists who could never be convicted because of a lack of evidence; the monsters who violently assaulted women in darkened parking garages; even the "boys' club" boys that felt that they were

190

entitled to the women who, in their minds, were lucky enough to be near them and their social and political power.

Just like Zilpher. Nothing ever changes.

It was getting harder to convince Indigo to keep things discreet, Amber had said. Discretion not being her own forte, I knew it had to be bad for her to bring it up to the young one. Indigo hadn't liked the suggestion to slow things down; to wait for the cases to drop out of the spotlight before striking; to allow the victims a false sense of security; to believe that they were going to get away with it before they were struck down and found dead.

"She left during the day while I slept," Amber told me. "I tried to track her, but she did her best to mask her scent, and it took me too long, and... shit, Opal, it's going to be on the national news, and I'm on *fucking* camera there!"

If I had a heartbeat, it would have skipped. My voice was a deadly whisper. "What. The. Fuck. Happened?"

"I heard the sirens first and figured I'd check it out. I knew Indigo couldn't have gone far, and she was always careless... so Goddamned careless, and I never did anything about it. *Shit!*" Amber took a deep breath to steady herself. "It was at the frat house. We'd read a story in an older school paper publication, an opinion piece that the boys at the house were using their parties to drug and rape any girls they wanted. One of the victims had written the piece. She'd woken up with no memories of the party and bruising and tearing that lined up with sexual assault. She tried to get help, but everyone turned her away. It was the classic case of 'Well, how drunk were you?' and 'What were you wearing?' They were never going to pursue it because the chapter brought in a lot of money from the national organization, and the University needed the money. So she wrote the piece and lots of women came forward with similar stories, but the whole thing was swept under the rug. Some women got paid off, others got smeared and slut-shamed until they withdrew their stories. It drove Indigo mad. She started killing anyone with Greek letters on their person so violently I had to physically restrain her some nights. They thought they had a serial killer on campus.

"She got away from me and went to the frat house. Every single man in there is dead. She drained a few, but once she was full, she started ripping them limb from limb... there's more blood than the time I tried to save her... Opal, this can't be covered up. The girls in the house saw her, and we were both caught on the school's security system."

"What did the cameras see?" I asked, dreading the answer.

"They saw Indigo, in all of her brutal, vampiric glory, and they saw me moving faster than humanly possible to stop her. And we had human witnesses. Some of the girls who saw us called us Dark Angels. They're drugged out of their minds, but they called friends and told them, they've put it online. Opal... I don't know how we're going to get out of this."

She wept while I was at a loss for words. I wanted to comfort my friend, to rush to her side, but she was right. It couldn't be covered up. It would have to be spun, and someone was going to have to take the fall. They couldn't both be allowed to live.

"Amber..." I said softly. "Keep Indigo with you. I'm going to do what I can, but you have to know..." I paused, not wanting to have to say it. "The Council is clear on this. It's too public. There will have to be punishment. I can't guarantee your safety. Be ready for this, Amber. Indigo is going to be killed. Probably very soon. But I'm going to fight for you.'"

"If you tell them, I'm dead! Don't do it, Opal! I can work with her, I can fix her. Don't tell them! Think about everything I've done for you! Give me a chance to get Indigo and hide! If you call them now, I will never forgive you! To the end of time, alive or not, I will hate you, and I will find a way to get back at you!"

Another pause. "I have to, Amber. This is too big."

She started to argue with me, but I hung up on her and immediately called Sapphire, hoping that, as Amber's sire, she would be of help. I explained the situation, but my heart fell when she spoke after listening intently.

"Madame Opal, thank you for bringing this to our attention. Amber broke the rules when she made this young vampire, and has been taking her along on errands of sloppy vengeance. Their activities have reached our ears more than once, but as you said, this is too big. We will put it to a vote. I take no joy in it. She was one of my first fledglings, my child, but know that our beloved Amber will likely never see another sunset."

I felt numb. I had thought myself so devoid of emotions that I could never be penetrated, that I was completely and utterly unflappable. But I knew that I *did* have love, whatever kind of love a "dark angel" could offer, for Amber. I felt nothing for her progeny, for my sister, but for my sire... I dreaded the coming vote.

Sapphire initiated a video call with every member of the Council in Eastern North America. Twenty four of us all remained silent as Sapphire spoke, bringing forth the charges against Indigo and her sire, Amber. They had been accused of being careless and wanton in their destruction, and had both been seen by living humans and had allowed themselves to be recorded. Their destruction was the recommended sentence. We would be given a chance to speak for one minute each in favor of or against the proposed sentence before we would vote.

Most of the Councilors had never had direct contact with either Amber or Indigo, and as such, merely made comments about the stupidity of allowing themselves to be recorded. Zilpher chimed in with some patriarchal bullshit about how they should have left the boys to their own devices, that their little crusade had no place among our people. It was the old "boys will be boys" line that even amongst humans was becoming less and less of an acceptable excuse.

My turn. I had one minute to convince them to spare Amber, and I knew I could never do it if I fought for Indigo too. Amber would hate me forever, but at least she'd have forever to do it. I needed to be as stoic and unemotional as possible. I didn't know I could be anything else, but I found it difficult to maintain composure in that moment. "Amber was spotted because she was attempting to restrain and remove her child from the scene. Indigo was mentally disturbed from the night of her transformation, something Amber had hoped would improve or disappear completely with time. It never did. Amber understands that Indigo is a danger to both humans and vampires, as well as to the delicate balance between our species. I do not believe she wants to see her progeny killed, but she knows the cost of what has happened. Amber should be spared, but the fledgling should be eliminated."

I knew for that to happen, the vote would have to have enough members abstain or vote against the sentence. Sixteen "yea" votes would seal Amber's fate. We would require sixteen "nays" to acquit. That would never happen, not with Zilpher on the side of convicting; he was too influential. Eight nays and/or abstentions would allow for a change to the recommended sentence. That's what I needed. Just eight of us to abstain or say no.

"We vote," Sapphire said.

If I could have closed my eyes without showing how much I cared and appearing weak, I would have. I wanted to shut it out, for my vote to be recorded and for them to leave me in my ignorance. I could be blissfully unaware if she was spared or not; I could live content in the knowledge that if I never heard from her again, that it was because she hated me and never wanted to speak to me again- not because I had caused her death.

Two ayes... six ayes... ten... The final count came. It was: four abstentions, three nays, and seventeen ayes. Seventeen votes for the death and destruction of my sire. My friend.

I maintained the look of indifference until the call ended. Zilpher would be sent to do the honors since it was near his area, and he was just so kind to volunteer. I hated him. I would always hate him.

When I was able to turn off the call, I called Amber back. No answer. Leave a voicemail. "Amber!" I screamed into the phone. "Get the fuck out! Leave Indigo there and just *go*! They're coming!"

I texted her the same words. I never knew if she got the messages. Zilpher sent out notice within the hour that he'd taken care of the problem and was already handling the PR surrounding the media reports of what had happened.

I had gone without hunting at all the next night for the first time in my entire afterlife. After paying a fledgling to finish disposing of my kill, I had gone to my bed and laid there for three days, becoming as weak as I had ever been, at least until I was brought down to this basement as a prisoner.

Zilpher had come to my door and I had told him to leave. Well, actually, I had told him to fuck off and die, but he threatened to call the Council and let them know my part in Indigo's creation, something he'd actually kept from them to use as leverage later. I let him in and he immediately drove me to my bed. I wanted none of it, told him again to leave, but he was relentless, ignoring my protestations. I would never let him know, but it was a distraction I desperately needed. He took full advantage, and I let him. Zilpher was exactly the kind of man Amber and Indigo had waged their war against, a fiend who used his own power and the weaknesses of others to get what he wanted. And here I was, honoring their memory by fucking him, the man who had killed them and then all but

195

forced himself into my bed, and I did it with reckless abandon to try to forget the overwhelming pain that had taken me over.

I hated myself.

But then, suddenly, I didn't. Because it turned out a tryst with Zilpher was just what I needed to put those feelings right back where they belonged, along with my shame, with the feelings of vulnerability that he had exploited. I shut them out, the myriad of emotions, knowing they would never be allowed in again; not in my mind, not in my heart, not in my actions. Madame Opal could deal with the death of her only friend because she simply no longer cared. And she was perfectly content to continue as though Zilpher had never killed Amber.

But now I knew that he never *had* killed her. She was alive and contacting him. Had she escaped, and they'd gotten in touch later? Or had he spared her, and if so, why? I spent hours and days alone in the basement, demanding these questions of the silence around me. I wish I could call her and not have her hang up on me if I did. I wish I could ask her what happened. I wish she could come and rip Cyrus's throat out for keeping me here. But then I wondered...

Would she? Or was I as dead to her as I thought she had been?

Chapter 25

Elsie

I was back at the beach, feet in the surf, being slowly, inexorably sucked down as though in quicksand. Cy's sad eyes held me right up until he reached out and held me with his arms instead. I felt the sand close over my head, and I awoke again, this time gasping for breath.

Was I really already in too deep with this guy, as my mind seemed to be telling me? I needed to get out and think.

I dressed in my running clothes quickly and ran into Mom in the hallway as she was about to leave for church.

"Morning, Elsie," she said a bit curtly without even looking up at me. "You were out late." Her tone would have been casual if it wasn't dripping with judgment. I looked down at my feet, feeling some measure of shame. I didn't feel shame for my actions (except when it came to Jack); rather it was for how my actions had affected my relationship with my mother. We had always been so close, but once I stopped being honest with her about what was going on in my life, we had begun to drift apart. There was always so much tension there these days. I was hoping I could fix some of that, even if I still had to keep some things to myself.

"It really wasn't that late," I said. "I need to figure some stuff out, so Cy's giving me a little space."

"Are you okay?" Mom asked, looking at me. Then she noticed I was dressed. "Going for a run?"

I shrugged. "I have some talking to God to do."

Mom half-smiled. "I wish you'd do that at Church with me," she said.

Growing up in a Christian home, some of my "activities," especially in my adult years, didn't exactly fit with Mom's vision for me. The problem with trying to fit a square peg into a round hole is that it will never work, and the peg just feels beat up, as though it has no value because it won't ever fit. I always believed in a higher power, in God, but as I began to explore life for myself, I realized the limitations and judgments that were put upon me by the church were soul-crushing. If God loved me, he wouldn't want me to feel so unloved just for learning who I was and trying to be that person. I'd created my own church. It was in my own mind, and I could go anytime I wanted or needed- not just when other people said it was time to do so. I even prayed, just not in the traditional, hands together, "Dear God, please send me a new puppy," kind of way. My prayers were usually wordless, a silent cry out to the universe that came from deep within me, voicing a need. Today, the call was so loud I could hardly think over the din, and I was hoping that allowing my soul to scream would help me find some clarity.

Mom gave me a hug. "I hope he tells you what you need to hear," she said before Dad grabbed the keys and they left for church.

Running the day before had been for fitness. Today it was medicine. I had no time or distance goals, and was only running to what my body needed to feel so my brain could work. As my legs ached, my lungs burned, and my mind raced. Was any of this worth it? I should just walk away. We hadn't known each other that long, and I had thought I was falling for him, but this was more than enough reason to end it. Done. The end. Or...

Could I get past a psycho (like, *actually* psycho) ex who seemed to be enlisting the help of someone I knew for a fact hated me, but knew me well? Was Cy quicksand? Had I gotten sucked too deep to pull away just like that? Did I actually love him back? And if I did... was it enough to make up for the rest?

I stopped to catch my breath, looking around at where I'd ended up since I hadn't been paying much attention; it had been as much as I could spare mentally to not run in front of cars. I was by the coffee shop, and the blue convertible was back in the lot. My breath caught as I realized I was staring at it, and it was running. I couldn't know for sure if Amber saw me looking at her, but I turned and ran as fast as I could home, my mind made up.

I jumped into the shower, letting the hot water scald my skin. Knowing I was home alone for at least another half hour, I took a deep breath and let the scream that had been building inside of me explode out.

"*AAAAAARRRGGGGGGHHHHHHH FUUUUUUCK!*" The water sprayed away from my face with the vibration of my voice. I allowed myself five more minutes in the shower to cry until I felt drained.

I laid across my bed, my wet hair soaking the sheets beneath me. I felt my phone vibrate. A glance told me it was the group message- the new one without Jack, but that included Cy. Something about karaoke Wednesday night, something new at The Watering Hole. The replies were flying faster than I even cared to read them, but nothing from Cy or me.

I opened a different thread. *Can we talk?*

Cy replied, almost immediately, *Of course. When and where?*

Chapter 26

Opal

Cyrus was late the next several nights, and we sat in complete silence, our previous banter dead in the shadow of our last conversation, argument, whatever you want to call it. I wouldn't talk to him until he answered me, and I refused to give voice to the heinous acts he refused to admit to or deny, not even to ask him outright. He, in turn, refused to answer the questions I wouldn't ask, and offered up no questions of his own. We stared at each other the way vampires can do, preternatural patience allowing us to not flee the moment, simply being still, learning every physical characteristic by simply studying their appearance. I could pick out a particular wave of his hair that never sat quite with the rest, creating a little ridge when he ran his hand through it; I saw a little tick he had where he would tap his feet down in a disjointed rhythm to fill silence; I found the slight quirk of one side of his mouth which sat slightly more curved than the other. In his annoyance, it became an angry curl that I imagined would be both frightening and sexy around the fangs he'd once had.

Quite often in the following days and nights, I found myself imagining him before I stole his blood, when he was a vampire like myself. I fought against the attraction I felt to my fantasized version of him. In my mind, his eyes were no longer the earthy hazel, but they were vivid and varied, changing with my imagination since I had no idea what color they'd been. In my mind, they changed as mine often did, a kaleidoscope of pleasure as we gave in to the passion, to our hate for each other, and brought this building down by its foundation... and then I'd drink from him again, this time all the way down to the last drop... and I'd claim his life, finally know everything he did, and I'd be quite possibly the strongest vampire who ever existed...

On the thirteenth night, I finally broke our silence. "Tell me about your eyes." I wanted to know, to see if it would help me understand something about him.

"Why?" He asked, his mind clearly elsewhere.

"Because you're holding me prisoner, keeping me weak, and torturing me with a silence louder than I hear all day in here by myself. I think you owe me conversation, at least. And as the only other person I have the possibility of seeing for the foreseeable future, I may as well know something about you."

He looked at me with that strange expression I could never figure out. It was several minutes before his shoulders relaxed and he said, "Fine." He took his sunglasses off and looked at his reflection in the mirrored lens. "I grew up in a little fishing village on the northeast coast of Ireland. The water we fished in was this... perfect shade of bright green-blue. It's not unlike the water you might see along the Gulf here. But it was my favorite color in life. Swimming in those waters, bringing fish in from them, even just sitting on the cliffs and watching the sun rise over them... I've only felt that at peace one other time in my life or afterlife." He looked at me, rage and sorrow fighting for control as tears gently fell from his eyes. "But she's gone now, the person who made me feel that way. And to add insult to injury, I've lost that color, my eyes, and any semblance of the peace I once knew."

I nearly felt pity again. What was this isolation doing to me? Was it the days alone with only my thoughts? The lack of blood? Was it the nights, filled only with the conversation and company of someone so decidedly *human,* regardless of any tiny spark of vampirism he retained? I didn't like it, the emotional response. I missed my easy detachment, my aloof view of humanity.

His eyes widened as he continued to glare at me, and suddenly his expression was bemused yet... rapt. "What?" I demanded, not liking the jitteriness I felt with him looking into my eyes like that. I wanted it to stop... and yet I didn't.

Without breaking his gaze, he turned his sunglasses toward me. I looked at my reflection. My eyes were an illustrious shade of green-blue. How curious that his story should resonate with me strongly enough for my eyes to match the color his once were. Maybe there *was* more than hate there. I didn't know how to feel passion beyond hate. I stared at the reflection, feeling the questions bubbling up within me.

"Why did you take me to the island?" I asked again, my voice quiet and gentle, unlike I'd ever heard from my own lips. I wanted to know. Needed to know. There was a connection, something I couldn't place. Something in me wanted to have been wrong about my origin, for there to be a reason for this strange affection I was beginning to feel. Something wanted to not have a reason to hate him- my current predicament aside.

"Why do you think I did?" Cyrus asked again, his own voice soft and pained.

We sat in silence for the rest of the night, until the sun's rays began to peek through my window.

He stood to leave.

"Wait!" I cried. He turned, startled by my outburst. A question was forming that I couldn't even quite get to. I didn't know why, but suddenly knowing was important. I needed to try to figure out what was so special about her. "Your lover, the one Amber killed... what was her name?"

His face crumpled. He hadn't expected me to ask that question any more than I had. Caring about her name, who she was... I didn't know what was happening to me in that basement, but it was creating a flood of feelings I didn't understand or care for.

He put his hand on the wall as if drawing strength from the stone. Without making eye contact, he told me.

"Her name was Elsie. Elsie Taylor."

Chapter 27

Elsie

Wednesday night rolled around, and instead of enjoying karaoke with my friends, I was sitting in a different, smaller, less crowded bar across town. We were the only two there except for a regular whom I knew lived close enough to walk, so I'd had no issue finding a parking space. I had opted for water, and I was sipping it slowly when Cy walked in, his sunglasses on. The sun had barely set, so I knew I wouldn't have to contend with his eyes looking deep into mine.

He sat, somewhat awkwardly, at the chair furthest from me at the table, which I didn't blame him for. He'd said he loved me, and I hadn't said it back. That in and of itself was a boundary, one he wanted to respect. But I felt that longing to reach for him the same as I'm sure he felt for me. We both resisted.

There was a very pregnant silence as we sat there, him not wanting to speak first, and me not wanting to say anything I didn't mean. I thought I knew what I'd planned on saying, but being in his presence made it hard to have the same resolve.

I took a deep breath and said, "I'm sorry about Fiona." It was true, and no matter what happened next, I wanted him to know that.

His gaze dropped to the table. "Thank you."

Another moment of silence.

"I..." I started. "Cy, I think I want this to work." His face snapped up, his hidden eyes trained on me. "But I need to know that there are no more secrets, and we need to find a way to make sure Amber can't hurt us or anyone else we care about. Until we figure that out, I don't want to give her any reason to target us. So..." I swallowed hard. "We can be friends. I don't want to lose you, but... there's nothing fun or sexy about all this. It's not exciting- i-it's terrifying. Christ, you'd think with all the crazy fantasy romance novels I read, I'd be a lot more into this, but I'm just n-not!" My voice was shaking so badly I could barely get the words out. I was in deep with this man, but I wasn't going to be pulled under.

Cy's expression was unfathomable. I saw a twitch in his jaw and wondered what he was thinking.

"Okay." *Like I said I wanted ice cream.* His expression had become resigned. "Okay. Elsie-"

Bzzt. I glanced down at my phone on the table. *Bzzt.* It was a call, not a text. Jess was calling me from karaoke night. I silenced the phone and waited for Cy to continue, but then a text came through- *Pick up the fucking phone!!!-* followed by another call. Jess was never this extreme. I frowned and picked up.

"What?" I asked, annoyed because I was having an important conversation.

Ashley was calling from Jess's phone and was sobbing. "Fuck, fuck, *FUCK*, Elsie! We're following the ambulance- Sam and Emily got run over in the parking lot- it was Jack's

Jeep, but the cops said it was stolen earlier today, and the driver took off, we couldn't even see his face- *shit*, El, Sam's in bad shape and I think Emily's fucking *dead-*"

The horror must have shown on my face because Cy's expression had gone from resigned to concerned.

My mind blanked for a few moments from shock, and suddenly Ashley was screaming again. "Elsie! Are you coming? Please come, I don't care what happened between you and Sam, he's fighting for his fucking life right now, and you need to be here!"

"Yes," I said numbly. "Yes, I'm coming. I'm on my way." I hung up and looked at Cy, knowing what I told him next would mean. "I have to go. Sam and Emily... Someone stole Jack's car and ran them over with it. Jack!" My voice was reaching hysteria. "Who was meeting with your psycho ex and has a grudge against Sam and me! She fucking did this! Cy, this thing here, you and me? It may have cost two people their lives! I'm sorry, I thought I could, but I can't. I gotta go."

I ran outside, hoping I could think well enough to drive. It was dark now. I dashed across the parking lot towards my car. I heard Cy follow me out, heard him call my name, but I ignored him. I shouldn't have.

Because the next thing that happened was that I was the third hit and run victim of the night.

*   *   *

My eyes opened to a stark white ceiling and the feeling of fabric beneath my hands. I looked around, my vision fuzzy. I was lying on a very soft, white bed. I could see a lot of white surrounding me and some artificial lighting. It looked very sterile.

I tried to move and felt pain shoot through my entire body. It occurred to me that my vision was fuzzy because one of my eyes was swollen.

"Am I in the hospital?" I asked out loud, hoping Mom would hear me and come hold my hand and tell me everything was alright. My voice sounded cottony, likely due to the swelling in my lips and tongue. I tasted blood. How badly had I been hurt?

"No," said a voice beside me- not my mother's. "I couldn't take you to the hospital."

My neck was stiff, but I turned my head as best I could. Cy was sitting in a white leather recliner next to the bed, leaning toward me with his hands clasped in front of his face. I could see behind him the view of the nighttime bay that had awed me just days before. Now I felt fear. Why was I here? I was hurt. I should go to the hospital. I looked at his eyes, now uncovered by the sunglasses. The color seemed duller than usual, and they were rimmed in red. He'd been crying.

"What happened?" I asked. "Why couldn't I go to the hospital?"

He dropped from the chair to the bedside and lightly grabbed my hand. There was a shot of pain, but it paled in comparison to the pain in the rest of my body. "What do you remember?" Cy asked.

Tears trickled from my eyes. "I don't know, Cy. Why can't I go to the hospital? I need to go to the hospital. I'm hurt, Cy," I pleaded, not knowing why he was keeping me here. "Please let me call my family."

"You can't go because you're going to be better before they could even determine what all needs to be fixed." There was a strange bitterness to his voice. "I made sure of it."

"I don't understand. Please, Cy..."

I heard him breathe a sigh. It was the sigh a teacher gives when their best student can't quite get the right answer- full of affection, restraint, and frustration all at once.

"Do you remember where we were?"

"Please..." I didn't want to play guessing games. I wanted to go to the hospital. I wanted my mommy.

"Do you remember?" He persisted. His voice was urgent but soft.

"I... I don't..." I thought about it. My head was pounding, but it seemed to be fading the harder I thought. "We were at the pub."

"Yes. What happened?" He asked. Why couldn't he just tell me? He obviously knew. Why was he making me try to remember when he could just tell me?

"We were talking... and then..." I gasped. "Sam and Emily!" I nearly sat up, but the pain forced me back down. "I need to go, I have to be there-"

Cy's free hand moved to my shoulder in an attempt to calm me. "They are well cared for. You, on the other hand-"

"But my friends think I'm coming! Cy, why are you doing this?" I was feeling like a prisoner, unsure why he was keeping me in his condo instead of taking me to the hospital where I could be treated, and be with my friends, whom I needed and who needed me.

"They know you're with me, but think you're unwell; I've told them that you're violently sick at your stomach and therefore should not be at the hospital. I sent them a message. Elsie, I need you to remember what happened next."

I sobbed through the pain in my face. I'd heard saltwater could help with injuries; I didn't think that tears counted, but they seemed to be helping. My eye already seemed to be focusing better, despite how hard I was crying. "I tried to leave and..." It was there, just beyond my reach. It was like the rest of the room. I could see it, but it was fuzzy, and I couldn't figure out exactly what I was looking at.

Then, all at once, it hit me harder than I'd been hit in the parking lot.

*   *   *

I didn't see it coming at all. I didn't hear it. I'd been running for my car, and Cy called my name. A split second later, I was skidding along the pavement, having been hit by what I thought was a car. I came to rest alongside a curb as my head made contact with it. I had a vague thought that I'd been hit by Jack's Jeep like Sam and Emily had, but that thing was loud. How had it snuck up on me? Was I just too upset to hear it roaring through the parking lot at me?

Then I heard Cy yelling. I couldn't make it out. There was a thud, and he cried, "No!" in a pained voice.

I was just about to allow myself to slip into unconsciousness, when I felt a hand grab me by the hair and yank my face upward, sending waves of pain through my body. "Hello, *Elsie.*" The voice was unfamiliar and dripping with venom. I opened my eyes as much as I could and caught a glimpse of tumbling aureate waves. *Ashley?* I thought, before I remembered the other person I'd seen recently with pale, shining hair like that. "Amber," I grunted.

She sounded delighted. "Ooh, so you've heard of me?" She giggled. It was a sweet, lilting sound. She really was a psychopath. "Good. This will be quick then. I don't know how much else sweet little Cy has told you, but you should be thanking me."

"For what?" I mumbled, the pain starting to get the better of me. I knew I wasn't going to last long.

I heard a thud and a grunt, but the way she held my head, I couldn't see what had happened. "Elsie..." Cy groaned from nearby. "Amber, don't you fucking dare-"

"Don't what?" She taunted him. "Don't tell her that she's been making googly eyes at a monster who doesn't even really love her?" Her voice was directed at me again. "Who's been pretending this whole time, just to get close to her?" She shook her head as though to say, "*What a shame!*"

"Not... a... monster," I spat. Talking was becoming nearly impossible.

"Oh, sweetie," Amber laughed, "you read enough of those silly books to know. Vampires *are* monsters."

My brain didn't make the connection to her words at first. "Not... real..." I was really fading now.

"As real as I am." Her voice was no longer lilting, but full of threats and danger. "As real as your boyfriend is." She turned my face to hers. She opened her mouth, and I felt adrenaline shock me back to consciousness as I focused on the twin fangs that had descended from her upper canines. Her eyes, as they surveyed my wounds, were the yellow-orange of a flame.

"No," I breathed, not believing what I saw, nor what she'd said. I tried to sound brave, but reality seemed to be shifting around me. "That's bullshit. Y-you... you're... lying..."

Amber had tightened her grip on my head and had leaned forward to lick the blood from my face. As I felt her fangs graze my cheek, I knew I had been so wrong about so many things, and I gave myself over to oblivion.

*   *   *

I sat up slowly, my eyes searching Cy's for any sign that I had imagined or dreamed that, some indication that it wasn't a real memory. "Amber," I said. "She... hit me."

"Yes," Cy confirmed.

"Not with a car. With her body. But as hard as a car."

"Yes."

"She... you... you're..." I felt fucking stupid even saying the word. "You're vampires?"

He stared down at the bed. "Yes."

I stared at him, my eyes beginning to focus better by the minute. "Was this what you were going to tell me tonight? When I asked you to not keep any more secrets?" Was it my imagination, or was speaking also getting easier?

"I don't know. I think I was going to try," Cy admitted. "But now that you know the biggest part of my secret, you deserve to know it all."

"Yeah, do you think?" I spat sarcastically.

He stood and walked across the room to a glass-topped table. The black metal frame stood out against the white walls and floor, the only pop of color being the glass that matched his eyes. He poured water from a pitcher and brought it to me.

I gulped it down, washing away the taste of blood and bringing moisture back to my dry throat.

Cy was staring at me sadly. "I want you to know..." he started. "Before I tell you this, please know that I know I've kept things from you, and I'm not sorry because it has kept you safe until now. But almost nothing I said has been an outright lie... not even when I said I love you."

I simply stared him down. I needed to hear what he had to tell me, but I wasn't going to just forgive him for putting me (and my family and friends) in danger.

He took a deep breath and began, "I *was* born in Ballycastle, just... earlier than I let you believe."

"How early?" I asked. I realized that wasn't my actual question. "Cy, how old are you?"

"I was born in 1701," he said matter-of-factly, as though his words weren't mind-bending. While I reeled from finding out he was over three centuries old, he continued. "Ballycastle was (and still is) a fishing village. I loved my home. I was young, strong, and skilled at bringing in fish. I managed to earn a small fortune for myself, which was lucky, because I'd fallen in love with a beautiful woman in the village: Fiona.

"She was so ahead of our time. She had a confidence that might have driven most men of the time away, but it captivated me. Her spirit was as free and fierce as the Irish wilderness. She was kind and warm, but could put the most stubborn men in their place with a word. She was a challenge," he chuckled. "And I loved a good challenge.

"I asked her father for her hand in marriage. I requested no dowry because she was all I wanted, and I knew I could provide for her. I managed to procure a little cottage by the shore for us. It was nearly my entire fortune, but I knew I could make it back, and Fiona was worth it. We spoke daily, and I honestly believed she loved me as I loved her.

"Our wedding day dawned with me finding a letter from her telling me she'd fallen in love with someone else- a merchant named Flynn who'd come to town to trade- and had left for Belfast with him. They were eloping to the Colonies."

"I tried to follow her to Belfast, but failed to find them. I knew I'd have to return to Ballycastle nearly broke and fully heartbroken. I spent hours and most of my money at a local pub to drown my sorrows. In my despondency and drunkenness, I found the area of the docks where men went for... company." Prostitutes, he meant. "I saw a woman with golden curls, and, with her back to me, she could have been mistaken for Fiona. I approached her. This woman- a girl really, not a day over twenty- had Fiona's hair, but her eyes were nothing like Fiona's deep blue. No, they were a vibrant shade of gold. It was Amber, of course.

"I paid her fee, and she took me back to the brothel where she worked. I had been denied my wedding night; I wanted so badly to pretend she was Fiona, to feel for one night that I hadn't lost everything. She seemed kind and listened to my story. I was so drunk that when she told me she could make it all better, I accepted without considering any possible costs. Before I knew what was happening, she'd cut her wrist and pressed the wound to my mouth. The taste of her blood was more intoxicating than the sweetest wine. Between the ale and the blood, I fell into a deep slumber, and she slit my throat."

I gasped softly at the nonchalance with which he described his own murder.

"When I woke, Amber explained everything to me and gave me my new name. By giving me her blood, and then killing me, she had made me like her. Vampire blood will save you if you are hurt and *might* die, but if you die after the blood is already bound to your body, you become like us."

"But..." I tried to wrap my head around all of this. "That's not possible. Vampires aren't real. And even if they were, you're very obviously alive. I've felt your heart beat, I've been with you in the sunlight, and I saw you get pummeled that night in St. Pete."

Cy gave a wry smile. "Vampires are real. We're just much better at blending in than some myths would have you believe. The sunlight only affects my eyes. That's the reason I wear the sunglasses; the degenerative disease I told you about was vampirism. If the sun's rays get into my eyes, it will burn the blood in my veins until I die. As for getting pummeled, I'm strong, but not unbreakable. I could have won that fight if I'd chosen to, but killing that lowlife in the middle of a crowded bar seemed unwise, since I had been trying to keep a low profile. And as far as the heartbeat..." he knelt by the bedside and took my hand. I nearly resisted, but he wasn't trying to be affectionate. He put my hand to his heart. I felt it beating, strong and steady. "Wait," he said, before I could say anything. Suddenly, the pounding of his heart faded... faded... until it was gone.

214

His heart had stopped.

Chapter 28

Elsie

"Bullshit," I whispered, trying to force myself to wake up from what was obviously a dream.

"Sadly, no," Cy said. "It's camouflage. A predator is much more successful when they can walk among their prey unnoticed."

"Are you a predator?" I whispered, my own very real pulse pounding in my ears. The adrenaline surge brought on by fear was causing the pain to fade deeply into the background.

There was genuine hurt and defiance on his face. "I was. I haven't been for a long time. Not since..." He broke off and turned his back to me, pressing his hands against the glass wall that looked over the bay. The sky was pitch black. What time was it?

He continued his story. "Amber had been jilted, like me. She was engaged, as I was, when her lover ran off with a girl from the next village. This was centuries before I was born.

Her family had sent her to a convent after her affair had been discovered. She never made it. Her story is tragic. I won't share more, but to say she was left for dead. She was found by one of our kind who gave her a new life..." His hands balled into fists. "But she's still driven by what happened to her in life. She saw herself as a crusader of sorts, making victims of those who hurt women the way she was hurt, as well as those she felt were headed down her same path, to spare them her pain. But she wanted a partner. She preyed on my pain by making me believe hers was so like mine. She convinced me that, as a superior species, we could save young lovers from our fate by killing them before one could hurt the other, and we could right the wrongs done to those who couldn't fight back."

I felt goosebumps up and down my arms. "You... you killed people?"

He wouldn't look at me. "I killed a lot of people. For fifty years, I joined Amber on her little campaign. She was as bold and vivacious as Fiona had been, but there was an undercurrent that always frightened me a bit. I never questioned her, even when I should have. She could be cruel. I killed, but I never wanted to cause pain. Amber lived for it. And then, every ten years, there was a strange pattern I saw emerging, and I confronted her about it. She was targeting young women- only young women- who all fit a certain type..." He hesitated, then continued. "She wasn't just killing. She was torturing these women. It went against everything I'd ever known or believed about her. These weren't vicious rapists or murderers, and they were often single, unwed; certainly not the young lovers we often killed, supposedly to save them from heartbreak. I tried to ignore it, but I couldn't. I asked her why she chose these women and why she made them suffer. I'd never seen her so angry. She was explosive. She had been choosing women who reminded her of the woman her lover had left her for... and torturing them out of a twisted sense of revenge to

217

commemorate the day her human life ended and her new life began.

"It was too much, even for me with all the blood already on my own hands. We fought, and she slipped up. She mentioned my name- my human name- which I'd never shared with her. I'd given her an alias, not wanting anyone at the brothel to know who I was, to come looking for me after I'd gone home. You see, our eyes change when we die; the colors reflect something in our souls, and mine became the color of the water that I had fished in my whole life, in Ballycastle. My name, my human name, was Cian. Amber took one look at my eyes and changed it to Cyan when she changed me. I had thought it fate, that my sire had chosen a name for me that was so close to my living name, but it wasn't. She had been watching me, watching Fiona; she had taken Fiona for her innocent victim and chose me to be her mate. I put the pieces together, and she didn't deny it; she had killed Fiona and faked the note I had received. Then while I believed I was following Fiona to Belfast, Amber was following me. Every event that led to me dying in that brothel was carefully orchestrated by the woman I'd stupidly taken as a partner."

He turned to look at me. Tears were flowing freely down his face.

"Fiona leaving me was unbearable. Knowing that she hadn't left me, but had been murdered..." Cy sobbed softly, then took a shuddering breath. "From then on, Amber became my enemy. I swore she would never be allowed to hurt someone like that again. I can't stop her from feeding, and I'm not particularly inclined to stop her from killing the malefactors and delinquents she so enjoys, but I can stop her from enacting her vengeance killings." He poured me another glass of water and knelt by the bedside, his head on his hands. He might have been praying. "I followed her for centuries, from country to country, city to city. I had spent enough time with her to discern her pattern, and by the turn of the 20th century, it had become a game for her. Outwitting me to claim her prize.

"I would observe her at a distance, making mental note of the people who were present where she went. I could easily pick out the women who were most at risk. Blonde hair... blue eyes... vivacious, joyful, kind." He raised his face to mine. "Elsie, you're her newest target."

It was warm in the room, but my body went cold. My hair stood on end. "How did you know?" I asked. A sudden realization hit me. "That's why you're here. That's why we met." My stomach churned. Anger began to creep in underneath the disbelief. Cy had been at The Watering Hole and in St. Pete because he'd been watching *Amber* watching me. "This has all been a setup."

He must have seen the apprehension in my face, and he reached out to take the water from me and held tight to my hand even as I tried to pull it away. He really *was* strong. "Yes," he admitted. "But no. I was never supposed to meet you at all. I was supposed to be a new regular at your usual haunts, someone you saw frequently enough to recognize, but never to speak to. I wanted to keep an eye on you and on Amber so I could keep track of her movements. She used to always strike on the exact anniversary of her death, but she doesn't care about that anymore. Now it's about besting me.

"You are the first one of Amber's victims to ever actually meet me. She planted the idea of having a cigarette the night we met. She'd found me and told me she was changing the game. When she walked by your table to leave, she whispered to you. We can speak low enough for a human to hear, but not consciously register, and she said that a cigarette sounded great, knowing you would at the very least look around and notice a smoker in the area.

"The next night, she told that man at the club, the one who hit me, that you were newly single and had been eyeing him from across the club. A terrible tactic, one which might have left you in his company, had I not been there myself, but not nearly as low as she can go," he said, his lip curling in disgust.

My rage was consuming. "You were *following* me, supposedly to save my life, and yet you were willing to *fuck me* in that bathroom while I was drunk? How the hell did you expect to go unnoticed after that?"

He released my hand and pushed his hair back, looking uncomfortable. "It never occurred to me that you would gravitate toward me as you did. And I knew it was wrong. I like to think I would have stopped you before things got that far, but when you kissed me that night... Elsie, I may be dead, but I'm still a man. And you... you are unlike anyone I've ever met. I've met a great many women over three hundred years. I had already been watching you for weeks, and had already started to feel something for you. I was so thankful when you prevented us from going any further that night because I knew I would have forever regretted taking advantage of you like that. I have lived over three hundred years, controlling my human and less-than-human urges, and you broke all of my training that night. You're smart and sexy and unafraid of being both of those things, and, even more unusual, you embrace them to the point that you show them to the world without shame. You never shy away from who you are, and it's beguiling. I knew once we met that I couldn't protect you at a distance. I had to be close. I *wanted* to be close.

"I meant what I said. I love you, Elsie." His gaze darkened. I realized that I hadn't imagined it before- his eyes *were* duller, less vibrant. "And because of that, I'm going to do what I should have done centuries ago and kill Amber, even if the other vampires kill me for it."

That was a lot to process. "I... you love... other vampires?" I stammered. "What other vampires?"

"Well, the ones who would carry out my sentence. We still have laws and a Council who enforces them. I'm sure some of the local vampires would be tasked with carrying out my sentence."

"There are other vampires here?!" I shrieked.

Cy looked as though he was being as patient as he could with my questions. "Yes, of course. You've even met one- Jett from Trusty's."

"*Jett* is a vampire?"

He looked at me with a mix of pity and amusement. "Why else would a five-star restaurant within viewing distance of a beautiful seascape offer no natural lighting or windows?"

I considered this, my mind struggling to comprehend what he was telling me, but it made sense... kind of. I thought I knew everything about vampires from books, TV, and movies, and yet here, in the presence of one who *loved me*, I couldn't believe what he was telling me. There was a block on my brain, as though I heard what Cy said, knew it had to be true, and yet I was stubbornly unable to accept it as truth. "I'm still so lost, though. Vampires kill to feed. Don't you? You feed on human blood."

Cy smiled humorlessly. "Yes, we do, but it's not a require-ment to kill. Killing certainly makes us stronger. It's why Am-ber usually bests me. I haven't killed since soon after I found out about Fiona, not even criminals; but we don't need much to survive. Refusing to feed doesn't even outright kill us, but it does make us vulnerable. Without it, the vampire blood in our veins begins to die until we essentially become human again. At that point, we age quickly- as though we're catching up to the decay our dead bodies may have experienced without our blood- and then we die. The process is painful, and instinct will more often than not win out in the desire to survive..." He trailed off. "I've tried it," he whispered. "Right after I found out that Amber killed Fiona. I wanted to be done, to die, to be with Fiona. I starved myself for weeks and nearly won, but the animal inside took over... that was the last time I killed. It was terrible... I completely lost control, hurt so many people... I refused to ever let myself get so weak or vulnerable again.

"Then, I met you. Suddenly I was protecting you not just because you were one of Amber's victims but because I cared about you personally. The night you came to me and asked me how I felt, I had to confront that I felt about you the way I've felt about no one since Fiona... possibly not even then. When we met the second time, I asked you to call me Cy, rather than by my alias. Because I refused to go by the name Amber had given me, I started to go by Cy after I left her, knowing I could never be Cian again but not wanting to be known by the name Amber had given me. It was a powerful thing for me to have you know my name, even if you simply thought it was a nickname. I started to take measures to improve my strength, knowing I would need to protect you, and soon. I increased my order from my contact at the local blood bank, knowing that I had to be as strong as I could be when Amber finally struck, so that I could handle her. I needed to know that I could not only defend you, but that I could end her torment of me and women like you forever."

"But why would the other vampires kill you?" I inquired. "You're friendly with Jett, at least. Aren't they... like you? Not into killing, I mean?"

Cy stared at something over my head, a million miles away. "Not all of them. And one of our laws is to never strike each other down- especially not our sires. But that's how this has to end. Amber has to die, and you need to return to your life, which you can't do if I'm a part of it."

I was floored by this unexpected declaration. The whole time he'd been speaking, I assumed he had been making his case for why I should forgive him, and we could be together, probably an assumption based on consuming too much vampire fiction. I never dreamed that he was, as he told me everything, plotting his own demise and expecting me to pretend I'd heard none of this and just go back to my normal life. I launched out of the bed to pace, not realizing at first that it should have hurt. It was several steps before it dawned on me. Once the thought occurred to me, I looked down at my blood-stained clothes and the wounds and bruises that already looked weeks old. Nothing hurt. I flexed my fingers. Not only was there no pain, they felt strong... I was stronger than I'd ever felt in my life. There was a sense of total control, over myself and my surroundings, like a drug coursing through my veins.

I looked at Cy with a question burning in my eyes. "What. Did. You. Do?" I could barely form the words for the anger and fear that gripped me.

He looked at the floor and rubbed a pink line on his forearm. "I told you. I didn't think you were going to make it to the hospital. My blood was the only thing I could think of to save you. It took a lot..." he looked back at me, the way the color of his eyes looked more muted suddenly making sense. He was depleted, and I was filled with his blood. I felt a chill run up my spine.

"Am I becoming a vampire?" I asked, my voice cold with terror.

"No!" Cy reassured me. "But... That's why I need to kill Amber quickly. If she gets a hold of you now... you won't die. You *will* come back. And I won't do that to you. You need time for my blood to fade from your veins, and you need to go back to being human, without some three-hundred-year-old demon keeping you from living your life."

I was furious, and I hated him. He was a murderer and a liar. He put me in danger. He put people I loved in danger, and two of them may not make it through the night. One of those people might have been my husband one day if Cy's very existence hadn't been enough to make me question my happiness with him. He had given me his blood, which could possibly damn me for all eternity. He gave me no choice in any of this. He just decided and acted, leaving me to deal with the consequences. But then...

If Sam and Emily had been safe and not fighting for their lives, wasn't this all I'd ever hoped for? Something passionate, thrilling, and dangerous? Hadn't I gotten exactly what I'd wished for? I had wanted him to fuck off and die moments before, but knowing that that was actually his intention created a feeling in my chest like my lungs had been deflated and my heart squeezed dry. He'd taken my say in all of this away from me, and was about to do it again.

I was deep in the sand, and it had closed over my head.

I hated him... and I loved him. And I hated myself for it.

"Don't," I sobbed. I hadn't even realized I was crying. I stepped toward him and reached for his hand; he grabbed it and pressed my palm to his lips. "Don't do anything stupid," I pleaded, kneeling before him, where he sat in the chair. I put my other hand on his chest. "Don't die. I fucking hate you right now, but I can't imagine my life if you hadn't come into it. I want to help you get rid of Amber, but not if it means losing you- not like that." I stared into his eyes. "I love you, Cy. I hate you, and I love you. I wish I fucking didn't, but I do. And if I might die, or if you have to leave me..." I trailed off, not even wanting to say it out of embarrassment. I rubbed the fabric of his collar between my fingers, feeling the texture, looking at the shirt rather than at him. "This may be our only chance for this."

His grip on my hand tightened and he pulled me up and into his lap. I gasped as his body pressed against mine, the saltwater scent of him filling my head. With no sweet little moments to lead up to it, he wrapped his free hand around my waist and kissed me hard.

If his blood had made me feel strong, it was nothing to how strong he felt to me. "Don't," I breathed as he kissed down my neck.

He pulled back slightly with a sly grin and a growl and said, "I promise not to bite."

I pulled myself closer to him and said, "Not that. Don't hold back. You can't hurt me tonight- your blood will make sure of it." I knew as I said it that it was true. He frowned and started to back away. "No!" I pulled him closer again. "When was the last time you didn't have to restrain yourself? You don't have to hold back tonight, Cy."

He struggled for a moment, and then raised The Brow at me. "In that case... I may have to break my promise."

When he kissed me again, I felt a roughness that hadn't been there before. Something else was different. I could feel them: his fangs. He had unleashed the animal inside, and I was as desperate for him as he was for me, for a thrill that had nothing to do with the fear I'd been fighting all night. Now I got it. I finally understood why people rushed into erotic pairings in times of high risk and danger. It made everything so much more intense, knowing it could be the last time you got to experience something like that. It distracted from the sheer terror of the actual situation, giving the adrenaline coursing through your body an outlet based in rapture rather than fear.

He stood, still clinging to me, and walked us toward the bed. He tore my ruined shirt from the neckline down and kissed along the soft skin of my breasts that showed above my bra. I felt a pinch as he gave a soft bite, his fangs drawing just a few drops of blood. The thrill of his hands, which had proceeded to relieve my lower half of its coverings, mixed with the sharp sting of his bite, nearly drove me over the edge.

I returned the favor, ripping his shirt and hearing the buttons land everywhere. He lifted me, my legs wrapping around his waist, as we'd once before done in this very house. This time, however, he laid me back on the soft bed rather than a hard kitchen counter. He entered me and I gasped as we finally came together.

I had once pondered about how, while things with Sam were good, I didn't know if they could be better. I had known different. This wasn't just different.

This was mind-bending. Every movement, every touch, every breath, every beat of my heart was its own climax. We wrapped ourselves around each other with every thrust and undulation as though nothing could ever separate us, physically or spiritually. Nothing I'd ever experienced came close, and I knew, as we gave in to the pull we felt upon each other, that nothing would ever come so close again. Each little explosion of ecstasy was blended with heartbreak in equal measure, and the passion was insurmountable.

I knew then that letting him go would be the single most painful thing I'd ever do, if I could even bring myself to accept him leaving me. The sand had covered my head. There was no escape.

Chapter 29

Opal

I looked at the blood I had accumulated. Tonight, the fourteenth night, would be the night I could break free. If it didn't work, it never would. This was a feast, and I would gorge myself upon it. I waited until just before sunset and took out every last packet, draining each one to empty. I felt strength I hadn't had for over a month returning to me. I only hoped it was enough.

Cyrus came down the steps and sat in his chair. His usual countenance of distinct dislike that he wore upon entering was gone, replaced with a careful curiosity. Our conversation the previous night had shifted something between us and we both felt it. But I'd be damned all over again if I was going to let it keep me from getting out.

I played the game for a bit, sinking into our silence, which was more charged than usual, but without as much of the malice. I needed time to make sure the blood had infused every part of me with strength before I made an attempt, or he might find a way to prevent me from leaving.

"Your eyes are emerald tonight," he commented, starting the conversation.

Emerald. Interesting. That was an adventurous color for me. I suppose I was no longer starving, and my body could feel the plan coming to fruition. I didn't reply. I couldn't think of anything to say in response.

"I liked them better last night," he said quietly, in the same gentle voice as his repeated question the night before. He didn't mention what color they'd been, knowing I would understand.

That was not expected. A compliment. Compliments to me were usually in the form of mortal men trying to get into my pants or from other vampires flattering my strength and power in hopes of entering my good graces. I felt like I should respond, but wasn't sure what was appropriate to say to your captor when he said something nice. I went with, "Thank you."

The silence returned. I felt the blood reaching a peak within me and knew I would break out soon. I had to keep him talking, keep him distracted.

"Should I ask again?" I said with little hope.

He smirked at me. It was actually a very attractive expression, full of impishness and humor without taking away from the handsomeness of his face. "Should I yet again answer with my own question?"

I laughed- a laugh with actual humor. I couldn't remember ever laughing like that. Ever. Not once. The basement, the isolation, Cyrus. It was all changing me, and I couldn't decide if I liked it. But I did know, whether or not I did, I couldn't abide it, at least not for long. I needed a kill right away. It had been two weeks of no contact with the rest of the Council, and I could guarantee Zilpher or some other Councilor or assistant was looking for me and would find me immediately, and I couldn't show that I'd been weakened. To show anything less than the strength I was known for would be as good as inviting death.

I looked at Cyrus, wondering if I could do it; if he would be the kill. It seemed unlikely, and not just because I'd grown fond of my jailer, like I swore I wouldn't. It was because he'd already eluded death by my bite once. What would stop him from doing it again? I'd need to take enough from him to get out, then find a kill out on the street. Yes, that was the way to do it.

I needed him talking, though. Not focused on my hands, which I needed to wrap in the chains, to increase the tension on them. "You told me about your color," I said, prompting him. "And I know of Elsie Taylor, your great love." I paused, as if the next question was precious to me, which I suppose it was, at least on some level. "What was your name?"

"Human name or true name?" He asked.

"Cyrus isn't one of them?" I replied. Anything to get him to focus on the words, not on me.

He smiled, but it was a sad, dry little thing. "I suppose it is now. It wasn't always." I could see his mind starting to time travel, and his eyes listed off to the side of me. Perfect. I slowly tightened the chains around my wrists and hands as he spoke.

"Before... when I was human the first time, my name was Cian. A strong, proper Irish name. When Amber changed me, she gave me a name so similar, only changing one letter to make a whole new name which reflected the soul shown in my eyes. Cyan."

I had completely frozen. He might have hit me for the look on my face. "*Amber* is your sire?"

He looked stunned, then frustrated. He'd slipped up. This was the most unexpected thing I'd heard from him other than when I realized he was the man from the island.

"Cyrus. Cyan. Whatever the fuck your name is... did you just say that Amber, my sire, the closest thing I have to a friend, lied to me? That she knew you before she found me on that island? That you and I share a sire?"

He remained silent, trying to figure out what to say next. Would he answer at all? Would it be the truth if he did? Lies? The revelation of lies I'd believed for a decade? The blood finally reached its apex, however, and combined with my heightening rage. I brought my arms forward as hard and as fast as I could, breaking open the chains around my wrists. His eyes widened, but before he could form a word, I growled, "Fuck it all. Fuck everything. Fuck *you*." And I lunged for him, my fangs making sweet contact with his skin and breaking through.

I sucked down the elixir of fresh blood pouring over my tongue, but there was precious little room left in my system after my feast before, and I needed a kill. The blood flowing into me was human, not vampire, and I couldn't risk failing to finish him off, so I threw him to the floor. He clapped a hand to his neck where I'd opened the vein, trying to apply pressure to slow the flow of blood.

"Don't think I've finished with you," I threatened, then bounded up the stairs.

Braun stood by the door and saw me fly out of the basement. His face was a mask of terror. I should have ripped him limb from limb, but I couldn't waste a second. Zilpher or Amber could be right outside, waiting. I launched out into the night and ran as fast as I could, becoming nearly invisible, a quick breeze to the humans I passed. I heard crying as I ran and sniffed the air. It was a girl, alone, and I could smell the combination of drink and drugs on her. I sniffed again. It wouldn't be enough to affect me, I decided. Most of the chemicals had already worked their way out of her system.

I found her walking down an otherwise empty road, a sweatshirt held tight around her. It was June in Florida. Not exactly sweater weather. She was suffering the effects of withdrawal already.

No matter, because I zipped up beside her and whisked her into a nearby alleyway. She looked at me with a mix of fear and hope. She opened her mouth to say something, but I had no time, not even for the apology I nearly uttered as I grabbed her tightly and opened a fount in her throat.

Her life rushed into me, filling me with all the lost strength I recognized as my own. The gurgling stream of her blood was soured slightly by the remaining drugs and alcohol, but I had been right. It was fading and wouldn't create unnecessary risk by slowing my reflexes or mental processes. I knew I was coming to the end of my capacity for more blood, and she to the end of her life. I pulled even harder at the opening, forcing those last ounces out. The blood began to slow and trickle, until I felt that last drop pass my lips, leaving her completely dry. I let the girl fall to the ground and stood. There was blood down my front- I hadn't exactly been worried about being tidy with this kill- and I'm sure I looked nightmarish because when I faced the entrance of the alley, Cyrus was there. He looked on the scene in horror. It was as I stood staring at him defiantly that several things happened very quickly.

The girl's memory filled my mind. I could still see what was happening around me, but it was like having a daydream. Her life had been fairly average, but lonely. Her name was Kara. She was younger than I'd thought, only fifteen. An outcast, a bookworm, a nerd, but this night she'd finally been invited to a "cool" party with the football team.

But she'd arrived and there was no one there besides her and the team. They had told her the party was just off to a slow start. They convinced her to drink, to smoke, to snort some kind of powder with them, and she obliged because she was finally fitting in. Once she was calm, compliant, and wholly unable to mount any kind of defense, the seniors told the newly recruited freshmen what to do. It was their initiation. They'd barely even had to hold her down, she was so inebriated... They even wore their jerseys... Smith... Perez... Molina...

The images came to me quickly, over the course of a few seconds at most. The horror of it caused me to lean over and vomit blood all over the alleyway. I had seen the aftermath with Indigo, heard the pain in Amber's voice when she talked about it. And now I had experienced it in the memory of a poor girl whom I had killed on the night of her greatest pain. Kara lay dead at my feet, that pain now part of me. When I stood again, Cyrus was still there, unmoving, but I saw a flash, for the briefest instant, of a different color in his eyes. They nearly glowed in the dark with their vibrancy. Cyan.

And then suddenly a second memory hit me, this one not from Kara, but from somewhere deep in my own mind, but connected to Kara's memory. A small boy, also named Molina, who'd looked up at me in adoration, the eyes the same as those which filled with laughter and malice as he violated Kara...

A second life's worth of memories filled my brain like a bullet. The irony of that thought barely cleared my mind before I lost consciousness, and...

I remembered how I died.

Chapter 30

Elsie

I awoke, at first not recognizing my surroundings. The feeling of fear quickly gave way to one of unease as the events of the previous night came back to me, and I sat up. *What,* I thought, *did I just do?* It had felt so easy and natural in the deep of the night- surrounded by exposed secrets and feelings, drunk on the power and strength I'd been granted by Cy's blood, feeling the thrill of surviving a near-death experience- to allow myself to be swept into a whirlwind of passion, but my decisions all seemed rash in the light of dawn...

Dawn. The sun was coming up. The wall in front of the bed faced east to the bay, giving a marvelous view of the sunrise, lightening the sky to soft azure, the sun glowing deep red at the horizon... blood red. I shivered.

I looked around the room. There was certainly a theme; everything was white (walls, ceilings, floors, rugs, furniture) except for any glass items, which were the color of Cy's eyes. The color of his childhood home.

I glanced beside me and realized I was alone. I opened my mouth to call for Cy, but then stopped. I could just leave before he realized I was awake. I climbed out of the bed, looking for my clothes. *Oh no,* I thought. They were torn and covered in blood. There was no way I could wear them out. I went to Cy's closet and pulled out one of his white button-downs. Thankfully my bra had survived the night, so I grabbed it and figured I'd go clean up in the bathroom and use a method I'd seen online once to fashion his shirt into a dress. I came out of the closet and ran right into a fully dressed and groomed Cy, nearly falling backward.

He smiled at me, steadying me with his hands. His eyes were back to their vibrant shade of blue-green that so reminded me of the Gulf waters I grew up swimming in; I guess we both related that color to a feeling of home.

He leaned down and kissed me. Part of me wanted to melt into the kiss, but the other part was very aware that I was wearing nothing and that I was having second thoughts about what we had done the previous night. Thankfully, it was a short kiss.

"Good morning," Cy said. The smile he wore was as sweet and carefree as I'd ever seen it. It was one of the most beautiful things I'd ever beheld, and was nearly enough to break my heart; he'd made it clear that we would never have a future together, and, despite my rash decisions the night before, I wasn't even sure I wanted one if we could.

"Good mor-" Something struck me. "Cy! Your sunglasses! Sunrise!" I looked frantically around the room for his protective eyewear, my momentary feeling of self-consciousness about my nakedness vanishing.

He chuckled, then took the shirt from my hands, wrapping it around my shoulders to offer me cover. After I'd buttoned it, he said, "I made you breakfast," and pulled me out of the bedroom and into the kitchen.

The smell was immediate and mouthwatering upon entering the room. He hadn't made breakfast- he had made a feast. The table was laden with eggs, bacon, sausage, toast, pancakes, fresh-squeezed orange juice, and coffee. It wasn't until I smelled everything that I realized how hungry I was.

I momentarily forgot my concerns; I crossed to the table and immediately started serving myself. I looked at Cy, who was joining me at a much slower pace. He placed a napkin on his lap and made his own plate, with much less food than mine.

I swallowed a large mouthful of bacon and asked, "Why aren't you wearing your sunglasses? I thought you said the sunlight would burn up your eyes."

He motioned to the windows and said, "Specially engineered glass. I don't need to worry about the sun within the walls of my home." The corner of his mouth quirked upward in a cheeky grin. "A little bit nicer than a crypt or coffin, wouldn't you say?"

I smiled back, but felt the unease creeping back in. "It's lovely," I said, trying not to convey the warring emotions within me and failing miserably.

His grin fell and a crease appeared between his brows. "Is the food okay? I haven't made breakfast like this in a long time."

I finished the bite I'd been chewing and set my fork down. I took a big gulp of coffee to buy a few seconds. "I..." my breath caught in my throat and I tried again. "I think we may have made a mistake last night."

Cy's face broke into a mask of pain. "Oh?" He asked. "I thought it was wonderful... I'm sorry if it wasn't for you."

Oh, the male ego. So fragile, even in a three-century-old immortal. I reached for his hand across the table. "It was the best I've ever had in my life. But that's not what I meant."

He traced the lines on my palm as he stared intently at our hands. "What do you mean then?" His voice was flat. He knew what I was going to say; he just didn't want to hear it any more than I wanted to say it.

I looked down at our hands as well, knowing I couldn't watch his face. "There's no future here. You said so yourself, and... I agree. Amber taunted me about my choices in fiction last night. She's right. I've been watching movies and reading books about vampire romances my whole life, never actually believing that they existed- vampires *or* those crazy whirlwind romances. I spent so much time in and out of a relationship with Sam, I never knew passion like what you and I have could exist. But it's not sustainable. I meant it when I said that I love you, but I also hate what comes with you. I hate the danger, I hate the choices, and I *really* hate not even having a choice. I don't even know if Sam and Emily survived the night!" I took my hand back and buried my face in my hands. "I could slit my own wrists right now and just be free of those worries, and I'd be like you, and we'd be together, but I don't want that either. I love my family. I love my friends. We have our whole lives ahead of us. And it would be wonderful if you could just... join *me*. But you can't do that either. We're Romeo and fucking Juliet," I laughed wryly. "Our story only ends in tragedy." I looked back at him. He was watching me with an expression full of as much sadness as I felt. "I love you. I really, really love you. But I have to walk away."

Cy looked at the food on the table. "Okay." There it was again. That same *"okay." Like I said I wanted ice cream.* Nothing more, nothing less. "At least finish your breakfast," he requested, a kind but sad smile on his face. "It will be wasted on only me."

We ate in silence; it was deafening. I was still so torn between all the emotions that fought to be on top. I was relieved that he didn't try to convince me that we could be together just a while longer, though I had almost hoped he would. A small part of me wanted him to tell me no, to grab me and kiss me with the intensity he had last night, to rip his own shirt from me, to make me forget about all the reasons I had for walking away...

"I think I'll go clean up," I said. "Do you have my phone? I need to call Ashley and find out what's happening with Sam and Emily."

"I do," Cy said, starting to clear the table. "I think the battery is dead, but I'll charge it for you." Then he leaned over and kissed the top of my head. The small touch was enough to send sparks up inside my chest and melt my resolve. I rose and turned away before I could make another mistake. "Take your time," he said. "And we'll leave when you're ready."

"Thank you," I said over my shoulder.

The bathroom was spectacular. All white, as with the rest of the condo, but the freestanding bathtub and walk-in shower were both made of translucent glass in *his* color. I pulled the shirt off and stared at my reflection, my eyes falling on nearly faded bruises and pinprick cuts across my neck, chest, waist, thighs. There was no evidence I'd been beaten nearly to death the night before, only of what happened after.

I turned away and decided, as tired as I felt from being up most of the night, I'd rather relax than stand, and started to pour a bath. I had just climbed in the tub when Cy came through the door looking panicked.

I reached for my towel, more out of shock than modesty. "Cy, what-"

He rushed over and pulled me out of the tub, holding me like a damsel in distress as he carried me back into his bedroom, as I soaked his shirt and dripped water everywhere due to my hysterical thrashing. "No, Cy! What are you doing? Stop!" He deposited me on the bed and stepped back.

"I'm sorry," he said, regret etched all over his face.

237

"Cy, I can't..." Suddenly the words were struggling to come out. "I can't just jump in bed with you one more time for the memories, it... it doesn't work l-like that, and-" I tried to stand up, but my feet felt unsteady. I looked at him in horror as they gave out under me. He caught me and laid me back down. "What did you do...?" I asked for the second time in twenty-four hours. My vision was starting to blur. He'd drugged me, I realized with a shot of rage.

"I'm not going to touch you," he said, attempting to sound reassuring, but failing in light of his choice to drug me. "I promise. I had to get you out of the water- I didn't want you to drown in the bath. But you can't leave. Amber's still looking for you." It was harder to focus on his words, and my eyes were closing. "I want you to have your life, and for that to happen, I can't leave you alone... yet."

And then sleep took me.

Chapter 31

Elsie

My mouth was dry. That was the first thing I noticed. The second thing was that my eyelids felt heavy, almost too heavy to lift them. I tried, but slammed them shut again as a brilliant red light assaulted my vision.

"Where am I?" I mumbled. Third realization: I was sitting up, and I was in motion.

I felt a hand gently brush my hair back, then fall down my arm to clutch my hand. "You're with me," Cy said.

"Cy..." I smiled. Fourth realization: Cy was here. My brain may have been working slowly, but having someone I loved nearby was a good sign, right?

I felt a stab of fear under my relief. Something was tugging at the corners of my mind. I tried to remember. It came back to me slowly: His confession about what he was; the fact that he'd forced me to drink his blood while I had been unconscious; our night together, pretending that we could actually make things work; the morning, when I'd told him I couldn't do it... and then he'd drugged me to prevent me from leaving.

My eyes snapped open, the awareness of my current situation banishing some of the grogginess, and the rest of the effects clearing up quickly as my pulse sped up, pumping vampire blood through my body. I yanked my hand away from Cy's. I looked frantically around. I was in the front seat of his car, fully dressed in clothes he must have purchased at some point since they weren't mine, and we were driving along the shoreline through a beach town I didn't recognize.

"Cy!" I looked at him in horror. "What did you do? What the *fuck* did you do?"

He stared straight ahead, his sunglasses hiding whatever his eyes might have shown. "I did what I had to."

"You fucking drugged me!" I screamed, tugging at the car door.

"Elsie, please stop," Cy said, an urgent note to his plea. "The door won't open, and I need to get you far away as quickly as I can. You need to be well hidden before I confront Amber."

"Are you a fucking idiot?" I cried. "She's been tracking us both, manipulating us this whole time, and you think that she won't find and kill me just because you take me somewhere else?"

He flinched. "I don't know what else to do. She changed the game by forcing us to meet. I told you, we were never supposed to do that. I don't know if she knew I'd fall in love with you, but if anything, it's made her more vicious. It's not just about her revenge ritual anymore- now it's about causing me as much pain as possible and about hurting you because you have my love and she doesn't."

I looked around again, hoping for a clue as to where we were. I couldn't tell if the sun was rising or setting, but it sat low on the horizon. Palms were whipping in the wind, and a dark cover of clouds was moving in from behind us. "Cy, where are you taking me?" I had started to cry. "Please... tell me."

"Not now. I can't tell you because I'm going to give you your phone to call your mother. You should know..." He paused, and his voice was strained as though what he was about to say upset him. "Cyrus Kelley doesn't exist. This car, my condo... they're purchased through one of the banks run by my... friends. They're untraceable. And if you tell her that I've kidnapped you, and she calls the police, Amber will find out and use that to draw you out." It was unnecessary, but he continued to emphasize his point. "She will hurt your family, or worse."

The thought of anything happening to my mom or dad, to Danielle, was like a kick in the stomach. "Why have me call her at all then?"

"Because your friend was hurt badly enough to be in the hospital and you were not there due to being ill (so they think), and by now, one of your friends will have called your mother to check on you. Since you are not there, they will have begun to worry. You need to reassure them that you're not hurt. You should tell them that we'd been having dinner at my place when you got the call about Sam, and then fell ill before you could leave; and that I've been taking wonderful care of you since you were worried the car ride home would have been enough to make you sick all over again; and that you'll be home just as soon as the worst of it passes. Which is true. Once I've taken care of Amber, I will take you home, and you will never see me again, something I'm sure you'll be fine with given my less than gentlemanly behavior," he finished with a grimace.

And there it was. He knew that if he'd laid this all out for me from the jump that I'd have gone along with any plan he had, so he took the choice away from me on purpose, knowing how I'd react. He'd drugged and kidnapped me to cement in my mind that it would be no loss when he was gone, to make it easier for me to let him go. It had nothing to do with him being a fiend- he was still trying to protect me. I wished I hadn't figured it out, because, through my anger at what he did, I felt a pang of sorrow cut through my chest at my understanding that this was all for show. Despite it all, that little part of me wanted him and everything that came with having him. He'd done unspeakable things. He'd lied, manipulated, and abducted me, and yet... I trusted him.

I was a fucking idiot.

"Fine," I said, taking the phone and turning it on. Cy motioned for me to put it on speaker. I hit the button, then dialed Mom, trying my best to sound like I was unwell when she picked up.

"Elsie?" She said. "David, it's her!" She had called to my dad. "Elsie? Are you there? Where are you?"

"I'm fine, Mom," I groaned. "I'm sorry I haven't called, I'm still just-" I threw in a fake gag for effect; thank you, acting classes- "I was at Cy's when I got the call about Sam, and I thought I was just sick from hearing the news, but then I couldn't stop barfing. He's been really great, making sure I'm taken care of." I paused, dreading the answer to my question. "What's the word on Sam?"

Mom's voice was sad and annoyed, which was to be expected after I vanished for... one day? Two? I wasn't sure, but it was clear the sun was going down now, as it was getting redder and lower. "He's out of surgery, but they don't know yet. Jack hit them both really hard. Sam's girlfriend, Emily... she didn't make it to the hospital. She died on the scene."

Something she said wasn't right. I nearly forgot to sound sick when I asked, "I thought Jack's Jeep had been stolen... wasn't it?"

242

"Oh, Elsie, that's what he said, but they found him within the hour, still driving the Jeep around. He said some girl named Amber had tricked him into giving it to her, but they have him on a security camera getting into the car before he drove it right into them. Who would have thought after all the time you spent with him... imagine if you'd still been with Sam!"

"I don't think..." I'd been about to tell her I didn't think Jack would have done that if I had still been with Sam, but that was a longer conversation that I didn't want to have, now or ever. I gave another gag, this one very nearly real, and said, "Thanks, Mom. I'll be praying for Sam. I think I'm about to have another round with the toilet... I'll call you when I'm up to driving home. Love you." And I hung up before she could say another word. I burst into tears. That might be the last time ever got to talk to my mother, and I knew it. And it was all lies. Cy, of course, having heard everything, took my phone and turned it back off before throwing it out the window. He then reached over and took my hand.

"I'm so sorry."

"Why?" I asked. "I knew he hated us, but I didn't think he'd *kill* any of us..."

Cy's lips were curled in disgust. "I'm certain we can thank Amber for that. I know quite well how she can convince a broken man to commit atrocities, all with the promise of feeling whole and earning her love. She's as close to a succubus as we have in real life."

I nearly began to laugh hysterically at the idea of "real life," since nothing in my life felt real anymore, but the tears wouldn't stop. The weight of everything that had happened since April (had it really only been two months?) hit me like a sack of bricks, and I broke down. Cy spoke to me, but I barely heard him. His voice was calm and compassionate, but none of it mattered because someone I liked was dead and someone I had once loved might be next; that is, if Amber didn't get to me first and kill me, turning me into a vampire since I was chock full of fresh vampire blood. And that was assuming she didn't manage to just kill me anyway.

I cried for so long that I eventually just ran out of steam, right as Cy pulled into a parking lot on a little island we'd crossed a bridge to get to. It looked familiar, but then, lots of state parks in Florida were set up in a similar way.

"Can you tell me where we are yet?" I asked, my voice worn out and devoid of any feeling.

"Caladesi Island," he answered without hesitation. That was surprising.

Curiosity crept back into my voice. "We're in Clearwater? How are we only in Clearwater if I've been unconscious all day?"

"We were only in the car for a few hours before you woke up," Cy said. "I drove in every direction for a while, trying to throw Amber off. I don't know if it worked, but I hope it did. We're going to park the car here, then go on foot through the woods. At the beach, we'll double back. There's an RV park where Jett arranged for us to have shelter and transportation waiting. From there... I'll figure it out." His usually unflappable confidence was shattered. His voice shook and his hands brushed his hair back nervously. If nothing else, *this* made me truly afraid.

Chapter 32

Elsie

Cy pulled my arm, trying to hurry me through the woods. The wind was picking up, and I wondered if we were going to have a storm. The clouds to the south had looked like bands of a tropical storm that had possibly broken apart as it moved north. I didn't know- my mind hadn't been too focused on the weather lately.

He ran ahead of me, never letting go of my hand. Thankfully, I'd been training for this, despite never knowing it was going to happen. All of my long runs (plus the healthy helping of vampire blood still running through me) had made this easier work than it might have been otherwise.

When we tore out of the jungle and onto the beach, we saw the last glimmer of light illuminating the waves, the sun having set before we'd even started running. I touched my hand to my neck, where two small cuts had already begun to heal.

When we'd parked on the island, I stopped Cy from opening the car door at first. "When did you eat last?"

He looked confused. "We had breakfast together this morning, but I don't need-"

"No," I interrupted. "When was the last time you had blood?"

Confusion turned to discomfort and annoyance. "You don't need to worry about-"

"Yes, I do," I interrupted again. "You need to be at your best to fight Amber, since I'm sure she's probably already murdered a few people tonight. I'm not suggesting you go kill anyone, but if a small dose would give you an edge..." I took a deep breath and put his hand to the tender skin on my neck.

"No," Cy pulled back. "Not like that. Once we make it to the RV, there should be a small supply waiting."

I scoffed. "You already tasted it last night. Remember?"

His eyes traveled to where I'd placed his hand. "More than you could know."

"Then just fucking do it! We may not make it to the RV without it. Just don't take a lot," I reminded him. "I still need to be able to keep up."

I hated to admit it, but him feeding from me was nearly as erotic as making love to him- nearly. It was one thing all the fiction got right. His lips and fangs pulling the mixture of my blood and his own from the sensitive area above my collarbone could have driven me to try for a moment of weakness if not for the fact that we had no idea how much of a head start we had, if we had one at all.

Cy looked over at me on the beach as I paused to observe the scene. The waves were shimmering in Cy's color, which might have given me a sense of calm if not for the sky, which, burning a deep blood-red, heavily contrasted with the water and made it glow eerily.

He saw my hand go to my throat and paused in his running. "Are you alright? Did I take too much?" He asked.

"No," I assured him. "It was just a reflex. I feel it healing. Your blood is really something."

He grimaced. "That it is. But we need to move. We're too out in the open. Catch your breath and let's go."

"I'm good," I told him. "I can run."

We took off through the woods again, and had just passed a sign leading toward the RV park when I felt myself thrown sideways, Cy's hand ripped from mine. I landed headfirst against a tree and lost consciousness immediately.

*   *   *

It couldn't have been long after I'd been knocked out when I came to. I felt the back of my head where a small lump was already starting to fade. I heard the nearby sounds of blows landing, groans, and even growls. I might have thought there were dogs fighting, but I knew it was a different kind of creature. I opened my eyes, stumbling to my feet. I was getting really tired of being knocked out.

I took a few steps while my vision centered and saw Amber attacking as Cy tried to stay between her and me. I could tell in an instant...

We were going to lose.

While Amber was graceful, moving with ease and seeming to require no effort, Cy was wearing down. I could see it in his missteps, the times when she bested him almost without trying. My heart pounded painfully again, as though it was trying to beat out of my chest to escape before it could be stopped by an outside force.

Amber saw me first. "She awakens!" She laughed. Her voice was terrifying in its beauty. "Cyan, your little girlfriend is awake and has come to your rescue." She lunged at him, swiping at his face with her nails, drawing blood. She used the momentary distraction caused by the pain to thrust her fist at the side of his head, knocking him down.

"Cy!" I screamed. He launched back to his feet, desperate to keep Amber from getting to me.

"Elsie, go!" He called. "I'll do what I can, just go!" He threw the keys to his car at me, and I scrambled to pick them up. I hesitated, not wanting to leave him. I'd love to say that moment of hesitation was what sealed my fate, but the truth was that what happened next was over so quickly, I'd never had a chance.

Amber, deciding the game was over, grabbed Cy by the throat and threw him as easily as if he'd been a rag doll. He landed against a large rock, where he slumped to the ground in pain. He may have been immortal and strong, but he could still be hurt.

Amber walked over to me and lifted me the same way she'd grabbed Cy, her hand around my throat, cutting off both air and blood flow. My head began to swim. Vampire blood or no, I was nowhere near strong enough to fight her. I was just about to accept what was going to happen, that I'd be killed, and I'd revive as a vampire- at least Cy and I could be together, as long as Amber didn't kill us for good afterward- when she dropped me at her feet. She spun and looked at Cy.

"Two and a half centuries, we've been playing this game, my dear," she taunted. "Two and a half centuries of me besting you much more often than you did me. I've been doing what we're literally *made* to do. I kill, and I feed. Humans hurt and kill each other every day, and I choose the worst of them for myself. My victims are *evil*, Cyan, and you know it!"

"Elsie's not evil," he panted. "And neither were any of the other girls you've picked over the centuries. Like Fiona."

"You don't know that! Women like this- like your precious Fiona- take things that don't belong to them! They're careless with other people! I was abandoned by my lover and my family because of a girl like that, and I became the victim. But I'm not anymore! Now I am the predator, and I feed on the worst of humanity, and, yes, once a decade, I take an innocent for my own pleasure. But you know as well as I that they don't stay innocent forever. You understood this. We hunted together, ending young lovers before they could break each others' hearts, allowing them to die, not knowing that pain."

I felt a jolt of uncertainty as I realized that I was beginning to understand her. Amber chose horrible people as her victims, it was true, but was it worth the loss of innocent life that she claimed as well? It was the age-old philosophical debate. Should innocent people suffer if it means that guilty ones are brought to justice? Or should they both be allowed to carry on? For Amber, it was an obvious answer; I personally found her choice ghastly. No innocent life was worth her brand of justice.

She pointed at Cy, continuing. "Then *you* abandoned me too- not just abandoned me, but you tried to take away the one thing that gave me purpose- killing these creatures." She curled her lip at the word. "And so I made it a game, a competition between us. It became *fun* again, a challenge. And in all that time, I never thought that if I just threw one of these *cattle* at you that you'd actually fall in love with her. I mean, come on! What's so special about her now? She's exactly like all of them. She's weak. She's nothing!"

Cy spat a mouthful of blood at her feet. "She's not you. That's something."

Amber's eyes widened with rage. "Well, if you feel so strongly about that, let's test a theory." She turned to me, a wicked gleam in her eye. "Let's see if you still love her as much when she's like me."

"You can turn me into a vampire," I sneered, "but I'll never be like you. Not knowing what you've done."

Amber suddenly looked ecstatic. "Well... there's the fun part. If this works... you won't remember what I've done. Or anything Cy's done, or anything *you've* done. You're going to be my blank slate. And then... we'll see if you end up like me."

With that, she pulled a gun out of a holster hidden under her jacket, and pointed it at my head. I looked at Cy and heard him cry, "No!"

I might have heard him say my name too, but it was cut off by the bang as the gun went off, and I heard no more.

Chapter 33

My head was pounding. I felt the gunshot all over again, even though I knew it had happened a decade before. In reality, I shouldn't have been able to have a headache at all, but my mind was being cleaved in two. I was Opal, and I was Elsie. I remembered both of my lives, so different from one another, with two very different people living them- different thoughts, different feelings. I was both of me, and I was neither. The two people now sharing my mind were taking turns floating to the surface, like oil and water. We both shared the same memories, but there was a battle for control in every moment.

I opened my eyes directly into a pair of very concerned hazel eyes. I knew him now, the name he'd asked me to call him. Not Cyrus. Not Cyan.

"Cy..." I breathed. I reached for his face. He grabbed my hand and squeezed it, his eyes going wide.

"Elsie?" He breathed right back. Hearing me call him Cy had given him hope, and it nearly passed into me.

I opened my mouth, my own shadow of a hope pushing me to say, "*Yes! Yes, it's me! I remember you! I love you! Thank you for finding me and bringing me back!*" But the words were stuck in my throat. I couldn't say them because, at the same time, I was furious at being held like this, the feeling of vulnerability. I tried to say, "*No, you asshole! Let go of me!*" My mouth opened and closed like a hooked fish searching for water, and my eyes blinked rapidly.

Cy's face darkened with worry. My silence made him question that tiny flicker of hope. "Opal?" He asked, his voice dulling as he deflated.

I tried to make some kind of answer, but I didn't know how to respond. He'd asked me if I was Elsie, and then if I was Opal. The answer to both was yes, and the answer to both was no.

This was the beginning of the madness.

"Cy..." I said again. It was the only thing I could get out. His brow knit together, and something in my eyes and in my inability to speak finally struck him. His face took on a resolute look, and he wrapped his arms around me.

God love him, Elsie thought as he lifted me from the ground and carried me out of the alley, leaving poor Kara to be found by someone in the early hours of dawn. He began to walk back to my home. No. It was *his*. I knew that now. Amber had given it to me- a cruel trick. Make me kill my lover, then disguise his home as a gift to me.

I buried my face in his shirt, not wanting anyone who happened to be out to see the gore all over me and call the police. That was the last thing I needed.

We walked into the lobby, Braun affecting an air of seeing nothing. Cy, arms still wrapped around me, had the elevator attendant take us up.

He set me down inside the door, but didn't let go. Probably for the best. The oil and water state of my brain came

252

complete with a sensation of a bottle shaken to see the effect of the two liquids fighting to be on top. I wasn't sure if I could stand. I possessed more physical and mental strength than almost any vampire in existence, and *human memories* were threatening to take me down; conversely and at the same time, I was a self-possessed and confident woman, yet the memories of the decade since my mortal death were going to break me.

Walking to the bathroom with his arm around my waist for support, he guided me directly into the shower without attempting to undress me. He'd always been so respectful of boundaries, but I didn't care. I didn't want the feel of soaked and bloodstained clothes on me and stripped them off even as they collected water around me. My movements were mechanical and only happened as the two halves of my mind came to an agreement and allowed it to happen. Elsie knew that Cy had already seen my body, and Opal was very free with my form regardless. He was seeing me at my most exposed- what was nudity compared with the nakedness of a mind stripped bare? I thought about all of the men I'd slept with and then killed in the last ten years, the others with whom I'd shared my body without a care. The sheer intensity of my newly uncovered human emotions came bubbling up, and Elsie began to weep, the horror of my existence spilling over the top, threatening to consume my entire mind.

Still in his own clothing, Cy held me, the water covering us both, letting the blood on my face, in my hair, drip onto his shirt, staining it.

"Oh, *God...*" I moaned. I nearly collapsed again, but Cy held me, washing me, then drying me and wrapping me in a large, luxurious towel. I'd bought it when I moved in here as Opal; it was the kind of thing I'd always loved but never wanted to spend the money on as Elsie. Luxury and practicality. Innocence and experience. Night and day. All in my own mind.

Once dried and clothed in a nightgown, Cy led me to my bed, to his bed. Everything was confused. It all made sense, and nothing did. My head spun and ached. My body felt like needles covered me, leaving my nerve endings raw and tingling.

I climbed onto the mattress, seeing the first light of day peeking over to light the water on the bay. The beauty of it amazed me, just now looking through my eyes as a vampire to see it the way I never had in my mortal years. Part of my brain knew that sunrise meant it was time to start the day, to shower, get dressed... to go to work. At a job. A job I no longer had or needed. Something about my job... The thought crept in to destroy the peace of the moment.

"Molina!" I cried, sitting up sharply as Cy had tried to cover me with the blankets. I threw them back, my agitation giving me enough strength to stand.

"What?" Cy was bemused by my outburst. I had said next to nothing other than his name since waking, and suddenly I was shouting a word- a name- with such conviction he must have wondered if something had come together for me, if I was fixed.

I was far from fixed.

"Molina!" I growled, spinning to face him. Then the bottle was shaken, mixing the oil and water, and I let out a wail of despair and collapsed to the ground again.

Cy came to my side, lifting me back into the bed. "No!" I shouted, snarling and sobbing.

"What is it?" He demanded, shaking me. "What is happening?" His own eyes reflected the confusion and terror I felt.

I sobbed gently into him, my face buried in his chest even while my arms tried to push him away. I couldn't control anything. I wasn't even "I." I was "we"- Elsie, Opal, and some consciousness borne of the combination of the two who had no name of my own. I wanted him to hold me and tell me it was all okay; I wanted him to fuck off and die. There was no in-between; there was no ability to quiet any one voice in my mind; there was no way to tell him what was happening to me because each voice wanted control of my mouth and none would relinquish my own claim.

We spent the day in a combination of embracing and battling. The only reason I didn't kill him was that the parts of me that had once been Elsie wouldn't let me. Cy was unable to discern from my incoherent growls and sobs what had happened in the alley, why I wouldn't or couldn't speak, why I was in the throes of a violent madness that I feared would never end.

By noon, I had burned myself out into a whimpering mess of tears and bruises from the wounds that I (both intentionally and unintentionally) had inflicted upon myself. Cy held onto me still, a comforting and annoying presence. I wondered what he would do, how he would feel about me if he knew that I no longer possessed the ability to reason. That the parts of me that had been Opal, which had begun to have affection for him in my own way, now hated him beyond the loathing I'd felt before. Because he'd done this to me. Abducted me, kept me chained, forced me to confront feelings I'd once only observed with a comfortable detachment, and ultimately forced me to escape recklessly, to kill a random girl to regain my strength, and to remember things I never wanted to recall to begin with. I didn't need human memories! They were what made other vampires weak, and now I was among them... lower even.

Meanwhile, my human side was screaming for Cy to comfort me, to hold me and never let go, to tell me it would all be okay even when I knew it wouldn't be because of the horror I'd seen in Kara's memory. In my mind, Jimmy Molina was just four years old, and yet... I couldn't even form the thought. The state of my sanity was fragile enough without going there.

But neither voice would allow the other through. Well into the day, Cy kept a vigil by my side, hoping for me to come

255

out of my state, to tell him if I remembered. I did remember. But I didn't know if that was a good thing.

Chapter 34

Cy had fallen asleep next to me on the bed. I realized this when I awoke and the sky was already an inky black. One of his arms was draped over my waist protectively.

The second realization that came to me was that I could control my limbs. I lifted my arm and looked at my fingers in the light. I- Elsie- was amazed and horrified by the sight of the strong tapered fingers that had brought death to hundreds. I- Opal- longed to let those fingers grab onto a new victim and vent my frustration through more bloodshed. It was in that moment that I realized I was making deals with myself without intending to. Elsie and Opal were too different to agree on what I could do or say, but I recognized that if I couldn't let each part of myself have their way, I would be reduced to a feral creature forever. I found the things that both of me knew I needed to and wanted to do. Something normal for both of me. Easy.

I stood up and went to the bathroom, where I looked at myself in the mirror. My hair was a mess and my eyes were shifting faster than ever, with a new color every few seconds. I tried to get a brush through the tangles unsuccessfully, and opted instead to just soak myself in a bath.

The clear glass of the tub was the exact color that Cy's eyes had been before I had drained him in the woods. It was strange to see Opal's memories through Elsie's eyes. It was surreal, that part of my mind still feeling very much human, yet being able to recall with perfect clarity the ecstasy of ripping into soft flesh and having the blood rush over my tongue and into my belly, filling me and strengthening me. It was pure joy and pure horror. Watching the memories, it felt almost like I had always been there, screaming at myself to stop and not hearing a word of it.

I tried my best to silence my mind, feeling the cracks in my sanity threatening to reopen and swallow me whole. Was this what my recurring dream had meant? The old one about the sand. I hadn't had the dream in ten years, but for part of me, it had only happened days ago. Was the sand not my love for Cy, but rather my own insanity?

I let the hot water pour over me and put my head all the way under the water. Vampires *can* breathe, but it isn't necessary, so I simply let myself be still, feeling the water enclose me and soothe me. I had a brief moment of panic, my mind flashing to being human when this would not have been possible, when holding myself underwater like this would have meant death. After a few moments of reminding myself this was not only okay but perfectly easy, I relaxed into the water and opened my eyes, the light in the room filtering through the glass and creating a world of perfect green-blue. It was like swimming in the ocean and seeing the light color the world around you. It was that perfect serenity that came with knowing how tiny you were compared to the sea, and knowing that it was okay to just be small.

I still didn't know if I was either of my selves any more or less than the other. It would take time to work through, and it occurred to me on both mental planes that I would need to figure it out quickly. Last night, when I had escaped the basement, I knew that the threat of a coup from within the Council or some other threat from Amber and Zilpher was very real as long as I was weakened. As long as I lacked the ability to even move or speak of my own volition, I was an even bigger target than I had been the night before.

I heard the ethereal sound of footsteps echoing through the water. They were approaching slowly, cautiously. When they stopped, I turned my head to the side and looked through the glass. Cy was sitting on the floor, staring at me through the tub wall. His face was an amalgam of a thousand emotions. Fear, concern, hope, love... I saw these and more as he gazed at me. I felt a stab of guilt that I couldn't tell him what was wrong, what I needed from him, that I needed nothing from him, that I *wanted* nothing from him, that I wanted him to hold me and never let go, that I wanted him to go away, that I wanted him to make it all go away and just lay me down on the bed that somehow belonged to us both and to make love to me and make me feel like I had control of myself and my body... to take away my mind... for just a short while...

But I knew he never would, and that I would never want him to. It was why I loved him and why he disgusted and confused me. We stared at each other through the glass, and I pretended the overlay of the color of the tub on his eyes was real, that he was back with me as he was ten years ago, immortal like I was, and we could try to make it through this together, through eternity.

I brought my face out of the water, unsure if I had the ability to speak yet. I stayed submerged to the neck, ready to dive back under the surface if I felt like I was drowning. I didn't want him to ask me about who I thought I was. I still didn't know. I feared I'd never know. The sand threatened to close over my head again, to reduce me to the sobbing beast-woman, and I felt myself start to shake. I couldn't answer that question. He opened his mouth and I nearly screamed, but he asked a different question.

"Why did I take you to the island?"

I stared at him, my body tense but no longer shaking. I'd been asking him this for weeks, and he never answered me. Now I knew. It was a good question. It might not give him the exact answer he sought, but it would certainly tell him if I remembered my life before. I sat up a little more in the tub, realizing I could answer this particular query honestly and without losing my head again. He leaned forward, crossing his arms on the glass edge and resting his head on them, his eyes level with mine. It was a sweet, reassuring posture. My mouth opened and I said, hoarsely, softly, "To save me. From Amber."

His mouth never moved, but I felt the smile. It was in his eyes, the relief, the joy that I had my human mind back; and it was the sadness, the pity, the guilt that I had to remember everything I'd done since I'd died.

I may have been stronger once I became a vampire, but my strength in my human life had been in the size of my heart, and in that moment, the heart won out. I turned my head, unable to look into his eyes as I reached up and grabbed his fingers, giving them a squeeze that probably hurt due to the disparity in our physical strength. If it did, he didn't show it. He reached out with his other hand and ran it over the wild forest of my hair. He stood and bent down to kiss it gently. Then he said, "I'll be right back," and left the bathroom.

I felt a flash of rage as I saw him go, not wanting him to come back, despising the vulnerability I felt. How dare he bring out this soft human side of me and then expect me to just accept it? My teeth ached like they were ready to lengthen and sharpen at any moment...

Yet when he returned, I felt a surge of affection. He *stayed*. He had found me and brought me back, for better or worse. Right now, it definitely seemed worse, but I had to hope it would get better as I came to terms with my two very different pasts, with my own paradoxical voices. I nearly scoffed at myself. Hope breeds eternal misery.

He had a packet of blood in his hand. "Here," he offered. "It's cold, but it's fresher than the rancid stuff you'd been hoarding for two weeks." His mouth quirked up in that sideways smile that once melted me to the floor. He'd known what I was doing, and let me get away with it. Had he known what would happen? I wanted to kiss him... and to bite him.

I discovered I could find my voice as long as I kept any emotion, one way or another, from being the driver behind the words. As soon as I felt something about what I planned to say, the war erupted again, and I couldn't speak. "Thanks," I said robotically, taking the pouch and biting into it hungrily, feeling the sweet nectar revive my body, if not my mind.

Cy turned his head, but kept his gaze reluctantly on me. He was trying to hide something in his expression. It took me only a second to figure it out. Even in the basement, he'd always given me the blood as he left; when he'd seen me over Kara's dead body the night before... he was seeing Elsie- soft, innocent, *human* Elsie- as the demon she'd been turned into. It was disgust. It was revulsion. It was sadness. And something else... guilt.

"It wasn't Amber." I contemplated the truth of my rebirth, only known to half of me up until now. "*You* were my sire."

Then he looked away. Suddenly my mind bore one emotion- anger. "You were going to keep me safe, prevent this from happening to me," I accused. "And when you *failed,* you came back and ruined me!"

I stood, splashing water all over the room. I rushed to him and pressed him to the wall, my hand at his throat. His expression had gone from a reticent sadness to outright fear and confusion.

"Elsie, what-?" He gasped

"I'm not Elsie!" I snarled. Even the parts of me that still felt like Elsie Taylor knew that this statement was true. My fangs had descended, aching at the proximity of his pulsing throat, of the power of his one last drop of vampire blood...

"But... You remember..." He pleaded, crestfallen.

"I remember *everything*. And I *feel* everything. I..." I started to choke on my words and I released him. I stumbled back into the bedroom and knelt by the side of the bed, my face buried in the down of my comforter, which hung over the side, torn completely from its place by my mad thrashing the night before. "Cy," I gasped, the sobs wracking my body again. "I can't be Elsie. And I can't be Opal. I don't know who I am!" He was by my side, wrapping me in a towel, and I looked at him with fire in my eyes. "I can't... I can't think... I can't feel... I feel too much... There are too many thoughts... I'm being swallowed whole by my own mind, by my own memories, and it's your fault!" I started saying each thought as it came to my mind. The words were true but without conviction, and I couldn't look at him as I said them. I stared off into the distance, certainly looking as mad as I felt. "But... It's not your fault. I hate you. *Fuck* you! I love you! And I hate you. Entirely and completely on both counts! I want you to grab me and make love to me again right now. I'll kill you if you try. I want to leave. I want to stay here forever. I want to kill. I want to die..."

He had sat back on the floor, putting distance between us without actually leaving my side. Tears had begun to flow from both of us as I rambled, my mad rantings showing him the extent of the damage that was done. The silence filled the room as effectively as it had filled the basement on many occasions, and for a moment, it nearly filled my mind as well.

"You're right," Cy said, finally shattering the spell of silence. I didn't look at him, worried if I did the din would overtake me again with thoughts and feelings I wished more than anything to not feel. Instead, I waited for him to continue. "It's my fault. But you're also right that it's not my fault. If I'd left you alone, you would be dead- truly dead. I wish more than anything this hadn't happened, that you had gone back to your life, that I never darkened your doorstep again, but *Amber* took that away from you. She targeted you. Her game cost you everything you cared about in life-"

"Not you," I interrupted. "She didn't take you, not completely... and I cared about *you*... I still care about you... and look at me now. I want to fuck you, and I want to kill you and finally take that last drop. I wish I never regained my memory. I wish I'd never lost it. I wish-" The words were spilling out of me again like blood from a wound. I closed my mouth to try to staunch the flow.

Cy waited until the moment had passed to continue. "She took you and twisted you. She made you into Opal-"

"Amber made me nothing!" I roared imperiously. "All that I am is *me*!" He waited several seconds before replying.

"Yes, that's true, too," he conceded. "Without your memories, your experiences, you weren't Elsie anymore. You couldn't be. You were simply a product of your awakening in the woods. You were a blank slate, save for the blood of the vampire... of my blood in you. That's all you could ever be without remembering your mortal life. So yes... that's my fault."

Was he accusing me of having or being nothing of substance since my rebirth? Did he not realize he spoke to his sovereign, to a Councilor? Did *I* not realize that I was no more sovereign than any other girl from the 'burbs? I tried to process these conflicting thoughts, and finally said, "I am and have always been more than just what's in my veins." The words came out cold and hard, with every fiber of my being rebelling against the idea that any part of me was due to anyone else- immortal or not- and not myself.

Yet again, the smile wasn't there, but his eyes were joyful, triumphant. Something in my chest seemed to awaken, a sleeping beast that was, itself, euphoric and proud. I may have been mad, but I was not weak. And yet...

My hands went to my face. The beast roared, wailed, thrashed... and again, I wept.

Chapter 35

I awakened again with the pressure of Cy's arm across my waist. It was comfortable and non-threatening, but a part of me longed for a less comfortable arrangement... well, both parts longed for that. The difference was one part wanted him closer, and the other wanted him dead.

I took a deep breath in and held it for longer than any human would be able to. When I finally released it, I kept blowing til long after there was no air left in my lungs. Elsie and Opal had finally decided to learn about each other, and I- Elsie- was amazed at my physical abilities. I thought back to things I'd done- running so fast I couldn't be seen by humans, holding so still I was a part of the night, the strength as I grabbed prey... better not think about that one too hard if I wanted to remain somewhat sane.

In return, I- Opal- began to reflect on the emotions, felt so strongly by my more human side, and how they came about, the reactions they elicited. I was stunned by how powerful a feeling could be if left unattended and unbound, as though an emotion itself could be a vampire, feeding on all it touched.

I looked to the window, where the sky was dark, but lighter, the higher I looked. It was twilight, the hour at which I would be hunting if not for the events of the last few weeks, and for the voice in my head that refused to accept myself as a "hunter." I went to the shower with a hairbrush and proceeded to attack the rat's nest atop my head. When I finally emerged, clean, combed, and calm, Cy was waiting at the end of the bed.

"Hi," he said. So casual for him.

"Hi?" I asked, my voice dripping with sarcasm, in equal parts meant to tease and wound. "I don't recall you *ever* being quite so informal as to say 'Hi.'"

I heard his breath catch. I was speaking calmly. Hope burst again behind his eyes, but he guarded it well. "Would 'hello' be more acceptable?"

I grinned. I felt my fangs against my lip as I did so and realized it could be encouraging or frightening. I needed to work on that. "Whatever works for you," I said kindly.

I walked over and sat down beside him without looking at him, choosing instead to stare straight ahead of me at the view of the darkened but sparkling city. The lights of boats returning from a day at sea glittered like little stars on the surface of the water. I watched them for a bit, just to think about something inconsequential.

"Are you okay?" Cy asked hesitantly.

I pondered that question. I wasn't sure if I would ever be "okay" again. What was "okay" when your mind, when your sanity was cracked like glass struck with a stone, ready to crumble into shards at the slightest disturbance? I decided it was kinder to him and easier for me to tell a white lie. "Yeah. I guess," I mumbled.

Cy cautiously reached out and touched my hand. I grabbed onto his tightly, still not looking at him. It crossed my

mind to crush the bones in his hand like kindling, but I waved
the thought away. I had other things that I saw as absolute
truths which needed to be dealt with, and I needed all the
voices of my mind working together to do that.

We sat there in silence for nearly an hour, me brooding,
listening to my own mind argue with itself about the things I
could do, couldn't do, should or shouldn't say, how and if and
when I should feed. All the while he looked on, when a
thought occurred to me, partially due to a low rumble I heard.

"Have you eaten?" I asked, finally turning to him. Then I
realized: "What do you eat now? Do you eat food? Or do you
still drink blood?"

He smiled- really smiled- and let out a snort of humor,
thrilled to be able to speak to me, to have a relatively normal
conversation. "I still drink blood sometimes. It doesn't satisfy
like it used to, but that one last drop seems to, I don't know,
spark or something when I do have it. I can get by with very little over a long period. I eat food again, though not much. I
guess I'm lucky in that the bit of vampire in me allows me to
take in very little of anything at all and be okay. You know- I'm
sure you do know- human food doesn't really appeal to vampires much, but I've found the joy in it since becoming mostly
human again. And let me tell you..." He leaned in close like he
was telling a secret. "Fast food is more devilish and seductive
than any works we demons could do."

I chuckled, the humor just barely reaching my heart,
which was still heavy-laden with the madness I struggled every
moment to keep at bay. "That it is..." I trailed off, the corners
of my mind seeming to close in on me, just enough to cause a
fear of ending up catatonic or violent again. I closed my eyes
and receded into myself, to quiet the noise until I could try to
appear normal- relatively so- again. After a few minutes in
which Cy waited patiently for the storm to pass, I asked him,
"But have you eaten? Since being here with me?"

He cocked his head, touched at my apparent concern, and gave my hand a squeeze. "I haven't. I've been busy."

"You should eat," I encouraged. "Go get something."

"I don't need much," he insisted, his stomach giving him away.

"But you're hungry," I insisted right back. "I can hear your stomach growling."

He raised The Brow at me. "Oh, really?" There was joy at the normalcy of our conversation, but also curiosity and just a hint of suspicion in the look.

"Yes. Really." I stood, looking over the bay through the glass walls. "You should eat. I think we have a lot to talk about, and I want us both at our best- not cruel with hunger- to do so." I felt powerful, confident, relishing taking charge of the conversation. Like myself- both selves- at my best. Thank God I was learning to work together with myself.

He stood and faced me, confusion overtaking the playful expression. "We do?"

"Yes," I replied. "I have questions, things I never learned from you or from Amber, other things I never even considered until recently, things to figure out, and decisions to make. But not until we've both fed."

I turned to my closet, preparing to get dressed, but he grabbed my arm. "What do you mean 'fed'? Elsie-" I snarled at the name. It didn't fit anymore, and I wished he'd stop-

"Whatever the hell you want me to call you!" He threw his hands in the air. "You can't go out there yet." He turned me to face him full on and held my shoulders. "You say you're okay, but I know better. I've been with you at some of your darkest moments as a human and as a vampire, and I've been here with you the last couple days, which have been pretty damn dark too. I don't even know how much you were aware of-"

"All of it!" I snapped.

"Good!" He threw back at me. "Then you know why I can't just leave and let you go out. You're still not all there. You'd have a body count that would bring the rest of the Council here faster than lightning!"

"Which is why I need the *kill!* I need to be ready when they come, because someone's coming no matter what and you know it. I have to be stronger!"

He winced when I said "kill," hearing the violent word from a mouth that no longer belonged to a sweet and innocent human he once loved. That was fine. I appreciated him helping me come to some semblance of sanity, but I didn't know if love was something I'd ever feel again, for him or anyone else. I didn't even know if I understood love anymore. I felt sick at the thought. I'd romanticized this most of my mortal life, the idea of being a vampire, of drinking blood, of living out eternity with my one true love, and never understanding the reality of it.

Now I had lived that fantasy, and it was nothing like I'd ever imagined. I had happily rejected connection, attachment, affection for others, and had come to relish the ecstasy, the power, the calm that came with the kill. It was a part of me, and I longed for it. Meanwhile, a part of me, the part trying hard to stay human, revolted at the idea, but I knew it would be necessary, and soon, for my own survival and for Cy's.

I glared at him. His hands clung to my shoulders like he had any ability to contain me. Eons might have passed while our eyes bored into each other. Finally, I said, feeling both pity and rage, "You know you couldn't really stop me if I wanted to leave. Right?"

Cy sighed and dropped his hands. One came back up to brush his hair back. "Of course. Of course, I know that." He looked at me, pleading. "Don't. Just... don't. We can figure some other way to bring your strength up."

I snarled softly, half-heartedly. I stepped back from him and went to go get dressed. I pulled on dark jeans and a flowing top with flat sandals, an outfit that was much more Elsie than Opal. I walked to the door, leaving Cy looking downtrodden and in despair that I was going out. I turned to him, the door open.

"Well?" I prodded. "Coming, human? We need to feed you."

Chapter 36

We sat on a bench along the Riverwalk. It was the exact same one where, ten years before, we'd been when musicians played us into a dance. Ten years. Yesterday. A millennium. Time no longer had any meaning or relativity to me.

I was on edge, trying to not freak out and end up huddled in a ball in public, or worse, to go on an insanity-driven rampage that would expose me and the entire vampire community; the thirst, combined with being out in the open, brought about anxiety like I'd never felt in either life.

Cy bit into his hamburger, either unaware of or trying not to draw attention to my little episode. I tried to focus on him instead, and took in the whole scene of him eating. I understood what he meant about food not appealing to vampires. I could eat the burger faster than he could blink, but it wouldn't satisfy me. It was strange that I knew I had gone ten years without an appetite for such things, and yet I could remember the mouthwatering taste of a burger I myself had eaten a week ago. Except I knew it wasn't a week ago...

He dug into the fries next. I caught a whiff as he did so. It didn't even smell like food to me; not bad, just not like food.

What *did* smell like food were the pounding hearts walking up and down the Riverwalk in the light of the early moon. Cy saw my gaze turning as people walked past. He laid his hand gently on mine, a reminder. That he understood my hunger. That he was there to help me like some Blood-Drinkers Anonymous sponsor. That he knew the desire to kill, and the equal desire not to.

"I could just take one," I growled at him. "The homeless-"

"Don't deserve to die tonight any more than those with roofs over their heads," he breathed back. "And you know you wouldn't stop with one." He made eye contact, trying to make sure I really heard him. "I remember it," there was a breath's pause while he tried not to say a name, knowing it would just spark the madness. "That thirst for more. That need to be soft, silent Death to as many as you could until you couldn't take one more drop. It was the purest and most sensual thing. But then it wasn't." He smiled sadly, encouragingly. "There are other ways to get stronger. We'll get there."

I had forgotten that he'd spent decades as a cold-blooded hunter at Amber's side. I wanted to ask him what those other ways were, but my mind drifted to Amber...

"What is Amber here for?" I asked suddenly, realizing he'd told me he knew she was back, and that she was planning something.

Cy stared at me, reluctance in his eyes. "We should discuss this back at home." Home. My condo... his condo... *the* condo. Would everything be confused and unclear forever?

I stood and started to walk away, with him at my heels. He struggled to keep up as I walked at a brisk pace when I caught a faint scent on the breeze. It was familiar somehow and filled me with a sense of dread and fury. I froze completely, not even my hair moving.

Cy was still eating and nearly ran into me since his eyes were on his meal. Upon seeing my stock-still stance, he began to look around in alarm, his hand reaching out for my arm. He had no way to protect himself if something was hunting us. He needn't have worried; I was the hunter in this case.

Without so much as looking at him, I took off, essentially vanishing to the humans around if any of them had been looking my way. I flew through the night, my feet lighter than air on the ground as I followed the trail like a bloodhound. I came to a stop in a parking lot near the sports and entertainment arena several blocks away. A show of some kind was letting out. Mostly men wearing jerseys with face paint... sports then. Didn't matter what the event was. My target was nearby. I had the scent, now I needed a visual.

Hundreds of voices overlapped, creating a din that might have drowned out the voices I was looking for had I not been able to pick out exactly what I needed from the roar. I heard them. They were laughing. Having fun. Enjoying the free-flowing testosterone cocktail of the aftermath of the home team winning. As if they had no worries, no cares. As if they hadn't violated and left a girl to be killed a few blocks away, just a few nights ago.

I saw *him* first. I saw those big brown eyes that had once looked up at me with reverence, which had once given me a feeling of love, of joy; and which I had seen just days ago committing an unspeakably evil act through the eyes of the poor girl who had paid the price for his crimes. I stalked around the edge of the parking lot as Jimmy Molina and some of the other boys from the football team (a small selection of the "party guests" I'd seen in Kara's memory) walked toward a guest pickup area. Of course. None of the ones there were old enough to drive. Not old enough to drive, but old enough to destroy someone. I may have been the one who killed her, but she only crossed my path in the first place because of what they had done.

I took stock of the situation, the crowds, the location. I couldn't drain them all fast enough to go unnoticed, but a part of me, the part of me that had happily followed Amber's example, didn't care. I wanted vengeance. I wanted to hurt them. I wanted them wiped off the face of the earth. I could snap their necks and be gone before they even hit the ground, and it would be done.

I stood watching them fist bump, slam their chests together, make strange war-cries that likely made sense in some context (I had no patience for sports before *or* after I'd died), but that just made them appear even more like the cavemen they were.

My heart broke, looking at Jimmy and knowing how his early childhood had been difficult. I'd felt like I was his safe space. Then I was gone- dead. Had the vacuum created when I disappeared filled with all the hate and rage he'd experienced at home? I'd tried so hard to be there for him and had ended up abandoning him. I wondered when he turned from the sweet boy who just needed that extra bit of love into a creation of evil. *Ha,* I laughed mirthlessly in my mind. *Takes a monster to know a monster...*

I had just about made up my mind to kill them all, just a handful of the fiends who'd hurt poor Kara but enough to sate my rage for now. It wasn't even a debate in my mind- the gentler human part put up a tiny fight, then faded away, the killer in me so much louder and in my element. I took a single step in their direction when a hand touched my shoulder.

I turned to see who it was, and of course, it was Cy. I'd waited too long, and he'd caught up. I had to ask, since I'd been too fast for him to follow by sight. "How did you find me?"

"Smelled you," he shrugged. "One of the few things I still have. It's not as strong or infallible as it used to be. Even harder because your scent is so reminiscent of magnolias, and they're everywhere right now. I had to really focus on you." I hadn't realized that my scent mirrored my favorite flower. Any other time, it might have made me happy. I felt far from happy.

He looked over my shoulder to where I'd been staring to see the boys- really, truly *boys*- and then looked back to me, The Brow going up, questioning. "I've watched you for a long time now," he admitted. There was a chiding tone to his words. "Years. I've never seen you seek out children." His speaking patterns had become much more casual and modern in the last ten years. I wondered vaguely if that was a result of being human again.

I spun back to face the boys, not wanting them to slip away while I justified my actions. "They're not children. They're barbarians."

I felt him tense and pull close to me. It wasn't an affectionate movement- he was trying to keep hold of me. People were all around, jostling us in their frustration that we were standing still when they were all in such a hurry to get to their cars. He didn't want to release me and lose me again. He was looking out for me. I wanted him to stop. I wanted him to hold me back. I wanted...

I turned to him, tears just barely contained. "Do you know what they did?" I demanded.

Cy's face was passive and sincere. He shook his head. "No. I don't."

I tried to find the words to tell him, but found it harder than I expected to. "That girl from the alley... my kill from the other night," I started, struggling to tell the story, the third set of memories jostling the other two, threatening to mix up the oil and water of my mind again. "She'd been at a party. No. It wasn't a party. It was a setup. They..." I trailed off, the words not wanting to be said aloud. But I needed him to understand why I wanted to hurt them. Why I needed to. "They got her drunk. They drugged her. Then she- Kara... It was all of them. Over and over and over, and she couldn't stop them. Initiation into their fucking boys' club. I saw it all... I *felt* it, in her memory... in the last drop. And that one," I pointed to Jimmy, "That was the worst for me. Because I knew him. Because I loved him... When he was little. Before he turned into this. He was my favorite student... before."

"Molina," Cy murmured in recognition of the name. "Little Jimmy Molina. That's what you were trying to tell me yesterday."

"I'm a killer," I said matter-of-factly. "But I don't torture. I don't bring undue or unnecessary pain. That girl is dead, and her final hours were spent in nothing but torment and agony, and they were the cause." I looked at Cy again. "If they were vampires, the Council would kill them for what they did. Kara's been dead for two nights, and they're out enjoying their lives like nothing happened. Like Kara was nothing!"

Cy frowned. "To them... she *was* nothing." His eyes took on a far off look. "I grew up a long time before consent laws were even conceived of. Women were often viewed as property, and a wife had no rights to deny her husband if she even had a mind to. Most wouldn't dare. And still, outside of the whorehouses (and select few even of those), what *they* did-" He pointed at the boys with a look of disgust- "would have appalled any of the men whose company I kept, even in those days."

I looked at him and nodded, my face a mask of resolution and rage. I turned and took a step, but his hand didn't let go of my arm. I turned to him. My eyes held a warning and a plea. "Let me go. Don't make me make you."

"Just wait," he said, revulsion curling his lip as he looked at the boys. His face was set, but his eyes were alive, thinking quickly. He raised his eyebrows and nodded his head behind me. I didn't see what he was looking at, at first, but then he said, "Get a phone. Anyone's phone. Quickly. It needs to be unlocked."

Confused and frustrated that the time I had to complete my task was slipping away, I didn't want to waste a moment, but he was so calm and the storm in me was so violent. The tiny, barely audible human voice in my mind begged me to listen to him, to give him a chance. Rolling my eyes at him and sighing, I dashed into a group of people shuffling through a crosswalk. I grabbed a girl's phone as she was texting and had disappeared back into the crowd just as quickly, her fingers still moving before she realized the phone was gone.

I brought it back to Cy, and he opened up a news website. He showed me an image of Kara from today along with a news story of how her body had been found in an alley, sexually assaulted and stabbed (it didn't mention the minimal blood at the scene or the fact that the stab wound was two small punctures in the carotid and jugular) and although only trace DNA from the suspects could be found on the body, they believed there were multiple perpetrators. *Of course, there were,* I thought, *and every single one used a condom to minimize the chances of someone proving what they did.* If anyone had any information, please call the Sheriff's office. There was a phone number.

"*This* is how we make it right- as much as something like this *can* be made right. They won't die instantly by your hand, never knowing what hit them- nothing that easy. They'll be subject to human investigation and laws. They'll be a scandal, and the story will follow them forever, convicted or not." Cy dialed the number and handed the phone to me. "Cry. You just heard about your friend Kara and you know who she was supposed to be with that night. Tell them as much as you can using what you know from her memory."

The dispatcher took my call and I began to sob. I had spent years faking various emotional states to hunt and had years of acting training as a human, but this was as real as it was pretending, being forced to remember the trauma she endured. "I have information about Kara Gable's last night alive."

Chapter 37

We walked through the door of the condo, and as soon as it closed behind Cy, I turned on him. "How fucking dare you?" The war in my mind was raging again, and the killer in me felt cheated.

He stepped back. "What?" He asked, completely nonplussed. I'd taken his suggestion, after all. He hadn't expected me to rage at him.

"They were mine," I snarled. "Their punishment was mine. *I* was their judge, jury, and executioner. How *dare* you rob me of that?" I was screaming, my mind at full volume with every voice; Elsie, the human, understanding Cy's actions; Opal, the vampire, cursing him for intervening; the new voice that understood and heard the voices of both of my pasts and my desires, feeling uncertain but conceding to the anger for the moment.

"I saved you from making a mistake!" He replied.

"So you say!" I roared, baring my fangs at him. He stepped back, actual fear flashing across his face. "Because the human legal system is so beneficial to victims. Because justice is *always* the result!" I threw myself onto the couch and sobbed. It was like being blackout drunk. My mind couldn't focus. I tried to convey the anger, the fury; and then another emotion, despair, intruded halfway through to take control, and the original thought was lost. All I wanted was to avenge poor Kara, and now I had left justice in the hands of men, rather than meting it out on my own terms.

I pulled my knees to my chest and continued to weep, in a way thankful for the excuse to do so. I had managed to appear functional, but my psyche was still fractured. Being around people, even Cy, was exhausting. The constant struggle to seem like I wasn't completely losing my shit made me want to curl into a ball and let it all out, and now, rational or not, I was given the outlet. Sweet catharsis...

Cy didn't move from beside the door the entire time I indulged the breakdown. He simply stared at me, the patient eyes of a centuries-old immortal full of pity, guilt, affection, fear... My brokenness didn't affect only me.

After I burned myself out and the tears had come and gone, and even after they'd dried on my face, he still stood like a sentinel, waiting for something to happen, for me to say something, do something.

"Why are you still here?" I asked hoarsely.

His eyes shut down and his voice was impassive as he asked, "Do you want me to leave?"

I studied him a minute, deciding if it was an offer or just a question. "Would you, if I said 'yes'?" Silence. Several pregnant moments passed before I decided not to test those waters any further, afraid of what would happen, and I sighed. "I wasn't saying that I *want* you to leave. I was asking because...why bother with me?" He continued to stare, unmoving and expressionless. Frustrated, I jumped to my feet and lashed out again, smashing a vase in my anger. "Is it because you want to torture me? To punish me for daring to die and become what *you* made me, whether you meant to or not? Or is it vanity? Narcissism? That you know you *failed* to save me, and now you've had to watch me become someone entirely different? Someone you hate because I'm just like you used to be? Like Amber is? Don't stay here if you think you can fix me because I don't fucking need to be fixed, and even if I did, it wouldn't work! I am a ruler! I am the strongest of our kind to be made in centuries, and the most powerful fucking vampire I've ever heard of!" I was panting with the current of the thoughts spilling from my lips so quickly I wasn't even sure they would be clear to mortal ears or if they would just be impossibly loud gibberish. Cy still hadn't moved, which enraged me so much that I kept going, just wanting him to fight back, to give me a reason to hurt him, to make him leave, and to be alone with my madness. "I could end you in less time than it would take for your heart to beat once, and then I could figure this all out for myself. I'm never going back to the miserable, weak human I was..." Tears started coming quickly again, the fire turning to ice. "But I can't do what I need to to keep my power anymore... And I'm *sorry* if you can't deal with whatever your issue is here. You can blame Amber all you want, but you're the one who gave me your blood. And Amber has been the closest thing I've had to a friend in the last decade! Why would she do that after trying to kill me? I have two lifetimes worth of memories, and neither one gives me any clue as to why any of you cared at all about me, and why you won't leave me alone now..." I finally faded out, falling back into my little ball on the couch, wiping the tears away like a child in time out. "Goddamn it, can you say anything?" I wanted so badly to kill him then and didn't understand why I just *couldn't.* But that's not right either. I knew why. It was the same reason I wanted him to leave, and it wasn't hatred. It was because I couldn't stand the thought that I might hurt him.

His eyes were still clouded with a deliberate lack of emotion. He was guarding something. His silence was deafening and infuriating. But it was also stirring something else I was fighting against. I couldn't pull it out of him with venom. I needed the human in me to be allowed to surface to get him to speak to me.

"Cy," I said, my voice small. I didn't want to allow myself to be this emotionally exposed, but I had to. "I... I don't blame you." No reaction. "Truly. I don't know how to explain any of this, but I'm sorry. I do need to be fixed, but it's not your job to do that. I don't even think it's something you could do for me. I have to figure it out for myself, and I don't want you to feel obligated to be here out of some kind of guilt. I could have walked away from this at any point when it started a decade ago, and I didn't. And who knows what would have happened. Maybe you'd have beaten Amber without me ever knowing, and I'd be alive and naïve and happy. Then again, maybe not. I never believed in fate, but maybe that's what this is. I mean, what are the odds that you'd live centuries and just so happen to end up trying to save someone and in the process make some kind of vampire titan? Maybe that's why Amber kept close to me, too. She was afraid." I looked at him beseechingly. "Are *you* afraid?"

The wall he'd put up to hide his emotions dropped long enough for me to glimpse something in his eyes. "Yes."

I looked at the floor. "Then you should go. Because you're right to be afraid. I'm insane, and I'm powerful. That's not a combination anyone should choose to be around. And as much as part of me just hates you, I can't stand the idea of anything happening to you. I guess that's Elsie's thing. Damned if I didn't love you... and look where it got me." I buried my head in my arms atop my knees, no longer crying, just prepared to stay here forever, or at least until Zilpher finally tracked me down and took me out, ending this farce.

I didn't hear him approach (was he that quiet? Was I that weakened?), but suddenly Cy's hand was on my back. It was a gentle pressure, full of comfort and protection. I might have laughed if I hadn't been so full of profound despair. I was the stronger of the two of us, and yet this tiny gesture made me feel safe for the first time in a long time. I leaned toward him, laying my head on his shoulder. He wrapped his arms around me, sweetly, softly, and I cried myself to sleep there in his embrace.

Chapter 38

I woke up alone. It was just past noon, and I was safe in my condo, but I was completely alone. I knew Cy had been here when I had fallen asleep- where was he?

I wandered the empty flat, looking at everything. It was strange to me that many of these things were mine, and yet they weren't. They'd been Cy's before Amber had claimed them as her own and passed them to me, just like the blood in my veins.

I had been out of touch for nearly three weeks now. Every day at first had been a risk to my safety. Now every hour saw an uptick in the risk not only to me, but to Cy and many other people from my past life whom I had only just remembered.

After nearly an hour of solitude with only my thoughts (the whole rainbow of them) for company, Cy came in with a cooler.

"I brought more blood," he said, taking the cooler to the fridge. "How are you?"

It was a simple question, yet my answer, if truthful, would have taken the rest of the daylight hours to convey-probably longer. I lied. "I'm fine."

He saw right through me and brought me a packet of blood. "Here. Drink." He'd gotten used to watching me feed over the last few days and no longer looked away in revulsion. Golly, we were just the very image of fairytale romance, weren't we?

I bit a hole in the plastic and drank it down like a grotesque juice pack. It wouldn't satisfy for much longer, but it was enough for the moment. When not a drop remained, I set the little pouch on the side table, not bothering to throw it away, and I jumped right in. I looked at Cy with a renewed fervor and asked, "What does my family think happened to me?"

It was like the floor dropped out from underneath him. His face went slack and his body seemed to deflate. He'd obviously hoped to wait a while longer to have this conversation, but the question was out there now.

"Do they think you did something to me?" I asked, imagining what I would think if I were one of them. I knew without a body they'd never be able to prove anything against him even if they did believe he had a hand in my disappearance, but it would be my assumption regardless.

He walked slowly over and sat next to me. He put his elbows on his knees and pressed his fingers together. "Yes. At first, most of them did, but... You have to understand. You didn't *die* to them. You disappeared without a trace.

"After Amber hit you, when I brought you here, your phone was going off nonstop. Your friends, your parents, they all wanted to know where you were. I sent texts at first, claiming you were sick, but they were demanding to speak to you, to know why you weren't at the hospital if you were that ill.

"I called them. I'm not proud of misleading them, but I told you back then how badly hurt you were. The internal

bleeding, the trauma to your head and spine were too extensive. You wouldn't have even survived a trip to the hospital.
Once I fought Amber off at the bar (which I later realized was
purely a gambit on her part to lull me into a false sense of security, one I fell for completely), I gave you my blood right there
in the parking lot. It allowed me to carry you safely. I brought
you back here. You were delirious for hours, your heart rate
speeding, your pulse weakening. I gave you as little as I could,
which still ended up being more than I ever anticipated. I never
wanted any of this for you. I hated that I had to do it to keep
you alive, but I wasn't prepared to lose you.

"I was able to convince your mother you were merely ill,
and that you would call her when you had recovered enough to
do so. When you awoke..."

I nodded, showing I remembered. We had fought. He'd
told me about how he and Amber were vampires, how Amber
had targeted me because I had reminded her of her once-lover's
bride. We had agreed that there was no future for us as lovers, a
human so connected to her world and a vampire with no connections to speak of. We had made love, the danger, the thrill
of it all making me feel as alive as ever, even as death stalked me.

"Well," he continued, clearing his throat. "The next
morning, I knew that Amber would have redoubled her efforts
to get to you, and I knew she had tracked down this place. She
hadn't yet come inside, but I had seen her looking up at the
windows in the night. It was the last place I knew of that she
couldn't find you, and she had.

"That was when I drugged you. I used your breakfast. I
needed to get you out, and I knew you'd never come willingly
while your friends were still fighting for their lives. You'd had
so much of my blood... I was no match for her without killing
over and over just to build up my strength, and if I lost, you'd
be like me." He put his hands to his eyes, as though he was

crying or had a headache. I knew he was simply feeling the weight of his decisions.

"I remember. You pulled me from the bath so I wouldn't drown. Then I woke up in your car twelve hours later."

"I drove up and down the coast, turning often, stopping to throw Amber off. You know I failed at that." Cy took a deep breath and pulled his head from his hands, putting his fingertips back to his chin, never once making eye contact with me.

"You had me call my mother," I said. "It was the last time I ever talked to her..." The realization of that hit me like a shot to the heart. I'd known at the time it might have been, but to have it be true was heartbreaking.

"And then I threw your phone out of the window, changing directions yet again. Braun had my phone. He texted your mother an hour later, telling her from me you were on your way, and again the next morning to check that you made it home okay."

It took me a moment to realize what he'd said. He'd set it all up ahead of time. "You knew I might not come back."

He looked at me with an intensity I could scarcely believe. His eyes bored into mine pleadingly. "I had to be ready in case. If Amber got to you, if you were turned, I needed to make sure that I had done everything to not be a suspect in your disappearance. You're on the Council. Imagine the fallout...

"You know what happened next. Amber found us. She shot you through the head, damaging your brain. It was the only thing I couldn't have planned for... The brain itself healed when you were reborn, but the memories were no longer a part of you as they once were. She'd managed to remove everything that made you Elsie, all of your memories, life experiences, the people you cared for. She killed you. She won.

"Then you fed from me. You drained your sire to the point of immortal death, taking in not only the blood that had

287

made you, but your own mortal blood, bonded to my vampiric blood. It's my own theory as to why you were born with more strength than others. It's because your first kill, your first blood, was ours. Yours and mine."

I sat back on my heels. It had never occurred to me, not that I'd had more than a few days to reflect on the truth of my rebirth. I had thought Amber was my sire up until then. His words, the analysis of my birth, made sense, though.

"When I was found on Caladesi, the campers who called emergency services saw the blood around, but assumed it was all mine since I'd lost so much. I received a transfusion and recovered, much to the bewilderment of the team of doctors who couldn't believe I lived. As far as I know, most of our kind still believe I'm dead, since they've not seen me since. Well, not that they know of. It's not like I smell like I once did- to my own knowledge. My eyes are decidedly human now, and the heartbeat isn't an illusion anymore... it's real.

"I had given a false name at the hospital, one of a number of aliases I've accrued over the years. It allowed me to disappear as you did. Naturally, as the mysterious vagabond boyfriend, I was the prime suspect, but the phone records showed I had been home when your phone was being used up the coast, and my doorman confirmed I had left to try to find you after the text was sent, but I never returned. Braun was kind enough to provide an excellent alibi and never gave a hint to another of our kind about the possibility I was still alive.

"I could never go back to your loved ones and let them know that I was still here, checking on them for you. If they knew I was alive, Amber would know. She's been keeping an eye as well... I allowed myself to disappear so she wouldn't know I was there, but kept close enough to watch them for you. I couldn't protect them any more than I could protect you, but three hundred years of living on the edges and trying to outwit Amber taught me how to go unseen when I needed to."

If I hadn't spent ten years as someone who had to plan for situations in a similar way, I'd have been astonished at the amount of thought he'd put into every step of my abduction.

"So I just disappeared... without a trace..." I parroted his words back to him. "What about the blood I left behind on Caladesi Island when I was killed?"

Cy smiled unhappily. "The police checked it when they found me. It had already bound with the vampire blood. It didn't even register as human in their machines."

I sat thoughtfully, processing this. So I really had just vanished to them. And even if they saw me, they wouldn't recognize me; my features had changed just enough to make me into someone familiar but different, just like with Indigo. Not to mention, I had spent ten years not aging a day.

"And..." I started. "How are they? My family? My friends?"

Cy held my gaze for a moment, then looked away. "Do you really want to know?" He asked, his voice guarded.

I opened my mouth to say, "*Yes! Of course! Why wouldn't I?*" But I hesitated. What could have happened that would cause him to ask? I thought longer than I expected, and finally said, "Yes. I need to know."

"Who would you like to hear about first?" He asked. When I didn't answer right away, he said, "Let's start with your friends. They don't see much of each other anymore, though they've been in touch lately. We can start with Sam, whom I know you have probably been concerned about since remembering him and his predicament at the time of your death," Cy said kindly and correctly. "Sam survived the crash. His leg had to be amputated, and he spent a few years in a wheelchair dealing with extensive damage to his musculoskeletal systems. He had dark periods, a few stays in mental health facilities, but he seems to have recovered for the most part. He got a prosthetic about six years ago and finished his physical therapy. He's been in a relationship with one of his old nurses for several years, but they don't seem to have plans for marriage just yet. He has become very active online, with a large following of people whom he inspires with posts about running while disabled."

That was interesting. Sam had always hated running; I could never get him to do a race or even just a little run around the neighborhood with me. There was a twinge of annoyance that with me (and one leg) gone, he suddenly took it up, but it was akin to feeling annoyance at a character in a movie who did something you disliked. I was no longer invested in his actions as I was in my mortal life.

"He's one of the few who doesn't believe you're still out there somewhere," Cy continued. "He thinks Jack killed both you and me, but it's never been proven. Not that it needs to be, for Sam anyway. Jack received twenty-five to life for the hit and run murder of Emily and attempted murder of Sam." This stunned me. I knew the hit and run had happened, but to hear it like that, with a prison sentence added in, had felt surreal.

"Couldn't happen to a better person," I mumbled sardonically. "What about Matt and Charlotte?"

Sad smile. "They got married about two years after you... left. Baby came another two years later... named after you. But they've been divorced for three years now. They co-parent well, from what I've been able to observe, but they seem much happier as friends than they did as husband and wife."

"Jess?" I asked.

Cy smiled. "She was laid off from her job and took to the church with enthusiasm. Now she's living abroad, working her way around the world as a missionary." He cast his eyes downward. "She asks all over the world, all over the country if anyone has information about you or me. She has little hope, but she does it mostly for your mother."

"For my mother?" I asked.

He grabbed my hand, squeezing it tightly to brace me for his words. "Your mother... she's convinced you're alive. She goes back and forth between thinking you're one of those life-long abduction cases or that you've run away and will come home one day. In both scenarios, you're with me..." He took a deep breath, steeling himself to say something clearly unpleasant. "Your father died a year after you left. They said it was an anomaly in his heart, but some of the doctors believe it was broken heart syndrome. Your sister moved home and finished her degree at a local university to be with your mother, so she wouldn't be alone."

I sat in silence for a while. My father was dead. Tears trickled from my eyes, but it was a muted, soft sadness. After all... I'd died first. Wasn't it his right as the parent to either go before me or to follow swiftly? It was a relief to pull on the detachment I'd perfected in my years as Opal to handle that piece of news.

Only one person left who really mattered. "What about Ashley?"

Pause. "I'm surprised you're asking," he said thoughtfully.

"Why?"

"Because you were following her when I found you."

Of all the information I'd heard so far, that shocked me the most. "What?" I asked, dumbfounded.

Cy looked thoughtfully out the window as though he could see so far over the water that another time was visible to him. "I was convinced you remembered your human life at that point. You were following her around town, watching her. I went to The Roof that night to see if you were there to see her... I realized I'd been wrong when you didn't recognize *me*," he finished bitterly.

"I thought she was Amber..." I murmured. "I realized I was wrong when I saw her... she saw me!" I burst out. "She was at The Roof the night you kidnapped me... again." I looked at him, offering as a teasing side note, "Please stop doing that, by the way."

He smirked at me. "I'll do my best," he chuckled. "And yes, she was there. So were many of your old friends. None of them noticed us; they were too busy celebrating. That was Ashley's engagement party- or the after-party for it, anyway." I smiled. It was just like Ashley to have an extravagant affair to celebrate another extravagant affair.

"She saw me," I repeated. The need to ramble was bubbling up in my throat. "In the bathroom, when I went to 'freshen up.' She came in, and I thought she was Amber. I tracked her for *weeks* because I thought she was Amber." I remembered the strange way she'd looked at me. I whispered, "She saw *me*. I think she recognized me... the way she looked at me. She looked like she'd seen a ghost. I just assumed she was one of those sensitive humans who could feel our presence. But it wasn't that. She recognized me. I just looked too different and too young for her to think I could have still been her friend who vanished." Tears were running silently down my face. My heart hurt to know how close I'd been to Ashley, and neither of us knew it. *Detach,* I ordered myself.

Cy leaned toward me. "We're lucky she didn't really recognize you," he said gently. "And even luckier she didn't recognize me. If any of them realized I was there, they and your mother would have raised the alarm in ways they wouldn't even realize, and I'd have been found out. Amber would have killed me before I ever got to you."

A small part of me still believed that would have been better, easier. But knowing what I knew at that point, I was glad to have remembered.

I curled up into a ball on the couch and pulled a plush blanket over myself. Cy touched my forehead, and I caught his hand before he turned away. He looked at me, a question in his eyes.

"I just... thank you. For helping me to remember them. For watching over them for me, even when you couldn't help. Thank you for telling me." I gave his fingers a squeeze, then let go and closed my eyes to the daylight.

Life went on without me. A little sadder, more somber, but on it went. Dad was gone, but everyone else lived on. I wished there was some way I could reach out to my mom and Danielle, to let them know I was okay, but I knew there was nothing I could do. Even if I could, it would be a lie. My friends... I missed them, but knowing that they were thriving was all I had needed.

Chapter 39

The next night, the thirst was brutal.

The last sun of the day was fading from the sky and I'd torn through every cold, stale, unsatisfying pack of blood Cy had brought for me.

"I need to, Cy," I told him, as I paced the room, my hands shaking. "I need fresh blood, and I need a kill."

"No," he replied casually from the couch where he sat with his legs crossed, like this was some kind of dinner party. "You don't."

"How do you know?!" I raged at him. "I'm stronger than you ever were, maybe you didn't need it as much as I do." I knew I was full of shit. I was jonesing and would say anything to go feed as I wished. Why didn't I? Why did I let him talk me into staying here? Why didn't I just kill *him* and sate this hunger?

Oh, right. Because a part of me still cared for him and wanted to try to be more like I used to be, which meant no killing.

"Amber and Zilpher could be coming for me right now, and you won't even tell me what Amber's plan is, and you think I can just sit here and wait for it? You haven't even given me back my phone, my tablet, my computer so I can try to track them, or to tell the Council I'm fine and they don't need to send out their own agents as well!"

He stared at me, waiting for me to stop. His unflappably calm demeanor was admirable, but it pissed me off. I hated how he wouldn't say anything if I was being (admittedly) unreasonable.

"Fine!" I snarled. "What can I do? Because I have never let the hunger and weakness get this bad before. It's starvation!"

He nodded and stood up. "Let's get you fed. You're right: we still have a lot to talk about, and, as you said last night, neither of us should be 'hangry' for that."

I gave him a cynical look. "I don't think I used that word, and I honestly can't believe you just did." But he was right. The depth of the ever-fluctuating madness I struggled with left little time for practical discussion, and I had the feeling that time would start ticking very quickly if I didn't get a grip and soon.

We were back at the Riverwalk, strolling along toward downtown. Cy had come close and wrapped an arm around my waist. It might have seemed affectionate, this posture of lovers, but I knew better. We might be getting along better, but this was his way of appearing normal to others while reminding me that he was here and not intending to let me out of his sight.

"Where are we going?" I asked, trying to make my voice light. I didn't like being out in the open for this long, as weak as I felt.

"Somewhere we can get you topped off," he mumbled.

I realized we were heading toward the Speakeasy. "Cy, no!" I breathed, fear constricting the words. "You said Amber is here, and with me out of touch for weeks, you'd better believe Zilpher's hanging around looking for me. If you take me there like this, they'll kill me. Even the fledglings could destroy me right now!"

"I don't think that's the case, unless they rose up against you as one. You're still stronger than most, but don't worry. That's not where we're going." He smirked sarcastically. "Don't you remember? I have a bit more of a refined palate."

He walked me along the Riverwalk and around the backside of Trusty's, where he rang a bell on the wall. A door that led to the kitchens opened to us. Jett was there and embraced me on sight. I realized I hadn't actually seen him at all in the last ten years as Opal. I knew of him, but we'd never interacted.

"Elsie," Jett said warmly. I bristled at the name but didn't correct him. I felt that it was too complicated to explain, and I was fading fast enough to be worried. "I didn't realize you'd joined us. It's been too long." He released me and reached for Cy's hand to shake it. "About a decade, I believe." He looked strangely at Cy. I knew why. He could sense what I did, that while I had "joined" the community of vampires, Cy had somehow left it; not only that, but he still hadn't aged, and he hadn't decayed from the loss of the blood. He didn't ask, but I worried about what that information might mean to others. I had been so concerned with my own safety, I'd forgotten his.

Cy must have seen my face and realized I wouldn't be able to maintain composure for long and decided to name drop a bit to help speed things along. "Actually, Jett, she doesn't go by that name anymore. I'm sure you've heard of the Councilor Madame Opal?"

Jett blanched. Realizing he'd just hugged a Council member and called her by her human name, he seemed to have recognized his faux pas. "I am so sorry, Madame Opal," he repented, giving a deep bow.

"It's fine, Jett," I said, trying to keep from correcting him on a second name I no longer recognized as my own. Would I ever have a name again? I knew I would, but it still felt unlikely.

Cy leaned in close to Jett. "We've been separated a while and have been... reconnecting." A wink. "We've been holed up, so to speak, and it's been a while since she's been able to feed properly. Can you help?"

Jett looked me up and down, noticing the withdrawal-like symptoms. He hesitated. "Of course," he said, shaking off his doubts. "She must be in rough shape for you to bring her here. And you know I'd do anything for a friend, even if she *is* a Council member." I wasn't hurt by the slight. Council members were feared, not loved.

He led us to a back corner of the dessert room and sat down with us in the booth. Jett closed the privacy barrier and then turned to the call system on the wall that could be used to ring for your server. He pressed a series of buttons that I had once thought were purely decorative, and suddenly the booth slid into the wall. We stood to face a doorway that hadn't been there before and walked through it.

I looked around in this hidden lounge and was amazed. It was decorated like a bar in a five-star hotel, complete with crystal chandeliers and leather couches. On these couches were a wide variety of humans with IV lines hooked into the crooks of their arms and the backs of their hands, but it was nothing like the atmosphere at the Speakeasy. These humans were awake and chatting casually with the vampires around the room. Many were walking around as though they weren't hooked up to medical equipment.

"What...?" I murmured.

Jett turned to me proudly and a bit sheepishly. "It's our best-kept secret. We know it's not allowed, humans who know about us and walk free. It's part of their training to work here. Our staff are exceedingly loyal because they know what I am, what some of my partners are, and they know what we could do if they were to tell. But most never even consider it. We hire the ones who have little to no connections, so we become their family. Some end up like us, but most just become aware of us and enjoy the idea of existing comfortably in the safety of a den of vampires."

Cy took my hand and pulled me aside for a moment. "I know it's not the same thrill as the kill, but here you can still achieve the same satiety. The trick is to take from as many as you can, filling up on not one, but dozens. It's like when humans say to eat the rainbow for optimal nutrition, something I never had to understand until I started eating again. But it goes for us as well. You can gorge on one good thing, or you can add variety and receive the benefits of all the different flavors." He handed me a small, sterile tube and mouthpiece wrapped in plastic. It looked like it would hook into the end of one of the IV lines.

I looked at him with disbelief. "You really expect me to believe if I just sip, sip, sip all night, it will fill the hole that killing left behind?"

He pursed his lips, for the first time showing the depth of his impatience with me. "Why don't you just try and stop being so fucking difficult?"

My head snapped back like he'd hit me. The words had stung. He'd never spoken to me like that in either life.

He sighed. "I'm sorry. I'm running a little dry myself- hungry *and* thirsty- and this whole thing isn't easy for either of us. Look, we're already here. Can you just try it? It won't *kill* you." He winked at me, trying to infuse some levity into the situation.

He had a point. The worst that could happen was that I'd still need to kill after we left, and we could just argue again then; but if this worked, I supposed it was a good thing.

I couldn't help mumbling grumpily, though. "Sure seems easy enough for you..." He raised The Brow to warn me we were heading toward another fight, so I sighed and said, "Fine," and sniffed the air. I picked out a scent, deciding on a

298

friendly looking man in his mid-40s whose blood smelled appealing to me.

"Hello. I..." I approached him awkwardly. I had never approached a willing victim to ask for their blood and had no idea what the proper etiquette was. I wasn't exactly a polite fiend, accustomed to asking permission before draining someone dry. I motioned to the man's IV. "Do you mind?"

He smiled civilly and sat on the nearest couch, reaching for the tube I carried. He clicked it into place expertly and leaned back as I put my mouth to my own end. The mouthpiece was surprisingly comfortable, fitting just between my lips with an area to cradle my fangs. It felt almost as natural as fitting my teeth onto a soft, tender neck, but it was undoubtedly less intimate.

My eyes slid closed as the blood began to flow. Oh! Warm, fresh blood; I let it nourish me, felt it moving through my body and reigniting the vampiric blood in my veins. The pulse of life began to make me feel stronger, more clear-headed. So powerful was the pull of that replenishment that it was with a great reluctance that I let the mouthpiece fall from my lips after just a short while.

The man and I exchanged pleasantries for a moment (Charles, I learned his name was), and then I left his side as he refueled with some snacks that were set around the room.

I looked around. There was certainly no shortage of variety in the room. I could smell every blood-type overlaid with the individual DNA of the person, as well as the food they'd taken in recently. It certainly helped to make them more appealing that they were fed with some of the highest quality and expertly prepared foods available.

I noticed Cy in a corner with someone who, in another life, could have been mistaken for his brother. The man was a few years younger in appearance, but had the same wave to his dark hair and a similar build- tall with just enough lean muscle that you could make out the definition of their arms and shoulders beneath their white button-downs. The man even had hazel eyes. They were laughing while Cy alternated between the snacks on the table and a mouthpiece. I noticed Jett watching him curiously from across the room and I became uneasy. I knew they were friends, but I had thought Amber and I were friends. The information that Cy was living in some state that was neither human nor vampire could be dangerous to both of us, and could be lucrative for the informant if they knew who to speak to.

As a nervous state settled over me, I began to move through the room, "sip, sip, sipping." I was filling up, but had not yet felt the climax, the spilling over of power that usually came with a kill. I was feeling more and more doubtful that this would provide that same apotheosis and felt disappointed that I would have to let Cy know it hadn't worked.

He'd had his fill apparently and had gone to a mahogany bar in the corner to order a drink. It looked like some kind of dark liquor, but I could smell it from across the room and there was no alcohol in the glass. He wanted to appear relaxed but be alert. That alone made my nerves worse.

The young man Cy had been chatting with before approached me as I looked around for my next... what was the right word here? Victim? Provider? Volunteer? It was all so foreign.

"Hi," he said with a relaxed smile. "I'm Frank. You're with Cy, right?" He nodded over to Cy, who raised his glass at us with an equally easy smile that was hiding an anxiety as intense as I was experiencing myself. It was coming off of him in waves. He wanted to go, to get back to the condo quickly, but didn't want to take me before I'd "eaten the rainbow."

"Nice to meet you, Frank," I said, affecting the same comfortable air as Cy.

Frank held his hand out to me, where his line had been placed. I hooked my mouthpiece up to the line. It was pure light, pure joy. His blood was the sweetest, richest I'd had all evening. My eyes fluttered closed, the last image I saw before I did so being Frank's eyes...

Suddenly I was pulling from the mouthpiece like I hadn't all evening. I was out of control, savage, feral. In my mind, I wasn't there in the hidden lounge at Trusty's. I was back at home, and the blood was Cy's. He held me close as I fed from him, his life flowing into me as it had done twice before, once in the basement just a few days earlier when I hadn't had a chance to savor the moment and, the first time, when I was human. I hadn't been conscious for that, but for this... for this, I was aware of every spark, every flash of light, every erotic pulse...

I heard yelling, and the blood supply was cut off. My eyes opened, and I was disoriented. A hand touched my arm and I turned, snarling and snapping at whoever had stopped me. I reached a hand out to shove them away and saw Cy fly backward into a glass table. It shattered around him. A flash of fear for him and concern that he was hurt suddenly brought clarity back to my mind and I realized what had happened.

The mouthpiece dangled from my lips, the line completely ripped free from Frank's arm. Frank, who was now dashing through a door across the room, herded by a couple of vampire bodyguards, had pulled the line out, afraid I was taking too much when I lost control, which I likely had been. Cy had come to try to help, but I'd lashed out and sent him flying.

Everyone was staring, Jett included. He helped Cy to his feet. Cy looked at me with fear and sadness, while Jett looked at us both in fear and anger. Fear. That's what I brought to people. I let the mouthpiece fall to the ground and went quickly to Cy, wrapping my arm around him. I wouldn't look at Jett, but I mumbled a nearly incoherent apology about

301

losing control, and I'd make sure he and Frank were both compensated for the trouble, and not to worry about the Council, that I'd keep the secret.

Jett's arms stayed crossed the whole time I spoke. He gave a stiff, "Thanks," and told me that I should get Cy cleaned up before we left so as to not draw attention.

I saw what he meant. The glass had cut through Cy's shirt and he had a number of slices on his skin which, while I could tell most of them were already beginning to heal, had left bloodstains on his white shirt. Jett led us to a bathroom near the door Frank had disappeared through and grabbed a black shirt from an adjacent closet full of apparel for the walking kegs.

Once inside, Cy went to the sink and leaned over it while I locked the door and slumped against it, sliding to the ground and covering my eyes. I was on the verge of sinking back into the madness, of letting the sand close over my head, and I worried this time I would never come out. I heard the sink start up, and, with great effort, I pulled my hands from my face and looked at Cy.

He had taken his shirt off and was standing in front of an ornate mirror by the sink, examining himself. He had tiny crisscrosses of bloody red lines all over his torso where the glass had cut him. I felt a jolt in my gut. I did that. It was my fault.

I stood and started to walk toward him. "Don't," he said. He was looking at me in the mirror. He was tensed from head to toe and his face was as blank as I'd ever seen it, but I felt the emotion pouring off of him. He was afraid of me. I didn't blame him.

I took another step and he turned to face me, his eyes warning me away. I ignored him. Without a word, I took a towel that was lying near the sink and ran it under the cool water. I dabbed gently at the wounds, most of which had already stopped bleeding. He was like a statue as I worked over his cuts, cleaning them and making sure they were healing properly. Some had closed completely, thanks to his little meal of blood before to bolster the drop of vampire blood in his veins, but there was one cut on his hand that was too deep. In a true human, it would have required stitches. Even for Cy, the bleeding hadn't slowed down yet. I asked him to hold the towel for pressure and led him to a chair in the corner. While he pressed it tightly to that wound, I worked on his face, wiping away the blood, and saw that there were tears mixed in. I paused.

"I'm sorry." At my words, he made eye contact for the first time since we were alone. His eyes were narrowed warily. I didn't blame him for being suspicious or angry. It was what I'd tried to warn him of two nights before, the reason I'd tried to encourage him to leave me. I spoke softly to him, despite the screaming voices fighting in my head. "I can't figure anything out. I don't know who I am or what I want or what I want to be. I can't decide if this is even real. I keep hoping this is a dream, and I'll wake up and be okay again. But I don't even know who would wake up. Would I wake up in Elsie's bed in my parents' house, having dreamt all of this up, and vampires aren't even real? Or would I wake up and be Opal with no memory of my human life? They both seem equally freeing and equally horrifying." I rinsed off the towel and kept wiping while he continued with the silent stare. "If we hadn't come here, I'd have killed tonight. I almost did anyway."

I lowered my eyes back to his hand to check on the cut there. It was still flowing. He held it to me reluctantly. He needn't have worried. "You were right," I told him. "I'm full. I didn't need the kill. And I'm not going to hurt you." I looked back into his eyes. "Not again. I promise."

As we looked at each other, a ghost of the past entered the room. It was an echo of another night, a decade earlier, in another bar bathroom. That night there had been booze mixed in with the blood; it had been a trashy establishment rather than a tasteful one. But here we were again, me cleaning him up, bewitched, bothered, and bewildered by feelings I couldn't muddle through and desperately wanted to both feel and to forget. His eyes had softened, and in the length of a blink, his eyes shifted to the color I'd known in my human years, the color they'd flashed to reignite the spark of memory.

His undamaged hand was at my back before I knew it, and he pulled me to him gently, giving me an opportunity to resist. I had no desire to pull away. I leaned in, and suddenly, his lips were on mine. It was as though ten years of separation, of forgetting him and who I was, of hating him melted away, and I knew that he would never let me forget again.

Chapter 40

I ended the kiss reluctantly. His hand was still bleeding. "I'm going to see if Jett has anything to help," I said, smiling, and left a small peck on his cheek before I walked out. I don't know if he knew I was lying.

I asked one of the humans where I could find Jett, and they pointed me to the door Frank had gone through. I entered without knocking.

Frank was sipping a cocktail glass with a small amount of what I immediately recognized as Jett's blood. Good. It would help replenish him faster than anything else he could give him. I had made a decision before I'd even left Cy's side about how to handle this, and he wouldn't be happy. It's why I left him back in the bathroom.

"Jett." The address was not friendly or familiar. It was a sovereign speaking to a subject, and he straightened at the tone.

"Madame," he said snidely with a curt bow.

"I think we should have a talk. Frank, you may go. You'll need rest to recover." I couldn't remember showing such generosity to a human in my entire afterlife, save for Indigo.

Frank left, unsteady on his feet. I actually felt bad and wanted to apologize, but knew that such a show of weakness- to show care toward a mortal- would negate everything I needed to say. "I don't know what you may know, what you may have guessed, but I think we need to recognize that at this point in time, we both could cause great harm to one another, in a political sense. And I believe you know that even without a fresh kill to my name, you would never win in a physical confrontation with me." He nodded. "Since mutually assured destruction is not on my agenda for the evening, I will pay you generously for the services rendered here tonight. As promised, Frank will be well compensated by me. How you choose to deal with him on your end is your choice, but know that the Council will turn a blind eye to this operation and to any action you take in response to the events of tonight."

He nodded again. I turned, but before I could reach the doorknob, he said, "Cy. He's not mortal, but he isn't one of us anymore." Statement. Not query. I turned to look at him, neither confirming nor denying. "Even a fledgling would sense it, *Madame*. I don't know why, I don't know how, but I know that as a Council member, tying yourself to a human will make you a target for a coup." Nothing I hadn't realized on my own. He realized that I wasn't going to give him any information and he shrugged. "Advice from an old friend."

"Thank you, *old friend*," I said, emphasizing the address to indicate both gratitude and a threat. "If you will have us back, we will return." It wasn't a request. I knew I couldn't kill (at least not often) and be who I needed to be to move forward, and I would need a way to circumvent the bloodlust. Hopefully, the "donation" I would provide would be enough to help Jett accept our company and not turn me over to Zilpher. But

306

if he wanted to cut off his nose to spite his face, there was little I could do to stop him, and we both knew it.

He nodded again and gave the same curt bow. I went back to the bathroom where Cy was standing over the sink, still holding firm pressure on his hand. He'd put on the black shirt, which was just as striking on him as the white had been; even better because any wounds that may still be weeping wouldn't show through his clothing. The hand was much worse than I had thought, to still be bleeding. He'd soaked through several towels. I looked it over and knew it needed attention that wouldn't be available here.

He had an impish glint in his eye despite the pain. "How did it go? Threatening Jett."

I placed my face against his shoulder, wrapping a hand around his arm since his hands were occupied. "I was nice. Ish. It was hard and went against every instinct, but I did it." I turned my face, speaking with my lips pressed against him. "Let's go home."

*   *   *

Cy went inside first, the fresh towel we'd grabbed before leaving half saturated with his blood. The wound had finally stopped bleeding, but he had lost a lot, and his skin and lips were pale, his eyes slightly unfocused. He threw the towel into the sink and pulled a bag of blood from the fridge. He pulled the cap off with his teeth and sipped it slowly, pulling back with a grimace every few seconds.

"Stop," I scolded. I went to him and took the blood. "You've lost too much. You're not helping anything by forcing yourself to drink beyond what you need."

"We should have taken an IV from Trusty's," he groaned, walking to and dropping onto the couch. "I could have given myself a transfusion."

I hadn't moved to him yet. I was making my mind up about something that could be rapture or ruin. There was only one way to find out.

His head lay over the back of the couch, his eyes closed. A sheen of sweat was breaking out across his ashen forehead. He'd lost at least twenty percent of his blood, then, for shock symptoms to be starting. Good thing I'd already committed mentally. I kneeled on the couch beside him and leaned forward to him. I gave him a soft, lingering kiss. He had energy enough for that, but his lips were cool. While his hands held my face, I took my hand to the base of my throat and sliced across the collarbone, freeing a stream of my own blood.

He pulled back in horror, pushing me away by my arms. "No," he gasped. His eyes were full of worry, but he couldn't hide the desire there too. "What are you doing? No!"

"Why?" I asked. I held his face as he'd held mine moments before, intimate and soft. "It's your blood. You gave it to me. I'm giving it back."

His eyes were glued to the trickle that was staining my shirt. "We don't know what would happen. Look what happened when you were changed, when you took my blood!"

"So take it back," I said. "Drink it, and we'll feed from each other," my fangs descended as my excitement grew, "and we'll be strong enough to never have to worry about the Council ever again! We could *be* the Council! Just the two of us-"

Cy stood with great effort. "Do you even hear yourself? A hostile takeover? The idea of changing me back crosses your mind, and the first thing you consider is a coup! That's the first reason I won't take it, *Madame*." He flung the address at me as an insult. It hurt as intended. "You don't even know what would happen! I'm not a human. I'm not a vampire. What if I weakened you, taking your blood, and something about my state as neither human nor vampire was... disrupted and it killed me? We'd both be fucked." He sat by me again and brushed my hair away from my face, a gesture he'd done dozens of times in a previous life, but now his hands were shaking with weakness. He whispered, "I'm not afraid to die. I've been alive for a long time. But I can't risk it until I know you're safe." I scoffed and he rolled his eyes. "You're strong and smart, and you've lasted a long time, not only surviving but thriving without me or any other man, woman, or creature to help you. I get that. But you're right that you need to figure out who you are before you can walk back into a den of vampires and expect to rule."

He was right on all counts. I hadn't thought of what might happen to him, only how it might help me to rise above Zilpher and the others, to take control of my life. I couldn't look him in the eyes. "I just want to be free of it all. I didn't want this power- the blood, the strength, any of it- to begin with. It was an accident. Kind of." I told him about Orla, about how my power was even more compounded by her blood in my veins. "I don't want you to die. I lived the last decade without you and look who I turned into. I mean, yeah, I was a badass-" a chuckle from us both- "but I think I have the opportunity to be better than either of the people I was before. I can be strong and ruthless, but know when to follow compassion and charity. That's because of you, because you helped me remember and sort through the muck in my mind." I held his hands in mine. "You don't have to take much. If it hurts you, stop. But you're fading. I could take you to the hospital, but how would we explain the blood loss from a healed wound?"

Cy's eyes drifted back to the now-closed line at my throat. He swallowed hard, the sweat pouring from him now. He knew I was right and nodded reluctantly.

I sliced the skin open again and pulled him to me. I'd never given my blood to anyone before. It was forbidden for Council members to do so, in case we used our strength to create a family of powerful vampires who would rise up- just as

I'd suggested Cy and I do- to overthrow the rest of the Council. I didn't care, though, because as his lips locked onto me and he pulled from the wound, it was a sensation so brutally sensual I gasped out loud. "Oh, fuck!" He started to pull away, startled, and I held tight to him, not wanting it to stop. "Fuck, yes!" At my positive exclamation, he gulped hungrily, the need in both of us rising higher the more he drank. I knew our entire fight had been pointless. There was no stopping it, and in reality, it hadn't even begun tonight. It started years before, right in these rooms, and we were just finishing what we'd started.

*   *   *

We spent the night and most of the next day in the throes of ecstasy. Our blood flowed back and forth between us, but never enough to bring Cy all the way back to immortality. He wasn't ready, he'd said. He wanted to wait. Nothing else was going to wait, though. We gave in to each other, more gently and lovingly than I had any memory of ever doing before, even as a human; our bodies, our blood, our voices combined and mingled in ways that I felt certain no one else in history had ever managed.

When the moon rose the next night, we lay in each other's arms, me staring at his eyes, which were shimmering. They were still hazel, but the shade of blue for which Amber had once named him undulated through the iris, like a fish swimming below a clear tide: visible, but hard to make out clearly.

Cy kissed me again, his arms holding me tightly. He was stronger than before. That was good because as I broke the kiss, I knew we'd both need to be as strong as possible. My mind had quieted during the night, allowing me to just be present, but the noise was starting again in earnest. I might never stop struggling with my inner voices, with the human and the vampire within me, but I was ready to know what I had yet to learn and to act on it.

I climbed out of the bed and pulled on a robe, tossing his shirt to him. "I think we need to talk now."

Chapter 41

We'd showered (together, of course. What was a few extra moments of pleasure before we dove into what was certain to be nothing but pain?) and had dressed, and soon found ourselves at the table, empty blood packets scattered around to fill what was lost the previous night, through Cy's wound and through the exchanges.

Cy was certainly closer to being a vampire than he'd been in a long time, with our shared blood coursing through his body, but we were careful to not let him have too much. I needed the strength of my own blood, after all, and I didn't need it diluted any more than it was. Then there was the concern over him changing. I didn't even know if he *could* become a vampire again. He would have to die with my blood in him, but he had already died once. I certainly wasn't going to make an attempt on his life in case... Well, I couldn't dwell on it too much, or I would lose my mind... again.

In addition to our empty blood packets, the table was covered with phones, tablets, and computers. He had all of his devices he had used while tracking my loved ones and me, and I had all of my devices I required as a Council Member, as well as a personal device that I kept secret from Zilpher and the others. It was a number only Amber had.

Before we get to that, though, let's back up to our conversation that began before we'd dressed and eaten, and what awaited me when I turned all of these items on.

"She's going to kill you," Cy had said, pulling on a pair of pants. His clothes were alongside mine in the closet, right where they'd been ten years earlier. I had no idea when he'd moved them in again.

I was stunned at his words, not because it was hard to believe, but because it was so obvious. "That's it? Amber wants me dead? What is this, ten years ago?"

Cy smirked at me, but then scolded, "You know better than to think that's it. You knew Amber for a long time after you died. You told me once she was your only friend. I knew you two had bonded and become close. I honestly think she had grown to care about you, in the way Amber cares, anyway. Then suddenly, five years ago, I lost track of her. She didn't contact you after that."

I told him about Indigo, how she'd been made, how the Council had ordered their death sentence, and how Zilpher had supposedly carried it out. I left out the part about Zilpher being my sometimes lover, though if Cy had been keeping tabs on me for that long, he likely already knew about it.

"Well, given what I know about Zilpher," Cy said, "he's just petty enough to actually spare Amber if it meant he had a chance to hurt you. To be sympathetic to his motives for a moment, you did kill Orla. He's no saint, and their relationship was always tenuous, but they were paramours going back before the birth of Christ." He looked thoughtful.

"But why the slow play?" I asked. "Why wait five years? Why not just strike right then?"

Cy laughed. "You're still very young, Love," he said, kissing my head. "Love" was the only thing he'd managed to call me that didn't cause me to have some kind of psychological revolt. Too bad I'd kill anyone else who tried to call me that, or I could have just accepted it as my new name. "Five years when you've lived for centuries or millennia is nothing. This is the opposite of a slow play for them. To them, this is swift vengeance."

"Then why now?" I demanded. Then it occurred to me. "Ten years. Every ten years, Amber reenacts her revenge on Sigrun."

Cy looked uncomfortable. "Yes. That's the heart of it, but... well, let's just say after hearing about her adventures with this Indigo, something else makes a lot more sense. And it's not good." His brow was furrowed in concern.

"What's that?" I asked, fearing the answer.

He hesitated, his shimmering eyes warning me about... what? Why wouldn't he tell me? Instead of saying anything, he turned and handed me a printout of a news article. A local university boy had been accused of rape. Well, that was right up Amber's alley.

"Okay, but how does this pertain to her hatred of me?" I demanded.

Cy pointed about halfway down the article to a highlighted line referring to the boy's attorney. *Attorney for the Defense, Public Defender Danielle Taylor, says her client is merely the victim of a he-said-she-said situation that has been blown out of proportion.*

Danielle Taylor. My sister.

The building could have collapsed underneath me for the sensation I felt in the pit of my stomach. Cy was talking. "This is the phone call I'd waited for that night in the basement, confirmation that Danielle was involved in this case. She started doing pro bono work for a while- not having the Ivy League degree hurt her prospects for a job- but your mom hasn't worked in years, and your sister had to pay the mortgage or they would have lost the house. Public defender was the first job she could get on the timeline she needed."

The air had gone out of the room. "Danielle..." We'd never been close, but I was always proud of her. She was so smart, so driven, things I had always wanted to be but never was. I was the artist, the free spirit. She would have been the sister anyone would have expected to end up in a position of political power, not me. Now she had to defend a probable rapist just to make ends meet, I was part of the ruling class of vampires, and these two things combined were going to get her killed.

"If she hasn't already, Amber's intention is to reach out to you, to pretend to make amends. She was going to convince you that Danielle is an enabler of these malefactors and that you should join her when she kills both lawyer and client."

I felt like I'd been slapped. "She wanted me to kill my own sister?"

Cy curled his lip in disgust. "All part of the game," he murmured. "I told you, it's all about the game now. The one thing we have going for us is that, to my knowledge, she thinks I died after she left me to rot back on Caladesi Island."

"You mean when *we* left you there..." I mumbled guiltily.

He looked down. "You didn't know who I was," he said, but the words still carried pain. I had never realized the true depth of what I'd done to him that night. I tried to see it through his eyes and had to detach quickly before it brought about another mad episode. I had enough of my own demons to contend with. Part of me wanted to hold him, to comfort him, to apologize, but I was already struggling with the information both in front of me and that which was still eluding me. I couldn't have the internal battle required to show such soft affection at that moment.

"No," I said instead. "I didn't." I needed to get back on track. "But it was about straight-up revenge before you left her and only then did it become a game- because of *you* specifically. I don't understand why she would do this, make such a big deal out of me."

Cy sighed. "I have my theories. Once I fell in love with you, it became about revenge again- but directly against you. The most likely thing I can think of is that she has been planning something like this from when you died, hoping that if she could get you to kill your own sister she would effectively be killing Elsie Taylor twice; the first time in ending your mortal life and the second in truly killing any remnant of Elsie that you may have held onto. Then she could enlist the help of someone like Zilpher to kill you a third and final time. It would be the ultimate victory over both of us. But I think there's more to it. I think that *was* her plan, but I watched you both for years. She truly grew to love you, and I think she was going to abandon the plan. She even stopped watching your family for a few years, but when you betrayed her-" I started to protest, but he waved me down, "her perception, not mine- she fell back on the original plan. It probably wasn't difficult to bring Zilpher in either, after you proved on your rebirth-day that you were stronger than he is, something he likely found humiliating."

I rolled my eyes, the gesture more casual than I felt. "Yeah, well, he's never been short on ego to bruise."

"There's more," Cy said. "She's been watching Ashley. She matches the profile Amber generally targets as well (though she usually goes for younger women than Ashley is now), and, while she's never done two revenge killings in the same year, I have a bad feeling about why she would be tracking someone else who was important to you. Then there's the one thing I can't figure out. She's given me the slip a handful of times, and I have no idea where she goes. She disappears from various locations, and reappears like she'd never left. I just don't know where she goes when she vanishes."

We sat in silence for several minutes. I went to the fridge and pulled out some blood for each of us. Cy had to open the lid with his hands, still lacking any kind of sharpness in his canines with which to puncture the plastic, though they appeared longer. His thirst was undoubtedly more present than it had been in the entire time I had been back with him. I tried not to think about what that might mean for him, for us, for a future, but was failing. This entire discussion made it very clear that a future for either of us, let alone for both of us, was not a guarantee.

We'd been apart for so long, and even before we were parted, there was the memory of everything between us that had nearly torn us apart. I couldn't give in to my feelings for too long. My mind was still volatile; I was a ship at the eye of a storm, and I knew any one event, even a word, that stirred the waters just the right or wrong way could cause the seas to churn and capsize me. If I dwelled too much on anything that produced any kind of intense feeling, the edges of my sanity would start to fray. I was glad for Cy and his company, and I wanted to be near him; I occasionally thought I even loved him. It had happened quite often during the previous night, the throes of passion working their magic. But I had spent ten years rejecting the idea of anything even close to love. Did I know what it was anymore? Did it matter if I did?

Faced suddenly with this very real possibility of a future, of eternity with Cy, did I even want it? If we prevailed against Amber and Zilpher and any others who stood against me, was what I felt for him enough to bind us together forever? I didn't know. I felt both my madness and my mixed feelings for him starting to creep back on me, felt the sand closing over my head. *Detach*, I ordered myself. Letting the calm, collected parts I'd developed as Opal take over helped when I started to feel the glass cracking.

Cy collected our devices and brought them to the table, running chargers from the outlets around the room until we looked like spiders at the center of a web. I took a deep breath. I had been offline for three weeks and had no idea what awaited me when I finally booted up. I grabbed another couple of blood packets for each of us and drained my own quickly while the machines loaded their operating systems.

Welcome chimes. *Here we go,* I thought.

The notifications came pouring in. Many were news reports that required my attention as Councilor. Possible killings from rogues. One was Kara. I looked away from the report and turned my attention to direct communications.

Dozens of messages from the Council were waiting for me. Sapphire, Zilpher, and half a dozen of the others. Zilpher's were the oldest, asking me if I'd tracked down Amber (*Why even let me know she was alive, and that you knew?* I thought. *Why open yourself up to my scrutiny? Is it all part of the game?*), then threatening to break down my door if I didn't answer him, angry messages that I wasn't around when he'd come by to say hello (*With his dick. Never again, though.*), and finally messages letting me know that the rest of the Council had been informed of my absence. The remaining messages from all of my contacts were some mixture of concern for my well-being (mostly Sapphire, though I trusted her only slightly more than I trusted Zilpher- she had the detachment I aspired to down to an art and rarely succumbed to petty personal connections or arguments, which included any emotional attachment to me), thinly veiled threats that I would be considered rogue if I didn't get in touch soon, and finally barely contained glee from Zilpher as he commented on how, if I wasn't already dead, I would be soon.

Cy was also tapping away at his own keyboards and screens with a deepening line between his eyebrows. I would have interrupted to see what he'd discovered, but decided we could share once we were both all caught up unless there was something urgent.

I took a moment to marvel at the strangeness of the moment, of us, two star-crossed immortal lovers frantically working side by side on computers and smart devices. I supposed it shouldn't have seemed so odd. Lots of couples worked concurrently in their homes. The abnormality was really due to our unusual relationship more than to the current moment, which for most, would be a very normal thing.

I returned to my screens, working on contacting all those who had sent messages, both of good and ill will, to reassure them that I was, in fact, alive and as strong as ever. I had created an alibi based on news and Council reports. Deaths that could possibly be attributed to vampires but were not covered in our internal memos were exactly what I needed.

My story was that I had uncovered a cluster of young and careless rogues in the area while investigating some of the killings that were baffling the police, and they had made a move against me as a group. I had to go into hiding quickly, and hadn't time to alert anyone. I had been tracking them for weeks, picking them off one at a time. They were no longer a threat, I assured the rest of the Council. I was sorry for acting without approval, but my methods were paramount to my safety and survival, and knew they would understand that I had acted in the best interest of our society as a whole.

I sent nothing to Zilpher personally.

I turned to the phone that was my direct line to only Amber, picking it up. I hadn't turned it on yet. I would never admit it to Cy, but discovering that she was alive had lit a small flame of joy within me. I knew now the ways she'd hurt me and those I loved, knew she'd lied to me about so much, but I had known her. I had seen her in moments of weakness and pain. I feared her, but I did love her, and so I also feared *for* her. I knew that I wouldn't hesitate to be the one to kill her if it came to that, but a small part of me wanted to try to reason with her before it did.

I pressed the button on the side, watching the startup logo brighten the otherwise black screen. I waited what felt like an eternity. The home screen sprang to life, and I waited. Then... *bzzt.* Message received one week ago.

Need to reach you. Call me.

Chapter 42

"No!" Cy shouted at me again.

We had been fighting for over an hour. I had told Cy that I wanted to go meet Amber, to feel her out. I needed to know if she was following through on the plan he'd predicted, but he wouldn't hear of it.

"You know it's a trap! Why even entertain this?" He looked like he might rip his hair out. It might have been comical if not for the wars raging between us and in my own mind.

I was dangerously close to losing control again. My love (if that's even the right word- what did I know of love?) for both Amber and Cy was conflicting and incompatible. I couldn't love Cy and accept Amber as a friend, and I couldn't love Amber and have Cy by my side. Amber had been my companion, my mentor, for years when I had no way of navigating my world. There was also the fact that, while I obviously found her selection of innocents to murder repulsive, I didn't entirely disagree with the tracking down of those scourges of humanity who slipped through the cracks of the human legal systems. A part of me believed there was something in her I could maybe reach, to convince her to focus on the one part of the crusade that was actually worthwhile. I *could* choose her, but I would be knowingly destroying others I loved, and she may still opt to destroy me as well. Once more, I was deprived of the choice; it was being made for me.

Earlier, after receiving Amber's message, I went to the fridge and tore through three packets of blood in quick succession.

"You okay?" Cy asked in concern as he watched my binge, not knowing the cause.

I braced my hands on the counter, looking away from him. "I'm going to call Amber."

He was completely silent for several moments. I looked at him as the silence grew, and his face was blank. Uh oh. That was never a good sign with him. "And say what, Love?" He finally choked out.

I snarled in frustration. "I don't fucking know! I know that I can't ignore her." I slid the phone across the table to him so he could see the message. "I contacted the Council already, so if Zilpher tells her I'm back in action and I *don't* contact her, she'll just get pissed and move up her timeline." Cy considered this and nodded. We both knew her impetuous nature and that unless I played to her plan, she would change it in frightening and unpredictable ways. "I can use this as a way to try to figure out where she's been and what her next steps are. If Amber thinks that you're dead and that I still don't remember my life, she has no reason to be suspicious of me and will want to move forward with getting me to kill Danielle. I can be our mole."

Cy shook his head, frowning. "I don't like it. It's too risky. We can track her remotely." He motioned to the wealth of computing devices on the table.

322

"And if we fail? You've already said she manages to disappear on you. Me not contacting her is just going to arouse suspicion. I have to call her. I have to be relieved she's alive and excited to hear from her." Never mind that a small part of that would be based in truth. He still looked worried, so I walked around to him and held his face in my hands. "It's just a phone call. I'm smarter than she is, and I can get information out of her."

Cy wrapped his arms around my waist and leaned his forehead against my chest. "You're probably right. I've spent centuries being afraid of her and what she might do." He looked up at me. "But you are smarter. If anyone can take her down, it's you."

I smiled and kissed him lightly. "Only with help."

He frowned, still not wanting me to do it, but after a brief tightening of his grip on me, he let go and waved his hand at me as if to say, "*Go ahead.*" Then he seemed to think of something. "Put it on speaker. I want to hear."

"Yeah, okay," I said sarcastically. "Let's just let her hear you breathing in the background. Because she won't know something's up if I call her with a human babysitter. You shouldn't even be here at all when I call her. Do I need to remind you how good our hearing is? Or have you forgotten in the last ten years?"

He glared. "Fine. But I'm not leaving. I'll stay in here. Go to the bathroom and close every door between here and there."

I turned to walk away and he grabbed my hand. I looked at him and his eyes were darkened with fear and worry. "I know you love her. I know how much she meant to you. And I'm sure a part of you even thinks she can be redeemed." He always knew just what I was thinking. "But she's dangerous. You know that. You know how many lives- innocent and otherwise- are at stake if we don't beat her at her game. Don't let her play you."

I was torn between gratitude at his concern and annoyance at his lack of faith in my ability to handle this. I wanted to say something witty, possibly biting, but I settled for, "I've got this. Don't worry."

I went into the bedroom, closing that door behind me. Then I went into the bathroom and shut that door too. If I had a heartbeat, it would have been flying. I was nervous, terrified, and excited to call Amber. I had to decide- and quickly- how I wanted to play this. *Fuck* these human emotions! I told myself that she wanted to speak to Opal, so I should let her talk to Opal. I did my best to stuff away any feelings that might affect how I reacted to the call. I needed the cold, uncaring, regal manner of Opal. I needed to be pleased, but like someone would be pleased that they received a free gift with purchase they hadn't expected. Nice surprise, but I could have lived without it.

I let out a long breath, effectively killing another two minutes while making sure I was ready for this. I sat on the edge of my beautiful teal bathtub and pressed the icon to dial Amber.

I put the phone to my ear and waited.

Ring. Okay, her phone is on and active. *Ring.* Why isn't she answering? *Ring.* What is taking so long? *Ring-click!*

"Opal," Amber said.

Suddenly my brain went blank. I forgot what I was going to say, how I was going to act. *Pull it together! Detach and act!* I commanded myself.

"Amber." I decided to aim for the power position. Let her come to me.

There was a silence while she realized that I wasn't going to say anything. "It's been a while," she said lamely.

"Yes. I was led to understand that you'd been killed," I said, trying to sound disinterested. I failed. Shit. Too eager, too formal; it didn't sound natural at all. I forced myself to calm and silence. I'd dragged information out of people for a decade with stoic and disapproving silence, I could do it now.

Amber gave a tinkling laugh. "Not that easy to get rid of me, girlie. Didn't think you'd care much since you made the call that nearly caused it." Her voice was sweet and airy, but I could feel the ripple of rage even through the airwaves.

I nearly made a comment to defend myself, but held firm. "Sure, Amber," I said, hoping I sounded bored of the game already. "You said you needed to talk?"

"I *did!*" She sounded delighted. "I found something fun for us to do to celebrate your birthday!"

"I don't have a birthday," I reminded her.

She laughed again. "You know what I mean! It's tomorrow night, you know! I was hoping to have more time before then, but you've been totally MIA, so we'll just have to do this on a rush timetable. Can you meet before sunrise? I'll text you where."

"Can't you just tell me where to meet you tomorrow?" I needed to stall. "I wanted to hunt and sleep. It's been a long few weeks."

"Oh, really? Were you faking your own death for half a decade because your progeny sold you out? No? Go hunt quickly. Then meet me. Trust me, this is so *us!*"

Then she hung up. I didn't have much of a chance to glean anything from her. Well, I did learn one thing. I had so much less time than I thought.

I left the bathroom and went into the closet to pick out something to wear. I had been in a loose-fitting tank and leggings since Cy and I had planned for a night in, but I could never meet Amber like that. I chose a body-hugging dress and heels. Cy wasn't going to like my plan one bit.

I went out to the dining room and motioned for him to join me in the bedroom. He smiled, completely misreading the situation. He walked in behind me, his arms rising to hold me, but before he could reach me, he saw the clothes I'd laid out on the bed. The Brow went up. Before he could ask, I started.

"I'm meeting Amber. Tonight."

The fight raged for well over an hour. Yes, I knew it was probably a trap; yes, I understood she had at least one powerful ally, and the two of them alone could very likely kill me before I ever even made it to the rendezvous. But I also knew that I didn't have time for anything else.

"Cy, it's tomorrow. She has something big planned for the anniversary of the night she killed me. You expect me to assume that it's anything other than my sister's murder?"

"And if you die tonight, or even if she lets you live until tomorrow and kills you then, your sister still doesn't live. We have to play this smart, Love!" He was reaching for me, but I wouldn't let him touch me. The entire time we argued, I'd kept my distance, showering and changing. I could still smell his scent on me, but it was faint, and I had to hope that Amber wouldn't recognize it as him since it wasn't a true vampire's scent.

"Then use the time I'm gone to find out more. Figure out if we have any allies we can call on, people who have a grudge against Zilpher or are afraid of Amber."

The phone buzzed and Cy grabbed it. "The Speakeasy, 4am," he read. Some of the wind went out of his sails and he sighed. "At least it's public. She could still kill you, but it seems a lot less likely if she's bringing you somewhere where a lot of other vampires who are hopefully loyal to you will be."

"Good," I said regally. "Then you won't fight me when I walk out the door now."

He cocked his head to the side in a combination of confusion and accusation. "It's only two o'clock. It won't take you two hours to get there."

"No," I agreed. I crossed my arms defiantly. "It won't. But I'm not going to see Amber without being at the top of my game."

He stepped toward me and I backed away again. "Don't," he begged. "We found another way, you could even just take from me, you don't have to-"

"How are you this dense?" I spat at him. "You remember your three centuries with the same abilities I have. You know she'll probably smell you on me as it is. Do you know if you smell like you used to? Because I used to be human and have no idea, and if she recognizes your scent, our gambit is over. I need to go out and do what I always do- did. Before. Otherwise, she'll know something's wrong."

Cy was crushed. He knew what I meant. I had to seduce and kill some drunken idiot. I wanted to wrap my arms around him and assure him that it was only this one last time, and I wouldn't like it, that there was no alternative. But if I was completely honest, it thrilled me to have an excuse to do it, and I hoped it *wouldn't* be the only time. So instead of comforting him, I turned and left the bedroom where we'd given ourselves so freely to each other just hours before. "Don't contact me until I say so," I called over my shoulder.

"Wait!" He cried back, rushing to stand in front of me. "Just... Promise me you'll come back."

I looked at him like he was an idiot. "I live here," I said. "Of course, I'll come back."

Cy shook his head sadly at me. "That's not what I meant. Promise me you won't let this destroy you again. Promise that if you do this, it won't take you away from me again. I know you're not Elsie anymore, not completely. But I do still love you. I probably always will. I loved you before, and I love who you're becoming now so... just don't let me lose you again. Please."

It was too much. It hearkened back to another life when, under the threat of danger, he'd confessed his love to me, and I couldn't reciprocate. Was I destined to hurt him over and over again for eternity?

I walked around him and simply said, "I'll do my best," and I left.

Chapter 43

It was my first hunt.

Opal had hunted, but I- the new I who was somehow Opal and Elsie and neither- had never hunted. I tried to let Opal take over, but the thought of Cy waiting for me at home was a constant nag at my mind and made finding easy prey difficult. I had gone to a few bars at which I always had success, but couldn't seem to seal the deal. I was running out of time. I suppose even though I was excited to actually get a kill in, a part of me was stalling so I wouldn't have time for the seduction part. Being this torn about something I'd done thousands of times was tearing at the fabric of my sanity... again.

I had passed up a couple of prospects simply because they were too drunk or stoned to be of use. I couldn't risk being impaired. Being out in the open was bad enough. I debated running as fast as I could up Nebraska Avenue to where the hookers hung out, figuring anyone trolling at this time of night would be no great loss to society, but even that would cut my time too short. I decided to stick close to the Speakeasy.

I walked that way, hoping some ruthless degenerate would jump me before I got there, thinking I was an easy target. It would certainly save me some effort and guilt; the more I wandered, the more I thought about Cy and his request. It was the reason I was impotent tonight. I struggled with the conflicting desires to find out what the future held for us and to just let my animal side take over and not care about him or any of the people who needed me... It would never happen, I realized. The sand was closing over my head, drawing me back into a life filled with human emotions, connections, and desires.

I saw movement ahead, a few blocks from my destination. Someone was stumbling around nearby. The scent was familiar, but the person was clearly drunk. I zipped over along with the wind and found myself in front of Frank from Trusty's.

"Fuck off," he slurred at me, stumbling until he came to a rest on the ground, barely sitting. "Vamp bitch nearly kills me then finds me here... gonna finish the job?"

I looked down at him in disgust and crossed my arms. I was the image of godly disapproval. "Why are you out here, Frank?" I asked. "Aren't you supposed to be in bed? Back at Trusty's?" It would be so easy to take him here, now, with his decadent blood that I could practically taste...

"Snuck out. You and Jett think I can be bought off. You think I..." His words trailed off and he turned and vomited on the sidewalk.

I rolled my eyes, annoyed. "I so don't have time for this," I mumbled to him as I lifted him by his arm and dragged him a few doors down to the kitchens at Trusty's. I knocked over and over, but no one came to the door. Finally, I dropped my burden and forced the lock. I deposited Frank in a corner of the wine cellar to sleep it off. He was belligerent and insulting to the very last moment of consciousness.

It was the least I could do for Jett after my incident.

As I walked back through the kitchen, I realized suddenly I wasn't alone. Someone had followed us in, the broken door having been as good as an invitation. I felt a knife at my throat. Damn all these distractions. I couldn't remember the last time anyone actually successfully snuck up on me- especially a human.

My attacker sniffed my hair. "Hello, gorgeous," he said in a guttural, unpleasant whisper. "What brings you here tonight? Doesn't seem like the place for a pretty little thing like you."

I rolled my eyes, fed up by this point. "Then let's get out of here," I said in my sultriest voice. I turned quickly, breaking the arm that held the knife. I dragged him outside, not wanting to leave Jett with the cleanup. He was wailing in fear and pain as he tried to hit me, to free himself. "Give it up, you dirty sack of shit," I spat at him.

We moved slower than I could have done alone, but still faster than humans were likely to notice, especially at this time of night. I deposited him on a bench overlooking the water. Other benches were filled with homeless people and with drunken couples who didn't realize that others could clearly see exactly how intimate they were getting. I turned to the thief and grabbed his face. I didn't even let him speak before I wrapped myself around him. To anyone looking on, it was a lover's embrace, my limbs merely desperate to be wrapped around his. He tried to cry out, but my mouth was at his throat before he could make a sound, and he sank into a state of semi-consciousness that often came over victims.

Oh, it was heaven, taking his blood and knowing I didn't have to stop, not for anything. Well, I planned to stop before the last drop. The last time I had gone that far... well, look what happened. I was certifiably insane as a result.

The little fight he had in him after I'd broken his arm faded as I took the hot, flowing life into myself. It was ecstasy. I had missed this, feeling someone's last breaths slip away...

feeling the heart race, then slow... knowing that I held their fate and snuffed it out quickly and without a thought. It was better than any human drug. I very nearly took the last drop purely out of the desire to keep draining well past the point of death.

I laid the body on the bench and stood to examine myself. Once I was sure I was clean of any blood, I took off toward the Speakeasy. I only had half an hour left and wanted to be early.

On the way there, I thought about the kill and how good it had felt. It hadn't been simply the kill; it had been cathartic, in a way, to know that I had actually removed someone danger-ous from the world. He'd put that knife to my throat. What could he possibly have wanted from me? Amber's words from the night I'd died came back to me. *"Nothing good, girlie."* Cy would have had me leave it to the law, but I *was* the law in Tampa, at least when it came to matters of blood. I could be judge, jury, and executioner to those who deserved it. But should I?

The questions plagued me my entire walk. I finally en-tered and sat myself at the bar. Colorado came over with a tiny bow. "Madame Opal!" He sang out cordially. "It's been a while. Usual?"

"Sure," I said, and watched him walk away to pour me a glass. I wanted a few moments to collect myself before Amber arrived. My mind was churning with joy, with guilt, with a de-sire to kill again, with horror at the murder I'd just commit-ted...

He would have killed me, I reminded myself. *And if not me, certainly someone else.* Even if I did love Cy, even if I wanted that future... I knew I wasn't done with my killing days. Not by a long shot. The more human parts of me hated that knowledge, but I had already allowed so much of who I was now to be driven by those softer, moral impulses. With the taste of my attacker's blood still on my lips, I knew that I could never give this up, not entirely, especially as long as I could justify the spilled blood by selecting only those who would harm others or myself. And I didn't know what that meant for Cy or for the two of us.

Colorado came and put the drink down in front of me. Something of my internal struggle must have shown on my face because he asked me, "Are you alright?"

I supposed it was better for Colorado to notice before Amber got here. It allowed me to correct the expression prior to her arrival. I tossed my hair back and took a sip from the glass. Heavenly.

"Fine," I told him. "My hunt wasn't as satisfying as I'd been hoping for."

He seemed to buy what I'd said, but then he leaned in to whisper to me confidentially. "You know... other Council Members have been here in the last few weeks. No one knew where you were."

I waved away his concerns. "I had business to take care of. I've informed my colleagues of my task. They shouldn't be disturbing you any more than usual from now on."

He smiled at me, but there was a hint of doubt. He knew me too well to be so easily convinced. Colorado had always been friendly and, I believed, loyal to me. I wondered if he would continue to be so if he knew that I was no longer the same person, at least not entirely. I was tempted to put it to the test, knowing how badly I needed an ally who could actually fight with me if needed. Cy was still nowhere near strong enough to join the fray.

I decided against saying anything, however. If he chose to stand against me for any reason, I would have yet another enemy to contend with; if he chose my side, I then had to worry about his safety in addition to my own and Cy's. At this point, until I knew what exactly I was facing, it was better to play things close to the chest.

I heard the door open and felt her even before I smelled her. I forced myself to detach, to adopt the stoic nature I felt so comfortable in for so many years.

Still leaning forward with my drink, I didn't move, even when Amber sat beside me, her foot hooked over the rail at the bottom of my chair. Friendly. Familiar. Lies.

She waited for me to say something, and when I didn't, she said sarcastically, "Hello, Amber, I'm so happy to see you alive after I nearly had you killed."

I took a long sip from my glass, allowing my preternatural patience to run the show.

"Opal, come on," she wheedled. "At least talk to me."

Without looking at her, I asked, "Why are you here, Amber?"

"Wow, this was *so* not the reaction I expected you to have when you found out I was alive. I half expected you to hug me, or cry, or at least smile!" She was pouting. But I knew better.

"You know me better than any of that," I reminded her lazily.

Amber let out an exaggerated sigh. "Yeah, that's true." She leaned in closer to me. "Come on, look at me! Talk to me! I've been 'dead' for the last five years! The least you could do is ask me how I survived."

"How did you survive?" I asked dully.

"Well," she started her story with relish, pleased to get to tell it. She always did love to talk. I had to wonder if any of it would even be true. "Zilpher came and he took Indigo first. She never stood a chance. Gone in a minute. Poor little baby vamp." There was some real sadness in her voice she tried not to let through as she spoke of her progeny. After all, she'd fought against me when I didn't want to let Indigo be made; she had advocated for the poor creature. "I fought Zilpher off. He's old and strong as fuck, but I'm no spring chicken myself, and thankfully I was gorged on a number of kills of my own that night. You know Zilpher. He would never admit that he wasn't the biggest and baddest bitch in town, and we were at a stalemate. Finally, he agreed to let me go as long as I stayed hidden from the rest of the Council. He got to save face, and I got to live."

"And you never thought to reach out and say, 'Hey, Opal, thought you should know I'm alive'?" I asked, my voice sounding bored. I turned slowly to look at her at last. Fear and relief mingled, creating a swooping feeling in my chest. She was really here. She was alive. And she wanted me dead.

"Figured you were just fine," Amber said, aiming for the same disinterested tone I had used. "But we're less than a day away from the tenth anniversary of the night you were born. I wanted to treat you!"

"How so?" I asked, finally getting to it.

She opened her mouth to speak, but as the door opened to another patron, she turned her head. "Oh, perfect!" She trilled. She stood to go greet the new addition to the party. "Opal, this is my new 'friend.' He's going to be joining us, so I figured I'd fill you both in on the plan together!"

Thank God for the decade of training to stay as calm and passive as possible, because my mind, which had been overactive to the point of nearly giving me away, was now leaden and filled with only one thought, one feeling. Dread spread through me like poison. He had changed, as all of our kind do when we die. His body had already been at nearly optimal fitness, so his figure was roughly the same. The face was older than I remembered, but full of the same handsome features that could be so cruelly twisted. The cold, hard eyes, now bright white instead of their former icy blue, surveyed me as I did the same.

"Opal," she said, "meet Candide. Candide, Madame Opal of the Council."

He reached out his hand to me, and I fought every instinct within me in order to grasp it professionally and nonchalantly, and not to strike him down instantly.

Jack was a vampire.

Chapter 44

I walked home after the meeting at the Speakeasy, trying to stop shaking. I managed to hold onto my composure while we talked, but once I was on my own again, I nearly broke down. I needed to get home to Cy. I needed to tell him what happened. I needed him to tell me it was okay, that we could still prevent Amber and Zilpher from hurting people I loved.

Amber had shown me the same news article that Cy had earlier about my sister and her client. She made an impassioned speech about how all the times we struck out against the "real monsters" was small-time. This time we'd take out the guilty party as well as the enabler- the attorney who worked so hard to release him back into society. My sister.

Jack spent the entire meeting with a shit-eating smirk on his face. I mostly ignored him except when answering a direct question. Amber had obviously told him I had no memory of my life before, because he made no mention of Elsie or anything that might have been connected to those years. Well, except for one thing.

Toward the end of the meeting, once the particulars had been ironed out, we sat and talked, cordially social. It was during that part of the conversation that Amber had asked me, "So no prequel to the sequel tonight?" She winked. Her double entendre was in reference to my earlier kill and the fact that I hadn't taken the man to bed before I fed from him.

"Ran out of time," I shrugged. "I've been dealing with those rogues for weeks; I guess I'm off my game. Not to worry. I am me, after all." I smiled confidently.

Jack- Candide- had been watching the exchange like a fat cat who'd gotten the mouse. He was very obviously a fresh fledgling, possibly only a few hours old, and had nowhere near my newborn strength. I knew he could still be dangerous if he wanted to be, especially with Amber and Zilpher on his side.

Amber said slyly, "Yeah, I'm sure you'll fill that void soon enough."

Jack then spoke up with a smarmy grin. "If you need a void filled, I'm sure I could be of use."

The rage I felt at that moment was overpowering. He knew who I was, knew our history, and thought that because I didn't know who either of us was (to the best of his own knowledge), he could make a move on me. I tried to disguise the fury, but decided it would perhaps be better to scare him a bit. It might help with the following night if he knew the true measure of my power. I reached over as though to run a finger down his arm sensuously, but grabbed on and snapped the bone like a twig. It would heal within the hour, but I wanted to inflict the pain, even for a moment.

"Young one," I spat. "You are very new and very cocky. If you plan to enjoy this new life for a period that can be measured in years rather than hours, you should learn your place, and with that, the respect owed to those whose station exceeds your own."

He was gasping with the pain but managed to growl a petulant, "Sorry."

I released his arm, flashing my fangs at him. "Good. Because you wouldn't be the first of our kind I've fed on." I turned to Amber. "Anything else I need to know before I go? Like I said, it's been an exhausting few weeks, and I need to rest if we're going to do this tomorrow." She shook her head, no. "Good. Then I'll see you at sunset." Amber turned back to Jack, laughing at him. I paused in my departure, debating keeping the next words to myself, but decided it was worth saying since I might never get to again. "Amber." She looked back at me. "I *am* glad you're alive."

She looked mildly stunned, but smiled at me. "You and me both!" That laugh like a bell cut through me like a dagger. I had spent so long with that sound being a pleasant one, and now it filled me with dread.

I walked out, waving a brief goodbye to Colorado, and walked back to the condo, the wave of emotions spilling over after being held in for so long. I knew once I got inside, I was going to break down, and had to hope that Cy would be able to help pull me out of myself quickly so we could prepare.

I walked past Braun, unable to even look at him for fear that the slightest deviation from my path would loose the flood, and I would drown in my own madness. I wish I had looked at him- he might have warned me.

I rode the elevator to the top floor and stepped out to see my door wide open, the jamb broken to splinters.

No! I thought, rushing inside. A million awful scenarios went through my mind. Our doors should be unbreakable except to the strongest of our kind, and the lock had been shattered. I looked around frantically. I nearly called out for Cy, but I could smell someone inside and it wasn't him.

No smell of death or blood either. I had to hope he had gone somewhere, though where he would be, I didn't know.

Once inside, I noticed he'd cleaned up before he left, making our little web disappear. At a glance, it was as if he'd never been here. Someone else was most certainly here, and he was sitting on my couch like he owned it.

"It was good to see you were back," Zilpher said, neither getting up nor looking at me directly. "I was so worried you might have been killed somehow," he said drily.

This was the last thing I needed when I was already so close to breaking. I tried hard to pull myself together long enough to make him leave.

"What are you doing here?"

Now he stood and walked to me, pushing the door behind me as closed as it would go with the splintered wood. "I came to check on you, of course," he sneered. He moved slowly on his leonine legs, his eyes now devouring the sight of me, that same expression he always wore here, that hateful glare combined with the intense desire. He grabbed me roughly and kissed me.

I found myself desperate to escape, but I was in my own home. I didn't need to get out- I needed him to leave. I didn't want him touching me like that. Our trysts had never been a source of happiness, but I had allowed them because the hollow, empty sex was all I knew. The idea of it repulsed me now, especially knowing how he was working with Amber to kill me. Mere hours ago, I had been in Cy's arms, and it had been full of meaning. My own indecision about what that meaning was didn't change the fact that Zilpher was too close, his hands too free, his hardening erection pressing against me through our clothes, and I didn't want it.

I pushed him away, and he used the opportunity to slide out of his jacket before advancing on me again.

"No," I said firmly. "Not tonight. I'm tired. I've been in hiding for weeks. I need to rest." I rattled off all the reasons I could give him for turning him away, knowing I should never have had to say more beyond the first word, but Zilpher was not used to being denied anything, and certainly not carnal desires of any kind. He held onto me even more strongly, pulling at my dress and ripping it from the top and the bottom, exposing most of my body, as though if he just kept going, I would relent. Unlike after I'd thought Amber was dead, I had no intention of relenting.

I felt a thrill of fear as I realized that I had never actually fought him physically before. I had been stronger than Orla, but I was freshly full of Cy's vampire blood at the time. Now I was barely pumped up from my single kill, and Zilpher, by what I could smell, had enjoyed more than a few deaths before he came to me. I had no idea if I could fight him off, but I couldn't bear the thought of playing along tonight. Not with the madness not so much creeping as stampeding back in.

I shoved him away again, and he loosened the neck of his shirt. "Get out," I growled, closing off my posture.

Zilpher laughed and stepped toward me again, not understanding that I was truly rejecting him. He reached for me and I knocked his hands away, stepping backward into a defensive stance.

Zilpher paused, his sneer becoming more pronounced. "I don't think you want to let me walk out of here without improving my mood."

"I don't give a fuck about your mood," I shot back, preparing to defend myself against an attack if it came.

He advanced on me slowly, making sure I felt the danger in each movement. "Your little lie about being in hiding isn't going to go over well with the rest of the Council when I tell them you've been shirking your responsibilities to hole up here with..." He gave an exaggerated sniff of the air. "A lover. A *mor-tal* lover, if my senses don't deceive me. Which we know they never have."

I stuck my chin out defiantly, taking another step back as he continued toward me. "You know I like to play with my food. I'm sure you also smell his blood."

His eyes glinted dangerously. "Hm... I also smell yours. You've broken the rules, giving your blood to a mortal. The sentence for that is death."

I knew he was telling the truth. He could smell the exchange of our blood, and he was absolutely right about the punishment for that. I nearly dropped my walls to show the fear I was feeling in increasing amounts.

I silently prayed to the God I'd once prayed to as a human that Cy would stay away until I could get rid of Zilpher. I wasn't sure if I could save myself, let alone anyone else.

"I can stay silent," he offered. "You know my price."

He lunged forward at me again, bringing his mouth to mine. The violence of the unwelcome contact made the fear bubble up, nearly boiling, until it finally burst in a ball of fury. I pulled my face back but held tight to him as I twisted my head to his neck and gnashed my fangs wildly, opening the flesh there as wide as I could, creating not so much a fount as a burst dam.

The bloody spray covered me, and I took in as much as I could, drinking it down quickly, not wanting anything of his in me but knowing I would need it to fight him. He fell back, putting a hand to his open throat. The blood was pouring through his hands. I knew it wouldn't last long- the flow was already slowing. I only hoped I'd done sufficient damage to weaken him enough that I could win if he chose to fight me.

"You crazy *bitch!*" He screamed at me.

"In the flesh," I said, wearing the insult like armor. I certainly wasn't sane, and I'd rather be *a* bitch than be *his* bitch.

Zilpher's face showed no evidence of his previous arousal. The only thing there was pure rage, which I returned in spades.

"I believe I told you to get the fuck out," I said. "Unless you want to test which of us is actually the stronger." I licked his blood off of my lips for effect. He seemed to be torn between the desire to rent me limb from limb and the uncertainty that he was capable. Well, that made two of us. "And you won't say anything to the rest of the Council unless you want me to respond by telling them about the little deal you made when you let Amber live." Shock. He didn't know she'd told me. Interesting. "Mutually assured destruction is not on my agenda tonight. So now... Get. The. Fuck. Out." I flashed my fangs at him again.

His lip curled with a snarl, and, without another word, he grabbed his jacket and left, making no effort to close the broken door.

Relief washed over me, crashing blindly into the fray of warring emotions that were trying to drag me back below the sand. I sank to the floor, letting myself be overcome by the weight of my insanity. The cracked glass was beginning to shatter, and I couldn't stop it.

Chapter 45

I heard him even before I smelled him, distracted as I was. After the meeting with Amber, after seeing Jack, with the kill fresh inside of me, and with what had nearly happened with Zilpher, my mind was fragmenting. It was as bad as it had been that night when I first remembered my life, possibly worse. Cy ran into the condo, calling my name, having seen the busted door as he exited the elevator and fearing, as I had, what may lay inside.

He found me shortly after sunrise, hugging my knees on the couch; Zilpher's blood had dried on my face and hair, staining the front of my body; my torn dress hung around me like a curtain in a haunted house. An appropriate comparison, considering I was barely able to speak from the ghosts which haunted my mind. He rushed to my side, hesitating to reach out to me, to touch me. "Braun said Zilpher was here... what did he do? Love, are you hurt?" I realized from his trepidation, reading between his words, that Cy understood what Zilpher had tried to do and had no way of knowing that I'd prevailed over his advances.

I reached for his hand and held it to me. He looked at me, asking the question without speaking. "No," I told him, that one word costing me nearly every ounce of sanity I had remaining to me. "No. I won." Then the sand closed over my head, and I sank into a jittery, wide-eyed catatonia.

Relieved, Cy carried me to the bathroom and cleansed me of the sanguine mess. I still felt the strength of Zilpher's blood in my veins, which was empowering, but having his scent all over me was certainly not helping with my ability to return to sanity. Being rid of the gore, being clean, was calming. I knew it would take more than a shower to get my shit together, but I also was able to recognize that I couldn't wallow in my deranged state for long. We had less than half a day before I had to meet Amber.

Cy dried me and walked me to the bed where he sat next to me and let me just be silent and still. It was a relief, to not have to speak, not have to act like I was normal, like I knew who I was or what I wanted, or even needed. To just have him there, ready when I was... it was all I needed to start working through the tangled webs of thought that I struggled to bring order to.

Finally, I moved, startling him. I looked into his face, my eyes pleading, and without a moment's pause, he pulled me close and let me weep against his chest. Once words came, I recounted everything that happened, speaking directly into his shirt. I told him about finding Frank; about the burglar I killed; about meeting Amber; about finding Zilpher and fighting him off. He held me close and waited for me to finish the entire tale. I was feeling the pieces of my mind beginning to mend the more I spoke, and he seemed to recognize that I was becoming more sound as well, because when I sat back to look at him, he allowed me to see the worry that grew on his face.

"What happened to *you?*" I asked. "Not that I wasn't happy Zilpher didn't catch you here. But where did you go?"

His face clouded over, and he tried to stand up, to release me, but I clung to him and wouldn't let go, worried if I did that the mending bits of my mind would shatter again. He looked down at me. "Frank is dead."

That got me to let go. I leaned back and stared at him. The shock of his words seemed to act like a glue, holding my sanity together. It was good. I'd need my mind functioning for tonight. "How? I left him in the wine cellar, in a back corner. No one should have found him unless..." Unless it was one of us. They would have had to smell him. The next thought that came to me was terrifying. I stood and began to pace. "Drained?" I asked.

Cy nodded grimly. "To the last drop. Jett called me, and I went. It was just before you were supposed to meet Amber. His alarm company had called about the broken door, but he didn't smell anyone other than Frank when he went to investigate. An hour later, he got another call from the alarm company. The door was open again. This time he smelled the death..."

"Does he know who did it?" I was filled with horror. Whoever it was, they now knew enough to destroy Cy and me, not to mention Jett. They knew I was unbalanced; that Cy was alive and human, though apparently still immortal; that I had not been in hiding at all, but had been with Cy; and they knew all about the back room at Trusty's, which could be trouble for a lot of vampires and humans who relied on the service provided there.

Cy shook his head. "He couldn't pin down the scent. But if it was Amber or Jack, we have to assume they know everything."

I kneeled by the bed and put my face in my hands, trying to hold my head above the sand. I couldn't be fracturing this badly and still manage to stop Amber, Zilpher, and Jack from hurting the people I loved. "We're outnumbered. Even if it wasn't them, I can't protect you *and* Danielle *and* Ashley *and* anyone else they might go after to hurt me."

He knelt next to me and kissed me softly, and in that moment, the gesture filled me like a warm drink. "Don't worry about me," Cy crooned. "I can take care of myself. And Jett was pretty pissed off about a murder under his own roof. You remember how mad he was at *you*, and you didn't even finish the job." He pulled me to my feet and sat me back on the edge of the bed.

"May as well have," I mumbled, feeling discouraged by our secrets likely being available to our enemies. "If I had, we wouldn't have possibly lost our only advantage in this fight."

"But we'd be one ally less," he said. "Which it sounds like we need. I didn't know about Jack-"

"*Candide,*" I corrected him with a sneer.

"Vampire or not, he's still Jack," he sneered right back. "Not that I derive any comfort from knowing who he was before. If anything, it makes me more nervous. When I spoke to Jett, I told him that I suspected an enemy of ours might have been the culprit. He may fear you, but he and I have been friends for a hundred years. I think we can count on him. There's loyalty there, as much as there can be loyalty among vampires."

"And how much is that?" I asked, my own experience with our kind not inspiring much hope.

Cy shrugged and grimaced. "Hopefully enough."

*   *   *

The golden light of the late afternoon illuminated our faces as we sat at the table and went over the plan again and again. We had written down lists of possible events and

347

outcomes, coupled with pros-and-cons lists for dealing with each until we had a long, comprehensive list of "what-ifs." It didn't matter, I was still filled with raging anxiety.

"There's so much that can go wrong here," I said for what felt like the hundredth time, rising from my seat and pacing. "If we have a single misstep, it could mean we all die painfully. Are we *sure* we accounted for every eventuality?"

"I certainly hope so," Cy said, rubbing his tired eyes, "but I'm not the one with the brilliant preternatural intellect anymore, so you tell me." He smiled warmly at me.

I tried to smile back, but I was still fighting against the tide of insanity that was pressing against me every single moment. More than once, I considered letting the madness take me in the hopes that it would be a complete and utter abandoning of all reason, and I could just cease to think about any of this. "The intellect works fine," I breathed. "It's the rest of my mind that isn't doing so hot. I'm not used to having to take other people into account anymore, and now I have to worry about a bunch of you at the same time."

The corners of his mouth fell. He reached for my hand as I walked past the table again and gave it a quick squeeze. "You'll pull through. And after we've come out the other side of this, when there isn't so much weighing on you, we'll work on what isn't doing so hot."

The guilt came bubbling up to the surface. "*We,*" he kept saying. And I still hadn't even responded to his declaration of love the night before, because I didn't know if I loved him, or if I *could* love him, or if I even wanted the future he was expecting. But there was one thing I knew that we needed to do that would only further confuse him.

"Well, you still won't let me put you on an airplane as far away from here as they can go, so we need to make sure you're as strong as possible," I repeated. "Even Jack- Candide- could take you out without even breaking a sweat. You need a lot more of my blood."

Cy shook his head, releasing my hand. "No, Love. You need every drop to face off against Zilpher and Amber. I could drink every ounce from you and never be up to facing either of them. I wasn't made for that fight when I was a full vampire, something that should be fairly obvious given the fact that you are not 38-year-old Elsie Taylor today," he said bitterly. Well, when he was right, he was right. "You have a better chance than I ever did of stopping Amber from hurting any more innocent women and ending Zilpher's reign of terror, both as a Councilor and a womanizer."

I laughed mirthlessly. "Gosh, you mean I'm not the first person he tried to rape?" I joked coldly, leaning against the kitchen counter. My words seemed to strike Cy more than I meant them to, and he flinched hard. I felt yet another pang of guilt as I realized how frightened he had been when he found me that morning, when he thought I had actually been a victim of such an assault. I nearly amazed myself at how casually I could already speak of it. One of the beneficial things about being fundamentally insane was that I could compartmentalize quickly and completely to appear functioning for short periods. Of course, when the pain and fear and sorrow and guilt all finally came back to me, I knew it would take more than a few hours to bring me back. In fact, I found myself longing for that moment, for a time when I had nothing to fear and could let myself sink into oblivion until I could emerge with my mind in one piece... maybe.

Cy quickly shook off his shock at my easy manner of talking about my ordeal. "From what I've heard," he responded to my comment, "you're not the first by a long shot, though you might be the first to be able to say 'tried.' Zilpher is well known for abusing his position."

Big surprise there, I thought. But we needed to get back to the task at hand. There were only a few hours of sunlight left, and I was supposed to be meeting Amber right after sunset. "Fine, but take just a little more. Please," I begged. "If they get the jump on you, I need to know that there's a chance..." My voice broke and trailed off. My feelings were unclear, but the thought of losing him before I had a chance to work through it was unbearable.

Cy walked to me and wrapped me in his arms, just holding me. "If it comes to that..." he sighed. "If it does, if it could even work a second time, I have enough." I worried that it would never be enough, that if it came down to it, his unique circumstances would prevent the blood from having any effect once his heart stopped. I pressed my face into him, allowing myself to revel in his embrace, his oh-so-human warmth; to feel the beat of the heart I couldn't bear to lose just yet. As I felt the comfort of his presence, a sensation came over me as though he was actually siphoning off the anxiety and fear. I leaned into him more heavily and let out a cathartic sigh. He bent his head down to kiss my hair, but I looked up at him to return the kiss. There was an urgency on my end, even as he went maddeningly slow. I wrapped one hand around the back of his neck and let my other hand drift toward his waistline.

"Wait, Love," he breathed, pulling back to look into my eyes.

"Why?" I sounded petulant. I was frustrated that he didn't understand what I had felt two nights before, when he had been inside of me, feeding from me and letting me feed from me in return. It hadn't been a distraction; quite the opposite. It had brought me a clarity, a peace I struggled to achieve on my own. I didn't want to stop. I wanted him to grab me, kiss me, touch me, fuck me, to help me to achieve that near-nirvana so that I could see clearly and perfect our plan.

I waited for Cy to speak. I hoped he wouldn't bring up Zilpher because I didn't want Zilpher anywhere near this moment. He stroked the side of my face, frowning slightly. "I love you," he said.

Shit, I thought, blindsided. *Please don't make me confront this now. I can't keep my brain on straight and figure out my heart too.*

He kissed me again, briefly but passionately, before locking me in with those rich hazel eyes, a muted, mossy, golden green and brown, with very little of the color for which he'd once been named visible anymore. For all his talk about how his blue-green eye color had reminded him of home, I imagined the Emerald Isle had no shortage of this color either. "That's all," he said. "I need you to know. I don't say that because I think you'll wake up one day and just be like you were when you were human. I'm not an idiot. Elsie is gone, but she is a part of you, and with her heart and Opal's strength, you could be so much more, so much better than the sum of your parts. I don't know what will happen if we make it through the night, but I love you, and I hope you can work through the maze of your mind, and eventually love me again, too."

I was stunned. So he knew, just like he always did. He knew the struggle I'd dealt with every moment since he'd come back into my life. He had, from the beginning, managed to know exactly what I was feeling, and to accept what I needed, when I needed it. All the times I had told him *"no"* only to be met with an *"okay"*, *like I said I wanted ice cream,* came back to me in a moment of rare clarity. I knew I would never, in a thousand lifetimes (if we were lucky enough to have them) deserve him. I could never earn, return, or even match the love he always poured into me. He had told me years ago, when I found out what he was, that one of us was undeserving of the other, but he had seen himself as the one unworthy of me. I knew the truth.

He had never been evil, I realized, watching the sunlight paint golden waves on his black hair. Petty occasionally, yes, but not evil. He had, at one time, hurt others, drowning in his own pain, but I had hurt people for my own pleasure. He saw the wrong in what he'd done back then, and chose to repent by taking the hurt he saw in others as his own burden. He was the epitome of good, removing bad from the world and only pouring love and kindness back into it, his one fault being that pettiness which stemmed entirely from his feud with Amber. I was no Zilpher or Amber or Jack, but there was a reason I suffered from lunacy. My struggle wasn't because of the inherent goodness within me. It was due to the demons who warred within me over and over, trying to make the "right" choices even when I craved the "wrong" ones, trying to avoid doing "evil" while feeling bound and tied to do "good." Despite the protestations of my more human side, I not only tolerated my evil acts, but actively enjoyed many of them, much like snuffing out the life of that nameless burglar at Trusty's.

Even now, as I pulled Cy back to me, a cruel, selfish part of me was only using him. His kiss, his touch- they served a purpose. Oh, I certainly enjoyed them and was glad that he was the one providing these things; because whatever my feelings for him may or may not be, I *did* care about him. But I needed to be clear-headed, and the erotic pleasures we were moving toward would drive the insanity back long enough for me to re-examine the plan for any holes.

Even now, I realized, regaining my capacity to feel things deeply wasn't entirely a recall to my humanity. If anything, the feelings had intensified the parts of me that dealt in pain and death. I could do these things more effectively and viciously now, because I could relish the fear, the agony. I didn't just want to win against my enemies. I wanted to *hurt* them. I wanted to hurt *others*. It didn't matter if I knew I would only go after people I felt deserved it- rapists, thieves, murderers- because I still wanted- needed- to cause them pain.

As Cy lifted me onto the kitchen counter, his lips leaving kisses along the length of my neck, and pulled my hips flush against his, a small part of my mind went back to a night ten years before. That night, I had refused him because this very act in this very spot had brought back memories of a tragic one-night-stand. I had no such qualms today. I was going to kill more than just the memory of Jack. I was going to kill *him*. Painfully.

Because fuck that guy.

Chapter 46

Detach, I commanded myself as I walked into The Watering Hole. The anxiety was reaching its apex, which made sense. Tonight would end in bloodshed. The only question was whose blood would be spilled by whom?

I had no idea why Amber chose here to meet. I may not be instantly recognizable as my human self, but the odds of someone in my hometown, in my old regular bar, taking notice of the familiar-looking young lady in the corner were astronomically high. I thrived flying under the radar. It was only when I chose to be seen, to be noticed, that I would suddenly be the belle of the ball, the beauty everyone couldn't help but stare at. I didn't want eyes on me tonight.

I planted myself against the very same outdoor table where I'd bummed a cigarette from Cy in another life. Maybe that was why she chose here. It was full of ghosts for me.

Detach! I repeated to myself.

I checked my phone. Cy was in his car watching from the parking lot of the grocery store across the street. I could just barely make out his scent from over here. The wind was blowing in his direction, and even recognizing it as easily as I could, it was faint. I could only hope that Amber wouldn't recognize it if she was able to pick it out from the others in the area.

Amber had asked me to meet her and "Candide" here. I had asked Jett to keep an eye on Ashley since I couldn't be in two places at once, and Cy was in no way equipped to single-handedly fight any of our enemies. I needed him to be my eyes at a distance, to see the big picture- literally.

The final rays of the sun shone through my sunglasses, and I felt her even before I scented her. I knew her aura from so many nights, so many hunts together. She couldn't be here without me knowing it.

"Yes, girl! I'm so glad you showed up!" Amber chirped at me, kissing me on each cheek and pulling out a pack of cigarettes. She offered me one and I took it, glad for something to do with my hands.

I smiled as though I was just here for the fun and took a long drag. "So, where are they?" I asked, getting right to the point. "And which one do I get?" I felt sick at my stomach at the thought of asking if I had the joy of killing my sister or her client.

"You get the lawyer," Amber said, as though she was handing me a gift. "I'll take the little shit, but you should get the big fish, the one who paves the way for this kind of pond scum to keep hurting more and more girls."

I wavered for just a second. She had a point. I knew Danielle was only in this job to support my mother, but she *was* helping abusers and rapists to walk free. Was I on the wrong side of this...?

No, I thought. *Detach a little less. That's your sister she's talking about. Amber wants you to kill your sister. And that boy hasn't been convicted. Innocent until proven guilty, remember? Human concepts.*

"Are they meeting *here*?" I asked, bringing myself back to the plan and exhaling a large cloud of smoke. "Kind of a shitty place for a lawyer to take a client. Doesn't she have some kind of office? And where's your little fledgling? His arm feeling any better?" I smirked.

Amber laughed. "I think his ego is more hurt than his arm," she assured me, enveloping herself in smoke of her own. "This is for us- you and me. He's off hunting while we have our fun. We'll have all night to play with the new toy once we've celebrated properly." She winked at me. Ugh. The only way I planned to play with Jack was how a dog played with a stuffed animal.

Amber nodded at the parking lot where a car had just pulled in. A nicely polished stiletto stepped down from the cab, followed by the rest of my sister. If I had a heartbeat, it would have skipped. She had grown into a gorgeous woman. Her hair, the same color mine had been in life, caught the fading rays of the sun and took on an ethereal gleam. She might have been an angel, with her halo above the dewy skin and sorrowful eyes. She was smiling, happy in the moment, but someone who has felt profound sadness can never entirely banish that from their aura, from their eyes. I was the reason for her sorrow.

"That's her," Amber said, oblivious to my reverie. "The charges were dropped today, so she and the client's family are celebrating over drinks."

"His family?" I asked, breaking my thoughts away from Danielle. "How many are we talking about?"

"Just him and his parents. I'll split those two with you, too."

"Why?" I asked. "Why the parents?"

Amber gave me a curious look, and I realized I'd slipped up. When, in all our time together, had I ever questioned her choices for a kill? "Why?" She asked suspiciously, mockingly. "Feeling sentimental or something?"

I laughed as coldly as I could. "For sure. It's my birthday, after all." I tossed my hair and beamed at her, taking an anxious pull on my cigarette that nearly brought it to the filter. She seemed mollified for the moment, but I had to operate as though she was pretending just as much as I was. Knowing that someone- some vampire- had full access to Frank's memories, including those about Cy and I, I had to assume Amber knew everything that he had. "What I meant was, how are we going to get all four of them? It's not our usual 'seduce and suck.'"

She grinned back at me. "I love the succubus in you! God, I've missed this. Here they come." She pointed to the latest arrival, putting out her own butt. A car was emptying of the boy from the news article and his two parents. The boy- really, truly, a *boy*- couldn't have even been a legal adult by more than a couple of years. I had to remind myself of what I'd experienced in Kara's memory that had been perpetrated by boys younger than this one. Age had no bearing on cruelty.

I watched them as they approached. The father seemed relieved to the point of giddiness. He was playfully shoving the boy, who was laughing back, but the boy's own laughter didn't reach his eyes. I wondered why for a moment; guilt perhaps? His mother looked somber and like this would be no celebration at all as far as she was concerned. I wondered if he'd really been guilty, and the evidence was too thin. Maybe that was why his mother was sad. Because she'd raised a monster. On the other hand, maybe she was just hurt that someone would falsely accuse her son. Maternal feelings were even less in my wheelhouse than regular, run of the mill human ones had been until mere days before.

They went inside. Amber motioned for me to follow her and we walked to the other side of the parking lot where we each enjoyed another cigarette. It was certainly helping my nerves. Here we leaned against her car- an upgraded and updated version of the same blue convertible she'd driven ten years before- and she told me the plan.

They weren't going to be here long. The mother had been against a celebration- I had been right about that- but the father had urged her to go for one drink. The boy would get anything he wanted from the food truck because he "beat this thing." Even Danielle had only put it on her calendar, which Amber had, of course, hacked easily, for one hour. So we wouldn't have to wait long.

When they came out, I would be well hidden in Danielle's back seat while Amber took off with the family. Once I'd finished with "the bitch lawyer," as Amber called her, I would go to the address Amber had sent me.

I sat for several minutes, trying to figure out where the catch was. It felt so straightforward- like Amber was really just offering me a great kill. If it hadn't been my sister, I'd have, by that point, rejected the notion that this was a setup. It couldn't possibly be this simple.

Half an hour had gone by as we watched our quarry through the large windows of the bar when we saw Danielle and the boy's father begin the dance over who would pay the check. Time to go. I went to the car Danielle had arrived in and climbed into the back seat, sitting as still as I could in the fading light, knowing that I would be nearly invisible if I chose to be. This would be fine. I would ride along, unseen, and as soon as she made it home, I would leave and figure out where Amber, Jack, and Zilpher were, then go from there. I nearly laughed, marveling at how easy it was turning out to be to protect my sister. I was so distracted by my own musings that I almost missed it.

As I sat waiting for Danielle, she had walked outside, not to her car, but to the outdoor table I had been at when we arrived. She was meeting a well-dressed man holding a single red rose. He was tall, slender, and looked not much older than she did despite his sleek silver hair. He gave her a tentative hug, as though he respected her right to say no. Clearly a first date. The eyes hidden behind his sunglasses, which I nonetheless knew to be argent and cruel, took her in with a smile, then moved to my own.

"Your move," Zilpher's gaze seemed to say.

Chapter 47

Amber left in her convertible, completely dropping the façade. The boy and his parents were forgotten and left to their devices. Good. I couldn't worry about people I didn't actually give a shit about if I had to deal with this.

I had been an idiot- a blind fucking idiot. Amber had taken me across the lot not to watch through the windows, but to get me away from where Zilpher had approached, downwind just like Cy. Did Zilpher walk past him and not notice? Or had he already moved against him, and I had lost Cy without knowing it?

I couldn't move from where I'd been tricked without Danielle seeing me. I pulled my phone out, intending to call Cy, not caring that Zilpher was close enough to hear if I spoke out loud, when I saw a video message.

I opened it and watched with the volume at its lowest, hoping it would be quiet enough to not be heard.

Amber was in her car, top down, wind blowing her golden hair all around. "Hey, babe!" She laughed, then blew a kiss to the cameras. "Gotcha! Are you enjoying the little show? I'm sure by now you figure you've made some wild miscalculations. Zilpher has your sister. Yeah, yeah, I know you remember who you were before, let's just breeze right on by that for now. It's a huge bummer, T-B-H!" She emphasized the letters as she spoke them, then gave an exaggerated sigh.

Every word was saturated with sarcasm. "But hey, at least you have 'allies,' right? To help save the people you *love*. I mean, Cyan is going to be a *huge* help, considering he's not only not dead, but he's actually human again and can't lift a Goddamned finger to stop us. That's one hell of a secret to keep! I mean, how fucking ironic that he would inadvertently turn you into a vampire, something he swore he'd never do, and then you'd unwittingly turn him into a bona fide human! I couldn't have planned that part better myself! And you know, I honestly didn't even know he survived. I really thought he died out there in the woods! He always *was* good at surprising me.

"I thought maybe you were onto us when you disappeared for a few weeks, but now I know you were just holed up fucking like little bunnies because you remembered your shitty little human life. But then you. Fucked. Up. You went to some weak-ass blood bar that, PS, Zilpher is totally going to have raided later, and you scared a little human who told Candide *everything*, including that you let yourself starve until you went savage. Well, he didn't mean to tell. His blood did it. He'd never betray Jett. Right, Jett?" She turned her head and looked down at the passenger seat. She turned the camera to show where Jett's disembodied head sat. I felt myself retch.

She aimed the camera back at herself. "Anyway, I think that's enough exposition until I see you. And I *will* see you. Soon. But for now, you have a choice. Your sister is with Zilpher, and out in the open where he can grab her and be gone before anyone would see. Yeah, you could follow him and fight him since you're probably stronger, but could you do it without him killing your sister? Or even worse, what if she *saw* you and the monster you've become, and you had to kill her after all? And then you would have to kill him, and the Council would have to kill you... such a mess!" She shook her head, mocking me.

"Candide, of course, is after your little still-human friend Ashley and plans to make her his 'vampire bride.'" She rolled her eyes. "So short-sighted, that one. And me..." She turned the camera to face the back seat. Cy was there, trussed and gagged, but otherwise unhurt. "I've taken back our lover. You stole him from me once- I want to see if you're arrogant enough to try again." Suddenly the gleaming smile was back. "I'll text ya the deets! Ciao!" Another blown kiss, and she ended the feed.

I sat, looking away from the blank screen to stare at Zilpher and my sister, but without really looking at them. I had no allies. I had no help. And three people I loved might die tonight. I thought I had covered every possibility. I hadn't thought that literally everything could go this wrong. I was completely on my own, and those who were still alive had only me to rely on.

Three GPS pins came through on my phone. One was right where I sat, watching Danielle and Zilpher. Another was The Roof with a photo of Ashley. The third...

"Shit," I whispered. The third was my condo with a big question mark over it.

Okay, I thought, my mind beginning to spiral into a place it wouldn't easily emerge from. *I can't afford to lose it now. I have to think. Think about what Amber said, think about what I know about each of these people, the ones I love and the ones I hate. I know them. Use that.*

Right. So what did Amber say? Jett's dead. That's a fact. Whether or not she killed him, that was unknown. And where did she get to him? He'd gone to check on Ashley. Did he ever even make it there? Was I too late to save Ashley already?

Too many questions started pouring in, and I felt my hands on the sides of my head, a scream building. I couldn't let go now. I had to hold it together.

Amber said I went savage, but not because I starved myself in my insanity. It was because she thought Cy and I had reunited and had hidden away together for a month-long bangfest. She said that he was human. She didn't seem to know that he still had some vampiric traits. That meant that, while she may have had suspicions before, she hadn't known that Cy was alive or that I remembered my human life until Jack told her what he learned from Frank, and that Jack, still new to this life, hadn't fully understood what he'd seen. It meant that her knowledge was incomplete and still fresh. She hadn't had time to work out everything that it meant... I hoped. I couldn't yet figure out how to use that to my advantage. I needed to stall...

My memory! My memory and my life as a human, and the things that came naturally to me that older vampires might not think about. That was the key. I looked down at my phone then back at Zilpher, who seemed so natural and at ease with Danielle. Looking at him, he could have just been a human man, just out on a date with just another human girl. But I knew he was a monster... not to mention a vampire.

I added the numbers I remembered to be Ashley's and Danielle's into a group text, hoping that they hadn't changed their numbers in the last ten years. *Is this Danielle Taylor and Ashley Fienne? If so, you are in danger. Both of you. Do not leave where you are! Get as close to the center of a crowd as quickly as you can. It might save your life. Go. Now.*

I hit send and waited. Danielle never looked at the smartwatch on her wrist or reached for her phone, but I felt a *bzzt*. I looked down.

363

Who is this? It was Ashley, or at least the number that was once Ashley's. She'd started a new private message.

Don't worry about that, I answered. That would never work. If it *was* Ashley, she was too smart for her own good and would never believe an anonymous text message. She needed more. I typed, *Is that Danielle's number? Please get this message to her. I can't tell you more but PLEASE! You are not safe!*

I saw the "..." as she typed back. The waiting was painful. What was she going to say?

Is this about Jack de Wilde? She asked.

I nearly laughed with relief. Thank God she'd heard that Jack broke out of jail- it would make this easier. Cy and I had seen the news report the day before while planning. Apparently, he'd vanished from his bunk at sunset. Literally vanished, with no witnesses. Doors and furniture were broken, guards were injured, and they had to fight off a riot in the aftermath, but the "escape" had happened instantly. What really happened was that Amber busted in like a bat out of hell, grabbed him, and left to make him a vampire.

I responded to Ashley, *Yes, but do not look for him. He has made a threat against you. If he thinks you suspect anything, he'll come after you. He is armed and dangerous.*

She was typing again. *Is he after Danielle too?*

That was hard. I couldn't say yes and risk her telling Danielle that Jack was the only thing she had to be afraid of. She'd get into her car and just leave, only for Zilpher to follow her home. Worse, she might get into a car *with* Zilpher. No, she had to know that her date was the danger. I did a quick search, easily cracking her dating profile password and finding that she had only been talking with Zilpher since earlier today. They'd agreed to meet that quickly only because they were both just "by chance" going to be in the same area. Good. The short time frame would work to my advantage. I texted Ashley, *No, she's on a date right now, and that person is a convicted rapist and murderer who escaped with Jack.* That might work. *Are you alone? If so, find a crowd. You need to be surrounded by people, preferably whom you know and who would notice if he grabbed you.*

More typing. *I'll tell Danielle. This better not be a prank.*

God bless Ashley's too-smart heart. She must be really scared to listen to me even when she didn't know who I was. I looked up and saw Danielle glance at her watch. I hoped she wouldn't freak out. She blinked heavily. *Shit,* I thought, *Zilpher's going to grab her and bolt if her heart rate spikes now.*

"I am so sorry, I have to use the restroom," Danielle said, her face still pleasant and passive, her heart rate not wavering. If anything, she seemed calmer.

Yes! I thought. All of her experiences dealing with the scum of humanity as a lawyer, being in a room with some of the worst criminals and knowing beyond a shadow of a doubt what they would do to her if they could, had steeled her so completely that she wasn't even really afraid in the traditional sense. But she was still getting out of there.

Who is this? The text came from a number I didn't recognize. So she *had* gotten a new number.

Where are you? I asked her.

At the bar. It's crowded and I have a gun. Who are you? She asked. I shook my head, smiling. Of course, she had a gun. Not that it would do much against Zilpher- or me, since she obviously thought I was a threat too, to tell me. But I wasn't going anywhere near her.

I put my phone deep into my pocket, hoping it wouldn't break since I would need it again. Even as I prepared myself for my next move, I heard the phone buzzing.

I gathered all of the strength I could muster into my legs, opened the car door, and burst out of the vehicle, flying at Zilpher at full speed. If Amber had been invisible at the prison, I was an unseen hurricane. I hit him, and for a split second, we might have been seen as the force of the collision slowed me for just a second before I forced him out of the public area. I was stronger, especially with his blood in me. I could beat him, I realized.

I kept the two of us moving until we were inside of a condemned office building. The concrete blocks that had once been the walls showered down around us, creating a halo of dust. I had Zilpher by the throat and kept pressing forward until I hit his head hard against the back wall. More of the building rained down, striking both of us, but through my rage, I felt nothing.

I turned, his body like a rag doll in my hands, and threw him to the ground. "Don't fucking move!" I screamed at him, fangs flashing, feeling simultaneously more like an animal *and* more human than I ever had.

Zilpher snarled at me. "I'm not going to fight you," he said begrudgingly. "I'd lose again, especially since you've had my blood. I'm sure you can imagine, I don't particularly enjoy losing." When I didn't relax my stance, he sat up to lean almost casually on his elbow, sighed, and said, "You can have the girl. I didn't think you were all that interested in 'girl on girl,' as they say these days, but if it's that important to you-"

"Stop!" I commanded him, confused. "Why did you go after her?" I demanded. "That specific woman. Why?"

Zilpher looked as perplexed as I felt. He looked at me sideways, suspiciously, trying to maintain his air of cold superiority and failing. "Because Amber said it would drive you insane, that you'd already claimed the kill. You wanted the lawyer because of some feminist bullshit reason. She said that if we could distract you by stealing your prey, she could find a way to finally kill you and get you out of my hair... The girl *is* yours, isn't she? That's why you dragged me..." He motioned to the detritus around us. "Here."

I was stunned. He knew *nothing*. Amber had played him as easily as she had played me- easier even. I sneered at him, realizing how superior I was to him in every regard. "You're a fucking idiot," I informed him. "Let's say the lawyer *is* mine. How is any single human that important to me? So much so that stealing her from me would allow me to be taken down by you and Amber and a fledgling when you're not even all in the same place? You divide. I conquer. Did you even think about this plan before you agreed to it? I always thought you were *smart*."

Zilpher looked like he'd drunk animal blood. We can do that, much like we can eat food. It's terrible and does nothing to strengthen us or to sate our hunger. If a vampire hurts an animal, it's a sure sign that they're a psychopath. All of this to say, his expression was an ugly one. His lips were pursed and his muscles were tensed. He didn't want to say any more, but seemed to understand that he had been played. "This *wasn't* the plan... not as I was presented with it, which I now understand to be how she intended. Amber and her new fledgling were going to be there with me, hidden in plain view. Once you came after me for taking your kill, they would hit you from the side and behind. But then Amber left and the little shit she made never even showed. Once I realized I was alone, I knew I had little chance of actually beating you."

I stepped back, allowing him to stand. We stood facing each other with our arms crossed, the halo of concrete dust swirling around us. I had a choice to make, and it entirely depended on whether I thought he was telling the truth. I couldn't imagine his ego ever letting him admit defeat that easily, but would he find it less palatable to fight and lose, or to forfeit?

"Why should I believe you?" I asked. I was tired of playing games and needed to fall back on my tried and true direct approach.

He glared at me for a moment, then kicked a broken brick angrily, adding more rubble to the pile around us. "Because I hate you. But... I love myself. I want to live to see sunrise tomorrow, and for many years after that, and if you kill me here, that won't happen."

I saw the anger in his face as he admitted it. Against all of my better judgment, I believed him. Zilpher was never going to win any congeniality contests, but he was right: he did love himself. I still needed more than just belief. I needed more information so I could win. "What do you know about the rest of Amber's plan?"

Zilpher dropped his hands angrily. "As you were kind enough to point out, I'm apparently a fucking idiot. I thought this *was* the plan."

I was shocked. "It's a terrible plan. I honestly can't even believe you fell for it. Are you telling me you're so arrogant that you fell for this simply because you believed no one would ever try to trick you?"

"You've made your point," he growled, his fangs finally showing. "Now, can I please go kill Amber, as I should have done years ago? I think she's finally earned it. I don't even mind if you tag along. In fact, I might prefer it. If I've learned anything tonight, it's that I might have underestimated her."

I paused. There. That was the information I needed. "Why *did* you let her go instead of killing her?" I asked. I knew the answer Amber had given me that I didn't believe. I needed to hear Zilpher's version.

"For the same reason I'm conceding to you now. I was defeated, and there was something I wanted. Back then, she beat me- I don't know how, I'd always been stronger than she, but something changed- and she said if I stood down, she'd play dead until she was ready to destroy you for betraying her, and I could help."

Something changed... what could have changed to make Amber stronger than Zilpher, who was more than twice as old as she was?

At least now I had the answer to how she made it out of that particular snag, even if it was still full of more questions. She'd simply bested Zilpher, and he could never admit she'd been better than he was, so he let her go to secure her silence.

Now he wanted revenge, which would be perfect except that I couldn't risk him knowing any more about my own situation than he already did. If, in the course of pursuing Amber, he found out about my human life, about how much I knew, he would never cease to use it against me when it suited him. Being willing to work with me tonight didn't mean he was suddenly a friend. It just meant we would have our fight another night. Because of that, I needed to keep him in the dark, and I needed to know that he couldn't come after me again- at least not tonight.

I took my phone out. Thankfully it had survived the impact of my attack on him. I flashed the screen to Zilpher, showing him what it said. "What am I supposed to be looking at?" He asked, annoyed.

I smirked at him, then turned the phone back to my own eyes. I typed away quickly while I explained. "I have just sent a recording of this conversation to my email outbox to be released at sunrise. I know you've never successfully gotten into my accounts- technology is really my strength, not yours- so you have no way of canceling it. You are going to stay here. I am going to go kill Amber." His eyes flashed as he started to protest, and I felt mine flare up even brighter. "If anything happens to me or to that human you were with before, or even to my 'mortal lover', as you referred to him, that email with you confessing your weaknesses and your crimes goes to the Council. If I require your assistance, I will call you. Until then, you have the night off. Lay low. No killing, not in my area.

Consider every human and vampire here *mine*. At sunrise, if you haven't heard from me, I'd go into hiding because Sapphire will definitely not be forgiving of this."

Our hatred flowed between us like a current. His lip curled. "Fine. But you owe me something in return."

I scoffed. "I owe you *nothing*!" I stepped toward him, feeling the rage build as I asserted my power. "You tried to rape me! Then you came after me to kill me, with a plot you didn't comprehend and an enemy you didn't understand. I am the only thing standing between the two of us and utter destruction right now, and you are just lucky that I might decide I need your help after all, because I could strike you dead here and now, and with the evidence I have against you, I'd get away with it!"

As I said the words, I knew they were true, and I briefly debated just ending him right then and there. But I knew I wouldn't. I needed to save my strength. I knew that, if I survived, he would live well past tonight to piss me off for years, likely centuries, to come. My thoughts flashed to the endless, nameless humans and vampires he would hurt in the remainder of his lifetime, and I just couldn't care. I devoted the length of about half a second to consider the effect this would have on my soul- allowing Zilpher to continue his reign of terror- and I found myself all out of fucks to give. I couldn't worry about people I would likely never meet when people I loved were still in danger; I had already resigned myself to the knowledge that, between Cy and me, I was the greater evil. Besides, with Jett dead, I needed a wild card in my pocket. I needed Zilpher available in case things got bad... bad enough that it would be necessary to expose my secrets to win.

I turned my back to him and walked out of the demolished building into the soft, purple haze of twilight. I spun and looked at him once more through the wreckage before I left. "If I call... answer. If you don't... that's the end of both of us."

Chapter 48

I had no time to celebrate my success in saving Danielle. I still had to find a way to save Ashley and Cy.

I stole Danielle's car to give myself some wheels. It had been easy to dash inside and snag the keys from her bag without her noticing. I needed transportation so that I wouldn't burn out all of my strength covering the distances I needed to in order to catch up to Amber and Jack. My sister was still inside The Watering Hole, hunkering down and waiting for me to give her the all-clear, something I wouldn't do until I knew for a fact that Amber or Jack wasn't going to circle back to murder both Danielle and my mother.

I put the car in drive and started for the freeway that could take me either home or into St. Petersburg, to The Roof. I had to decide, and quickly, where I was going to go first. Amber was obviously the more significant threat. That was obvious. The question I needed to answer was really about which victim had more time. I wanted to go straight to Cy, to save him first, but I had a gut feeling that Amber would wait for me, that she would want me to witness his death, or him to witness mine. I had no idea if he could die, or what it would do to me psychologically if he did. As it was, my single-minded focus on saving him and Ashley was the only thing holding me together.

Amber had a millennium of patience and a desire to not just kill, but to cause pain. As much as I didn't want to leave Cy with her a moment longer than necessary, I knew that young, brash, impulsive Jack needed to be my next target. And he would not be offered amnesty like Zilpher had been. Jack would have the pleasure of dying at my hands. I would drink all but the last drop of the blood Amber had given him before I killed him, both to ensure he never came back and to imbibe me with the strength I'd need for my final battle.

I drove the car at breakneck speeds past my exit and over the bridge. I prayed I wouldn't catch the eye of a traffic cop while flying at double the speed limit. It was the second time that I had spoken to God (in my own personal way of screaming my needs in my mind, and all the voices were in unison) in as many days, something I hadn't done since my days as a human, but if He *was* there, He seemed to be listening because I didn't have to outrun a single police cruiser. I pulled the car screeching into a public lot, launched myself from the vehicle, and dashed around the back of the building, leaving a flabbergasted group of onlookers with the fleeting image of a young woman in torn clothes, covered in dust and dirt before she vanished from view.

In the alley, I looked up and saw the lights of The Roof overhead. I felt a flutter in my chest, echoes of the heart that had once beat there. I'd been here many times as both a human and as a vampire, and now I was back for the first time with years of memories once lost to me, and knowing that someone I truly loved- someone who had been my best friend and confidante in those lost years- was up there and needed my help. I looked at myself, knowing I'd create a commotion if I was seen up there looking like this, and also knowing if I was seen by anyone who knew me (human *or* vampire me), it would be disastrous.

I closed my eyes, allowing my other senses to take over, to hunt for the vampire that was once Jack. If I could figure out where he was exactly, I could figure out the best way to get to him. He was definitely up there on the sixth-floor rooftop terrace- I could smell him. Where precisely within that facility he lurked, I couldn't tell. I listened for individual voices, for a heart beating faster than the others around it, anything that might give me a hint, but couldn't pick out anything distinct. They were too high up and too densely packed for me to discern what I needed. I would have to go up, and I needed new clothes and to clean up before I could do that.

I walked a block away and happened upon a young hooker- way too young, I noticed with pity- but in the right size clothing. More revealing than I would usually choose, but not out of place at a bar. I held her close and drank until she lost consciousness, then lifted her, carrying her like she was drunk to a hotel a few doors down. I booked a room, paying enough that no questions about either of our states would come up, then took her up to the room and laid her on the bed. I showered quickly- even faster for the speed with which I could move- and shook out my hair which quickly settled itself as though dried and styled. I took the tragic creature's clothes and left her a brief note telling her to get out of that life and some cash I had on me to help her get off the streets, if only for a couple of nights. Maybe I wasn't as evil as I thought...

I took the elevator up to The Roof and, as soon as the door opened, I began scanning the scene. I picked Ashley out quickly from both her voice and the pounding of her terrified heart. She was in a group of people, including Charlotte and a man I assumed to be Ashley's fiancé, given their intimate posture. He was holding on to her protectively. *Damn it,* I thought. The problem with my half-lie about her attacker being Jack was that she felt comfortable enough to tell those around her, which put them at risk. Jack wouldn't hesitate to kill anyone who stood between them. Most fledglings were reckless to begin with. He had cornered the market on that in life, and I had no doubt he would be exceptionally dangerous if only for his lack of inhibition.

I tried again to sense Jack in the crowd, but couldn't pinpoint him. It was almost like he was everywhere and nowhere. I caught his scent on several humans who walked by, but smelled no blood other than that in their veins. He was hiding somewhere and hadn't fed from anyone yet.

I glanced back at Ashley, who was saying something to her fiancé. They had a small argument, but then he kissed her and squeezed her hand before she and Charlotte left the group together. *No, no!* I thought. *Where are you going?*

Keeping eyes out in opposite directions, they slipped into the ladies' room. They thought if they went together, used the buddy system, that they would be safe. I needed to pinpoint Jack quickly before he could trap them in the bathroom. I went back to scanning for my adversary, when I heard a sound that only I or another vampire could have discerned over the heavy bass and chatter. It was breaking plaster, glass, and wood, and it had come from the bathroom.

I flew through the crowd, no more than a sudden breeze to those around me. I pushed against the door and found it locked. I checked the men's room on a hunch and found it locked as well. Not wanting to waste more time, I pushed against the door, breaking the deadbolt out of the wood easily.

I had heard right. The wall between the men's and women's restrooms had been obliterated. Charlotte lay on the floor, a trickle of blood dripping from somewhere on her head. I still heard her heartbeat, which was strong; he'd just knocked her out. While I took brief notice of Charlotte, my eyes were on Jack, who was holding Ashley by the throat, cutting off any screams she may have let out. She was staring at him in horror. He ran his free hand over her body possessively as he slowly squeezed the air from her windpipe.

She hadn't noticed me since I was behind her (and she was a bit preoccupied), but he had. I was in a bad position. If I moved, he could break her neck. If I didn't, she was going to die anyway. I couldn't risk being seen; Ashley might not have recognized me when she saw me the time before, but she had obviously noted the resemblance to my human self. It would be even harder to ignore the familiarity if she saw me defending her against Jack.

Jack glanced at me, a smirk spreading over his face as he realized how little I could do to help without him killing her outright or exposing me. I looked frantically around the room. It was a very run of the mill bar bathroom, however, and other than broken bits of wood, glass, and drywall on the floor, there was little for me to reach for that I could realistically use. Pieces of shattered mirror were everywhere, just like the night I killed Orla, which gave a terrifying funhouse feel to the room; I could see every angle, but it was disjointed and crooked. Just like my psyche.

Ashley was beginning to lose consciousness. I needed to distract him. I lowered my voice to the timbre only he would be able to hear and asked him. "I thought you wanted her for yourself- to turn her into one of us. Not to kill her like a common thug in a bar bathroom."

He gave a slight shrug. He didn't bother to mask his own voice, or maybe he didn't know how to yet. "Oh, I'm not going to kill her yet. Once she's unconscious, I can do anything- anything at all." He licked his lips, and I nearly gagged at the implication. "And if you try to stop me, I will just kill her." He gave a short, cruel laugh as she struggled weakly against him, then turned his attention back to her. "You know, I always liked you, Ashley. You never gave me the time of day. Not like *some* people... who got what they wanted and then threw me under the fucking bus, ruining my Goddamned life. But then I had the joy of learning new and exciting ways to *hurt* people in prison. I learned from the best in class there. And by a miracle, after *years* being stuck in that hellhole, someone gave me the best gift ever; now I have knowledge and means, and no reason anymore to hold back from my more... primal instincts. And once I've finished with you, you won't have a choice but to give me a chance..." He bit his lip, letting a trickle of blood come down and leaned in to kiss Ashley, to force her to take it. She pulled her head back, away from him, away from the blood, which was exactly the opening I needed.

I reached into the back of my top and pulled out the gun I'd stolen from Danielle's bag when I'd stolen her car key before I left The Watering Hole. Then I put a bullet through Jack's snow-white eye.

He dropped her to the ground and screamed, clutching his face. I knew it wouldn't kill him, but it had been the pain and distraction I needed. Ashley gasped for air, trying to get away from him, not yet realizing why he'd let her go. Between his cries and the gunshot, I was grateful for the loud music outside.

"You crazy *bitch!*" He yelled at me, his burst eye socket now a fount of blood.

No longer bothering to keep my voice low, I kept the gun trained on him and said, "You know, you're the second person in, like, a day to call me that. Got to be honest, though- it's kind of growing on me. I'm thinking I may have my name legally changed."

"You don't have a legal name!" he roared at me. "You're fucking dead! You're nothing anymore!"

"Neither are you, *anymore*, 'Candide,'" I sneered, bored already of his uncontrollable temper and his need to talk too much. "Which is why it won't matter when I kill you now."

Before Ashley had a chance to even turn to look at me, to see who I was or what I was doing, I launched across the small bathroom and knocked Jack to the ground. He was pinned beneath me, nowhere near my level of strength, and therefore helpless. I didn't hesitate at all before I dropped my fangs to his neck and ripped at the flesh there just as viciously as I'd done with Zilpher the night before.

Unlike with Zilpher, I did not release him. I drank until there was only one last drop within him. I wanted no part of his memories, but knew that he could survive if I didn't finish the job. As he lay there, his eyes glassy, I grabbed a long shard of broken mirror and cut his head clean off, throwing it across the room to join a pile of splinters.

"Oh, God," Ashley whimpered through the damage to her windpipe. She was still on the floor behind me. "Oh, my fucking God." She started to vomit. I wanted to turn and look at her, make sure she was okay, but I couldn't let her know who I was, who I had become; especially since, for her own safety, she'd have to take that information to her grave, and it might drive her mad to do that. Because I would never bring her over to this life. Ever.

I heard her stirring, getting to her feet and walking to me. I began to shake, the madness clouding my mind as I fought against the weak, mortal desire to see her face, to have her hold me as friends do. I put my hands to my temples, hoping to calm the storm long enough to get out of here without making any more of a scene, but she was between me and the door. I felt her hand on my arm and turned my face as far away as I could, trying to shrug her off. She couldn't make much noise. Jack had really done a number on her throat. She would need to see a doctor. But she tried to speak, and I heard her, my ears picking up the little sounds that would be otherwise inaudible. "You're the one who sent me the message, aren't you?" She pulled at my arm, trying to turn me. She'd have done a better job trying to tug at a brick wall. "Who are you?"

"Doesn't matter," I mumbled. "Call 911. Get help for you and your friend."

Too-smart Ashley responded stubbornly. "Charlotte. Her name is Charlotte, and somehow I think you know that. Look at me. Talk to me. What was wrong with Jack? Why were his eyes white like that?"

I swallowed hard. I wouldn't look at her, couldn't tell her. If I looked into her eyes, told her about Jack, if she realized that his eyes had changed for the same reason mine had, if I had to behold the recognition and horror there, I might never regain my focus. I might dive headfirst into insanity and Cy would be left to Amber.

"I've seen you," Ashley said. I realized she could see a ghost of a reflection in the piece of mirror I held before me. "I thought for a minute, when I did…"

Unable to hold out a second longer, I turned to her, my eyes ablaze with defiance. "You thought *what*?" I grabbed her and drove her back to the wall. I didn't want her that close to me, that comfortable, and I needed her to see me for the dangerous monster I was. Just because I had saved her didn't mean I was safe. "That I was someone you used to know? I'm not." I flashed my fangs at her, still descended from the kill, to drive home what I was trying to convey; that she should walk away now and not dig any deeper.

Tears poured from her eyes, physical and emotional pain overwhelming her. Her legs shook beneath her. "Holy shit… Elsie… Christ, it's you… I thought when I saw you before, it couldn't be you… your eyes were wrong, like Jack… But it really is you, isn't it?" Her eyes took me in, including the blood all over me. Speech became even harder as she sobbed through the pain in her throat. "I thought you were dead... we all thought you were dead..."

I looked at her as coldly as I could, fighting back the flood of memories and the desire to be as far as possible from a mortal who knew who I'd once been. I took several steps backward and away from her. "I'm not Elsie. You were right- she *is* dead. And she has to stay that way if you or anyone else she ever loved wants to stay safe. Do you understand?" Ashley reached out as though to embrace me, but I shoved her arm down. "Ashley, no." She gasped when I said her name. I knew why. Her name in my voice was so familiar it hurt, for both of us. "Ashley..." Now my voice broke, and a tear escaped the corner of my eye. Over her shoulder, I saw my reflection in a dangling piece of mirror. My eyes looked like they had when I was human: sharkskin and gold. I might have held out eternally if not for that little reminder of a past life. There was no mistaking me for who I once was. For the first time since my rebirth, I could be recognized easily. The familiarity of my reflection hit me like a truck. The human in me won out.

I began to cry in earnest, the tears falling hard and fast. Ashley took a tentative step toward me, and, despite my better judgment, I let her come to me. We embraced, weeping into each other's hair, holding so tightly we may as well have been trying to squeeze ten years worth of hugs into one. Once we had gotten past the worst of the blubbering, we stepped back, our hands still locked on to each other's arms, taking in the sight of each other. She looked over my features, completely changed in death, and yet just the same as they'd been a decade ago. I looked at the new lines of her face, still mostly unnoticeable, but forming beautifully and naturally around her mouth and eyes- smile lines. Lines I would never have.

The madness was closing in as I gave into this extravagance of humanity, but I tempted it anyway. The demon in me would have complete control once I found Amber; I could allow Elsie this moment of weakness before I crammed her down deep in order to do what I had to. I stroked Ashley's hair gently, then smiled sadly. "I mean it, though, Ash," I whispered through more tears. "And I tried so hard not to see you tonight because I don't want this burden for you, but you can't tell *anyone*. *Ever*. If you do, the best-case scenario is that they lock you up for being crazy. Worst case, you're killed for even having been here now and living to talk about it."

"But why?" She asked. It wasn't whiny. It never would be with her. She just needed to know. "What happened? *How* did this happen? It's not even possible!" I could see her mind trying to come up with reasonable answers and hoping I'd confirm one of them. *It must be nice,* I thought, *to have a brain that tries to protect you from impending madness instead of welcoming it with open arms.* "I just don't understand... why you wouldn't come back." Her voice was small and hurt.

I released her, frustrated that she wasn't getting it and feeling the cold anger that could only be borne of Opal rising to the top. "Because I can't. Because I meant what I said before, that I'm not Elsie. She died ten years ago. Literally." I bared my fangs again to drive the point home. "Ashley, the only reason I was here tonight was because I couldn't let Jack do *this* to you too."

"Why not?" She demanded. "What exactly-"

I turned on her before she could even react, my hand gripping her face at the chin. I would have gone for her throat to prove the point further, but she didn't need any more injuries there and my intention was to frighten her, not hurt her. I glanced briefly at the bruises blossoming along the flesh where I could so easily drink... maybe I should. Then she would understand...

I tore my eyes away, forcing myself to abandon such thoughts. I screwed up by letting her see me and know who I used to be; I needed her to understand the consequences of that knowledge. "Do not ask those questions. Do not seek those answers. If I could make you forget this, I would. You have a beautiful human life with years of beautiful human experiences ahead of you. I will never have that again. Even if I could, I don't *want* it. I'm not that girl. I haven't been for a decade. Look at Jack! I killed him right in front of you. And he's not the first person I've killed- not by a long shot. You're smart, Ashley. You know what you're looking at right now, and it's not your friend. Be smart enough to not follow the Devil into Hell, because *that* is who I am, and that is where I'm headed, and if you seek me out, I won't have a choice but to drag you down with me." I pressed my fangs against the skin of her throat, not enough to break through; just enough that her heart rate spiked and she knew how dangerous I was.

I let her go with a small shove and turned my back, going to the door. Hand on the knob, I hesitated, and looked at her over my shoulder. She was shaking with sorrow and fear. I sighed, saddened by this botched farewell. "I'm sorry. Please, Ash. Forget this. Don't look for me. None of this has a happy ending unless you just forget." I wondered if Cy knew any vampires who were particularly good at psychic manipulation (something very few of us could do at all, let alone well) and could make her forget. Then I realized I'd never have the opportunity to ask him if I lingered here forever and Amber killed him. I nodded at Charlotte. "Charlotte needs a doctor, and quickly. You do, too. Call 911. Do it now." I opened the door just a hair, then bit my lip. My voice caught as I said, "Bye, Ashley," and I vanished before her eyes.

Chapter 49

I allowed myself more tears as I drove. It was the lesser of the two evils I could choose between, the other being allowing my psyche to completely fracture, and I needed to get to Cy quickly. It was just past midnight and the state troopers were out looking for drunk drivers, forcing me to drive maddeningly slow. Thankfully I wasn't too far from my building.

It had been heart-wrenching to see Ashley, and even more so to have her see me, to know what I was now. The human mind was a marvel. She watched me feed on someone's blood and then decapitate them (I mean, sure, that person was trying to kill her and worse, I'll give her that), she saw the fangs that had done the damage, she heard my warnings about how knowing who I was could mean her death, and yet she still believed that I could just go home, be Elsie again, pretend I still belonged in that world. Call it what you want to, hope, denial, delusion... I longed for it. I wished I could simply let that desire for things to just make sense and be simple override the warring of my ever conflicted personalities. It would be bliss to just ignore the perpetual tide of insanity I had to fight against.

I spent the entire drive putting my human connections away in the dark corners of my mind, letting them go like feathers on the wind. Danielle, Ashley, Charlotte, my mother, Jess, Sam... anyone who could distract from my mission was systematically reduced to a ghost of a memory. I knew once the night was over, if I lived through it, the ghosts would return to haunt me. But for tonight, I needed them out of my mind. I couldn't keep worrying for the humans I'd left behind if I wanted to save the person who could possibly be part of my immortal future.

I left the car in a parking garage a block away, hoping that it would afford me the opportunity to get a little closer before Amber realized I was there. I dashed into the building, thinking I could at least make it to the top floor without announcing my presence until I saw Braun, unconscious and bleeding on the floor. He'd recover, which I was glad for, but I knew then that any chance of surprising her was negligible.

I took the stairs, not wanting to wait for the slow mechanism of the elevator to move when I could be at my landing in half the time. I stood outside my door, listening, smelling. Amber had been here, but she wasn't anymore. *Shit*, I thought. *Where did they go?* I opened the door and walked in, looking for any clues, but it didn't take long to find what she'd left me.

In the middle of my bed was a single chain with a broken manacle attached. I recognized it instantly. It was one of the chains Cy had used when he'd held me captive in the basement. I ran faster than lightning back down the stairs and burst through the basement door, but I didn't smell them here either. I did smell someone, though. It was faint, but familiar; almost like whoever it was was so barely there that they didn't have any scent to give off. I walked down the stairs, a thrill of something like fear slowing my steps.

At the bottom of the stairs, I looked around and saw the mattress I'd been prisoner on for two weeks. The sight of that item alone filled me with a lingering dread, even though I knew now why it had been done. I didn't like to think about those weeks, the starvation, the helplessness... It occurred to me briefly that I could just leave Cy to Amber out of revenge for keeping me prisoner down here. I shook my head, banishing those thoughts, because whatever my issues were with Cy, I needed him alive to figure them out. There was also the more pressing matter of the unconscious, nearly-dead woman lying on the mattress, one arm bound by the chain.

I knew her.

It was like being in a dream as I moved to her side. I looked over her dark hair; once so lustrous, it now hung unkempt and straw-like. The luscious red lips I recalled in my memory were pale and cracked. Her frame, slender to begin with, had become skeletal. And I knew the reason I could barely smell her. It was because there was but a solitary drop of blood- vampire blood- left in her body.

I took out my phone and dialed.

"What?" Zilpher was annoyed but smug when he answered. "Realized you can't do this without my help?" I nearly hung up, but decided in that moment to let the human part of me reach out to the human part of him. I know I'd said I owed him nothing, but this was the only possible exception, since it had been my fault she was here in the first place.

"No, but you need to get to my building as fast as you can, and bring blood with you. You're going to need it."

"I'll eat on the way," he said.

"No. Get it from a blood bank, and get a lot. You're going to be making a donation of your own tonight."

He scoffed. "In what world would I come all that way to give you my blood? If you needed it, you should have just taken it before. If you need my help-"

"I don't need your fucking help, Zilpher! And I don't need your blood." I looked down at the mattress again. "But Orla does."

*　　*　　*

An hour later, Orla was awake and alert enough to take small amounts of Zilpher's blood on her own.

"How are you alive?" I had asked her brusquely. "And tell me everything you know about where Amber went tonight. Cliffsnotes version."

Orla glared at me as she told me everything. I didn't blame her for her hatred. I *did* try to kill her, and actually believed I had succeeded without a shred of remorse. Had our situations been reversed, I would hate her just as much.

Cy had been right. Amber had been plotting my eventual final death from the night I was made. When she'd pulled Orla and Zilpher aside to discuss my challenge to Orla, she was telling them I'd killed my sire in the woods, a cardinal sin amongst vampires. But she could already sense I was strong enough to not go down easily, and perhaps I could be a useful tool if they allowed me to live and controlled my existence through their own physical and political power. When I fought Orla, I had indeed failed to take the last drop, just as I had with Cy, thanks to my inexperience. Unlike Cy, who was essentially an immortal human with some enhanced abilities, Orla was still a vampire. This was likely due to Amber's calculated care of her. After I had decapitated her, Amber brought her head and body back together, which healed when Orla was given a rather quick meal of Amber's blood, since she'd held onto the last drop of her own. Amber, realizing my immense strength had come from nearly draining two vampires much older and stronger than myself, kept Orla as a prisoner, too weak to fight or even remain fully awake most of the time. Amber made sure that there was always enough blood to feed on, drinking from Orla almost constantly, building her strength up little by little. It was how she had managed to beat Zilpher years before. I couldn't even imagine how strong she was after another five years of slowly draining Orla nearly every night.

"Where is Amber now?" I demanded. "Or where is she headed?"

Orla pulled back from Zilpher's throat, where she had been latched on as he drank yet another plastic pouch of blood to replenish his own reserves. She wiped a trickle of blood off of her delicate chin. "Why should I tell you?"

I crossed my arms. "Because while I was the one who nearly killed you in the first place, I very possibly saved your life tonight. And the only reason Zilpher was able to come and give you his blood to bring you all the way back is because I spared *his* life earlier."

She continued to glare at me, her eyes sharp and alive again, in that shade not so far off from Amber's. "You tried to kill me and then took my mate as your lover," she accused.

I snorted. "'Lover' isn't exactly the right word. Love had nothing to do with anything that happened between us, believe me. You can have him back. Please, feel free. But if you don't tell me where Amber went, Zilpher will die because I will let him, and I'll come for you again."

Zilpher explained about the recording I had sent and the threat I'd made. Orla seemed to realize she had to help or risk actually dying- for real this time. With no less hatred in her eyes, she sighed and reached into the pocket of the shapeless pajamas she'd been dressed in. She pulled out a bullet and handed it to me. It was old, bent and covered in dried blood. Then she handed me a note.

Returning this to you. Little anniversary present. -Amber.

I held it in my hand, realizing what it meant. This was the bullet that had gone through my brain and ended my mortal life. It had robbed me of my human memories and paved the way for my current madness. It also told me where to go... somewhere I had never set foot as a vampire, but for once, ten years ago to the day.

I stared at the bullet as I spoke, my voice sounding like it came from someone else, someone who wasn't spiraling out of control. "I have to go," I said. I broke my gaze from the bullet and looked at Zilpher. "Take her upstairs to my flat. Get her cleaned up." Looking at Orla, I said, "Help yourself to anything you want in my closet. You're taller than me, but some of the dresses should work. I owe you at least that much."

They both looked at me strangely. I realized I sounded sentimental, which would be perceived as weak. I was almost too tired, too angry to care. I growled, frustrated that they weren't doing what I said. "You need to get her out of here and somewhere safe in case I lose to Amber. I need you on call, out in the city for me, and you'll draw too much attention out there with Orla looking like that," I said, hoping they would just be grateful and not focus on my slip up. Zilpher's cold eyes sized me up briefly, but then he nodded and helped Orla to her feet. They went up the stairs and, once I heard the door close behind them, I sat on the mattress, staring at the bullet. I was running out of time, but, I hated to admit it even to myself, I was scared. I didn't want to go there and relive it all, especially knowing that, yet again, Amber was stronger than me, stronger than Cy.

I closed my hand around the bullet and squeezed it until I felt the metal biting into my skin. The sensation grounded me as my mind began spinning out of control. So much of my existence for the last ten years had been based on falsehoods and manipulation, and I struggled to contend with the ever-unfolding lies I had for so long believed in. I didn't even know if I finally had all the pieces, but if I did, I was no closer to figuring out the puzzle. I felt the sand closing over my head and I pulled my knees to my chest, trying to drown out my inner voices as they argued and screamed unintelligibly. I put my hands over my ears as if that could silence the din, to no avail. I found myself reaching for Cy to calm me, but he wasn't here this time, and he never would be again if I couldn't get my shit together. I couldn't lose it now- I had to rally. I knew where Amber had taken him and I needed to get there, but I had to be ready for her. I had to be stronger, faster, smarter than she was, and couldn't see how I could do it. The screaming in my head reached a fever pitch, then suddenly stopped.

All at once, the pieces of the plan fell into place. Suddenly and without any joy, I realized I knew what to do. A tear fell from my eye as I resolved to follow through, knowing what it might mean, what it would likely mean.

Mutually assured destruction.

Chapter 50

An hour later, I was driving the car up the coastline toward Caladesi Island, fat droplets of rain breaking through the blanket of humidity. How fitting that the weather would mirror that of the night I died.

It was only a few hours until sunrise and I had been getting messages from Amber for hours, taunting me.

You're late, bitch. Where are you?

Don't even fucking tell me you actually rescued the humans first. I'm so disappointed in you!

He's going to die! Do you even care? Get here!

I had ignored these messages, knowing that the angrier and more frustrated Amber was, the less in control she would be, giving me an opportunity to gain the higher ground. Her emotions were her downfall, as I'd seen time and again over the years.

I'd changed out of my bloody and torn clothes and then made a stop before I left Tampa. I hated to waste more time, but I had to make sure I had everything I needed to give myself the best chance. My plan was not foolproof, but if I could pull it off, I would win. Well... I would survive.

I parked the car in the lot. The wind was picking up, and thankfully I was downwind, which would offer me at least a small advantage. Thank God for my preternatural memory because I knew the exact spot where she would be and it wouldn't take me long at all to reach it. I grabbed the large duffel bag I'd brought with me and looked around, checking to make sure I wasn't being stupid and had somehow missed Amber sneaking up behind me, downwind, waiting to ambush me. Thankfully, I could smell both her and Cy on the gusts that pelted me with warm rain, and they were right where I thought they'd be. Once I was satisfied that I was alone in this part of the island, I dashed to a small area not far from where Amber and I would have our final showdown and stashed the bag. I just had to hope the wind wouldn't kick up in another direction before I got to them and spoil the surprise. I tried to cover my tracks by going back to the car and approaching from that direction. Everything had to go perfectly, or the game was lost. I shouldn't have been so hopeful considering that I'd already failed to foresee every single failure on my part all night, but I had almost nothing left to lose.

I stayed hidden in the trees and the headwind blew my hair out behind me. A fire was set up in the tiny clearing, barely staying aflame in the storm. I saw Amber pacing impatiently in front of Cy, who had been tied to the very tree in front of which I'd been killed. She must be thrilled with this storm. She did have a love of symmetry...

Against the tree, Cy was barely sitting up. He was conscious and alive, but the black eye and the still seeping twin punctures on his neck let me know that he wasn't okay. I nearly abandoned my plan and just dashed forward to grab him and run, but I knew it would never work, and I had to abandon those impulses. Everything depended on me not giving in to that side. She'd hear me coming, see me, smell me, and I couldn't face her in a one on one battle. Not yet.

My mind had been unnervingly quiet since coming up with my plan. If it worked, if I lived through the night, the noise would start again; the madness would return worse than before. If there was one certainty regarding this night, it was that the me who emerged, if I did at all, would be forever changed from who I had once been. My body might endure, but there was no chance my mind or my soul would remain whole after what I would have to do. I steeled my nerves. I took a few moments to speak into the silence of my mind, consoling the parts of me that would be entirely broken by the end of the night, apologizing to them. I pulled down walls and released demons I'd fought against for weeks, and then stepped out from the trees to let myself be seen, careful to remain downwind. Amber turned to face me, then threw her hands up in the air.

"Fucking finally!" She cried in mock exasperation. "I honestly thought you were going to leave loverboy here to die. You had me worried!"

I said nothing, just stared at her, the dancing and flickering flames creating shadows on the trees. I could only hope I looked as menacing as I was trying to, a goddess of the island, enraged at an intruder to her domain.

After waiting several moments for me to speak to no avail, Amber broke the silence. "Oh, come on!" She whined, stepping to the side to place herself between Cy and me while still making sure I could see him. "Say something! I put *so* much work into all this. The least you could do is acknowledge the level of genius and patience that went into it all."

I cocked my head to the side, my lip curling. "The only thing I'll acknowledge is that you were right."

Amber smirked. "Oh? About what? Because I can think of so many things I've been right about, and you don't even know the half of them."

I glanced at Cy. His eyes were barely able to focus on me. He was badly injured, and his blood was weak. She'd taken more than I thought she would. A tear fell from his uninjured eye, his expression defeated and pleading. He wanted me to run, to leave him to Amber. I wouldn't do that. I couldn't. She'd proven she was too dangerous to be let go. I needed to kill her or die trying. Leaving him and running wasn't an option.

Small puddles were forming in the sand and dirt, creating little pockets of mud. Palm leaves slapped viciously at each other, and the crashing waves could be heard even this deep into the woods.

"You once told me about your life as a human. You told me about yourself, and you were absolutely right," I taunted, calling to her over the sounds of the island storm. "You are *not* the smartest."

Amber laughed, a sound that out in the human world would have turned heads for its beauty. Out here, it was eerie and haunting, bouncing off the trees and raindrops. "You really think so? I got you here, and you have to admit- I've got you in a sticky spot. I'm sure you're here because you found my little gift? I've been feeding off of Orla for years, ever since-"

"Yeah, I got the rundown already," I interrupted roughly. "No need to bore me again."

Amber's face turned sour. "After all I've put up with from you, you could at least let me say my piece!" I gave her a bored look, then crossed my arms and leaned sideways against the nearest palm. I unenthusiastically waved my hand to tell her to go on, knowing she couldn't help but monologue at me. She looked like a child having a tantrum at my disinterest.

"Trust me, babe, you don't want to make me any angrier, not unless you want me to just kill Cyan now so you and I can get down to business."

I snickered and said, "Sure, Amber. Go ahead. Get your words in. I may as well let you speak since you'll be dead come sunrise."

"Listen, little girl," she said, trying to sound superior. I rolled my eyes, enraging her further. "With everything I've been through and lost in my time on earth, with everything I've survived, you think that I'm going to be taken down by *you?*"

I shrugged. "That's exactly what I think."

She stepped toward me as though to attack, but then pulled back. I wasn't the only one in a sticky spot. She wanted the game to go on, but if she attacked now, it would all be over. "You think you're going to win here?" She growled. "You underestimated me!"

I raised my eyebrows thoughtfully. "Oh, I don't think I did." I remained silent otherwise, knowing that my refusal to say more would begin to eat away at her. She wanted the fight; she wanted to eviscerate me with her words before she did so with her hands. I wasn't going to let her.

She turned and put her fist through a tree. Several coconuts rained down around her. Perfect. She was already unraveling. I just needed her to go a little further...

"Neither of you ever understood me!" She raged. "You never understood what I tried to do! The people I tried to help!"

I faked an exaggerated yawn. "Okay, Amber. Is that all?"

I thought she would start pulling her hair out at that point. She was swelling with fury, reaching her peak, and I would need to throw my wrench into her plan soon. I had hoped for more time, time to try to come up with an alternate plan, to convey the plan to Cy, anything, but I knew I couldn't.

"No, that's not all!" She shrieked. "I beat you! You may have saved your little human friends, but now I know that you are and always have been weak and human! And tonight, I'm going to kill both of you!"

My stomach felt like it had filled with lead, knowing the time had come. I forced myself to detach as I gave her the last of my long silences, but couldn't do it without one final act as Elsie Taylor, one little indulgence of humanity. I looked at Cy, unwilling to let Amber out of my sight, but needing to see his eyes, to know he understood what I was about to do and to forgive me for it. I held back my tears and told Amber, without looking away from Cy. "No, you won't, Amber. I won't give you the chance." I swallowed hard and directed my next words to Cy, my voice breaking, "I *do* love you."

Then I pulled the gun out, put two bullets in the man I loved, and watched him slump down dead.

Chapter 51

I used the moment while Amber reeled from what I'd done to rush her and deal a hard blow, but she recovered quickly, throwing me to the side. I flipped back to my feet, gun still in hand, and adopted a defensive stance, the gun pointed at her face. Amber stood up, her hands going to the sides of her head, a gesture I had used frequently in my bouts of insanity. It certainly looked as crazy as it felt.

"What the *fuck?*" She screamed. "You just killed him!" Then she laughed, a wild, deranged cackle. "I didn't think you had it in you!"

I shrugged, trying to look like I didn't care, hoping that the tears on my face could be mistaken for rain. "One less distraction."

Amber glanced back at Cy's body, the laughter dying on her lips. One bullet had hit him in the head, leaving a trail of blood from his ear down his neck. The other had gone directly through his heart. I saw a flicker of sadness cross her face. She had loved him once too, and I supposed there was at least a small amount of regret there. Who knew if she actually intended for him to die tonight or if it had been a ploy just for my benefit? Didn't matter. It did the job; I needed her emotional and off-balance for this to work, and I couldn't defeat her while trying to save Cy. He was beyond my worrying now.

She turned to me coldly. "That goes for both of us." She looked at me curiously. "You know I didn't leave him enough of your blood to bring him back, right? I know you smelled it, the weakness of the blood. Even if he could have come back, you shot him in the head! Just like I shot you. He wouldn't remember anything if he *did* come back, but he can't even... He was *human*, utterly human. Now he's just... dead." I shrugged and stared at her, a sob building in my throat, knowing she was certainly right, that he was dead and that I had done it. Amber tried to center herself, but her rage was tangible. "Why don't I just kill you now, then? Since you've gone and ended the game."

It was my turn to laugh. "Oh, I think the game's just getting started, babe!" I shot at her in that tone she so loved to use herself. I let the gun hang limply at my side, still available to use but not actively trained on her. "You see, Amber, I knew I couldn't beat you in a physical confrontation tonight, especially not if I had to save Cy too. Well, you threatening him is one thing I don't have to deal with now. Now I can just worry about you and me."

Amber slunk toward me, her limbs keeping tension to launch at will. "I don't think you're worried enough," she growled, her voice barely audible above the gale.

"Oh, sweetie," I mocked her. "I'm worried as much as I need to be. It's *you* who isn't worried enough."

Before she could respond, I ran, not toward her, but into the woods, away from the flames. I hoped that knowing where I was going would be to my benefit, since Amber had to rely on her senses to figure out where I was headed, and by moving downwind, I robbed her of one.

I circled back to my bag and reached down to yank it open, grabbing the first thing my hand fell on. I gripped the handle, the weight resting against my hand comfortably, then I turned around and launched the axe at Amber who had just burst through the trees, the slightest hint of the fire visible behind her, creating a halo by which I saw the blood spray arcing upward upon impact.

The axe hit her on the collarbone, bouncing away after making a cut several inches deep. She staggered back as blood gushed out in a stream for a moment, and then promptly ceased, healing immediately. But the shock was evident. Perfect.

"What the *fuck*?!" She screamed, grabbing the area where she'd been hurt. Then she turned on me, her face no longer able to be mistaken for a human's; she was entirely an animal, a demon, bent on my destruction. I should have been terrified. I was calm, numb even. I had to be, or I'd break down before I could take her out.

While she recovered from the first blow, I launched three knives at her in quick succession, opening more wounds. Then I pointed the gun at her, shooting at her throat, her heart, the fleshy parts of the abdomen, the upper thigh, anywhere I knew to have a large blood vessel that would release a substantial amount of blood before the wound could close. By the time I finished, she would hopefully be weakened enough from blood loss that I could beat her. She continued toward me, but paused to claw at herself where the bullets didn't exit before the skin healed. I imagined that must be painful. Good.

Her blood soaked the sand and mud around us, creating a pink river in the running rainwater. By the time she reached me, I had nearly accomplished my goal. I'd been hoping for more blood loss, but our strength would be fairly evenly matched. I was almost glad. The thrill of a physical fight would help keep my mind away from the clearing, where my lover lay dead.

As we exchanged blows, She tried to taunt me, to throw me off, but she was getting more and more desperate as the fight progressed. "I- won't- lose- to- stupid- fucking- Elsie- Taylor-" she grunted between hits.

"Good news," I snarled at her. Her need to talk during the fight, to have her say, gave me the opening I needed, and I slipped under her arm, getting a hold of her and pinning her to the ground. "You can't. Because you *did* win that particular game. Elsie is dead. You get me- not Opal, no, not the cool and collected Councilor who thought you were her friend. You get the mentally unstable demon who remembers both lives. So tell me," I whispered, my lips at her ear. "How does winning feel?"

I sank my fangs into her throat, ripping a large hole and pulling her blood into me as hard as I could. She pushed against me, but the moment I took in her blood, Orla's blood, thousands of years worth of immortal strength on top of my own immense power, she had no hope of winning. The gun was beyond her reach, as were the axe and the array of hunting bows and knives I'd brought just in case, compliments of a friend who dealt in weaponry. She had no way to win, and even closed her eyes, losing her grip on consciousness as things seemed to grow darker around us...

I realized too late that the added darkness was not due to her life slipping into me (which it was), but was due to a shadow hovering over us. By the time I looked up, I was roughly shoved off of Amber, and, though I could have easily fought the new arrival, I allowed myself to be moved. I saw the soaked mop of black hair descend on a comatose Amber, opening the other side of her throat. I watched in amazement, horror, rapture as Cy drank deeply.

This was new to watch. We'd shared blood. He had drunk from me, but I'd never *seen* this, not from him; never seen him attack prey; never seen him imbibe someone's life without hesitation. He held her tightly, his limbs arranged in a way that, if one didn't know better, it might have appeared that they were making love. Even just as an observer, it was a sensual, breathtaking experience.

I sniffed the air and realized Amber had very little blood left, so I stood and went to the pair of them, placing my hand on Cy's shoulder to stop him before she lost too much to reawaken. He turned to me, a snarl on his lips, but when his neon eyes met mine, he softened and smiled. Amber was fully unconscious but still alive when Cy rose to his feet and grabbed me tightly around the waist. I could feel in his arms the strength I remembered and then some. Our blood combined had once again done wonders, giving him power possibly equal to my own. His scent was closer to mine now with my vampiric blood in his veins; that fresh smell of seawater that I associated with him was now laced with a floral undercurrent, like the magnolias I so adored. He looked into my eyes for just the length of a gasp, then bent his face to mine, kissing me, holding me, pulling me to him so tightly I thought we might merge. Drops of Amber's blood, which remained on our lips, in our mouths, flavored the moment. *Oh, yes!* I thought in ecstasy. Yes, he was alive, and he was immortal with me, and we- I- had won!

The intoxication we both felt from gorging ourselves on Amber's immortal blood was dizzying, and made it hard to focus on the present, but there was more to do. I pulled away first, ending the kiss, but not letting him go. I held my head to the place where I'd shot him, feeling the healed skin with my cheek. I was working hard to force my mind to stay silent, knowing we weren't finished here yet, but wanting to savor this moment and to say what I hadn't been able to before in front of Amber.

"I'm sorry," I breathed, my mind mostly quiet but my mouth as vocal as ever. "I couldn't think of anything else to do. I realized earlier she thought you were completely mortal, and I knew there was no way I could save you *and* kill her, not when she was that strong from feeding off of Orla's blood for so many years, and I just hoped that you'd had enough of my blood to heal, and I was so worried when she took so much from you, I thought any chance we had of you coming back was lost, and when the second bullet clipped your ear, I thought I'd actually hit your brain, and you'd forget me and-"

"I know," Cy said, cutting off my rambling in his soft way, the animal I'd seen moments before fading back into the gentle lover I knew. For several minutes, he just held me like that. The intensity of the night was being washed away with the rain, and as the tension lessened, I felt elated. I had beaten Amber. Me. Just me. I'd overcome every obstacle she'd thrown at me, and now she lay at my feet, utterly defeated.

"I did it," I said with a laugh that blossomed into near hysterics. "I beat her. I did it! Me. Just me."

"Yes," he said, still speaking tenderly. "You did." As if on cue, we looked down at her, still and silent with the rain beating on her. I released Cy and lifted Amber over my shoulder, then dragged my bag along behind me and back to the fire. He didn't even reach forward to help, and I was glad for it. I needed to finish it on my own, just how I'd done it all. Me. Just me.

Smoke was drifting in swirling currents, fighting against the raindrops as the last embers of the fire held on. I laid Amber at the foot of the tree where two of the present party had died. She groaned as I pulled the chains from the basement out of the bag. I wrapped them around her tightly. She began to stir as I did so.

"Crazy bitch," she mumbled, shifting her weight, trying to throw the chains off but failing in her weakened state.

"In the flesh," I acknowledged with a grin.

"I can get out of this, you know," Amber said. "The chains are strong, but trees break easily." She hadn't even opened her eyes. I vaguely wondered if she had enough strength left to do even that.

"Not when you're this weak," Cy said, staring at her, his lip curled in disgust. "Not when you have so little blood within you."

Her eyes snapped open and she looked at him in shock. So she wasn't aware that he'd been reborn again, that he'd fed from her. She stared at him with a mix of fear and joy. "Cyan!" she whispered. "Your eyes... You... You're immortal again!"

"No thanks to you," he said. There was none of his usual warmth. He was as cold as I could be. It made me want to shiver. "You're going to stay right here, where you murdered Elsie and where you left me to die ten years ago. You get to wait in this spot until the Council comes for you." I glanced at him, hoping he didn't notice the guilt in my eyes. Cold, he may be, but, as I already knew, he was too good. Despite everything she'd ever done to him or people he loved, despite his unquenchable need for revenge against her, despite how he loathed her, he was willing to walk away and let someone else have a hand in her fate. I couldn't let that happen. Never again. And I hoped he wouldn't guess what I intended to do.

Amber pulled against her chains, struggling now, appealing to Cy. "But you didn't die! You survived! You're a vampire again because of me!"

"Because you tried to kill me *again!*" He roared at her, shocking both of us with the unfamiliar sound of his rage.

She began to cry, a weak, pitiful sound. "I never wanted you dead. I needed *her* to believe I did. I would have saved you. *She* shot you. She was willing to let you die-"

"And I was willing to die if it finally meant your death," he said softly but coldly, his harsh words shocking Amber into silence. He looked to me. "Is it secure?"

I pulled on the chains. "As much as it can be," I replied. I stood and looked down at Amber, then said to Cy, without moving my gaze, "I have a phone in the car, and sunglasses. Can you get those while I stay with our friend here?" The sky would be lightening soon. Especially in a storm, when the sky seemed to stay dark so much longer, the UV rays could sneak up on you, and we would need to protect our eyes before that happened.

He looked uneasy, his hatred for Amber not reaching deep enough to affect his soul as strongly as mine had been, to give him the peace of mind to deal the final blow, or even to allow me to do it. He thought I would finish the job if he left, and that he'd lose me forever. He may already have, but I didn't want to let him know that... yet. He glanced between us. "Don't worry," I assured him. "She'll still be here when you get back. I won't touch her. Promise." Cy nodded and took off at a run- a nearly invisible, supernatural, vampire-speed run. I was sure he'd missed the feeling of that, but I also knew it meant I had less time with Amber, and I had more to say, more to ask.

"You know why you lost," I said in the quietest voice I could, hoping Cy wouldn't overhear as he got closer. It hadn't been a question. I knew she knew. I wanted her to say it, but she gave my own brand of silence back to me. I chuckled and sat next to her, still feeling drunk from the physical boost her blood had given me, as well as from the relief, exhaustion, and the ever lingering madness on the edges of my mind which wouldn't remain quiet for long. I figured I'd take this last opportunity to drive the point home. "You lost because, after a thousand years, you're still ruled by the weaknesses which were a part of your mortal life. You lost because you assumed I suffered from the same plight. Unluckily for both of us, that's not

402

the case. Oh, I have issues, that's for sure. It may be weeks, months, even years before I emerge from the profound insanity that *will* overtake me within the next few hours. And that will happen because I'm not Elsie, but I'm also not Opal. You didn't fight either of your old enemies tonight. You fought a new one that you didn't understand. You thought I underestimated you, but you were so far off. *You* underestimated *me*."

"You told him you love him." Her voice was quiet, tired, and her eyes were unfocused, staring into the distance.

"So?" I asked. Did it suddenly matter to her that I actually loved him? It certainly hadn't stopped her from killing me before.

"Did you know he'd come back?" Not the question I expected.

I could lie to her. I could refuse to answer. But it no longer mattered. "No. I didn't."

"Then why would you do it? If you love him, why would you kill him?"

I was confused. Amber's sentimentality was so foreign, not because I had so effectively detached from that feeling, but because it was coming from her. "Because I had no other way to beat you," I said. "Now, you get to answer my question." Her gaze rolled lazily to me. "Why me?"

She narrowed her eyes, unsure of what I meant.

"Why did you choose *me*? Ten years ago. You chose me. I know what Cy said, about your 'type.' But there are probably millions of women who fit that profile. Hell, my best friend fit the profile. Why did you choose me?"

A ghost of a smile crossed her lips. "Why do you think it *wasn't* your friend?"

I blinked. "Was it?"

Amber shrugged. "Maybe it was. Even if it had been your friend in the beginning, I'd have targeted you anyway. Because of Cyan. Because he fell in love with you before you ever spoke to each other, just from watching you. But it doesn't matter now."

"It matters to me. Tell me. Tell me why you came into my life and drove it so far off course," I demanded, no longer caring if she heard the desperation and despair in my voice.

She chuckled, and when she spoke, she almost sounded like herself again. "One thing I've learned in a whole millennium, babe... Your life can't go off course. If you ended up here, that's because this *is* the course of your life. Sure, you can make choices, react to things, but that's all part of it, too, part of the journey. And I get the feeling, though you'd never tell dear Cyan, that the Council is never going to make it here. Which means *my* journey is at an end."

I nodded crisply, confirming her suspicions. "You should know," I told her coldly. "That you could have had me for an ally in your crusade. I think you're right. Some people should not be left to the law, should be taken care of by those who can. I would have let you live. I would have joined you, but you will die today out of pure and simple revenge, because you came after me and those I love." I stared at her, watching the words sink in. A thousand years of life should have given her plenty of practice in appearing to not care, but her eyes were filled with a fury she couldn't hide, and I could feel the current of fear undulating from her.

I looked away when I heard Cy approaching. He had three pairs of sunglasses in his hands and the phone. I took the phone and got into my email quickly and deleted the outgoing email to the Council. Zilpher would be spared for tonight, as promised. Then I sent a message to him to confirm it was done. I put the phone into my pocket.

"Do you want to say goodbye?" I asked Cy, just a hint of sarcasm coloring the words.

"No," he said, and turned, walking at only a slightly faster than human pace back toward the car, making sure Amber could clearly see him as he left her behind and didn't look back. She was crestfallen. She had obviously hoped to at least say one final thing to him, for a final farewell, and was crushed by his cold rejection.

It was even crueler when I held the extra sunglasses out to her, then dropped them in the sand, several feet out of reach, and crushed them underfoot. She had less than an hour until the sunlight would burn what little blood was left in her veins, and she would die. She had been right: she wouldn't live until members of the Council arrived for her, and I didn't have to lay a hand on her to do it. I kept that promise to Cy. When the rain stopped, and humans re-entered the park, she would be nothing but dust, a corpse decayed for a thousand years. I looked at her one final time and turned away.

"Bye, Amber."

*   *   *

I climbed into the car and Cy held my face in his hands, looking into my eyes. I stared back, reveling in the vibrancy of his irises. The hazel had been warm and comforting, but the intensity of this seashore shade of green-blue was gripping. He leaned in and kissed me again, softer than before.

I felt a pang of guilt, knowing that, while he might have guessed what I'd done, he didn't know for sure. I tried to detach from it, but it held on. With the indulgence of that one emotion, by allowing that flicker of guilt to manifest, the rest came flooding in, and I felt the sand closing over my head quickly. I'd kept it at bay for too long and the noise was overpowering.

My body tensed and Cy sat back, looking at my face, seeing the insanity darkening my eyes. "Hold on, Love," he said urgently, starting the car. "Let's get you home. We can figure things out from there."

I nodded my head, terrified at the impending madness that was beginning to swallow me whole, but grateful that he was with me still. "Okay," I said as casually as I could. *Like he'd said he wanted ice cream.* He smiled at me through his worry, trying to reassure me.

Then I blacked out.

Chapter 52

I had been right that it would take me a long time to piece things back together enough to come back to myself, whoever that was. Cy told me it was just shy of seven weeks before I spoke at all, and another month before anything I said even resembled sentences. All told, I spent close to half a year lost in the catacombs of my own mind.

Even once I broke free from the catatonia, I still struggled with remaining anchored in reality. I would be functioning almost normally, and then something would trigger a fracture and I would lapse back. Not for too long; sometimes minutes, sometimes days, but certainly long enough that Cy knew better than to take me far from home- or out at all.

Sometimes his presence brought me more clarity; other times, it made things worse. I never knew which way the day would go. Every time he trained his crystal clear, oceanic eyes on me, I relived shooting him, knowing at the time that it would have in all likelihood been the end of him. And every time I had to relive the guilt in my decision and the knowledge that had I weighed the loss of him as less important than besting Amber. It was all the worse because I knew when I shot him that I hadn't lied when I told him I loved him. I meant it then, and meant it even more every time I told him thereafter. His forgiveness for my actions and his patience during my frequent mental breakdowns was something I could never begin to thank him for.

He spent a lot of time away from me, but it was never longer than the night. It was something I didn't quite understand while I was unreachable in those early days, when I was unable to bring my head above the sand. I never made an attempt to leave and find him, or to subvert his requests that I remain at home for not only my safety, but for the safety of humans and vampires in the area. I could barely walk to the fridge for blood most days; there were mornings when he'd have to hand feed me when he came home.

Cy later explained to me that he had stepped into Jett's position at Trusty's to keep the operation running. I was glad to hear it- he had a true passion for making bonds between humans and vampires that were mutually beneficial, as well as for providing vampires a way to feed that didn't force us to take life. He didn't like that I still craved the kill, but he never said anything. When I realized he was likely avoiding the fight so as to spare me a deeper trip into insanity, I got even angrier and melted down. We finally agreed that, as long as even going out was out of the question, the argument could wait.

Lots of arguments ended- or didn't- in this unresolved manner.

I often asked him during this time, when I was aware enough of what was happening, why he didn't just leave me. He had his life- well, afterlife- back, and he could be enjoying it for once. He had no Amber to deal with for the first time. He shouldn't feel responsible for me, shouldn't bind himself to the mad vampire who kept him from all the joys of life. He always responded the same way: he ignored the question and carried on with the status quo.

Soon after my butterfly-like emergence from the cocoon of my psyche, Cy had insisted on an embargo on sex until he felt like I was sound enough in my mind for such things. I was furious, threatening to go hunt like I used to, to fuck some human in an alley and kill him, letting the sex, the blood, and the death revive my mind.

"You won't do that," Cy had said softly. He wasn't giving me an order or telling me I couldn't. He wasn't horrified at the thought, or even hurt that I said it. He simply knew I was full of shit and wouldn't. "It wouldn't help. It would make it worse."

He'd been right, of course. I may have had good days, but most were still spent with me battling the internal voices which tried to bring the others (and therefore all of me) down. As such, our bed had become a place where we talked and held each other, and where, occasionally, on nights when things were clear for me, I tried to break the rules. Sometimes he let me (and thank God for those nights, because they made me feel almost real again), but most of the time, he didn't.

This particular morning, when he finally told me about the things I needed to know, had followed a full rebellion against his prohibition. I could always tell how crazy I seemed on the outside based on whether he let the walls down and acted like my lover rather than my caretaker, though in reality, he was both.

That night, he thought I was very, very sane.

As the first light of day illuminated our motionless but still entwined bodies, Cy kissed my head sweetly, then looked at me, frowning.

"Haven't you wondered yet why you're able to just be here? Why we have this peace? Why no one on the Council has come for you yet?" He asked.

The truth was that I had thought about it- repeatedly. In fact, it was like a song that kept playing over and over in my mind, meshing with and overlapping a thousand other dismal tunes at once. I figured it was best not to ask and stir up those voices, so I had just assumed he'd tell me when he thought I was ready. It seemed he had decided it was time.

In my extended absence, Orla had reclaimed her seat on the Council, which was rightfully hers anyway, since it turned out I had never actually killed her. I was thrilled about this since it meant that I no longer had the responsibility to the Council I had always loathed. It also gave me the time and freedom I needed to deal with my own issues without fear of being taken out by the rest of the Council or any other vampires who saw me as vulnerable.

It hadn't always been particularly safe for me, though. Apparently, in the early days of their reunion and my disappearance from public life, Zilpher and Orla had decided to take my treasonous attempted murder and usurping of a Council member to the rest of the Council to have me sentenced and executed. It had become common knowledge by the time they planned to act on it, but most of the Council had decided to overlook my crimes, knowing that I was perfectly content to step down and be left alone. Zilpher and Orla, however, planned to expose everything they knew about me- from my hand in Indigo's creation, to my taking a mortal lover (even if he wasn't mortal to begin with or anymore), even to my indulgence of Trusty's which they planned to expose as well- in order to have me killed. Cy had learned of their plan before they could follow through, thankfully. He'd gone through my phone for anything he might need to keep me safe after my mind shut down. He had found and sent them the audio recording I'd taken where Zilpher admitted to letting Amber go, and had created a fail-safe system where that recording would be sent out once a week if we weren't around to stop it, keeping us safe from them indefinitely.

Cy had also found in my phone a video recording I'd made. When he told me, my heart sank. I'd hoped he'd never see that video and know that I'd lied; that while I hadn't dealt the killing blow, I had personally and directly caused Amber's death, and hadn't left anything to the Council.

While he'd gone to the car in the early hours of that morning, as Amber and I had talked, I'd set up a camera nearby to record where I'd chained her and had the feed forwarded to my phone, along with a timestamp in case I ever needed it. The video started by showing Amber and I talking, though there was no sound (thankfully; I couldn't bear it if he knew what I'd said to her on top of what I did). I saw Cy come with the sunglasses and my phone, saw him leave. I saw myself taunt Amber one last time, then crush the sunglasses into the ground, destroying the very thing that could save her from the burning. I saw Amber appearing resigned, calm, yet sad as I left. But as the sky started to lighten, she began to struggle, the reality of what was going to happen and the fear of that realization setting in. The storm never let the light shine in earnest, but her thrashing slowly began to change from terror to pain. Her eyes were clenched tightly, fighting against the sun's hidden rays, but her veins were already beginning to darken under her skin as the blood boiled within her. She opened her eyes into the cameras, screaming, and I saw the blackened, shriveled things where her golden eyes had once been. The scream seemed to go on forever, her pain reaching through the screen to touch me. As her wail finally faded, she slumped against the tree, her body returning to the earth even as I looked on. I watched the whole video intently, making sure I saw it right up to her death. A part of me had been convinced she may have found a way out, at least until I saw her body decay in front of my eyes.

"I wish you'd told me what you were going to do," Cy said sadly to me after I saw it.

"You would have tried to stop me," I said, not looking away from the now blank screen.

"Probably," he admitted. "But you shouldn't have had to deal with that burden alone." He brushed my hair away from my face. "You can share those things with me, you know."

I leaned against him, taking in that fresh saltwater and magnolia smell of him. "I do know that. But sometimes things that are mine just need to be mine. I beat her without any help. I had to finish it the same way."

We lay in silence for a while, then he changed the subject just a bit. "Your sister was fine, by the way. She made it home safely, thanks to you, I assume. But you should know," he said with a grin, "someone anonymously called the bank and paid off your mother's house, and Danielle is returning to pro bono work now that she doesn't have as much to worry about financially."

I nodded. I was glad that she could quit the job she hated, but I felt little to no connection to his words otherwise. I couldn't tell if I was protecting my mind from another wave of madness or if I honestly no longer harbored any strong feelings for those humans who had once been my family; it left me only with a kind of grief, not for them, but for the connection we'd once had.

He continued: "Ashley and Charlotte recovered well after their... mishap. The police have no idea how Jack got into The Roof, hid out in the bathroom, broke through the wall, decapitated himself on the broken glass, then ended up with his head and body on opposite ends of the room- nicely done, Love. But given the testimony from both Ashley and Charlotte, as well as the fact that he was a fugitive murderer, they've let the case drop with that being the official explanation."

"Good," I said, still not able to tap into any kind of raw emotion about what he was saying.

He paused for a long time, fighting with what he said next. "I have to ask... Ashley saw you, didn't she? When you saved her. She realized it was you. You know, I still don't know all the details of that night, but... I need to know about Ashley, at the least. It could be a problem."

I felt a hint of what might have been concern. It was true, I hadn't told him about that night, not in its entirety, because reliving it seemed like a surefire way to book myself on the first flight to Crazytown. That morning, however, I felt safe, detached enough to not lose control while I recounted every moment, the parts with Ashley and without. Once I'd finished, he sighed.

"Well, that explains it," he said. "Ashley has been making comments around town. Things that would just seem odd to other humans, but that have gotten around to us. She's nearly been killed a few times, though she doesn't know it, and so far, only my threat of personally draining and beheading anyone who hurts her has kept her safe. But it's raising questions about my attachments to humans, which could be bad news for Trusty's, especially if the Council found out."

I put my hands over my eyes, finally feeling the flame of something... anger. "She's a fucking idiot. I told her this would happen." I growled, my frustration driving my madness. "I can't believe I let myself get that close. Stupid bullshit feelings! I should never have even spoken to her. I should have just left. Now she thinks she can-what?- get through to me? Get me to come home? Maybe we *should* just let her be killed."

Cy gave me an indulgent smile. "To what end?"

"To *her* end!" I snapped. "If she wants to flirt with death, maybe I should just let her. Or I could do the honors myself, just so she knows how serious I was since she obviously thinks this is a fucking joke."

I felt my emotions kicking into high gear like they hadn't in months, but the warring voices of my psyche were merely background noise. It was invigorating and made me want to do something rash.

"Actually," Cy said with a grimace, seeming to read my mind, "that might not be a bad idea."

Chapter 53

I stood with Cy in the darkness of the parking garage, blending into the shadows while we waited. Ashley had come to the mall after work to shop for honeymoon clothes. Her wedding was only a few weeks away. Why, I wondered, with such a joyous event to look forward to, would she spend so much time and energy trying to draw the monster out from under the bed?

It was late and dark; the winter sun had dipped below the horizon hours earlier, but there was a brilliant full moon, which provided lovely shadows to add to the effect. There were very few cars left, which almost guaranteed we would get her alone. I could practically taste the coming fear.

Cy had come with me to make sure I didn't succumb to the madness again. He leaned casually against a cement column with a view of Ashley's car. His usual white shirt was covered with a casual but sharp black blazer with the sleeves rolled up to the elbows along with the shirt. He looked every bit as sensual and mysterious as he had when I'd met him, and it fanned flames of desire within me. I really did love him, and I *really* hoped I wouldn't lose my mind here because I was already planning out the rest of our night, and, due to the nature of my plans, he wouldn't go along with it unless I was clearheaded.

Ashley emerged from the light of the nearest department store, laden with bags and distracted. She was trying to manage her phone, texting frantically while balancing her purchases. She may as well have a bullseye painted on her; she would have been easy pickings even for a run of the mill human degenerate. She was almost lucky that *I* was the danger in the shadows.

Almost.

She made it to her car and threw the bags into the trunk. When she walked around to the driver's door, she jumped and put her hand to her purse, where I knew she carried a gun for protection. She had seen my eyes, bright red that night, flash in the moonlight, which was exactly what I had intended. I stepped out of the darkness and let her see me.

I had played up the "vampire" look. I wore black leather pants and a matching corset-style top. My makeup was dark and striking with exaggerated contouring, and my hair was pin-straight and severe. The sky-high heels on my boots completed the ensemble, making me look like I'd stepped out of some-one's fantasy illustration of a modern vampiress.

It was several seconds before she realized it was me, the look being so different from anything I'd ever sported in life, and not even close to the streetwalker's clothes she'd seen me in over six months earlier. I needed her to see me for what I was, to understand the danger she'd been courting.

"Elsie!" She gasped, a hint of a smile breaking through the fear she had felt. She stepped toward me, and I bared my fangs.

"No, you absolute Goddamned idiot," I said. "I'm *not* El-sie. I told you that the last time you saw me. You just don't fucking listen."

Ashley looked stung. I was certain she thought we'd have another sweet reunion. It had been a mistake to let it happen the first time. I knew it then and felt it even more strongly now.

She stammered, "I j-just needed to..." She trailed off as she saw Cy, his leaning form looking like an ancient statue in modern dress. "Holy shit... Cyrus?" She breathed. She looked at me, flabbergasted. "What...?" Her eyes were wider than I'd ever seen them. "Oh, my God..."

I knew what was going through her mind. She now had her answer to how I had gone from her friend to a fiend. But she still wasn't understanding that the friend she had hoped to see again was really and truly gone.

"Stop looking for me, Ashley," I growled. "I told you it would get you killed. It already almost did, several times, and you didn't even know it. Get married. Live a life. Stop talking about me. Stop letting others know what you know because as of today, my protection is withdrawn. The next vampire who comes after you *will* kill you, and I won't lift a finger to stop it."

Silent tears streamed down her face. "But I-" she started.

"But nothing!" I shrieked, grabbing her by the throat and throwing her back, pinning her to the hood of the car. "I could kill you myself. Or I could turn you into a vampire like me. Is that what you want? You want *this*?" I bared my fangs at her.

She tried to shake her head to say "no," but my grip was tight, probably too tight. She would have started to struggle for air if I hadn't released her. She clutched at her throat. "I'm sorry," she coughed. "I didn't... I'll stop."

I regarded her coldly, hearing her rapid heartbeat powering the fear and sincerity in her voice. But I knew Ashley. Soon the fear would fade, and she would try again. This wouldn't stop her; it wasn't enough.

"Only if I don't give you a choice," I snarled, then grabbed her roughly and bit into the deep, luscious vein in her throat.

She cried out only once before she lapsed into the vague stupor that my victims always seemed to adopt while I fed. Her blood was rich, smooth. I hadn't fed on an actual live human since the last time I'd seen Ashley, and here she was, filling me with her life.

I felt her heart fluttering beneath me, the organ itself recognizing that I was very close to taking enough to hurt her, when Cy grabbed me and pulled me off. I snarled at him like a feral creature, but he flashed his own fangs at me in warning. Then he turned to Ashley, who had not, in fact, lost too much blood to recover her senses quickly. Her hand was covering the wound and her face carried no trace of hope anymore. She was staring at us in pure horror.

Cy turned to her and slowly, deliberately pushed her back down to the hood of the car. To drive the point home, he leaned forward and licked a large drop of blood from the hollow of her throat while she whimpered softly. "You get to live tonight," he told her. "But your stupidity isn't putting only you in danger. The only reason you're still alive now is because we're strong enough to stop the ones who have targeted you so far. There are others, much stronger than we are, who have caught wind of your careless questions. And I won't die or watch *her* die because of a simpleton who thinks she's safe from what lurks in the dark. You aren't. I think we've proven that." Ashley nodded, a terrified grimace pulling her mouth wide. "Go home. And don't ever- *ever*- speak of us again."

He released her. Ashley spared me only one more glance, but there was no affection or longing in her eyes. She finally understood what I'd tried to tell her, and the only thing she could feel for me was fear. She peeled out of the lot and was gone.

I leaned heavily against the wall and sighed. Then I looked at Cy, who was watching me with worry. "Well," I said drily, "I think that went perfectly."

He smiled grimly. "I couldn't agree more. I think dear Ashley is done asking questions."

I ran my hand through my hair, the straight style giving way to the natural wave. "I certainly hope so. I don't intend to dissuade anyone of the notion that she's under our protection, but I won't help her if she does it again." I meant it.

He raised The Brow at me and reached out to put his arms around me. He looked down into my face, searching. "Are you okay?" He asked. "We can go home if you need some time to process everything." If I was going to lose it, he meant.

I grinned thoughtfully. "I think... I *am* okay. Actually, really okay. I mean, I don't know if I'll ever be all there again, but I don't feel like the sand is covering my head. I feel clear. I can hear all the voices telling me different things, but I have control over them. I think... I think a fresh start, without the human connections and without all the Council bullshit, is what I need." I smiled mischievously at him. "But yes," I insisted, pressing my body against his suggestively. "Take me home."

"Okay," Cy grinned back, The Brow going up in agreement. *Like I said I wanted ice cream.*

About the Author

Lara Ann Dominick is proud to share her inaugural novel *Oil and Water*. She has spent most of her life enjoying supernatural and paranormal literature and is pleased to showcase her own take on the myths and legends. A graduate of Rider University, she now makes her home in the Tampa area. Her love of the Gulf Coast and its beauty inspired much of the imagery found in the novel. Lara is a fitness enthusiast whose love of running can be found in her work and on social media.

Made in the USA
Columbia, SC
25 June 2020